GIDDY BARBER EXPLODES IN 11

To Shawn.

For you I would slay dragons.

Published by Peachtree Teen
An imprint of PEACHTREE PUBLISHING COMPANY INC.
1700 Chattahoochee Avenue
Atlanta, Georgia 30318-2112
PeachtreeBooks.com

Edited by Ashley Hearn
Jacket design by Maggie Edkins Willis and Lily Steele
Design and composition by Lily Steele

Printed and bound in August 2024 at Sheridan, Chelsea, MI, USA.
10 9 8 7 6 5 4 3 2 1
First Edition
ISBN: 978-1-68263-714-2

Library of Congress Cataloging-in-Publication Data

Names: Havranek, Dina, author.
Title: Giddy Barber explodes in 11 / Dina Havranek.
Other titles: Giddy Barber explodes in eleven
Description: Atlanta : Peachtree Teen, 2024. | Audience: Ages 14 and up. | Audience: Grades 10-12. | Summary: Overburdened with responsibilities at home and struggling with school work and toxic friends, fifteen-year-old Giddy embarks on an eleven-day challenge to confront the escalating challenges within her life and her own mounting anxiety.
Identifiers: LCCN 2024006225 | ISBN 9781682637142 (hardcover) | ISBN 9781682637159 (ebook)
Subjects: CYAC: Stress (Psychology)—Fiction. | Anxiety—Fiction. | Family life—Fiction. | High schools—Fiction. | Schools—Fiction. | LCGFT: Novels.
Classification: LCC PZ7.1.H38748 Gi 2024 | DDC [Fic]—dc23
LC record available at https://lccn.loc.gov/2024006225

GIDDY BARBER EXPLODES IN 11

a novel

DINA HAVRANEK

PEACHTREE Teen

0

At the age of fifteen, Giddy Barber knows two things: she's going to become a mechanical engineer and she can't remember the last time she smiled.

Normally she wouldn't think about smiling, but her mother has tasked her with going through old videos—birthdays, anniversaries, vacations. Giddy's mom wants to make a virtual scrapbook. It's 5:14 in the morning. Giddy is awake and dressed, lying atop her covers. She swipes her thumb and the video plays again—Jax, eight; Giddy, five. Jax sets up red and green dominoes on the floor of the room they once shared, and small Giddy uses the legs of a caped, yellow-booted action figure to knock the dominoes down every time Jax makes a neat row of five. Giddy yells: "Superdoo!" The dominoes fall. Jax says: "You never let me finish!" He complains to the camera. "She won't let me do this!" He sets up five more dominoes. Giddy knocks them down. “SUPERDOO!” She laughs with a force that sets her off-balance, her chubby form teetering to hit her head on the mattress behind her. The camera jiggles, the person behind it sets it down, uttering her own small chuckle.

Giddy replays this video four times, frowning. Then she gets out of bed and quietly slips into the hall, changing the thermostat from its subzero nighttime setting to a more appropriate seventy-two degrees, and then softly opens the door to the room shared by seven-year-old Tad and five-year-old Tigs. Both are hunkered down in their respective twin beds, sleeping or pretending to. Giddy kneels, has to press her belly to the floor to squeeze her arm and shoulder under the bed where the yellow-booted action figure lies covered in dust bunnies. Like most of her toys, it wasn’t hers to start out with. It was Jax’s before it was handed down to her and then, without Giddy’s input, given to Dougal, then later to Tad, meaning it’s destined eventually for Tigs’s toy box, probably soon, because Tad’s interest in the figure has clearly waned. Giddy first noticed it weeks ago while walking Tad and Tigs through the process of cleaning the floor of their room.

Giddy sits cross-legged to the tune of Tad’s soft breathing. The figure’s head has been chewed on since her ownership. One leg flaps, busted at the knee’s articulation. The cape wants to pop up like a vampire collar. But even new, it would be unremarkable, not even a name brand, just a knockoff like most of Giddy’s old toys. She can’t remember the name it had when it belonged to Jax, but Giddy had wanted to call it Superman, except she changed the name when Jax pointed out Superman’s cape is red. Giddy thinks she renamed the toy Superdude, but it came out “Superdoo,” so . . .

Superdoo. Jax had told her mother it's like *poo* only with a *d* and way more "super."

Giddy goes back to lie on her bed and examines Superdoo, unable to remember why the toy gave her so much joy. She's still examining it when her five-thirty alarm goes off.

Giddy slips Superdoo into a front jeans pocket, leaps out of bed, unscrews a bottle from her nightstand, and pops a morning antacid. She bangs on Dougal's room first, hitting the door with increasingly louder knocks until he screams at her from within. Then it's back to Tad and Tigs's room. Tigs sits up obligingly at Giddy's first shake, then throws her arms around Giddy's neck. Giddy groans. She hugs her back and stands, Tigs hanging on her until she forcibly sets her down. Giddy grabs a brush, works out a few tangles before binding the left half of Tigs's short brown hair into a tiny topknot. She kicks the mattress behind her. "Get up, Tad."

Tad, still wrapped in blankets, doesn't move. A familiar burn begins in the pit of Giddy's stomach. It's just a small one, a hot pinprick, and she can imagine the antacid jostling around in her digestive juices. So Giddy kicks the bed again—harder. She makes another topknot on the right side of Tigs's head and says, "I'm serious, Tad!" as Tigs raises her fingers to touch the topknots with reverence, awestruck by Giddy's abilities.

Still not a sound from Tad.

Giddy drops the brush and yanks the bed up so hard, Tad hits the wall. Tigs jumps up and down, laughing.

Tad yawns. "Well, I *was* getting up," he says slowly, throwing one arm out from under the blanket, "but now I have to remake my bed, and it's going to take me *so much longer*." He reads Giddy's face for signs of responsive rage.

Giddy doesn't give it to him. "Breakfast is in ten."

Tigs is already halfway into the blue jumper that Giddy set out for her the night before. Giddy kicks Tigs's sneakers out from under the bed and heads down the stairs where their golden retriever, Bodie, crashes into her and seesaws back and forth. Out into the backyard goes Bodie and into the kitchen goes Giddy, where she sets the coffee on, splits apples, and fills a four-slice toaster with frozen waffles. Back up the stairs to bang with both fists on Dougal's door.

Dougal, age fourteen, flings the door open. "Christ, Giddy!" As his booted feet thunder downstairs, Tigs bursts out of her room shouting, "Second waffle! Second waffle!" and shoves past Giddy. Tad sidles out behind Tigs, then stops to lean in the doorframe, folding his arms with exaggerated slowness.

For a moment he and Giddy stare, squared off against each other, neither moving. Downstairs, Giddy can hear Dougal and Tigs in the kitchen.

She says: "There were five waffles left in the box. Four are toasting."

Tad yawns.

"You're not going to get two now. At most you'll get one. And you'd better hope Dougal doesn't take the last waffle out of the box and toast it so he gets a *third* waffle."

Tad doesn't move. One corner of his mouth twists up.

Giddy rips her eyes away and motors down the stairs to where the four waffles in the toaster have vanished. Tigs has two and she's made space between a stack of potholders and some junk mail to eat at the Barbers' woefully undersized kitchen island. Dougal has the other two waffles in one hand and he's shoving them into his mouth as he moves about the tiny area. Tigs squeezes out loops of syrup as Giddy scoots around her siblings, draws her elbows in, sits on a stool, and opens the waffle box again.

There are actually *two* frozen waffles at the back of the box. Giddy blinks, surprised. She looks to the stairs to see if Tad is watching. Then she slips one waffle into the trash while popping the other into the toaster.

Giddy puts a hand to her belly. Her stomach *burns.*

The fridge door smacks the back of Giddy's head as Dougal opens it. "Could you not?" she yells at him.

"Could you scoot up?" he snaps back, speaking around mouthfuls. He grabs some juice and uses it to swallow the last of the waffles before sucking in his chest to squeeze out of the kitchen. He goes to the door and peels winter coats back on a rack to get his backpack.

Giddy is eating instant brown rice with egg whites. She chews thoughtfully and her stomach shrugs off the meal, its low simmering line of acid receding in its pit. A thump from the stairs draws her attention. Giddy locks eyes with Tad as he takes one stomping step down; then the second foot joins the first on the same step. Then one more loud step down.

"Coffee! Coffee!" Giddy flinches as Tigs shoves her cup forward. Giddy pours her a quarter cup and watches, elbow propped on the table, chin in her hand, as Tigs pours about six tablespoons' worth of sugar into the cup before stirring it with a fury that jettisons little droplets over the rim. Out of nostalgia, Giddy pours herself a small amount of coffee, holds it to her nose, reveling in the smell of chemically induced power. She thinks: *Maybe with a little half-and-half?*

But her stomach lurches at the thought, and the burn rises up to the back of her throat. Giddy sighs and dumps her coffee down the drain as Tigs licks a circle of syrup around her mouth.

Tad has reached the last step on the stairs. He waits, watching Giddy for several long seconds, before rapidly stepping down and bolting to the table where Giddy slides him a small cup of coffee and his plate with a single waffle. He looks at Tigs's plate of two waffles and smirks. He grabs the syrup, squeezes out a half cup onto his single waffle before declaring: "There's something wrong with the toilet again."

From over at the coatrack, Dougal chokes back a laugh. He and Tad exchange a smile.

Giddy drops her fork. "Are you serious?"

Tad stabs his sopping-wet waffle and lifts the whole thing up, syrup dribbling over the sides of his plate.

"Did you use too much toilet paper again?"

He shrugs, takes a giant bite, forked waffle quivering. The quirking corners of his mouth are now coated in syrup.

Giddy folds her arms and leans back. "Well, I'm not fixing it right now."

Tad doesn't stop chewing, but his lips droop into a gratifying frown of disappointment.

Dougal is still grinning as he opens the door to leave. Giddy yells: "Bus stop!" and he slams the door in the middle of her sentence. She dumps out the rest of the coffee and springs into action, cleaning up and grabbing sack lunches from the fridge. Giddy crams them into Tigs's and Tad's backpacks. Bodie starts crying at the back door, a high keening sound that splits Giddy's eardrums. She winces, then calls out: "Coats!" before running to let Bodie back in. The dog shows his gratitude by jumping up all over her, cold nose running, tongue licking at Giddy's face. "Not now! Not now!" Giddy pushes him back down and says, "Guys, coats!" with renewed emphasis.

Tigs has only one arm in her coat and she's spinning and humming, letting the rest of the coat unfurl out around her like a cape. Tad's coat is on the floor, covering his feet, and he appears to be digging in his backpack for some of the lunch Giddy just packed.

"Nope!" Giddy swoops down from behind and zips up Tad's backpack. He scowls as she picks up his coat and forces his tiny arms into the sleeves. Tigs holds her arms out very elegantly for Giddy, as if she is a princess and Giddy her most trusted lady-in-waiting. Giddy grabs her coat on the way out the front door, where the winter air forces all of them to pop up their hoods and shove their lower faces into the necks of their shirts. The Barbers march to the bus stop, shivering, feet crunching through frozen brown grass and slipping on sheets of ice on the sidewalk.

Superdoo pokes Giddy's fingers with a rude abrasiveness when she shoves her frigid hands into her front jeans pockets. At the end of the block, Dougal sits on a curb a short distance away from the corner. He's flanked by two other high schoolers, and to Giddy's irritation they are vaping. Tad doesn't seem to notice.

He's found a broken wedge of concrete and is using his heel to work it out of the pavement.

When the bus pulls up, Dougal hops up and gets on. It's not lost on Giddy that his friends don't board the bus but instead head down the road toward the flashing open sign of a convenience store. They disappear inside and reappear with chips and drinks. They sit outside, eating, talking. Giddy shakes her head.

Her stomach gurgles with unpleasantness and she presses a hand to her belly, disappointed. She had high hopes for this morning's modified "white diet" breakfast.

"Giddy!" Tigs tugs her sleeve.

Giddy puts a fist to her mouth and belches.

Tigs pulls at her harder. "GIDDY!"

Giddy looks down.

Tigs holds up her fingers so Giddy can count them. "I have *five* questions today."

A great weariness settles on Giddy's shoulders and she sags a bit, her eyes scanning the end of the road to see if she can spot Tigs and Tad's bus yet.

Tigs yanks on her sleeve again—hard. "I said I have five!"

"OK!" Giddy disengages Tigs's tiny hand. "What are they?"

"Where does mud go after you get it off your shoes and it gets thrown out and why does everyone hate it so much?"

Giddy rolls her eyes. "Mud gets washed into the ground, and if you're a bug, you probably don't hate mud."

"Why do people like water more than mud then?"

Giddy hops a little on her feet to stay warm, checking the time on her phone. The elementary school bus is late. "Who says they do?"

Tigs shrugs. "Why do mermaids not live in mud then?"

"Actually, I'm pretty sure mermaids do live in mud and that's why we can never find them."

Tigs goes over to a tree and studies it before wrapping her arms around it and putting one foot up to see if she can get traction to climb. She loses interest after a few slides of her feet. Giddy sends a GIF to her friends of a cartoon cat slamming its head into a wall over and over.

She waits. Two minutes go by with no response. Tigs has decided to sit facing the tree and is making a game of involving it in a conversation. Tad has resumed digging into his backpack. He opens the chips Giddy packed in his lunch and starts eating them.

Giddy texts, *Any good music out there?*

That gets her a K-pop video and a hip-hop song, which she puts in an earbud to listen to. A third incomprehensible audio track sounds like it was recorded in somebody's garage. She frowns, unable to tell if what she's listening to is really bad or if she just doesn't get the style.

That's Kara, right? Trinity texting.

Oh yeah. She's great. Asia texting.

She's meta with her talent. Jess texting.

Giddy has never heard of this Kara person, but she is in the process of trying to figure out where she can download more music by her when the elementary school bus pulls up, sixteen minutes behind schedule. Giddy glares at it.

Tigs breaks away from the tree and complains. "That was only four of my questions!"

"Ask them faster next time," Giddy says, giving her and Tad a light push up the steps. As soon as the door closes, Giddy turns and takes big flat-footed steps so as not to slip on the icy pavement. But it's slow going, so when she hits the curb, she steps on the grass and runs. The soles of her sneakers kick up frozen ground slush, and within seconds her lower jeans legs are coated with a cold, muddy mess. Inside, Bodie jumps around her ankles as she goes up the stairs.

It's 7:02. If she hurries, she'll only be five minutes late to school.

The upstairs toilet has a tube sock in it, the pale end floating up through murky water like a tapeworm. Giddy invents new curses as she plunges it out, throws the sock in the trash, and disinfects her hands.

At 7:10, Giddy rolls a heavy bike out from the side of her house. It's a guy's—Jax's before he got a car. She stands on the pedals, which move slowly and arthritically, chain clicking and threatening to lock up. *Jax's bike is vintage*, said their mom, as if vintage were a thing to be proud of and not just code for cheap and secondhand. Her calves burn as she pedals, sticking to sidewalks when she can, feet splayed out for balance every time she hits a patch of ice. She switches to the road when the path becomes too clogged with joggers and dog walkers. On this particular morning Giddy is subject to a slow chain of traffic lights, and every time one turns green she has to stand on the pedals again to get them to resume movement.

By the time she pulls up to her school, locks up her bike, and enters the big double doors, it is 7:32 a.m., meaning she is currently seven minutes late. There's someone new at attendance, answering phones and writing messages on sticky notes.

"Barber *a-r* or *e-r*?" she asks, typing. "And is Giddy with an *i* at the end or an *ie*?"

"Barber like the haircut," Giddy says quickly, "and Giddy as in *happy*."

"Ah." A pass prints and Giddy takes off in a jog down the hall in the direction of the school's south wing. The muddy slush she accumulated on her jeans has hardened and is breaking off in little jagged pieces of dirt. Giddy slows long enough to reach down and slap most of the rest of the mess off with her hands. Her backpack knocks against her spine and Superdoo worms his way up to peek out of her pocket like a kangaroo kid. Giddy makes it to first-period art class *twelve* minutes late and slows her steps, softly opening the door to a room that smells of clay and cleaner and is filled with smudged tables instead of desks.

Students are already at work on the sculptures the teacher assigned them yesterday. The teacher is carving his own masterpiece at the front of the room: an elephant sitting on its hind legs, upward-turned trunk defying gravity.

Giddy holds up the pass. The teacher gives her a perfunctory nod and she crumples it up and throws it into the trash. She quietly heads to the back of the room to remove an art folder and a chunk of clay from a drawer.

Giddy delivers everything to her table, sits down on her stool, unslings her backpack . . .

And for a moment all she does is rest, elbows propped up, chin in her hands. Giddy allows her eyes to close, her breaths to even out.

After a few seconds she looks down. The assignment instructions, written on easy-to-clean laminated paper, read: *Sketch five things from life that are not dishware or sculpture. For example: buildings, trees, plants, people, animals, furniture. Use each sketch to inspire the form of a piece of functional pottery. DO NOT use as inspiration: cell phones, tablets, televisions, or cars.*

Giddy takes some ibuprofen out of her backpack and swallows two without water. Then she opens the art folder and rolls out her clay into little balls. She thinks she was pretty smart in sketching a piggy bank yesterday because it can be made with only balls of clay of varying sizes. Also, there's no texture work and no real concern for stability apart from a hollow interior, which Giddy solves by making the body as one solid lump first and then carving out the middle from the top. She molds a lid over the top before cutting in a small coin slot. The top sags into the interior twice before she gets the thickness of the sides just wide enough to support a top that tapers. The rest of the body is relatively easy, except for the curlicue tail, which concerned her until she allowed it to lie flat, curling up atop the pig's rear. She accomplishes all of this in eight minutes, which is two minutes faster than she thought she could do it in. There. Functional pottery finished.

Then her teacher leaves the elephant long enough to lower the lights and click on a screen. The class simultaneously groans and giggles. The screen reads: *Addendum! On a sheet of notebook paper, explain your personal connection to the object you chose to make.*

And Giddy thinks, *Well, dammit!* She looks around the room. There are things like mermaids and faces at the other tables and at least one rather impressive bong. Giddy doesn't own a piggy bank. She's only seen them in cartoons, so she lies and writes: *For Christmas I once received a piggy bank as a gag gift. . . .*

The bell rings. Giddy hastily sets the piggy bank on a high shelf, puts away the notebook paper and art folder, and washes up. A great sense of tiredness overcomes her at the thought of her next class, so out in the hall, she drags her shoulder along one wall in a slowdown maneuver Tad would envy. She forces herself through the door of English right as the bell rings. Most of the desks have been moved into a semicircle at the center of the room to facilitate discussion. A few remain in their original locations along the walls, an option for shy students who don't like to be front and center during discussion. A big sign reads, *Free seating encourages free thought!*, which might have been the case the first two weeks of school, but now everyone pretty much takes the same seat they are comfortable in whether it's a discussion day or not. Giddy has hers. It's at the very back of the room, just behind the corner of a bookcase. It's partly hidden, so she's almost never called on. Plus, the bookcase corner can be used to surreptitiously and illicitly prop up her phone.

The prompt on the board says: *Write a quick email advertising something you want to buy. You must describe one attractive quality about the item and explain why you need it.* Giddy takes out a piece of notebook paper and tiredly writes, *I want to buy a piggy bank.*

Must be bank-like. She thinks a moment before adding: *I won't need the bank after I buy it, so never mind.* She writes her name on it and drops it into a tray in front of the teacher's desk and collects this week's assigned reading from the bookcase. The teacher steps out from behind her desk and sits at the apex of the semicircle. Hands go up when she asks what people chose to advertise. Giddy takes off her jacket and arranges it into a barrier that will further conceal the light from her phone as well as make a comfortable pillow. As if anticipating this, her screen lights up.

Do we have eggs? Mom.

Giddy texts, *No.*

We had five yesterday!!

Tad and Tigs had two each. I used one this morning.

The teacher asks: "So what if you don't know what you need? How can you advertise for something if you don't know what it is you need?"

Mom: *Store w Jax. Pronto!*

It's Tuesday. Giddy's older brother will be out too late to take her to the store. "Pronto" will have to mean "Thursday." *OK.*

Giddy puts her phone face down, props up her elbows comfortably atop the cushy hoodie that's lying in a C shape on her desk, and allows her eyes to unfocus. The teacher walks around, holding up a slender copy of *The Yellow Wallpaper.* "As you read this short story, I want you to ask yourself how our protagonist, Jane, advertises her needs without fully understanding what those needs are."

Giddy closes her eyes and lets her thoughts meander to that state of being in between peaceful sleep and wakefulness.

Her phone gently buzzes. Giddy doesn't open her eyes again until she feels the bump of a student walking past. Everyone's packing, leaving. She didn't even hear the bell, didn't read *The Yellow Wallpaper*, which is still splayed open in front of her. Giddy sluggishly fumbles, dropping her stuff once before returning the short story to the bookcase and getting around her desk.

As she exits, the teacher regards Giddy with a curiously neutral expression that somehow always infuriates her. But Giddy's steps quicken as she heads outside to Pre-AP Algebra II, possibly her favorite class. Her eyes lock on the second hands of wall clocks as she bypasses a gridlock of students around the restroom water fountains, hurrying to be first through the door. Victorious, Giddy slides into her chosen seat, front row and center, and sits up straight. Her lips twist in excited determination at the question on the board: *Explain the steps required to simplify a rational expression.* Giddy is already writing the answer in her composition notebook while everyone else is still finding their chair. Then, because she has the time, Giddy creates a rational problem and uses each step to simplify it. Because there's *still* time, Giddy creates a second problem, making it a little more complicated than the first.

Giddy snaps her notebook closed and sneaks a sideways glance at Katlyn, who sits next to Giddy in the front row. Katlyn, with her neat little line of brand-new, brand-name pencils and a rotating menagerie of animal sharpeners—panda today, tomorrow a giraffe? Katlyn, with her shiny alligator Mary Jane pumps, who taps her foot with a *tink tink* against the desk leg as she writes, brow furrowed in concern. Giddy leans over to look. Katlyn's only half finished.

"How's the problem going?" Giddy asks, tone innocent.

Katlyn stops tapping and pinches her lips together. She doesn't say anything. She thumbs backward in her composition notebook, checking and rechecking the notes the teacher gave them last week.

Giddy sneers.

Katlyn's eyes flicker tensely off the page and up to the board. "Can anyone tell me," the teacher asks, "the three steps to—"

Katlyn's and Giddy's hands shoot up.

"Ms. Barber, can you give me the first step?"

"There are three steps in simplifying rational expressions," Giddy says. "The first is to factor both the numerator and the denominator of the fraction."

"Great. Can anyone give me the second—"

"I actually have an example problem," Giddy tells the teacher before Katlyn's hand can finish rising a second time.

"Oh. Lovely! Why don't you write it on the board while the rest of us finish up." He holds out a dry-erase marker for Giddy. "The second step?"

"You have to reduce the fraction by canceling out identical expressions in the numerator and denominator," Katlyn says. "I have an example too."

Katlyn points with her pencil to the board as if ready to write her example up there too, but she wilts when Giddy starts writing hers in a way that takes up most of the spare space. The teacher instead indicates that Katlyn should hold up her composition book for him to see. "Yes. Well done." He turns to see what Giddy has on the board and brightens. "Ah! The leading coefficient in your problem is a negative number."

Giddy stands up a little straighter, and Katlyn, troubled, turns back a few more pages in her notebook.

The teacher says: “And what do we do here, Ms. Barber?”

“Because it’s a negative coefficient,” Giddy says, “you also need to write the expressions in descending order to factor out the negative number.”

“So let’s do that. Let’s simplify Ms. Barber’s nicely creative problem.” Giddy sets the marker on his desk and takes her seat as heads incline and other hands shoot up with answers. Giddy tosses another sidelong look at Katlyn—Katlyn who never makes lower than a ninety-eight in any of her classes except algebra II, her weak point, in which she finished the last semester with only a ninety-one. And Katlyn wants to be valedictorian in two years.

Disappointingly, the teacher doesn’t call on Giddy again, though Giddy does have the pleasure of watching Katlyn’s vexed expression as she copies the example she wrote. Giddy grabs a set of extension problems from the teacher’s desk.

And gasps as she sits and Superdoo pokes her again. She pushes the action figure down. The algebra II extension problems are meant to be completed over the course of one week. Giddy breezes through half of them by the end of class.

From algebra II, it’s on to Pre-AP Chemistry. Giddy sits up straight front and center again while her teacher delivers a mini lesson on chemist Antoine Lavoisier and the value of experimentation. “By showing that the mass of phosphorus and sulfur *increased* through combustion, Lavoisier raised doubts about a popular alchemical theory and challenged the status quo."

Which is all well and good, but Giddy is eager for some actual practice problems. Her fingers drum on the table, restless and anxious for something to do. There's an equation for the formation of phosphorus pentoxide on the board. Giddy starts copying it into her composition notebook when her phone buzzes.

She reflexively takes it out of her back pocket and holds it under the desk. *Her voice is vomit. What u writin?*

Giddy looks over her shoulder to where Trinity and Jess sit at the very back, having taken Pre-AP-level Chemistry only because on-level conflicts with their dance elective.

Giddy sighs. She texts: *Hydrogen Oxygen Radon Potassium*

???

Giddy rolls her eyes and texts: *H, O, R, K, get it?* She slides her phone back into her pocket as three laughing emojis pop up. Giddy's irritated because her teacher has moved off Lavoisier and she missed the last thing she said. Zach, sitting one table over, leans to tap her table with his pencil. "Hey."

"Hey." Giddy is copying *combustion* and *reduction-oxidation* as the teacher adds them to the board.

Zach scoots his chair toward the aisle. "I don't know if you've got plans Saturday—"

"I'm busy," Giddy says. "Also, I can't date until I'm sixteen." The year is half over and Giddy's already had to use this line on Zach twice.

"Yeah, no, I know, but—"

Giddy looks up at Zach and he stops talking and starts fidgeting with his pencil instead, twisting it around in his fingers and tapping it against his knee. Giddy thinks if he leans forward any farther, he's going to somersault off his chair. "It's, um . . . not a date really. It's more like a study group."

"No," Giddy says. "Busy." And Zach scoots his chair back.

The lecture segues into a more interesting lesson about redox reactions, a demonstration involving magnesium and a burner, and instructions to diagram what the students believe happened to the electrons during the magnesium fire. That diagram takes up most of the remaining class time, and while some students are furiously wrapping up as the bell rings, Giddy has already turned in three finely detailed redox diagrams. She files out the door, Jess and Trinity behind her.

Asia's already at the cafeteria table when they all sit down for lunch. She's wearing an old jean jacket covered in a chaotic riot of bright patches and she's playing with a home-design program on her phone. She flashes a big smile at them all that earns her a flinch from Trinity and is completely ignored by Jess. Jess props her phone up, grabs an oversized hoodie out of her bag, and promptly disappears into it, pulling the strings tight around her face, hands sticking out just enough to press play on a video.

Trinity leans over, watches the video on Jess's phone, points to the screen, and giggles. Jess shoots her a cold look. Trinity's smile dissolves like cheap toilet paper. She lays her own phone flat and tries to carefully type something into a *Vote now!* post she's made with her press-on nails still intact. Giddy's phone buzzes.

She takes it out and checks it. It's a link from Trinity to her post: *Trend it or end it?* There's a picture of her nails and two buttons. *Vote now!* And Giddy thinks, not for the first time, that

Trinity's sitting right there, and if she wants to know Giddy's opinion on her nails, she could just ask. But Giddy sighs and clicks the *trend it* button, which sends a resulting ding to Trinity's phone, and Trinity smiles at her screen.

Giddy's started digging in her backpack for her lunch when Asia sets her stylus down, looks at them all, and says: "I'm thinking about house flipping as a career."

Automatically, Giddy's and Trinity's eyes turn to Jess for a reaction.

Jess fixes a cold, laser-level stare at Asia. So Asia starts speaking faster: "I'd know what kind of tile to pick out and I'd know how to buy it on the cheap because of my uncle. Also, I'd use a lot of vinyl flooring because it looks just as good as wood."

Giddy unscrews the lid of her lunch thermos. Today's designer meal is low-sodium bone broth with a few chunks of chicken breast. A burst of laughter explodes from the other end of the cafeteria and Giddy looks up, watches a line of seated students talking and laughing. One of them tosses a chicken nugget across the table to another student, who tries to catch it with his mouth.

Asia goes on: "Also, I know how to match colors and I'm passionate about trends." She stops long enough to take a quick sip of soda.

Jess says: "Are you finished?"

Asia frowns, swallows, sets her soda down.

Jess slides her arms out from her hoodie and leans in, half emerged from her dark cocoon. "Because if you're done explaining why you'd be so awesome at this, I should tell you that flipping a house is *hard*," Jess says, "and that most people who think they can do it fail."

Asia looks stunned. Giddy thinks she shouldn't be—Jess is never impressed by Asia's creative pursuits. Asia shoots an imploring look at Trinity, but Trinity's still typing around her nails. Trinity's voice sounds vacant as she says: "I dunno. These things are always more complicated than they make out on TV."

"Guys, I know it's hard!" Asia says. "But I think I would love—"

"Wi-Fi sucks here!" Trinity angles the phone to make it easier to tap the screen with her finger, but the GIF she's trying to add to her post is frozen.

"I would love flipping houses!" Asia says. "Also, most people don't have my experience."

"Actually, people with experience fail at it all the time. They lose everything," Jess says. "You would need to be something special."

"Yeah, special," Trinity whispers. Then her face brightens as her GIF unfreezes.

Asia shoots a dejected, hurt look back and forth between them, and Giddy doesn't know why Asia bothers or what she thought they would all say to her. Giddy's not sure if there's really such a thing as a social hierarchy in a group of friends, but if there is, Asia is definitely on the bottom.

Giddy's eyes slide back to the table of laughing students. So far the one trying to catch chicken nuggets in his mouth hasn't succeeded in doing anything more than getting a smudge of ketchup on his cheek.

Asia sounds wilted yet hopeful as she says: "Giddy, what do you think?" Then she snaps her fingers and hisses: "Giddy!"

Giddy blinks and looks at Asia. She tries to remember everything she knows about house flipping. But before she can say anything, Asia stands up. "I know! I want you to look at the pattern on my dress and imagine this same pattern but as fireplace tile."

Jess shoots them all a quick look swimming with subtext. "OK. You're a fireplace. Now what?"

"Imagine painted brick, white with a matte finish and over the mantel a bold tangerine—"

"Oh God? *Orange?*" Jess sticks out her tongue.

Trinity glances quickly at Jess then back at Asia. "I can't believe she went with orange," Trinity says, shaking her head.

"I'm not trying to discourage you from your dream," Jess says as Asia sits back down. "I'm just being realistic."

Trinity adds, "Everybody thinks they understand color, but it's really just their own taste and it doesn't match anyone else's unless— Oh, Giddy, look!" Trinity flips her phone around. "Watch this." It's a music video of a boy band with lots of flashing lights and a strong percussive backbeat. When the camera starts spinning, Giddy drops a hand to her stomach.

"Oh God," Trinity says, yanking the phone back, "did that make you sick?"

"You should know better," Jess snaps at Trinity. "Flashing lights trigger epilepsy."

"They *do* trigger epilepsy," Asia says just as sharply to Trinity. "Don't you pay attention? You don't do that when somebody's stomach is sick."

"It's fine." Giddy's stomach is doing its familiar flip-flops. She opens a ziplock bag and munches delicately at the edge of a cracker. Then she covers her mouth and burps.

"I hate that you have to eat crap all the time, Giddy." Asia sadly shakes her head. Then she takes another bite of snack-bar-issued pepperoni pizza.

"I would personally kill myself if I had to eat the crap Giddy eats." Jess types something into her phone. "No offense, Giddy."

"It makes *me* sick watching what Giddy eats," Trinity says.

"What did you eat this morning?" Asia asks. "It's stuff in the morning that makes people sick in the afternoon, isn't it?"

"Egg whites and brown rice. A little butter in the rice for flavor."

"You should *not* have used butter," Asia says, and Trinity is nodding in agreement. "That's grease. You need to eliminate greasy food."

"Yeah, you're kind of doing this to yourself, when you think about it," Jess adds. "You need to plan your meals."

Giddy tilts the thermos back and downs the rest of the soup in one big gulp. Her stomach roils against the invasion. In her mind, Giddy sees a thousand tiny warriors with spears poking little holes in her insides. "I found some more Kara music," Giddy tells them. "I downloaded a few more of her songs."

"Who?" Asia asks, and Trinity seconds with a shrug of confusion. Jess doesn't weigh in at all for a blinking second before: "Oh, that was just something we found this morning. It was random. We're not into Kara or anything. We were kidding about her having talent."

"You're not into Kara, are you?" Trinity asks.

"Because she's so derivative!" Asia insists.

Another *huge* burst of laughter from the table behind them, and this time it's not only Giddy's head that whips around to look at the nugget-tossers. "Basic idiots," Jess says.

"Thank God we are not that stupid." Trinity goes back to her forum. Jess snuggles deeper into her hoodie and pops earbuds in. Asia returns to her design program, though now she's chewing her lip, worried.

At this moment Giddy feels a shift inside her, a blessed weight lifted. *This* is why she likes sitting with Jess and her crew—it's when the earbuds go in. Everybody's comfortable not talking and no one expects anything out of anyone. For those first few glorious seconds, Giddy doesn't listen to anything. She just uses the earbuds to soften the noise around her. Then, for variety, she clicks on Kara's music. After a few nods to the beat, she concludes Asia was right: Kara is derivative. She doesn't know why she didn't hear it the first time. Giddy covers her mouth for another unpleasant burp, and when the lunch bell rings, when everybody else at the other tables is finding excuses to linger, Giddy and her friends just part with no goodbyes, which Giddy thinks is easier. And who wants a chin of ketchup from tossed nuggets anyway? She sneers at the table, and Superdoo, in his singular brutal expression of himself, decides to jab Giddy in the upper thigh right as she stands up.

"We're going to destroy this course tomorrow," Patrice says. It's fifth-period robotics, and today's timed course challenge involves using rocks and magnets to avoid obstacles and construct a tower. Giddy quickly surmises the real challenge will be disengaging the blocks from the magnet on their robot. Patrice pulls her thick curls back and lines up a ruler as she helps Giddy build a second attachment, one designed to help the bot gently withdraw from the block tower without knocking it over. Giddy's other teammate, Deb, runs an anxious finger along a laptop, crunching numbers as she programs. A boys' group is first to get the blocks stacked, but when the robot's reversal causes the whole tower to tumble down on top of the bot, Giddy's team chuckles with satisfaction.

Then Patrice asks Giddy: "What's wrong?"

"What?"

"You look like somebody murdered your dog."

Giddy shrugs. Her phone buzzes with a text. She takes it out of her back pocket.

Jess: *Ms. Cooper hates me.*

Giddy sends Jess a meme of somebody vomiting on the floor in front of a teacher.

Jess: *That's why I dont study. Fail me anyway.*

Giddy surfs the Web briefly, trying to find a humorous video clip to share. Something under a minute. Trinity was right about the school's Wi-Fi.

Jess: *Im so depressed.*

A little alarm goes off inside Giddy, but she doesn't respond. Instead she spends a couple of seconds eyeballing the stacked blocks. They look smooth. Should she add rubber grippers to her bot? She scrolls through GIFs before sending Jess one.

Jess: *Its probably my meds do you think they work am I just a bitch?*

Giddy mutters a curse because this text came just as she forwarded a clip of a Korean pop star face-planting onstage. She meant it to be funny. But now maybe it's going to read as her being exasperated with Jess?

Jess: *Im probably just a bitch I probably don't deserve meds cuz I SUCK AT EVERYTHING!!*

"Christ!" Giddy mutters.

"Everything OK?" Patrice asks.

"Yeah." Giddy's looking up something else—anything funny but not offensive funny. Something cute. Like maybe a stupid cat. Possibly a ferret.

Then Jess sends *her* a picture: *OMG GIDDY!! Asia just sent this she made this in graphic design her dream fireplace member? look*

It's a computer-rendered illustration of a tiled fireplace. The tile is a bright glassy tangerine with some kind of black inked flower design. The accompanying carpet and overstuffed chairs are vaguely Southwestern. Everything is brightly chaotic.

Jess: *OMG her design sucks so much HA HA.* Giddy sees that Trinity is now included in the text thread.

Trinity: *Poor gurl thinks this is good??*

Jess: *We have to be xtra nice now.* Then: *Giddy see it and be like . . .* and a resend of the GIF Giddy sent just now of a student vomiting in front of a teacher.

The bell rings.

It's on to seventh-period world history, where the teacher hands out index cards, and on the board it says: *Write down everything you think you know about World War I and then collect your textbook and QUIETLY read pages 154–159.* Giddy slumps in her desk because how the hell is she supposed to know anything about World War I when he hasn't taught it yet? Giddy writes *Hitler was a bad man* on one of her cards and drops it into the box at the front of the room, where the teacher sits at his desk clicking through emails. Giddy collects a class textbook, turns to the page written on the side of the board, and goes back to her seat.

It's always too warm in this class, but Giddy wears her jacket anyway because it's thick, and the collar, when she creases the back, acts as a neck pillow. Giddy hates her seat, which is dead center in the middle of the room, but sitting in the back would put her next to Hunter. Hunter, who sits with a kind of jackass smile on his face that wouldn't go away even if somebody died across his lap. Hunter, who is tall but likes to act like he's taller by slouching and stretching his legs out so they block the aisle and you have to step over them to pass while his idiot friends giggle over every little thing he whispers. Hunter, who likes to try to talk over the seats to Giddy even though she's pretty damn near sure she's never started a conversation with *him*.

Giddy flips her hood up, cracks open the book, which smells like earth and old coffee. One of Hunter's friends snickers as she pretends to focus really hard on what she's reading. The chapter title, *The War to End All Wars*, sounds promising, but most of it ends up being really boring and Giddy's eyes glaze over after just a paragraph.

She doesn't realize she was asleep until she hears the teacher say, "So, who was Ferdinand?"

Silence. It stretches out, long and uncomfortable. Giddy makes a pretense of being fascinated by a textbook photo of the archduke with his wife minutes before their assassination. Giddy's teacher is looking at the right side of the room, which means he's going to call on somebody over there and then Giddy and then somebody else and then she can sleep again.

"Mr. Carr? Who was Ferdinand."

"The archduke."

"Great." The teacher nods. "That's good. So why was he important?" He points to Giddy. "Ms. Barber?"

"He died," Giddy says.

Hunter raises his hand. "What was the guy's title?"

"Archduke."

"OK." Hunter lowers his hand.

"And why did it matter that he died?"

Silence.

"Come on, guys." The teacher throws up his hands. "Monday was yesterday! Let's see some life in here."

Hunter raises a hand.

"Mr. Blancovich."

"What was the archduke's name?"

Tittering from around the back of the room.

"You know his name, Mr. Blancovich."

"I forgot."

"Reread page one fifty-four then." The teacher scans the room. "Ms. Longren, why did it matter that Ferdinand died?"

Hunter raises a hand.

The teacher snaps his fingers as Bella blinks at her desk. "Ms. Longren? Come on! Why do we *care*?"

Hunter waves his hand. Emphatically. Giddy stifles a small sigh.

"Yes, Mr. Blancovich."

"I just remembered his name. It's Ferdinand."

More tittering. The teacher smirks. "That's great."

"It helped me learn that you said it just now."

Mild laughter. The teacher sits on the edge of his desk and levels a stare. "So we're going to do this today, huh? That's what you want, Mr. Blancovich? You want a whole rest of class full of essay work for everybody?"

This is the standard punishment for disrespect in history, but since Giddy's never gotten back a graded essay, she's not worried so much as mildly annoyed that there's going to be a lot of expected writing.

Hunter looks innocent. "I was just asking a question."

"Know what? Hold your questions to the end of class and we can discuss them privately." The teacher points to the note card box. "You can write it on an index card if you think you're going to forget." A few students snicker. To everyone else he adds: "I'm going to turn the lights off and we're going to watch a short video. Don't fall asleep, because you're going to have to answer questions about it."

The video, a brief illustration of the preexisting conflict between Serbia and Austria-Hungary, is narrated with such a soothing voice that Giddy has no problem drifting off while sitting straight up. When the lights come back on, the teacher kicks the legs of the desks of a few students who'd put their heads down, but not Giddy because her head was only lightly leaning against her neck-pillow hood and she wakes up fast.

"So what was the big thing that started this—actually, four big things. I'll write them on the board. I want you to write this down. *M-A-I-N*. Militarism, alliances, imperialism, and nationalism."

Giddy's phone buzzes.

Asia: *12?* Asia's sent a picture of the bottom half of her algebra homework.

Giddy reads it over and texts *x = 3 not 5*

Asia sends her a GIF of a fist-pumping kitten.

"So what is imperialism? Somebody tell me what imperialism is? Mr. Collier?"

"Um. A policy of defending a country's power through diplomacy or military force."

"Way to read it out of your textbook," the teacher says darkly. "Would have been nice if you'd put that in your own words, Mr. Collier. How about nationalism? Ms. Dabney—in your own words?"

Rhea has an index card in her hands. She's reading it, and something on it is making her laugh. "Um." Another giggle escapes her before she composes herself. "OK, it's like when you care about only yourself and that's it."

Giddy's phone buzzes again.

Asia: *13?* Another picture.

The teacher looks pleasantly surprised. "Yeah. If you were a country and you only cared about your country, sure."

Asia: *So lost w this one HELP!*

Rhea raises her hand. "I have a question."

"Go for it."

"Why did the prince kill Ferdinand?"

"Princip," the teacher clarifies. "Princip was the name of the man who killed Ferdinand."

"So he wasn't a prince?"

"No," the teacher says pointedly, rolling his eyes.

"So he wasn't a royal asshole?" Rhea asks the question fast and then bursts into giggles. She holds up an index card. "I'm sorry! That's so dumb, I know. It's just, Hunter handed his card to me and it's his question."

Laughter ripples through the class. It is a stark contrast to the teacher's cold and silent stare.

"Essays it is," he says after a beat, and there's a class-wide groan. "I'd like everyone to turn to page one sixty-five. Summarize what you know about Germany's relationship with Russia prior to the conflict. Then explain the domino effect of Austria-Hungary's declaration of war. Make sure you fill two pages." As the groans increase, the teacher adds: "Oh, is this a lot? Maybe you should have thought of that before you started passing note cards around and acting like you're still in middle school." He writes his assignment on the board, goes behind his desk, and sits at his computer. Giddy looks at her phone. There are only nine minutes left in this cursed class.

Hunter says: "Hey, Giddy."

Giddy doesn't say anything, so he says it louder. "Giddy! Move your big, fat head. I can't see the board over your hood."

Giddy ignores him. She's going over Asia's homework on her phone screen.

"I'm serious, Giddy. How can I complete my assignment if you keep putting that big-ass hood up like you're cosplaying a Jedi?"

Giddy whips her head around and glares at him.

"Thanks, Giddy," Hunter says. "Now I can see the right half of the assignment. Maybe if you leaned a little left, I could see the left half."

"Nobody thinks you're really going to do the work," Giddy says, "so why don't you shut up?"

Hunter assumes an affronted look. "It hurts for me to think that one of my peers doesn't have confidence in my abilities as a student."

Asia: *Giddy u there?*

Giddy turns back around and texts: *Sorry*

Asia: *13??*

Giddy expands the screen and holds it closer to her face to better read Asia's chicken-scratch handwriting when Hunter says: "Giddy, would you really please move your head down so I can see the board?"

Giddy ignores him.

Hunter shouts: "Giddy, is that porn?"

The teacher's head whips up, and as Giddy stuffs her phone into her pocket, the teacher pops open a drawer, fills out a form, gets up, and slaps it on her desk. "Sign it!"

"A write-up?" Giddy says. "For checking the time on my phone?"

"This class has a no cell phone policy. You should have powered it down or kept it in your pocket."

Giddy swears under her breath as she puts the phone and the paper in her pocket. When the bell rings to dismiss school for the day, Giddy jumps out of her seat. In the hall, she says: "Jackass."

"I don't make the cell phone policy in world history class," Hunter calls over the heads of students as she stalks off. "I just try to honor it!"

Giddy holds her backpack tight against her chest, using it as a shield as she mini-steps in a slow-moving crowd that clogs the very egress it craves. One final brutal crush expels Giddy out the double doors and into the sunlight. She unlocks her bike and heaves it out of the bike rack, rolling it to the sidewalk, where the chain locks and the wheels seize up. Giddy rolls it back an inch, then forward, then shakes it violently. The chain clicks into place, and as she climbs on the bike and stands, pressing down with all her might, she remembers her mom saying, *So it's tough to pedal? It's good cardio!* Giddy rides her bike home listening to a K-pop mix Jess recommended, thinking it might give her something to talk about tomorrow.

Nobody else is home yet and all is quiet except for Bodie, whose vicious wags knock a bunch of mail off the coffee table as he leaps around, trying to lick Giddy's chin. She lets him out in the backyard and restacks the mail. She checks the time: 3:25. Giddy takes a boxed casserole out to defrost. Two-day-old meat from a roast becomes tomorrow's sack lunch sandwiches for Tad and Tigs. In the pantry, she stares at the Tetris maze of reclipped chip bags before drawing one out and emptying its contents into three separate ziplocks. She labels the lunch that has mustard instead of mayo on the sandwich as Tad's and turns back to the pantry for something for herself to eat. She settles on a can of condensed beef broth, instant rice, and low-sugar applesauce.

Her phone buzzes.

Asia: *Got a 55 on my math homework*

Giddy texts back: *I'm sorry*

Asia: *What are u doin?*

Making lunches

Asia: *Jess is being a bitch again prob off her meds*

Giddy keeps her phone in her hand as she goes out the front door and begins walking to the end of the street. It's 3:39 p.m.

Trinity: *U there?*

Yes

Trinity: *Chemistry tonite?*

Sure

Giddy puts the phone away. Now that she's no longer heated up from bike-riding, she's feeling the cold again. Her breaths puff in the air and she bounces on her feet as she keeps an eye on the end of the street. She shoves her hands deep into her front jeans pockets.

When her fingers scrape painfully against plastic, Giddy yelps and pulls her hands free. Superdoo's head pokes out of her pocket, grinning up at her. Giddy groans and shoves him back down. She puts her hands in her coat pockets instead.

The high school bus pulls up and Dougal jumps out and stomps past Giddy, cold breaths pumping out of him with the fury of a hoard-guarding dragon. Giddy glares until she's verified he's made it to their front door, then she scrolls through forum posts on a quack website Jess once signed her up on for fun. It specializes in spiritual healing and other pseudo-nonsense that Giddy figures she and Jess can snigger over together.

But her thumb pauses over one post:

I'm healthy but my stomach isn't. Giddy clicks the link. It takes her to a flood of posts that seem geared toward a vegan lifestyle and/or gluten-free products. Giddy mentally adds coconut water to her next grocery run, then sees a bolded response that appears to have nothing to do with food.

Have you tried opposition therapy?

Giddy's thumb slides past that statement. She scrolls, seeking additional info about coconut water. But she slows until the bolded words hover at the top of her screen, just one flick from disappearing.

Giddy taps the post to expand it.

I used to struggle with depression. But it didn't make me cry. I had a sick stomach a lot and I couldn't sleep much. Also life just seemed "gray" to me and if you've ever battled depression you know what that feels like ha ha!

Giddy frowns.

I tried medication but it didn't work. So I set up a plan to snap myself out of it. I call it my "opposition therapy." Basically, I stop doing the things I want to do and try to do the opposite. For example, I like hot showers but they weren't doing anything for my depression so I switched to cold showers, which I also didn't like but I did it anyway. I started changing my hobbies, doing things I'd never normally do: I took an improv comedy class—

A pop-up advertising a self-help book to "a better you" blocks the screen and Giddy spends a few irritated seconds finding the hidden X to close it.

—to cure stage fright and had a miserable time the whole way but here's the deal . . . I was feeling things again. Maybe not good things, but having experiences that somehow affected me. And I realized nothing had really affected me for a long time and maybe this was good.

The pneumatic whoosh of the elementary bus door jars Giddy. Tigs slams into her, hugging Giddy's legs with a force that almost knocks the phone away.

"I thought of my fifth question," Tigs says. "How come—"

There's a collective yell as every student on the bus gets out of their seat and rushes to the back. The bus bounces. Tad bolts off the bus, grinning ear to ear. He's holding a backpack up high, and a boy with a black eye is chasing him. "That's mine! It has all my Legos!" Tad darts behind Giddy and Tigs, grinning viciously.

Giddy thinks it's hilarious her little brother believes she will protect him. She yanks the stolen backpack away so hard, she hurls Tad to the ground. As she thrusts it into the hands of its distraught owner, Tad sits up, scowling and rubbing his shoulder.

"Why'd you do that?" Giddy demands.

Tad grins—wider and wider. Giddy stares back, forcing him to hold the smile until she's pretty sure it hurts his face. Only when he winces does she take Tigs's hand to walk home ahead of him.

Beside her, Tigs beams at being chosen. "How come nobody ever makes cheese?"

Giddy frowns. "I don't understand your question. People make cheese, Tigs."

"No, they don't! They buy it at the store."

"OK. But somebody made it first." Giddy opens the door of their house and helps Tigs out of her jacket.

"No, they don't, Giddy! They all just buy it!"

"Fine. They just buy it." Giddy goes into the kitchen and preheats the oven. Bodie's dish is full, and in the den, Dougal is watching TV. He's let Bodie in from the backyard and the dog is now sprawled over his lap on the sofa, tail thumping quietly. "Have you done your algebra yet?" Giddy asks, slipping her jacket onto the rack on top of Tigs's. "Ms. Russo gives homework every day."

"Have you done yours?" Dougal asks.

Giddy gapes and points outside. "I've been busy."

"So have I."

Giddy walks over, Tigs hot on her heels. "So my fifth question is how does the store get the cheese?"

"Tigs, go take a bath. I'll be up in a bit." Behind them, Tad stomps upstairs, feet loud and deliberate. Giddy collects the remote and cuts the TV off. "Busy doing what, Dougal?"

Dougal throws up his hands and Bodie lifts his head. "Seriously?"

"Busy doing what?" she asks again. "You ride the late bus. You have nothing to do but sit and wait for like twenty minutes outside school before the last bus picks you up and there's all those stops on your route you could be, like, getting it done at the red lights."

"You know I can't work in a moving vehicle," Dougal tells her.

"Well, what's your excuse right now?"

"Christ, Giddy!" Bodie hops off Dougal and jogs away, tail lowered. "I just got home!"

Giddy sets the remote on top of the TV, crosses her arms, and waits. Dougal mutters something and grabs his bag. He puts his fingers to his forehead like he's developed a sudden headache. "You dropped something," he says. As Dougal goes upstairs, Giddy looks down.

Superdoo is sprawled across the tip of her sneaker.

Giddy rolls her eyes and collects him. She almost puts him back in Tad's room, but at the last second she ducks into her room to deposit her backpack, grab a pencil, and toss the action figure on top of her bed. She hears Tigs splashing around in the upstairs tub. Giddy opens the door to Tad and Tigs's room. Tad pokes around in his backpack. "I've got five minutes to help you with math," she tells him, "and then I've got stuff to do."

Tad stares blankly. Then he upends his backpack, spilling the contents all over his bed. Giddy sighs and sits on the bed next to him and watches as Tad picks up a piece of paper that was crushed underneath a binder and then smooths it out with his hands.

"You're repacking that bag when we're finished," Giddy tells him, and he mutely nods. Giddy hands him the pencil and sits down. It's an odd-and-even matching worksheet. As Tad draws lines connecting numbers to groups of apples and butterflies, Giddy asks him again: "Why'd you take that kid's backpack?"

That same stupid grin spreads across Tad's face and Giddy decides it might just be easier to drop the whole thing because she doesn't have the energy for it and anyway, the kid got his bag back.

Tad seems like he's got this, so Giddy starts to stand, but he grabs her hand. "Wait! This one?"

"You already did that one. There're seven butterflies. Seven's an odd number."

"No"—he taps the pencil emphatically on the page, as if she's an idiot for not understanding—"*this* one!"

"How many squirrels?" Giddy asks.

Tad counts. "Five."

"And is five odd or even?"

"Five is ev—odd! Five is odd."

"Great. When you're done, kick Tigs out of the bath and clean yourself." Giddy leaves for her room. There's the sound of hip-hop trickling through the walls from Dougal's bedroom. Giddy flops onto her bed and yelps as something hard cuts into the center of her back.

Superdoo lies on her bed, a twisted, broken mess. His head has popped off and the cape has come unattached except for where it's caught in an elbow. One arm has dislocated completely at the shoulder and the legs are bent backward.

Giddy spends a few minutes reconnecting him and straightening his yellow cape. She positions Superdoo, seated, on the edge of her desk and gets out her binder. Giddy breezes through the rest of the algebra II extension problems, her brain easing. She has always enjoyed numbers. There's a dependability in them, a comfort in their fundamental sameness and unchanging value.

Her algebra II work is over too soon, as is Giddy's input into the chemistry forum, which she really did just to give Trinity academic points on their teacher's discussion. Giddy is slower to work on her world history reading assignment. She's already a chapter behind. After a few paragraphs she decides to put it off again. Bodie pops open her door and hops onto her bed. She scratches his belly while perusing a series of English-assigned open-response questions about the conclusion of *The Yellow Wallpaper* by Charlotte Perkins Gilman. Giddy hasn't read it, so she copies a couple of answers from a summary she finds online. She's also supposed to read act 1, scenes 1 and 2 of *Hamlet*, which she has in an app on her phone. Giddy skims over the first few pages, which seem to involve nothing more than a couple of people talking about what it's like to guard a tower before deciding online summaries will probably do for this one as well.

Her stomach hurts. Giddy has a sample pack of prescription antacids her mom snagged from a doctor at work. She said she could get Giddy a full prescription if it helps, but since it hasn't, Giddy hasn't bothered approaching her mom about it. She's fallen back on an over-the-counter brand, but now she wonders if antacids lose their strength over time, so she picks up her phone again to look it up.

The opposition therapy post she was in the middle of reading pops up. Giddy frowns. She googles "opposition therapy quack science" but finds nothing related. She tries "opposition therapy" and "reverse therapy," but neither sounds like what the guy on the thread was talking about. Giddy concludes it's probably his own invention, not worth her time. She starts to go back to researching coconut water.

And for some reason finds herself returning to the forum to read more of the guy's post:

I started exercising, even though I hated it. I changed everything I ate but not to be healthy, just to be "opposite." I ate things I never would have considered eating. I actually ate crickets.

This comment leads to a lengthy side discussion on the merits of cricket flour. Giddy is reading it when she hears the front door open. Giddy goes downstairs as her father shrugs out of the jacket he wears over his scrubs. He has a phone against his neck. He says: "Well, are his teachers following Dougal's accommodations, because if they're not, that could explain why he's acting out?"

Giddy puts the casserole into the oven and sets a timer. She flops onto the sofa, phone in hand, reading:

Then after I started doing things I would never do (hang gliding is for another post) I started making a list of the responsibilities I take on and the duties I regularly avoid. I have roommates and they were mostly agreeable to trading out chores for a while when I told them what I was trying to accomplish.

Her dad ends the phone call right as a damp Tigs hops downstairs two steps at a time, bundled in koala jammies and looking perturbed. He scoops her up into a quick hug before setting her down and going into the living room, squeezing behind the sofa to sit at a tiny computer desk tucked away in a crowded corner. When Tigs tugs at his sleeve, he disengages her fingers: "Papa's busy, honey."

"But I can't find my koala hat!"

He swivels the chair, a half smile on his face. "Do you know where you lost it?"

Tigs shakes her head.

"Did you look for it in your room?"

Tigs shrugs.

"Well, I'm not finding it for you, babe." Dad pulls up the high school website. "If you want that hat, you need to find it yourself. Barbers solve their own problems. Actually"—he clicks a screen and grades pop up—"the problem is, your room's messy, so after supper I want you to clean it. The whole thing."

Tigs frowns. "Even Tad's side?"

"Tad's not the one losing things, so, yeah, the whole room." He turns his attention back to the screen, starts looking over grades, and shakes his head. Tigs frowns in consternation. Upstairs, Giddy hears the bathroom door open and Tad's small feet as he runs into his room.

Have you ever counted up all the little things you do on a schedule without really thinking about it? Like, I don't smoke, but I compulsively floss my teeth, after each meal and maybe six or seven times through the day total. So I quit flossing so much and bought some mouthwash, which I swore I would never use because it burns my mouth. I changed where I sit in the apartment. I changed the route I take to work in the mornings. Small things you wouldn't think matter. But it turns out making these changes annoyed the hell out of me!

Tigs grabs a tablet off the coffee table and sits on the sofa, the missing hat apparently more trouble than it was worth.

"Christ almighty." Her dad shakes his head in horror at what he's reading on the computer screen.

It was like a security blanket was being taken away from me, a security blanket I didn't even know I carried. Like phones, for example—what would happen if you just put your phone away?

The oven timer sounds and Giddy goes into the kitchen. She opens the corner of the instant rice bag and pours a couple of tablespoons of beef broth inside before setting it in the microwave. To Giddy's surprise, her dad is hastily clearing off the island table: more junk mail, plastic grocery bags, six-packs of soda. He piles everything on the coffee table. "We are all going to eat together as a family tonight," he tells Giddy. He sits on a stool and texts. "I'm trying to reach your mom. Has she texted you? Her shift ended at noon." Tigs ambles past Giddy to sit with the tablet in the kitchen at her dad's feet and her dad and Tigs are a pair, both staring into their selected screens with purpose.

Anyway, if you want to do what I did then—

"Giddy, I asked if your mom texted you?"

"No," Giddy says. "The only thing she did was text earlier that she wanted eggs."

"How'd we end up out of eggs? So she didn't say if she was picking up a shift tonight?"

"No."

"Maybe she texted Jax." Her dad starts texting again.

—I recommend starting with this framework: Step 1—Reverse all your habits.

Dougal comes down, Tad right behind him. Tad's making a game of kicking the back of Dougal's feet before Dougal moves them to the next stair. Dougal is moving slowly to accommodate this, smirking as Tad giggles. At the last step, Dougal waits for Tad to catch up then kicks viciously backward, striking Tad's unprotected toes. Tad yelps and staggers, grabbing the railing as Dougal grins and goes into the kitchen. Tad sits at the base of the stairs, rubbing his foot. "Ow!" He grins.

Dougal opens the oven. "Casserole looks done. When do we eat?"

Tad limps over to the table as their dad says: "We're waiting for your mom. Just sit down."

Tigs and Tad are already seated. Giddy and Dougal take their respective places, and Bodie weaves his way under Tigs's legs, belly pressed to the floor in a hopeful position. Giddy looks at her phone under the table: *Step 2—Think of a thing you must always be in control over and let that control go. Put someone else in charge or abandon it entirely.*

"Dougal," their dad asks, "have you looked at your grades?"

"Yeah."

"Recently?"

"No, not recently."

"When?"

Dougal shrugs.

"Because you're failing three subjects."

Dougal nods, processing this information. "That's bad," he agrees.

Step 3—Do an activity you would never, ever do and keep doing it even though you hate it. If you can, do something unexpected each day.

"OK, guys, put the screens away." Her dad waves at Giddy's phone and Tigs's tablet. "I think we can live without phones for five minutes." To Dougal, he says: "Are your teachers reading your tests out loud to you?"

"Which ones?"

Her dad rolls his eyes. "All of them, Dougal. Are all of your teachers reading your tests out loud? Because you get that provided to you."

Dougal leans back in his chair and appears to think. "Ms. Prince always reads them, Coach Loftton." He shrugs again. "Yeah, they're doing it."

"What about . . ." Her dad scrolls across a page on his phone. "What about 'breaking your assignments down' and 'helping you organize'?" He looks up at Dougal.

"Are you looking at my accommodations on your phone?" Dougal asks, sounding incredulous.

"I'm just trying to be thorough. Hang on"—their dad runs his thumb across the screen—"can't believe your mom hasn't texted. What about your colored overlays?"

Dougal: "What about them?"

"Do you have them? Do you use them? Do you put the overlay on the page when you read—"

"Yeah, Dad," Dougal says, sounding tired. "I use them. I use everything I'm supposed to use. I take breaks. I organize. I double-check my assignments before I leave."

Giddy and Tigs have their devices on the table in front of them, screens dark from disuse. They lock eyes. Tigs sticks her tongue out at Giddy and Giddy repeats the gesture.

"Are you missing any assignments?" Dad asks. He's texting as he speaks. "Geez, your mom. I can't even . . ." When Giddy reaches a slow hand toward her own phone, he says: "Not you! Come on, guys, bear with me here. I'm just sending your mom another—"

"Yeah, I turn all my stuff in," Dougal tells him.

"Really?" Dad's head snaps up. "Because I checked your school grade book on the computer tonight and your grades are littered with zeros."

"OK." Dougal barks out a laugh. "I haven't turned everything in."

Dad gives him a horrified look. Then his phone buzzes. He checks it and tosses it onto the table in disgust. He gets up and takes the casserole out of the oven that Giddy turned off minutes earlier. He puts it on the table. There's a viscous frustration to his knife cuts. "Your mom picked up an extra shift. Go ahead and eat."

Giddy microwaves her rice. When she comes back to the table with her rice and applesauce, Tigs and Tad are already digging into the casserole. Giddy eats her rice and applesauce slowly, measuring the impact of every bite as it slides into her stomach, braced to stop if necessary.

"Do you know what assignments you're missing?" Dad asks.

"Yeah," Dougal says between bites.

Dad looks at him sideways. "Do you really?"

Dougal shakes his head. He's still smiling a little. Dad sighs. Dougal clears the rest of his plate in three bites then hops off his stool. As he walks upstairs, Giddy sees him slip his earbuds in.

Tad and Tigs are still slowly making their way through their meal. Dad wipes his mouth and looks at Giddy. "This was good. It really was. We don't sit down enough together." He gets up and goes to the couch. A second later the television is on.

Giddy takes the entirety of her dad's hour-long crime drama to finish the applesauce and most of the rice. Tigs and Tad have long ago finished eating and are in the den, where Tigs is finding new ways to try to hide under the cushion of an overstuffed chair. Giddy holds her plate under the water in the sink, rinsing it. With her other hand, she's on her phone.

Make yourself do this for a sustained period of time. Do not waver, even though at times you may not like who you become.

The post ends. Giddy stares. His program over, her dad switches to news, while Giddy, disappointed, scrolls through the forum looking for anything else posted by the user, but after searching for almost thirty minutes, she can't find anything. She's still leaning on the counter, searching archives, when her mom comes in. She peels off her coat and tosses it onto the overburdened rack, which wobbles under the strain. From the couch in the den, Giddy's dad gives their mom a silent, reproachful gaze, but her mom isn't looking at him. "Giddy, did you get eggs?"

"It's on the list."

She's wearing scrubs and Crocs. She kicks off the Crocs. "How's robotics going?"

"It's fine."

Her mom walks into the den and curls up on the other side of the sofa. One finger extends to touch the back of her dad's head, playing with his hair as he watches TV. He looks over at her and she smiles. He says: "You could have texted."

"I can't drop everything to check my phone all the time."

"One text. That's all. Wouldn't have taken a lot." Her mom sighs.

Her dad says: "The school wants to sit down about Dougal."

Her mom's eyes widen. "Did you tell them that we both work and we're busy?"

"I did, but they need at least one meeting to update his accommodations this year and the year is already half over—"

"Oh my God!" Her mom lets her head drop back against the sofa. "They're just trying to waste our time. There's no update! Obviously, Dougal needs to keep everything. If he didn't, his grades would have improved."

"I know."

"Have they asked the teachers if they're doing their part?" her mom asks. "That could be the problem." Her mom sighs again and nestles a little deeper into the sofa. Her dad switches the channel to a contestant singing her heart out before a panel of dispassionate critics.

Tad and Tigs head upstairs as Giddy puts the dishes in the dishwasher. Her mom is saying: "They just want to shift the blame to him. But it's not his fault. Dyslexia is a disability."

Her dad lowers his voice. "They said he flipped off one of his teachers."

"He did *not*!" her mom says, and stares ahead in soft surprise. "Why would he do that? Is he lashing out? That's not OK."

"No, it isn't."

"My God," her mom says. "He's hurting so much."

Giddy goes up to her room. Next door she can hear Tigs tearing up her own space, probably looking for her koala hat again. Giddy flops onto her bed, and the vibration courses through the floor and up into the desk to jar Superdoo, knocking him sideways. Giddy picks him up and resets him, lifting a spiral notebook out from under him so he'll sit more evenly. Giddy looks at the spiral and then back at Superdoo. She shakes her head, opens the spiral, and grabs a pen.

Because there's no harm in making a list just to pass the time, Giddy writes: *Step 1—Reverse all your habits.* Then she lies back on her bed and thinks: *What are my habits?* She looks at Superdoo's face, frozen into an eternal can-do attitude, and she thinks: *School, home, school.* But that seems so mundane, if not true. Giddy decides the key is to go in order and be specific. *I wake up before the alarm. I get everyone up. I make breakfast . . .* What's the opposite of that? *Not* wake up? *Not* make breakfast?

So she takes a cue from the author's list and writes: *Cold morning shower!* There's a reverse. Giddy always takes a hot shower before going to bed. What else? Giddy frowns. She could write *Skip school* next, but the thought of being stuck in her own house confronted by a commitment to nonactivity bothers Giddy, so she writes: *Leave bike. Walk.* Which would take a stupid-long period of time to get to school. What about classes?

Giddy chews on the end of her pen. She makes a two-column chart labeled *Good/Bad* and organizes her subjects. She ends up with:

Good: Algebra II Pre-AP, Chemistry Pre-AP, Robotics

Bad: English, World History

She needs to add art, which she has an A in, but everybody gets an A in art as long as they turn in their work, so she puts it under *Bad.*

Good: Algebra II Pre-AP, Chemistry Pre-AP, Robotics

Bad: English, World History, Art

She'd need to flip this, to start doing a terrible job in the good classes and a wonderful job in the bad ones if she was going to reverse her habits at school.

Giddy yawns.

Step 2—Think of a thing you must always be in control over and let that control go. Put someone else in charge or abandon it entirely.

Well, that's pretty simple. Giddy writes: *Put Dougal in charge.* That idea is hilarious because putting Dougal in charge means nothing would ever get done.

Step 3—Do an activity you would never, ever do and keep doing it even though you hate it. If you can, do something unexpected each day.

And Giddy thinks step 3 is redundant, because if she's doing steps 1 and 2, isn't she already being unexpected all the time?

What else would she do that's different? Play sports? Shave her head? *Not* complete a list?

Make yourself do this for a sustained period of time.

Giddy writes *10 days* and then sets the list on her desk and scrolls on her phone for a while. It's past nine. Tad and Tigs are quietly squabbling from their respective beds, their voices muted. They won't leave their rooms to bother Mom and Dad anymore tonight because they don't want a chore. Dougal's room, on the other side of hers, is ominously quiet. Her mom's in the shower, preferring, as Giddy usually does, to clean up at a time when there's no competition for hot water. Afterward she'll retire to her and Dad's room at the end of the hall next to the upstairs bath, and on nights when they forget to close the door all the way, Giddy can sometimes hear them quietly discussing things in bed before they fall asleep.

Only now downstairs does she hear the door open and her older brother, nineteen-year-old Jax, putting his coat on the rack. She lies there and listens: Jax opening the fridge and grabbing food, Jax eating by himself. Jax walking upstairs and turning left at the hall to go the direction of a short set of stairs up to the attic that used to be storage but was converted into a bedroom for Jax just before Tad was born. Jax's feet plodding on the floor above her, the noise coming through the ceiling. It's still early to her, but Giddy, who used to stay up past ten, feels her eyes sagging. She should shower. She always showers late at night when there's lots of hot water, but she's tired. The words *Do not waver* hover in hazy lines at the edges of her brain because that was half the sentence of what the person in the forum said at the end of their post.

The other half was: *Even though at times you may not like who you become.*

She falls asleep.

1

Giddy wakes fifteen minutes before her alarm, her phone buzzing in her hand. She blinks dumbly, realizes she never got dressed for bed but just fell asleep as is. Giddy sits up and opens the text:

Mom: *Scrapbook videos?* 😊😊😊

Giddy lets her head drop back on the pillow, closes her eyes. The phone buzzes again.

Giddy opens one eye.

So cute that last one!! Four smiley emojis.

Now a link, which Giddy's thumb brushes over. A video opens. There's small Giddy again with Superdoo, knocking over dominoes and laughing her ass off.

Giddy closes her eyes again. Drifts. When the alarm goes off, she jerks upright and her clumsy fingers fumble with the clock. Her head itches. She never showered, and now there won't be any hot water because her mom keeps it freezing at night and their water heater is crap. Giddy staggers into the bathroom and tosses her phone next to the sink, where the video of small Giddy plays in a loop. Giddy hears the crash of the dominoes, small Giddy laughing, as she steps into the shower and puts her hand on the hot water tap, knowing that it's going to be lukewarm at best.

For a moment she just can't manage. She presses her forehead against the tile and closes her eyes, and from behind the curtain she can hear small Giddy screaming, *"SUPERDOO!"*

She needs to move. She needs to get going. She has breakfast to make and she thinks, *I've got to get it done fast in case Tad clogs the toilet again. Get the shower over, then the bus stop, then you can sleep a little in English, and if you're extra quiet in world history, maybe Hunter will be too busy bothering someone else to notice you. Get home. Get back to bed.*

Her hand is still on the hot water tap and for some reason it's not moving, not turning anything on. She can hear small Giddy moving, though, knocking over dominoes and laughing her way into hiccups.

Step 1—Reverse all your habits.

Giddy stares at her hand on the hot water tap before taking it away in dumb confusion. This won't be a hot shower, despite the tap's promise. It's going to be a lukewarm sucky shower that leads to a lukewarm sucky day and it occurs to Giddy that all her days are pretty much like this and they aren't getting any better and why isn't she moving?

Small Giddy: *"SUPERDOO!"* Crash of dominoes.

Just take the damn shower!

Small Giddy: *Crash!* Laughter. Hiccups.

Take the shower!

"SUPERDOO!!!"

Giddy grits her teeth, drops her hand to the cold water tap, and turns it all the way up in one violent twist.

The water hits her with cannonball strength and Giddy screams, *"Shit!"* Only, the word stretches out into a long ribbon of shock. Her hands pump against the tile as she backs away from the water, into the tub's far corner, feet almost slipping out from under her.

"Shit, shit, shit . . ." Giddy spins in place, shower rings rattling, and slaps the water onto parts of her body, alternating with soap. Her hair gets the fastest wash imaginable as the sensation of cold sinking into her scalp is one of the most regrettable things she's ever experienced. Giddy vaults out of the tub in less than thirty seconds, toweling off and feeling no cleaner than when she stepped in.

Giddy stumbles into the hall, where the floor is super cold. She barrels past the thermostat and into her room to wriggle into a heavy sweater and jeans. Giddy sits on the edge of her bed, arms folded around herself, shivering, feeling like an idiot. And then her eyes lock onto the college posters on her walls.

One's from MIT. Another Stanford. There're a couple of regional universities with higher acceptance rates. They all came for free this past summer after Giddy sent a series of emails requesting information on the schools' mechanical engineering programs. The one thing they all have in common is the students pictured are either smiling or contentedly focused, whether they're molding thermoplastics or gripping soldering irons with confidence over wire-riddled breadboards. Not one of *them* looks like an idiot, and Giddy can't imagine a single one sitting on the edge of their bed shaking and shivering in a freezing cold house.

Superdoo watches from her desk, a comically optimistic smile on his plastic face. She grits her teeth, grabs the pen, and crosses out *10 days.* Everybody does things in periods of ten. Base ten is the most common system of counting, used on everything from money to the metric system. Giddy writes *11 days* because 11 *isn't* what's expected. It's also a good solid prime number.

Step 2—Think of a thing you must always be in control over and let that control go. Put someone else in charge or abandon it entirely.

Giddy stands up. She goes out into the hall and marches straight past the thermostat without adjusting it, bangs on Dougal's door with her fists, waits a second and bangs on it again. Pause, repeat. Pause, repeat.

There's the sound of Dougal's headboard hitting the wall as he swears and rolls over in bed. Giddy says loudly: "I'm leaving for school and I'm not walking anyone to the bus. Lunch is in the fridge, but you'll have to make Tad and Tigs breakfast."

She doesn't hear anything. For all she knows, Dougal is already back asleep, but a thrill of excitement rushes through her at the thought, the very thought, of Dougal having to do all these things instead of her. And it's not too late to just go downstairs and start setting up breakfast for everyone as normal. But her teeth still rattle with cold and she feels *charged*, which is new and different. Giddy can't remember the last time she felt like this.

She says through the door: "I'm leaving you in charge, Dougal."

Now there's a very small sound, like somebody repositioning themselves on their bed. Giddy rushes into Tad and Tigs's room and hastily shakes them awake. "I'm leaving. Walk with Dougal to the bus, OK? Don't forget to grab your lunch from the fridge."

Tigs wipes one bleary eye and sits up in bed with a sleepy disconnect. Tad nestles farther into his covers, blanket under his chin, eyelids slammed into deliberate lines and a smirk on his lips.

"He's pretending," Tigs sagely whispers.

"I know." Giddy exits, hitting the stairs so fast, Bodie doesn't have time to trip up her legs. He barrels down after her, a surprised whine emitting from the back of his throat. Giddy grabs rice and chicken broth from the pantry—

Reverse all your habits.

—and slowly puts them right back. Giddy stares, regarding them for a moment not as a meal but as the pair of white flags she waves at her stomach. Instead she pops open her phone and goes back to the post again. *I actually ate crickets.*

Giddy makes a face. Didn't Tad say there were toasted crickets at his museum field trip last year? She searches the pantry but can't find any. The absence of crickets leaves her with an odd sense of dejection and relief. Giddy grabs some smelly rye bread instead and closes the pantry door.

Into the kitchen next to raid the fridge. She avoids the Tupperwares of tame dinner leftovers—store-bought rotisserie chicken and pizzas—and starts pulling out condiments: ketchup, mayo, hot sauces . . . all things she refuses to touch. She sets them next to the rye and pushes her way to the back of the fridge. There're bottles of pickles. There's old cream cheese, maraschino cherries, a variety of salad dressing, ancient hummus. . . .

She slides a jar of sauerkraut aside, revealing a bottle of pickled sardines behind it. Their gray heads are still attached, vacant eyes staring, and they jiggle from Giddy bumping the bottle with her hand. She yelps and jumps back out of the fridge, ramming her hip painfully against the kitchen island.

Giddy starts to slide the sauerkraut in front to cover them up again and pauses, hand on the bottle. Her dad likes sardines. He eats them on crackers. This bottle is new and looks untouched.

Giddy thinks, *I could make a sauerkraut and ketchup sandwich.* Which would be pretty radical for her, all things considered. But also she's eaten sauerkraut, so besides it being virtually guaranteed to upset her stomach, there's no risk. It's just a normal food from the normal Barber food stocks.

And a second ago, she was going to eat crickets.

Giddy slides the sauerkraut aside and reaches a hesitant hand in for the sardines. She uses a spoon to pop the lid. Inside, it smells like pickles. They can't be terrible, right? Giddy makes a face and slathers one rye slice with at least two tablespoons' worth of mayonnaise and the other slice with equal amounts of ketchup. Then she tries to get some sardines out with a spoon. But they keep slipping along the glass edge until Giddy, frustrated, dumps the jar over a strainer in the sink. She uses a paper towel to pick up three sardines and nest them into little cradles of mayo-ketchup. Then she wraps the sandwich in so many layers of plastic wrap, she can't see its contents anymore.

Into her sack lunch and backpack it goes before she can change her mind. Giddy teases her jacket off the rack and has her hand on the front door when Bodie rushes the back door, scratching and whining. His eyes beseech hers.

Giddy shoots a glance upstairs at Tigs's and Tad's room and at Dougal's still-closed door. Bodie spins urgently, scratches the door again.

Giddy snaps her fingers and points. "Go get Dougal up. Go get Tad and Tigs."

Bodie stares at her. He plants his butt down and waits.

Giddy rolls her eyes and shoves the front door open where, to her surprise, it's still dark outside, the sun a good thirty minutes from rising. The icy air slaps Giddy's still-wet head and she throws up her hood, digging out gloves and bouncing in the chill. She gets to the bus stop corner, currently pooled in yellow light from the streetlamp, and she stares at it because she's not used to seeing it all dark and quiet. She checks her phone. It's only 5:52. On a normal day she wouldn't notice how dark it is because she'd still be inside making breakfast and getting Tad and Tigs out the door. Giddy pops in earbuds and scrolls through music. She puts some K-pop on and nods to the beat. A few cars scoot past. A jogger winds his way around her. Her breaths puff out and the yellow streetlights reflect patches of black ice. There's an air of repressed calm and graveyard quiet, of a world sleeping but on the verge of waking.

It takes her just under an hour to reach school by walking, and when she arrives, she still has about forty-five minutes before class starts. Almost nobody's at the front of the school building—all the early risers are out on the track or sitting on benches with their phones. The bottoms of her feet feel a little numb in that warning way that says there might be pain later. Giddy shrugs it off and stares at the time, mesmerized: 6:41 a.m. On a normal day she'd be waiting to put Tad and Tigs on their bus.

What to do? Giddy sits cross-legged against a wall feeling oddly exposed, but no one seems to notice or care, so Giddy pops her earbuds back in and scrolls through K-pop.

Do an activity you would never, ever do.

Giddy stares, thinking. She googles "opposite of K-pop" and frowns her way through Korean terminology before trying "list music genres." "Rock 'n' roll" and "country" sound promising—Giddy cannot think of a country music song that wouldn't result in her leaving the room. Her thumb pauses over "classical/opera."

Giddy finds "40 most beautiful arias" and smirks. It takes a while to download on the school's crappy Wi-Fi. It isn't until the doors have opened and Giddy's making her way to art class before the first song starts. She supposes she should have guessed that she wouldn't understand a word, because what she's hearing is in Italian. There's no way for Giddy to describe the man's singing except it's slow and incomprehensible and there's no beat. Giddy mentally checks off *new activity* and sits outside of art.

When the bell rings, she gratefully pops her earbuds out, goes in, and takes her ceramic piggy bank and instructions to her seat. Then she looks up because the room is filled with a weird silence that comes from being the first and only student. Her teacher stares back at her, tool held up over his clay-worked elephant sculpture.

"Giddy," he says. "This is a surprise."

Giddy doesn't say anything, but apparently silence isn't acceptable, because he adds: "Did you get dropped off early?"

Giddy's eyes flit to the door. Everybody's procrastinating in the hallway and Giddy hates it when teachers do this—try to make small talk to fill the air—so she just shrugs in a way she hopes is loud and elaborate and filled with enough meaning for him to interpret.

"OK then." He turns to his work. A few students finally trickle in. Drawers open and close as they retrieve their designs and rip paper towels off holders. At last comfortably lost in the chaos, Giddy checks over her perfectly adequate piggy bank. It's sagged a little, clay legs depressing and widening into chubby folds of skin. Giddy rereads the instructions and looks at the wall calendar to verify that she has three more days to work on this. She eyeballs her pig again and sighs.

Giddy only chose art because she had to pick a second elective after robotics. And it's not difficult. Do the minimum. Turn it in. Easy A.

Reverse all your habits.

Giddy puts one fist over the coin slot and slowly and deliberately crushes her pig. His chubby legs splay out and his blank-eyed head tilts at a disbelieving ninety degrees. As she kneads the clay into anonymity, she thinks *functional* and *personal connection.* Instead of balls, she starts making little squares so she can stack them into a robot, but halfway through the building process it occurs to her that the robot resembles something from a cartoon, not the faceless motoring bot she helped design in her other class. She smashes it, rolls more circles, and tries to make Bodie. Bodie's head looks like the piggy bank's but with irregularly sized flap ears. She doesn't know how to make it functional. She thinks *dog bowl*, but somebody on a table nearby is making a food dish for their cat and Giddy doesn't want to be derivative. She looks around, and apart from Bong Sculpture Guy almost everyone is making dishes or pencil holders. Maybe she's drawing a blank because she's not aiming high enough?

She finds a picture of an ancient teapot on her phone, notes the sculptural challenges involved in attaching the spout and handle, and resolves to make a teapot first and worry about personal connections second. She goes for an egg-shaped body because it's less likely to cave in, but forming a spout that's both hollow and stable turns into a comedy of errors with Giddy sticking what looks like a crude bendy straw into the side.

She's so caught up in her design, she doesn't hear the bell ring, doesn't notice anybody putting their stuff away until the last exiting student bumps her table with his hip. Giddy scrambles to get her half-finished teapot onto an upper shelf where she hopes no one will bother it in the next twenty-four hours.

On her way out the door, her teacher says brightly: "First in, last to leave!" and Giddy thinks, *What the hell am I supposed to say to that?*

In the hall she tries to hurry to get to English class, but the first-to-second-period transition isn't one she's fine-tuned and Giddy finds herself swimming upstream against a crowd of students pouring into the amphitheater. She still manages to be one of the first through the door, though Giddy looks at the continued semicircle seating arrangement with disappointment. Discussion formation. Giddy knows where the teacher likes to sit, so she chooses the seat right next to it at the front of the room.

The writing prompt reads, *Explain what makes you nervous during class discussions*, and Giddy grits her teeth and writes *Nothing!* and then, because it might look like she's not trying, she adds: *I have concluded after much reflection that nervousness is not an emotion I suffer from while doing class discussions.*

"You're in my seat."

Giddy looks up at a kid named Avery, who coldly regards her with an unslung backpack ready to dump on the desk on top of hers.

Giddy says: "It's free seating."

"I always sit here when it's discussion day." Now Avery's voice dials up a concerned notch, and he looks around the room as if seeking confirmation. "Ever since the beginning of the year."

Giddy honestly can't remember where Avery sits. She's never cared. But this is an up-front seat, a seat for eager students, so Giddy shrugs. "Find someplace else."

Students are filing in, largely ignoring Giddy and Avery, so he leans forward a little and says: "Why are you being such a bitch about this?"

Giddy gives him a look of exaggerated pity. "I think the bitch is the one without the seat."

Avery leaves then, settling for a side seat, where he glowers at Giddy. When the person who usually sits in *that* seat sees Avery, they blink a little, step back, and move around him. Somebody takes Giddy's old seat at the back of the room. They abruptly toss their own jacket on top of their things and lower their head.

Giddy turns in her quick write and waits for the teacher to begin. When the teacher sits in her usual seat in the circle, she gives a quick eyebrow raise at Giddy and Giddy sits up straighter. *Do an activity you would never, ever do.* Giddy has *The Yellow Wallpaper* open in front of her for quick reference, though she doubts she needs it because she already found a summary online. She also has the first couple of scenes of *Hamlet* on her phone in her lap for reference.

"OK." Her teacher has a series of note cards in her hands. "How many people finished both *The Yellow Wallpaper* and the first two scenes of *Hamlet*?" Some hands go up. "There's a reason I wanted you to read these in conjunction, but I won't say what that reason is yet. I know you haven't finished all of *Hamlet* yet"—at this a few enthusiastic hands rise, including Avery's, and her teacher smiles— "*most* of you haven't finished *Hamlet*. So I'm just going to start with *The Yellow Wallpaper.* How'd you feel about this piece?"

Hands go up, including Giddy's, and the teacher points to a girl at the back of the room.

"I liked it. I thought it was creepy."

"Why creepy?"

"Because the girl goes crazy at the end."

Giddy hasn't made it to the end yet of *The Yellow Wallpaper*, and she's trying to remember what the summary said about the protagonist's state of mind when the teacher says: "How about you, Giddy? What did you think of Jane?"

Giddy doesn't remember anybody in the story named Jane. Wait—was Jane the maid? Giddy says: "I liked her."

"OK!" This must be the right answer, because the teacher leans forward. "What is it you like about her?"

One beat. Two. Giddy says: "She's really got it together." Giddy likes her answer. It's suitably vague and her teacher's always saying there's no wrong opinions, so she punctuates it with a bright smile. Discussion achieved.

Yet for some reason the teacher frowns and about a dozen hands furiously rise.

"Kyle." The teacher points.

"Jane has *not* got it together," Kyle says emphatically. "She is literally losing her mind every second she stays in that room."

A flush of aggravation floods Giddy's cheeks. She scans the pages as discreetly as she can, but sitting up front she feels exposed. She flips to the end of the short story and reads a few lines. The maid's name is Jennie. The husband is John. The protagonist is . . . Where's the name of the protagonist? Ah. The crazy lady telling the story is Jane.

Giddy raises her hand.

"Giddy."

"She should listen to John," Giddy says.

"Really?" Eyebrows up again. "Why should Jane listen to John?"

"Because he loves her." Giddy's finger rests lightly on a sentence in which the woman telling the story says her husband loves her dearly. "And he wants her to get better." Good answer. Giddy is confident enough to keep looking the teacher in the eye and not read the room for confirmation, even though she can see hands going up out of the corner of her eye.

"So part of Jane's problem is she doesn't listen enough to her husband, John?" her teacher asks, and when Giddy nods, adds: "And John's suggestions are good ones?"

When a teacher asks one follow-up question, it might mean you've done such a great job, she wants to make sure everyone understands your answer. But two follow-ups is never a good sign, and Giddy presses her hand against the page to keep her inner rage in check. All in. "Yes. I liked his suggestions."

Total quiet from the class.

"Can you tell me which one was your favorite?"

No, Giddy most certainly cannot, because all she knows is John is the woman's husband, loves her, and apparently (according to Kyle) she still goes crazy. Giddy doesn't know why Jane goes crazy. Giddy only scanned this story and read an online summary that was apparently crap. So she starts slowly, eyes on the page. "He . . . tells . . . Jane . . . that she should . . . try to make some . . . changes. . . ." Giddy stops, not just because of the teacher's face but because of all the other faces in class, because now Giddy *is* reading the room and the students are smirking and one of them overdramatically slaps his forehead.

"Did you finish reading *The Yellow Wallpaper*?" the teacher gently asks Giddy, and Giddy, given the choice between appearing lazy or looking like a moron, slowly shakes her head.

"Maybe you could refrain from commenting on a story before you've finished reading it." That condescension comes from Avery, and her teacher shoots him a warning glance.

"Well, Giddy, I look forward to hearing your opinions once you've finished it." She speaks in a kind of bright voice, the kind teachers use when they're trying to encourage a student who just doesn't get it. Giddy always smirks when she hears it used on struggling students in chemistry or algebra II, but it's never been used on her and Giddy thinks, *I could get it. I just didn't read it, and I didn't read it because you assign boring things!* So when the discussion switches to *Hamlet*, Giddy doesn't raise her hand once, because even though she read part of it, her answers will just look stupid. And anyway, she's not asking for things Giddy memorized, like *What is the name of Hamlet's friend?* (Horatio) or *Where does this story take place?* (Denmark). She asks things like "Why is it appropriate that the play opens with two confused characters?" Or "How do you think Hamlet feels about his mother?" After a while, even the guy who took Giddy's old seat raises a hand to say something that gets nods of assent and Giddy thinks, *Shit, am I the only one who doesn't care about these two stories?*

When the bell rings, she is first out the door, a class copy of *The Yellow Wallpaper* still in her hand. As she hurries down the hall to algebra II, anxiety abates, and she slides into her assigned seat with a sense of ease and gratitude. There's never free seating in math, just calm, collected order and plenty of repetition. Giddy gets the practice problems off the teacher's desk, looks to the board, at a rational in need of simplification next to a graph and the new term, *asymptote*. Giddy could simplify the rational in her sleep.

She lifts her pencil to do just that.

Reverse all your habits.

Giddy reluctantly puts the pencil down. The problem on the board is never for a grade, not in algebra II. Neither are the practice problems that her fingers itch to complete, to reassure herself that she's good at something. But, Giddy reasons as she slides the papers away from her, she doesn't have to prove anything here. She's naturally good at math, always has been. This is the day to stay quiet, to think of anything other than numbers. So Giddy opens *The Yellow Wallpaper* and reads past the first two pages as the other students work. And when her teacher starts explaining how an asymptote is just a line a curve approaches but never reaches, Giddy doesn't write anything down and instead trains her eye on a blank section of the dry-erase board over his shoulder, tuning him out, thinking that, in a way, it will be fun to still beat Katlyn's grades without even trying. When the teacher asks them to graph a rational and describe the resulting asymptote, Giddy judiciously skips the problem and goes back to reading. That is, until the teacher discreetly taps the edge of her desk with a rolled-up paper, making her set *The Yellow Wallpaper* aside. "I need a volunteer to come up to the front of the room and graph this for me." He writes an expression on the board and turns to face the class.

Several heads pivot automatically to Giddy, but she doesn't raise her hand. Katlyn does, of course. With enthusiasm. The teacher hands Katlyn a marker and lets her go to work. When Katlyn turns back around, he asks the class: "So what is the value this line will never reach?" He scans the room, makes eye contact briefly with Giddy.

Giddy doesn't raise her hand. A boy somewhere behind her does. "I think maybe five?"

"Are you sure?" More hands rise, but not Giddy's, and now the teacher gives her a little frown. "What do you think?" he says to someone over Giddy's shoulder.

"Three."

"I agree that *x* cannot equal three," her teacher says, taking the marker and allowing Katlyn to sit back down. Katlyn has a breathless expression of superiority on her face. She shoots a sideways glance at Giddy, but Giddy is ignoring her and everything else by staring at the wall.

"I want you to look at the line," the teacher says. "Notice how it's horizontal?" The teacher writes another expression. "I need someone to graph this one? Giddy?" He holds out the marker.

Giddy looks at it and shakes her head. He frowns again. "Really? OK. Someone else."

Katlyn's hand hesitantly goes up again, but he adds: "Someone new. Anyone? There's eternal gratitude in it for you."

A smattering of laughs. A boy sighs and gets up, graphs it. "That's not bad. This won't end, though." Her teacher extends the line off the graph. "To infinity. Is this one horizontal? What is the behavior of this line?"

Giddy's eyelids sag and she blinks in surprise. She usually naps in English. Maybe that's why she's tired now. Giddy figures there's no harm in it. She slips her jacket on and pushes the hood under the back of her neck, lets her mind wander, her head tilting gently to the side. . . .

"Ms. Barber." The teacher taps the corner of her desk again. Giddy blinks awake. He's past demonstration, and now there's a series of new projected expressions on the screen. Giddy looks around. Everyone's moved to individually graphing. "Not get any sleep? You seem unfocused."

"I'm fine." Which is true, because Giddy is right where she wants to be. When he moves on, she gets out graph paper and puts her pencil to it.

And discovers she's not sure how to do the problem. It's math, though, so she ought to be able to figure it out. But Giddy is still frowning at her graph paper when the bell rings.

She's still puzzling over the problem as she enters chemistry, where the instructions ask students to choose lab teams. Trinity and Jess are on their phones at their usual back-of-the-room table. Their jackets and one of their backpacks droop over the table's third stool. Giddy starts forward. Usually she relocates their stuff to sit next to them. Usually.

Do something unexpected.

Today she turns in a slow circle until her eyes connect with... Zach, who doesn't have a partner today. Usually Javier or Nathan slides over to his table. But Javier has been tapped by the teacher to help a table that usually argues and Nathan is absent.

Giddy looks around the room for literally anyone else. Jess and Trinity still aren't looking at her. All the other tables are full. Zach also looks around the room, sees the lack of empty spaces, looks at Giddy, his face a conclusion of bright hope.

Giddy takes a step forward and mentally kicks herself as Zach's expression eases into a kind of slow, flattered confidence. "Oh. Giddy. Hi. Good to see you."

Giddy sits on the stool next to him.

He says: "So, partners?"

"Yeah, partners." She thinks, *Let him lead the lab.* She drops her pencil so it lies impotent in the open spine of her notebook, and leans forward, elbows on the table, hands propping up her chin. Numbers and lines race around in her brain superimposed over graph paper. In front of the class, her teacher titrates an indicator into a solution of sodium carbonate and vinegar. There are gasps of approval throughout the room as the clear solution suddenly turns pink.

"This is all about finding balance," her teacher is saying. "If you add too little, you won't see a change at all. Add too much and it turns red." She grins darkly. "Don't let it turn red."

"Thanks for working with me," Zach says.

Giddy shrugs. Then her phone goes off.

Jess: *WTF Giddy???*

Giddy looks over her shoulder. Trinity stares open-mouthed. Jess is still focused on her phone. Giddy can't help but notice that the third stool, the one she would sit on if she worked with them, is still covered with all their stuff, and she thinks, *If you want my help, why is it I always have to move your things?*

But she texts: *Sorry. Explain at lunch*

She looks over her shoulder again. Jess is leveling that laser stare at her over the top of her phone. Meanwhile, Trinity looks to be collecting all the lab supplies by herself and bringing them to their table. Trinity holds the instructions close to her face, mouth moving as she reads.

Jess doesn't help her. Jess just keeps staring at Giddy.

"Do you want to read the instructions and have me do the first step?"

Giddy flinches. "What?"

Zach's holding up the lab instruction sheet. "Do you want to read or do the first step or—"

"You can do it."

Zach unscrews the cap of a plastic container. "Which step?"

"All of them." It's a very basic indicator lab, one that starts with *Put less than one-eighth of a teaspoon of sodium carbonate into the first flask.* Giddy thinks nobody really needs a partner for this, so she lets her head get heavy, and for some reason, she's still thinking of asymptotes and trying to conjure up her math teacher's instructions as if it were possible to process them postmortem. She never slept in English and she barely got a nap in algebra II, and it occurs to her that in her excitement to leave her house early, she forgot to eat any breakfast, not even a little instant oatmeal. Now that she thinks about it, that's probably why her stomach isn't killing her, but it's also probably why she's low on energy.

"Um, OK." Zach looks uncertain. Then he brightens as he dips the measuring spoon in. "It's really great, actually, because we never get to talk. Probably because of all the other students and you're just really busy all the time." The spoon emerges heaping with powder and Giddy thinks, *That's not a one-eighth teaspoon, you idiot*, but she doesn't say anything.

The next instruction says to put six drops of phenolphthalein solution in the second flask and three dropperfuls of vinegar in the third. Giddy knows that a *drop* and a *dropper* are two very different things in chemistry, which is why it's so interesting to see Zach putting so many dropperfuls of phenol into the glass, he might as well have just upended the bottle over it.

"Think this is about six?" Zach asks, pipette shaking as he squeezes, sending phenol red splattering like a murder scene all over the inside of the flask. Giddy is horrified.

"It's fine," she says. She sneaks a glance over her shoulder. Trinity appears to be doing the entire lab alone and she looks shaky and confused. She keeps glancing at the door, where the bathroom pass that hangs on the wall is missing because Jess has clearly taken it and just left. Trinity shoots a desperate look at Giddy.

Giddy turns back around. On the lab paper it says: *Add a few drops of water to flask 1. Stir to dissolve.*

"So," Zach says, "your parents are strict, huh?"

It takes Giddy a moment to figure out where he's coming from. Then she remembers and says: "Yeah. Strict."

"But your birthday must be coming up."

Giddy can't take her eyes off the seven dropperfuls of water Zach is adding to the sodium carbonate. She says: "Does Javier usually measure for you?"

"No, Nathan likes to do the measuring. I usually write everything. My penmanship is—well, not to brag—pretty extraordinary. So your birthday? Just curious—when is it?"

The thought of a surprise birthday present from Zach with the implied obligation of a date is an outcome Giddy isn't ready to deal with, her eleven-day list notwithstanding, so she lies: "Not until August."

"Oh." *Using a pipette, slowly combine the phenol solution with the sodium carbonate solution until it turns a light shade of pink.* Zach dips the pipette in and fills it. A dropperful goes into the sodium carbonate. No change. "Still clear." He frowns.

Javier's table already has a solution the color of rose quartz. Two other tables have a slightly brighter pink. Zach adds another dropperful and then, without waiting for results, a third and fourth. "The thing is, I really think we could go out if it was labeled something else, like we were supposed to be studying. But we could watch TV or go somewhere. Oh!"

Without warning the clear liquid turns a deep and unapologetic shade of dark red. "Maybe if we pour it out, we can—" Zach is cut off by the teacher, who laughingly swoops down on Giddy and Zach's experiment and holds up the flask for everyone to see.

"There's one in every class." She swirls the liquid around. "You go too far too fast and you get something you can't undo." To Zach she says: "Add some vinegar. That'll clear it. But if you want pink, you'll have to start the lab over." To Giddy: "I'm surprised you had this trouble. You're usually so careful." She takes out her phone and snaps a picture of the flask seconds before Zach dumps in vinegar. "For my website. This is just too perfect an example of what not to do."

"This isn't for a grade, though?" Zach says hopefully, and she laughs again.

When the bell rings, Giddy doesn't bother packing. She scoops up her stuff and holds it under her chin as she rushes out, nauseated by the conversation, by the loss of a lab, by Zach's breath, which is the kind of peppermint that hits you over the head with a hammer. Trinity and Jess are quick to follow her out.

"You left us hanging, Giddy!" Trinity says.

"Sorry," Giddy says.

"You helped *Zach*," Jess says, glaring. She takes out her phone and starts typing into it. "I couldn't believe what I was seeing."

Giddy doesn't point out that Jess left the room for most of the lab or that joining their table would have forced Zach to go solo. As they walk into the cafeteria, Giddy says: "It was part of an experiment."

"What experiment?" Trinity asks, and Jess actually pauses her texting to look up.

Giddy tries to shrug it off. "Just an experiment."

"What for?" Jess asks, eyes narrowing.

"It's just a thing I'm trying."

"What kind of a *thing*?"

As they reach the table where Asia's already sitting, Giddy snaps: "It's to feel better, OK?"

Asia's mouth pops open into a little *Oh* and she shoots a look at Jess. "You're *depressed*?" Asia asks.

Trinity says: "You can't be depressed! That's Jess's thing."

"Yeah," Jess says. "I don't know if you've noticed, but there's a lot of that going around, so you're not special." As Giddy gapes, she adds: "Still not sure why you didn't do the pink lab with us."

"I'm not depressed," Giddy says quickly. "This is just an experiment."

"Wait," Asia says between mouthfuls. "You did the lab where you try to turn the liquid pink?" She puffs up. "We did that yesterday! I got pink!"

Jess and Trinity regard Asia sourly. "You know, Asia," Jess says, "that's really something. That's really great. Good for you."

Asia's smile drops into a thin line.

"*Really* good," Jess adds, doing a small clap with her hands that Trinity joins in on.

"So good!" Trinity says. "So impressive. Amazing."

"I've never been more impressed than right now," Jess says.

"This *experiment* I'm doing," Giddy says, "there was this other guy who did it and the way it works is—"

"You guys suck!" Asia says to Jess and Trinity, a catch in her voice. "I was just saying it was something cool we did in chemistry instead of something boring!"

"No, you were rubbing it in," Jess says, "and you need to own that."

Giddy opens her brown sack lunch and the sandwich rolls out. *The* sandwich. Giddy had forgotten. And now her creation lies before her, squished and irregular. The mayonnaise and ketchup leaked into the plastic wrap, creating pools of arterial red and bone white.

"Oh God!" Asia scoots a little away from Giddy. "What the hell is it?"

"It looks like a crime scene," Jess says.

Giddy begins unwrapping, slowly, exposing seeds of rye. She hadn't even bothered to cut the sandwich in half. She lifts it, and a couple of gray sardines poke their fish heads out. And that's what finally gives Giddy pause—the fact that her sandwich is looking at her with a stern, almost reproachful gaze.

Her eyes flicker to Jess and Asia and finally Trinity, but they are all rapt with attention and waiting, almost eager. Giddy decides the key is to not look at the sandwich that is looking back.

Do something unexpected.

A smaller, potentially saner Giddy voice wheedles: *But it doesn't have to be this, right?*

Keep doing it even though you hate it.

Giddy shuts her eyes tight as she takes a bite, going all in for size and speed. The chewing is surprisingly easy, and for a moment Giddy thinks maybe she actually did a good job.

Then the taste hits along with some little prickling slivers of sardine bones. Giddy swallows, and that gooky, prickling sensation follows all the way down the back of her throat. She didn't think to bring a soda or anything to wash lunch down with, and now, oddly, she finds herself buoyed by the horrified stares of her friends. Giddy can't remember a time when they all just looked at her and weren't talking about something else at the same time.

Emboldened, Giddy takes a second and third bite, shoving as much of the sandwich into her mouth as possible, counting the seconds it will likely take to finish it.

She has only a quarter of the sandwich to go before something catches in the back of her throat. She tries to swallow, coughs instead, and spittles of sandwich spew on her friends, making them rear back in their seats in outrage. Her throat is just pumping and pumping, pushing and pushing back . . .

There are three industrial-sized gray trash cans at the center of the cafeteria. Giddy gets up and sprints for one of them. As she does, her feet slip on the sticky floor and she veers sideways into a table, striking her hip on one corner as students lean out of the way and a few indignantly lift their lunch trays. Giddy grabs the trash can, leans, and it pushes away from her—she didn't account for the rollers at its base. Giddy runs forward with it rolling on plastic black wheels, leaning in, retching. Once the first bite is out of her, her stomach surges and everything else follows.

Giddy's entire body trembles as she stands up. She's pushed the trash can all the way to the side of the cafeteria, so she starts rolling it back to the center where it belongs and the wheels sound so very loud because no one's talking and this is just what rolling trash cans sound like in a cafeteria gone deathly quiet. Even the custodian stares as she replaces the can, grabs some brown napkins off a nearby table, wipes her mouth, and returns to her seat.

Asia, Trinity, and Jess stare quietly at her for a few long moments.

Trinity breaks the silence. "Wow, are you trying to lose weight, Giddy?"

"There're better ways of doing it," Asia says. "Have you tried jogging? Or you could do what I do, which is eat raw or if not raw, at least green."

"You are eating a *burger*," Trinity says, astonished.

"A *plant-based* burger," Asia corrects. "Anyway, what would you know about it? You haven't done anything about your weight since the seventh grade."

Jess snickers. "You did pack it on that year," she says.

Trinity's face burns hot, and Giddy gets up to throw away her lunch, still shaking and tired but relieved that her friends have moved on to criticizing Trinity. Giddy notes all the stares from everyone else in the cafeteria in a disconnected way like they're observational footnotes at the bottom of a lab paper. She leaves the cafeteria to rinse her mouth out at a water fountain. But when she turns around to go back inside, she stops at the entryway.

She watches her friends from a distance. Even from here she can see that Trinity is agitated and on the defense, probably because they're still harping over her weight. And Jess and Asia have these little smiles at the edges of their lips. There're ten minutes of this lunch left. That's ten minutes of not being in class, ten minutes of total phone-freedom.

Yet Giddy feels no impetus to recross this threshold.

So walk away.

She's stupefied by the thought. Can she do that? Just walk off. Won't they notice she didn't come back? Won't that be fodder for next time?

It will be. But she's too pissed and embarrassed to deal with them now. So she turns and walks until she reaches robotics. There she sits, back to the wall. Her stomach feels . . . Actually, she can't feel her stomach at all. It's walked off the job instead of protesting, its emptiness a perfect mirror for the deserted and quiet halls.

After a few minutes, kids start meandering around corners. Then the bell rings to end lunch and Giddy stands up and goes into robotics and plugs in her phone. When Patrice and Deb arrive, they connect the bot's magnetic arm and Giddy stares at the skeletal design of a program she laid out last week for running the course in under five minutes. It's a good basic program but one that needs tweaking because she can already tell the added weight of the arm is going to make the robot lean as it rounds corners and possibly result in it getting stuck. It's only a test run—nothing they do today is for a grade—so Giddy is comfortable telling her team to run the program as is. They do. They lose by thirteen seconds, right behind the boys' team they made fun of yesterday.

"Our poor little guy." Patrice makes a face over the robot's arm. "We need to shorten it maybe? What if we make the arm more vertical?"

They look at Giddy.

Giddy doesn't respond. They wait for an answer.

Deb says: "Earth to Giddy."

"Sorry, I thought everything looked fine." To Giddy, the lie is painfully transparent, one she'd improve if she'd had more time to think about it.

"We know it looked fine." Now Deb sounds irritated. "How do we fix it?"

Patrice says: "We only lost by thirteen seconds and only because it kept getting caught at the turns. Let's reduce the time it takes to make the turns and see if it stays on course. I'd rather try that than take its arm apart."

Giddy sinks into her chair as Patrice and Deb hover over their laptop. She tries playing on her phone, which is what the other students who aren't that invested in the class do. She ends up completing yesterday's world history assignment and moves on to read a short article about atrocity propaganda that targeted the German and Austro-Hungarian armies. Giddy preps some questions that might be great to ask in world history later. But during the last fifteen minutes, the teacher interrupts to tell everyone of a change to this year's regional competition.

"They want to add a student-designed course. At least two objectives and a timed completion. I know you're just sophomores, but entry next year qualifies you for a scholarship program for the following year. No groups! This design is individual work. I'd like to choose *one* to submit from this class."

Teams split up almost immediately, and Giddy opens her notebook, draws a rectangle and pencils in two sections divided by a circular pit. At the bottom of the page she makes a short list that includes rubbing alcohol, oil, and fire. Giddy can't think of a worse combination than pyrotechnics, flammable hazards, and circuitry. After all, there's no danger in her design being considered *good.* No teacher in their right mind would pick a course that could destroy a robot, not when the parts used to build it are school-issued.

Giddy returns to reading the propaganda article, frowning because she didn't know people used cartoons to dehumanize the enemy and aren't cartoons for kids because some of these war comics are *gross.*

Her teacher clears her throat. Giddy looks up in surprise. The class is empty. Her teacher sits alone behind her desk. "I was wondering when you were going to look up and realize we dismissed. I thought about waiting, but . . ." She gives Giddy a good-natured grin.

Giddy blinks.

"The bells are down," her teacher clarifies.

Giddy shoves her phone into her back pocket and turns to run out the door. Two minutes after? How can it be two minutes after the bell? And world history is all the way on the other side of the building. Giddy has to go against traffic, shoving her way down the side wall. When she gets to the last hall, the crowds clear and she breaks out into a run, her side hurting.

When she finally makes it into world history, she heaves her backpack off and slams it angrily on top of her desk. The resulting sound is like a bomb detonating. Giddy takes a step back from her desk in surprise, and Hunter, who'd been leaning across the aisle talking, sits bolt upright, a half-shocked smile on his face. Students bump into each other at the door and the teacher stands from his chair, a sword behind his words as he yells: "Ms. Barber, sit down immediately!"

Giddy does so, slowly, apologetically. She quietly opens her binder, turning to all of her notes. On the board it says, *What happened in 1914?* Giddy takes out an index card to write a response as someone kicks the desk two seats behind her and, subsequently, the student behind her kicks *her* desk.

"What," whispers Hunter, "the fuck was that?"

Giddy shakes her head. She has a plan for this class, good questions from that article she read in robotics. The teacher, unwilling to be parted from his computer prior to the ringing of the bell, is leaning over his desk chair checking his email again, but now he has a glare on his face, a glare that Giddy put there.

Two seats back, another desk kick. Then *her* desk kicked again.

"I said: 'What the *fuck* was that?'"

Giddy's drumming her knuckles on the desk. She hurls a hand back and very quickly shoots Hunter the finger just as the final bell rings.

"OK," says the teacher, coming out from behind his desk to sit on its edge. "What happened in 1914?"

"They invented zippers," Hunter says.

"Gee, I'd love it if after ten years of education you learned to raise your hand. We're looking for key events involving the war." Some snickering. Giddy is among those with her hand raised, but the teacher points to another boy. "Yes?"

"Declaration of war."

Someone kicks the desk two seats back. When Giddy's desk gets subsequently kicked, she almost bites her lip. She whips her head around. Hunter flashes his phone at her real fast so she can see the letters on the screen: *WHAT THE FUCK WAS THAT?*

"Not to mention alliances," the teacher is saying, "getting others to help you carry out a strategic attack." Giddy turns back around in her seat and waves her raised hand a little. The teacher pauses and looks at her as if afraid he might regret his choice. "Yes?"

"The, um, invasion. Germany."

"And who gets invaded?"

Giddy flips a page in her notes. "Luxembourg."

"Good. Where else?"

Giddy frowns, runs her finger along a page. "Belgium."

"Good." The teacher's eyes don't waver from her. "Where else?"

Giddy blinks. She goes back to her notes, but she could have sworn Germany only invaded Luxembourg and Belgium. She says: "Russia?"

"No, Ms. Barber. Germany did *not* invade Russia." He smirks before scanning the room again. Points to a girl. "Yes?"

"Austria-Hungary invaded Russia, not Germany."

"That's very good, Ms. Irvin!"

She beams.

"What else happened in 1914 that we should care about?"

Hunter raises a hand. The teacher's eyes dart off him and onto someone at the front of the room. "Mr. Fowler, you haven't raised your hand. What do you think?"

Aaron has been nodding off against his hand and has a thin line of drool down his cheek to prove it. He sits up fast, looks at the drool on his hand, and wipes it against his blue jeans. "Umm . . . I guess . . ."

"Sanitary pads were invented that year too," Hunter says.

There is general sniggering, mostly from the back of the room, but even a few students in the front bite their lip and grin as the teacher puts thumb and forefinger to his temple, closes his eyes, and takes a steadying breath. "We are talking about World War I. The discussion will stay focused on that and not on you, do you understand? Can you maybe go five minutes without a desperate bid for attention?"

"I thought we were talking about things in 1914 we should care about."

"Nobody cares that sanitary pads were invented in 1914!" the teacher snaps back.

"Giddy might," Hunter says, shrugging. "Just seems like she could use one today."

"Are you kidding me!" Giddy spins around in her desk to the students' sharp intakes of breath.

"I'm not, actually, I really thought . . ." Hunter looks helplessly around.

"Stop acting like you don't know exactly what you're doing, and stop kicking my desk!" Giddy kicks the desk of the student behind her and he flinches back in his chair.

"Ms. Barber!" the teacher shouts. "End it!" And then to Hunter: "You too, Mr. Blancovich!"

"He's doing all of it," Giddy says. "I haven't done a thing!"

"Well, you're the one who came in and slammed your stuff down." He sighs. "Steering back to 1914 with *no more comments* from Mr. Blancovich. About anything." He turns to the rest of the class. "What was France's response during all of this?"

Giddy raises her hand emphatically. She knows this one.

Her teacher points to someone else. "They invaded . . ." The student frowns. "I can't say it . . . All-sock-ee?"

"Alsace. What was the response from Great Britain?"

Giddy's arm goes up again. Her teacher points to the boy behind her, who says: "Britain sends its soldiers to France."

"Great. All of which led up to the First Battle of the Marne, which will be the subject of your *essay*." Groans from all around. A few sluggish students shake themselves awake. "Grab a textbook. You've all got fifteen minutes." The teacher goes back to sit at his computer. Giddy, glowering, grabs a book and sits back down, turning to a page number written on the board.

She's only a third of a way down the required reading when her seat gets kicked again, this time so hard, the legs creak. The teacher glances up. "Ms. Barber, resist wriggling around in your seat. You're making a considerable amount of noise."

In fifteen minutes, the bell rings. Mercifully. Giddy, late to put her textbook back because she was trying to do well on her essay, is one of the last out the door. The hall is already crowded and Hunter and his friends file out close behind her.

"Stop wriggling in your seat, Giddy," one of them says.

"Giddy, stop wriggling."

"You're being very distracting, Giddy."

Giddy pops her earbuds in and the noise around her disappears, replaced by an assertive baritone who rolls his *r*'s as he sings. She pushes through the open doors and out into the sun, where it's way colder than inside her history class. Giddy starts off in a run for the bike racks and then curses and winces. Her side still aches. She's starting to think she pulled something.

Only when she reaches the racks and has trouble locating her bike does she remember that she walked to school, and Giddy's flurry of subsequent curses and foot stomping coincides with a generous swell of operatic strings. Giddy shoves her hands into her pockets and starts walking. She keeps her hood up and her head down, counting seams in the sidewalk, measuring the varying distances of blocks just for the sake of measuring. She breezes through five arias, every one an assault on her eardrums, the attacks varying from adamant bursts of thunder to an almost begging, wheedling whisper, and Giddy thinks, *Drama much?*

She stops at the skate park and takes out her earbuds. Not because her side hurts—walking actually seems to make that better. But because amid the crowds, the grinding of wheels, the clips of boards being kicked up into hands—everyone's *smiling.* They all look so damn *happy.*

A falsetto voice chirps staccato as Giddy puts her earbuds back in and pulls her hood around her head. She hurries the last few blocks home, glad to have made it, thinking her bad day is almost over.

She puts her key in, turns it, frowns. The door is already unlocked.

She pushes it. Something blocks the door. There's a smell—dog poop? Also, it's terribly cold—in fact *freezing*—inside the house. Giddy pushes the door harder and now she sees the coatrack has fallen. She kicks the piles of winter coats and sweaters out of the way and pushes the door open.

Tad and Tigs are in the living room. Tigs has her favorite red jumper dress on over her onesie even though Giddy distinctly remembers seeing it in the dirty clothes hamper last night, and she's wearing her thick coat over it. But when she sees Giddy, she stands and the onesie falls to her ankles. Tad, wearing his own big coat over his jeans and shirt, has made a battle tank out of dominoes on the floor, where action figures burst out from the inside, guns hot.

Every corner of the den floor and sofa is covered with Legos, action figures, and ripped-out pages from Tigs's sketchbook. The stairs, for some reason, are draped in toilet paper, and on the upstairs landing one roll lolls over the side like a streamer. The smell of souring milk and fruit punch draws Giddy's eyes to the overturned cartons and fruit juice jugs on the kitchen counter, to the gobs of red-and-white peaks of toilet paper being used to soak up liquids.

Bodie shoots out from behind the sofa and, whimpering, runs to scratch at the back door. His soulful eyes implore.

Giddy snaps to attention. She stands the coatrack up, runs to the back to let Bodie out, then navigates a minefield of toilet paper to come back into the living room and stare at Tigs and Tad.

Tad silently builds another domino tank only to have an enemy soldier come in to crush it. Without looking at her he says: "I'm hungry."

Tigs throws back her head and emits an ear-piercing wail. She runs and wraps herself around Giddy's legs. "Bodie pooed! I tried to clean it and the toilet upstairs did its thing again so I tried to clean that, too, and *we don't have phones*!"

"You didn't go to school." A numb part of Giddy's brain adds up the time. "Where's Dougal?"

"The bus didn't wait and it just left us here!" Tigs pulls her face back enough for Giddy to see her eyes and the top of her nose. "And we don't have phones and we couldn't call!"

"Tad!" Giddy says sharply. "Where's Dougal?"

Tad shrugs. Giddy swears under her breath, disengages Tigs, and vaults up the stairs, tiptoeing over the toilet paper. The bathroom floor is wet as Giddy kneels to grab cleaning supplies and a bucket out from under the sink.

And she stops. Giddy slowly stands, plunger in hand. She takes a step back from the toilet, where the water is high and jam-packed with poop and puffy little islands of toilet paper. Her mind is still engaged in a game of calculations, adding up how long it will take to restore the toilet, to bleach-clean the upstairs hall floor and stair runner, to wipe down the kitchen counters and floor. Her arms prickle because it's *freezing* from the thermostat never being adjusted this morning.

And she is gobsmacked by a sudden rush of calm. Giddy doesn't know from whence this beautiful well springs, only that it seems rooted in a generous absence of personal investment in this current situation. Giddy opens her hand and lets the plunger drop to the floor. She says loudly: "Tad!" Then, when he doesn't respond: *"Tad!"*

He comes up the stairs, but he steps loudly on the edge of a piece of toilet paper and makes a game out of dragging it down the hall behind him. He smirks at the filled toilet, then up at Giddy.

Giddy points to the fallen plunger. "Pick that up."

He looks from the plunger and up to Giddy. "Why?"

"Pick it up," she repeats.

Still smirking, Tad lifts the plunger, turning it, fascinated by the bulb-shaped end. Giddy says: "Now put the plastic end in the toilet."

Tad's smirk vaporizes. "I'm not supposed to be doing this!"

There's a plastic cup on the counter that Tad and Tigs share for oral hygiene. Giddy grabs it and dips just the edge into the filled toilet bowl. Tad's little mouth pops open in horror as milky brown liquid trickles in to fill the void.

When it's half full, Giddy tilts it back and carries it down the hall, Tad in a panicked run behind her. She opens the door to his room and holds it over his bed, which is an unmade mess of old pink sheets and the Spider-Man comforter he got for Christmas.

Tad loves his Spider-Man comforter.

"Giddy, no!" Tad thunders around her and throws himself on the bed, scooting as much of the comforter under his butt as he can manage. "Giddy, don't! I'm sorry, I'm sorry, I'm sorry!"

"Out of the way, Tad," Giddy says. She tilts the cup almost all the way sideways until the brown liquid bubbles, held only at the edge by the miraculous surface tension of water.

"No, no, no, no, Giddy, Giddy, Giddy, Giddy!" Tad bounces on the bed and reaches up as if ready to block it.

"Today you're going to learn how to unclog a toilet, Tad," Giddy tells him, cup still weaponized.

Tad's lip curls in a little pout. "But, Giddy, I'm too small."

She was expecting him to say something like that. With a flick of her wrist, Giddy jolts the cup and little brown drops spatter sideways to dot Tad's exposed pillow, where they expand and lighten as they sink into the cotton pillowcase.

"No, no, no." Tad grows very still. He puts his hands in his lap and stares at the head of his bed.

Giddy says: "You can do what I tell you to do and learn how to unclog a toilet or I can put the rest of this on Spider-Man and maybe I'll do it when you're not looking, Tad, the way you like to clog toilets when I'm not looking. Maybe I'll put it on the *underside* of the comforter. You'll be sleeping with dog poop and you'll never even know it."

Tad's eyes unlock from his bed. He looks at Giddy. With a quiet seriousness, he says: "What do I do?"

Giddy inclines her head to the door and Tad gets up and backs out of the room, worried eyes watching the cup. Giddy tilts the cup back upright and follows him. In the bathroom, she dumps the dirty water into the toilet and tosses the plastic cup into the trash. She points to the plunger.

Tad hesitantly picks it up again. He touches the red bulbed end to the water's surface, sending the paper islands spinning, and draws back. "I can't put it in there because the water's going to go over."

"No, it won't," Giddy tells him. "There's still a little bit of room."

Tad looks unconvinced. He sinks the plunger in inch by inch and the paper swirls around it. Tad flinches as it hits the base of the toilet.

"Move it around until you feel the hole in the bottom. Do you feel it? Push the plunger in until you feel it. Like this—" Giddy touches the end of the plunger and guides it and then sharply warns: "Don't take your hands off, Tad! You're still doing this yourself. Feel that? Feel how it doesn't want to move backward? That's suction. OK, pull it back and keep pushing it back down.

Do it two more times." Giddy takes her hands away and Tad is doing it, tiny fingers white-hot in their grip on the plunger, face squirming in concentration. When a little water splashes up to hit his arm, he stops and gags. "This is gross," he whispers.

"Yes," Giddy snaps back, "it certainly is!"

Tad flinches and resumes. After about three more plunges there's a rushing sound, the water spirals down, and the islands of toilet paper form an ugly corsage over the hole. Tad drops the plunger in the toilet and whirls around, his breaths coming in short, startled gasps.

He looks up at Giddy, his small face an odd mix of shock and admiration. Giddy is telling him, "From now on you're being more care—" when he explodes forward and throws his arms around her.

"Giddy, I did it!" Tad is jumping up and down, shaking Giddy. Giddy stares down at her brother, dumbstruck, and thinks, *This is so weird*, because Tad's not a hugger. In fact, he likes to shrug out of hugs. Giddy, unsure of protocol, disengages him the same way she did with Tigs and pulls a plastic trash bag out from under the counter and a pair of plastic gloves. "Put these on," she tells him, and a moment later: "You need to take all that paper out of the bowl and I'll hold the bag as you drop it in."

Tad draws his gloved hands back in alarm. "Giddy, no, please. There's probably still dog poo in there."

"There's almost certainly some dog poo," Giddy agrees.

Watching Tad grab up the dripping paper and drag it over the rim is its own brand of slow comedy, and when he's finished, Giddy flushes the toilet and Tad heaves a huge sigh of relief. When he tries to leave, Giddy hands him a spray cleaner and a roll of paper towels. "Clean the floor. Clean the hall. Throw everything in the plastic bag, including the gloves. When you're done, come downstairs and use the same cleaner on the kitchen floor. Then put all your toys upstairs."

"Tigs messed up the kitchen," he says sourly.

Giddy points to the trash. "Tad, I swear to God, I will take the toilet paper out of the trash and straight to Spider-Man—"

"OK, OK!" Tad starts wiping the floor outside the bathroom. "Look!" He puts both hands on paper towels and leans forward in a run across the hall. "Look, I can do it super fast like this!" He runs back, sprays the floor, does it again so that Giddy has to step into her bedroom to get out of his way.

Giddy watches, stupefied not by his cleaning but by how cheerful he seems. She quietly closes her door.

It's only half after five in the evening. Giddy exchanges a brief glance with Superdoo on top of the desk and looks around her room. It occurs to her she doesn't have anything she treasures the way Tad treasures his Spider-Man comforter. Now that she thinks about it, almost everything in her room is there because it fulfills a basic need—bed, dresser, small desk and chair, tackboard over her desk. Giddy examines the tackboard more closely, because it occurs to her she hasn't used it since—when? Two years ago when she got a phone with a calendar app? So Giddy starts pulling down each colored slip of paper and reading forgotten messages to herself. But she can't remember why she wrote them, so she wads each one up and throws it in the trash, until in the end, there's nothing but loose tacks and bits of torn-up cork. Not even a birthday card. Nothing she's interested in keeping.

Next, she turns to the mechanical engineering posters on her walls. She must care about those because they represent her future. But just to see how it feels, Giddy eases the stapled corners out. The posters roll obediently into cylinders and Giddy sets them on the dresser. Gone are the fresh faces, the breadboards, the college logos representing Giddy's bold new chapter of existence. She looks at them, curled inward, anonymous. . . .

And she doesn't care that they're not on her wall anymore, so she picks them up and sets them in the trash can, gently, just in case she changes her mind later. Now the wall is bare except for several bright squares over the paint where old things hung, probably drawings from when this was Jax's room and Giddy was in the room that now belongs to Tigs and Tad. Giddy's eyes trace the forgotten geometric echoes of childhood.

Then she lies back on her bed and takes out her pilfered copy of *The Yellow Wallpaper.* She's just a few pages in when the downstairs front door opens and she hears Dougal shuffle in and curse. He runs up the stairs and throws open her door. "It's freezing and it smells like piss! What the hell happened?"

"Bodie wasn't let out, so he pooped in the house," Giddy says over the top of her reading. "Tad's cleaning up."

"Tad's in his room!"

Giddy corrects the tense. "*Cleaned* up. If you don't think he did a good job, redo it. It's mostly the stair runner. The toilet backed up."

"I'm not cleaning the stairs!"

Giddy gets to the bottom of a page and shakes her head at her earlier answers in English class. In *The Yellow Wallpaper*, Jane's husband, John, is an effing moron who shouldn't be giving advice to anyone.

"Giddy, I said I'm not cleaning the stairs."

Giddy turns a page.

"It smells *bad* in the house, like really—" He throws his hands up.

Giddy says nothing.

"Also, what are we eating?"

"Whatever's in the fridge."

Dougal stomps down the hall, and seconds later the AC clicks off and the heat comes on. Giddy gets up and quietly closes and locks her door. When she's finished with *The Yellow Wallpaper*, she takes a break from English and turns to her online world history quiz, but she has a chapter to read for that first. Giddy learns all the reasons people in Austria-Hungary hated people in Serbia, though most of the reasons seem like stupid things to go to war over (the ban of pork products from Serbia being the exception, because in Giddy's experience people will do literally anything for bacon).

Music cuts on in Dougal's room. Giddy's knob rattles. "Giddy?" Tigs says through the door. "I have four questions today!"

Giddy sets the book down. Tigs has an invisible pull like a rope attached to Giddy's muscles. Giddy looks to Superdoo. The action toy regards her in stone-cold silence.

"So the *first* question is can you grow more sea sponges from sponges if you put them in water?"

Giddy can't fathom how Tigs even knows what a sea sponge is. She says: "Maybe. Is the sponge alive?"

"Of course it's alive!" Tigs sounds disgusted, like the thought of a dead sea sponge is an affront to nature. "It's from the *ocean*."

"Then sure." Giddy reaches for her book, but the knob rattles harder.

"My second question is how many babies does a tiny piece make and my third question is do the tiny pieces make tiny babies?"

"I don't know, Tigs."

"I had a fourth question, but that's if it needs soil."

Giddy doesn't say anything. She goes back to reading her book. The door rattles a third time, and Giddy says: "Tigs, I'm not going to do questions with you. I'm doing homework."

"Giddy, I'm hungry!"

"So make yourself a cheese sandwich. You know where the cheese is—it's in the door of the fridge."

"I'm scared I'll make a mess again."

Milk and fruit juice. That invisible tug grows in strength.

"Then try harder not to make a mess?"

Silence from the door's other side. Then, in a voice filled with utter sadness: "I'll just wait in my room."

Giddy rolls her eyes and grabs her book, tearing fiercely into the next chapter. After a little more reading, she takes the online quiz and to her mild surprise gets an eighty out of one hundred. There's an extension read for world history, a book called *The Guns of August.* Giddy's reading an online summary about it when her parents come home.

"OK," her mom says, "but I'm working during that time, just so you know!" The door slams. The rack creaks under the weight of thrown coats.

"So trade with somebody."

"This isn't my thing! When we got married, you said you'd take care of all the boy issues and I'd handle the girl issues." Her mother's hasty steps are followed by a knock at Giddy's door. "Giddy, the school sent me a pair of absence texts for Tad and Tigs, if you can believe it. Would you clear that up at the office tomorrow?" A sniff. "In the hall it smells like lilacs and . . . something. I can't tell . . ." Her mom walks away as Tigs throws open her door and barrels down the stairs.

Her dad says: "Hey, squirt!"

"Daddy, I'm hungry!"

"Oh really? How about I get you some yogurt, huh? Must be going through a growth spurt." A laugh.

Then her mother, going downstairs: "Do I have to do *everything* around here?"

"I think they want us both at the school at the same time. I think—" Her dad lowers his voice then, and the rest dissolves into quiet conversation over the rising audio of the television. Giddy changes for bed, turns out the lights, and once under the covers, takes out her phone and reads more of *Hamlet*, figuring she won't get through half a page without falling asleep. She has been sleeping a lot lately. It stuns her to find she's still awake at eleven reading Shakespeare long after her parents have turned in and long after Jax has slinked home, making his usual quiet way down the hall and up into his bedroom.

When she falls asleep, she dreams of Laertes's dad in *Hamlet*. He's going through her trash bin of posters, saying: *Don't lose these! I know what I'm talking about!* But Giddy thinks maybe he doesn't. Giddy thinks maybe he's just as stupid as Jane's husband, John.

2

Giddy's aching stomach wakes her at 5:14. As she rolls over and shuts off her alarm, she remembers: she never ate dinner, didn't even consider it, didn't even get past one bite of sardine sandwich. *Step 1—Reverse all your habits.* So today she'll *finish* a sardine sandwich.

Her insides buckle at the thought and Giddy pops two antacids before plucking the spiral out from under Superdoo. She clicks a ballpoint and suspends it over the page, reading rapid-fire: *step 2 let control go step 3 do an activity you would never, ever do and keep doing it even though you hate it. If you can, do something unexpected each day. . . .*

Into the bathroom she goes, where her foot knocks over an empty can of air freshener, and she thinks, *Dougal.* She can just detect dog poo, buried deep under the smell of canned flowers.

Giddy glares at the showerhead like it's public enemy number one. It's not like she doesn't need a good *hot* shower. She barely let the water touch her yesterday and her scalp's even more itchy, plus who showers cold in winter? Giddy grabs the handle for cold, averts her head, and turns it on full.

Giddy's mouth pops open in shock as thousands of tiny ice picks drive into her spine. When she steps out, she towels off hair that still feels like it has soap in it. The tinned flowery smell from the air freshener extends all the way to the top of the stairs, making Giddy wonder just how many cans Dougal tore through last night. She stops at the thermostat that her mother always sets to a cold sixty because she says she can't sleep with the heat on. It's fifty-four degrees in the house. Giddy's breath puffs out in quick little protests as she runs into her room and grabs a heavy sweater.

She is halfway down the stairs when she realizes Bodie is barking *outside*. Dougal's in the kitchen, back to her, face in the fridge. Giddy ducks into the pantry and grabs bread. When she comes out, Dougal's on the sofa, feet propped up, eating cereal. Giddy starts making another sandwich and her stomach pitches at the smell of the jarred sardines. She tells him: "You need to wake Tad and Tigs and make sure they get to the bus stop."

When Dougal doesn't say anything, she speaks up: "I said you need—"

Dougal puts his spoon down long enough to shoot her the finger. Giddy rolls her eyes. She decides today's sandwich will have mayo only, no ketchup, and a hefty chunk of red lettuce on top of the sardines. She pops it into a Tupperware instead of cellophane and grabs one of Tigs's juice boxes. She also shoves a slice of bread into her mouth and downs it with a glass of water. Everything goes down like fire, just as she knew it would.

"Giddy, Giddy, Giddy!" Tigs jumps the last four stair steps two at a time, hair disheveled from sleeping in pigtails. She's weirdly wearing her red jumper over jeans. She has sneakers on with way-too-large socks that belong to either Dougal or Jax. The cuffs pool over the ankles like melted marshmallows. Tigs twirls. Giddy sighs.

Tigs stops spinning and one pigtail smacks her in the eye. "I dressed myself!"

"I can see that." Giddy plucks her coat out from under the others.

"So will you wait for the bus with me?"

Giddy regards the adorable little train wreck that is her sister. Also, she wonders if she should have added sliced boiled egg to her sardine sandwich because that's at least a protein her stomach can keep down.

She tells her: "Wake Tad and leave with Dougal," and Tigs rockets up the stairs like a gleeful shooting star. It occurs to Giddy as the outside air slaps her in the face that Tigs might have only rushed because she believes Giddy will reward her by walking them to the bus again. Giddy pops her hood up and doesn't go back inside to correct her.

Instead she puts her earbuds in and walks to the tunes of a Chicago opera house.

At the school library, Giddy checks out a copy of *The Guns of August* and then goes to art class, where she finds her teapot's spout sagging and a crack in the egg-shaped dome. Giddy crushes the whole thing and goes back to trying to make something in the shape of Bodie. This time she decides to start with a sculpture and make it functional later. She goes for realism, pulling up a picture of Bodie on her phone. His whole body is too big to go for, so Giddy focuses on just the head. But the nose is either too long or not long enough and attaching flap-like ears to the sides makes the eyes appear small. In her mind she dubs it *the abomination* because the variances in scale could signal one of so many canine genetic disorders.

"Maybe make it a cartoon head?"

Giddy twists around on her stool. There's a girl at the next table who's never spoken to her before. She's wearing a T-shirt with a UK flag that says LONDON, and her water pitcher has an intricate otter sculpture for a handle. It's good. Really good. Giddy compares the scale of the otter's head with Bodie's and tells the girl: "I was going for realism."

"OK. Just a thought." The girl turns back to her work with a purpose that Giddy interprets as judgmental and her brain boils. She works faster, trying different ways to get Bodie's ears, nose, and eyes right. Now he looks like a wiener dog instead of a retriever. Now he looks like a Muppet. When the bell rings, Giddy stashes her Frankenstein on the upper shelf and furiously washes her hands. As she heads to English, she thinks that what really galls her is she would have had an A with her piggy bank except it wouldn't have followed the rules of personal connection. Also, it's art class, which means it should be easy, not difficult. She's still pondering this as she takes a seat up front for English class discussion.

Avery walks in, sees Giddy's seat, and says: "Oh, come on!"

Giddy pointedly ignores him. The quick write on the board reads: *How intelligent is Polonius?* And Giddy writes *Bricks are sharper* before folding her card up and dropping it in the box on the teacher's desk. Then she mentally smacks herself because her answer is flippant and she's trying to be good in this class, and anyway, the answer is probably that Polonius is a genius. They have Chromebooks today and a quiz, and the first question is from *The Yellow Wallpaper. What are some ways in which you are like Jane?* Since Giddy shares no qualities whatsoever with a crazy woman, she lies: *I had yellow wallpaper in my last house and I also found it annoying.* The next question is equally vexing: *Describe some ways in which you and Hamlet are the same.* Giddy chews on her nail. She punts: *Hamlet lies.* She's not sure if it's true, but wasn't there a part where he was nice to his parents and he didn't like them? Giddy isn't sure. She deletes it and writes: *Much in the same way Hamlet feels, I, too, believe in ghosts.* She doesn't, but who's going to know? Better to write that than to go with something the teacher can prove is inaccurate.

The rest of the questions are simple, and Giddy sighs with relief because she knows things like character names and scene numbers (and can quickly look them up on her phone if she doesn't), and in a few minutes she's hit the submit button. Giddy looks around the room and sees a few students still puzzling over the quiz and one girl typing an entire paragraph comparing herself to Hamlet, and Giddy feels a pang of regret because maybe the parts where she lied weren't being true to Superdoo's list. The quiz ends and as the Chromebooks are collected, the teacher announces they are about to discuss act I. Giddy can't remember how act I ends, so she opens her book and is running her finger along the part where Hamlet is about to meet the ghost as the teacher asks everyone: "So what do you think of the character of Hamlet?" and hands go up. Giddy ignores them and continues to skim the page.

"Giddy Barber."

Giddy looks up. The teacher and everyone else is staring at her. The teacher says: "I'd like you to close your book. We're discussing, not reading."

A cold fury creeps through to the ends of Giddy's fingers and she snaps the book shut with a thud. "So, Giddy, what's your take on Hamlet so far?"

"Polonius seems smart," Giddy says.

"I'm asking about Hamlet, though." Somebody snickers. Giddy whips her head around and angrily canvases the back of the room, but the offender remains hidden.

Her teacher shoots an annoyed look at the room but a kind look at Giddy. "Giddy, I'm just asking for your opinion."

"And I'm just about to give it to you." Ouch. That came out sounding bad, like she's annoyed, which she is. Giddy draws back a little in her seat, the air between her and her teacher potentially weaponized. She expects a rebuke because her tone deserves it.

Instead the teacher just waits. As the silence extends, a rush of heat blooms in her cheeks, and Giddy knows this is the meanest thing the teacher could do to her, that if she really cared about Giddy, she'd just call on somebody else.

"Hamlet," Giddy says, "is a bad person who I don't like." Chin up. Hands pressed resolutely to the desk.

"OK," her teacher says. "That's valid." She turns to the rest of the class. "Anyone else share Giddy's feelings about the main character and maybe want to explain your reasoning?"

A few hands shoot up and Giddy blinks. She's been ejected from the spotlight, and that wasn't supposed to happen until the teacher had skewered her. The next question should have been *Why do you feel that way?* Or *Give me three citations from the text that prove your argument*. Then snicker, snicker, class laughs as Giddy flips through her pages. But to just leave it like that, to just let her off the hook? *That's valid.* Giddy's fingers curl against the book's edges as she fixates on a word she almost never hears. What does that even mean? What is she supposed to take from that? The teacher doesn't call on her again, and Giddy is still fuming when the bell rings, so when she leaves class, she makes sure to throw some trash at the wastebasket in a way that it will miss and bounce back under the teacher's desk. Her teacher sees it and Giddy locks eyes with her as she files out the door. Her teacher's gaze remains frustratingly neutral.

Giddy feels better walking into algebra II until she gets a look at the starter problem on the board, which is *Graph this asymptote*, and Giddy, disheartened by her ignorance, stares at her graph paper, telling herself this is temporary, that she'll catch up on math when the eleven days are over. At the last minute, she looks off another kid's paper and he doesn't hold his hand up to cover it, probably because nobody's expecting Giddy to copy anything in math class. As her teacher collects an answer she isn't even certain is right, he talks and points to a graph on the board. The weight of words like *slant* and *end behavior* and *points of discontinuity* drag her eyelids down and before she knows it, she's micro-sleeping. When the bell rings, a sluggish Giddy packs her stuff and heads out the door behind everyone else. Her teacher gives her a baffled look, but Giddy's battle-weary eyes slide away.

In chemistry, the teacher wants everyone to explain why table salt is a redox reaction and Giddy, still groggy, knows this one but writes some nonsense that deliberately confuses isotopes and ions in a way that makes her snicker. On a pop quiz she writes *fluorine* as a response to a reaction between iron and oxygen and hopes her teacher finds her answer as hilarious as she does. Her phone buzzes:

Jess: *Asia is being hopeless again.*

Giddy: *Why? What'd she do?*

Jess: *Just thinks she's got talent lol*

Giddy: *Graphic design?*

Jess: *thinks she's a cartoonist now*

Giddy draws a little face with its tongue sticking out in the middle of the electron diagram printed on her quiz. Jess sends a picture of a drawing of a squirrel talking to another squirrel, and this would be why she's doing so bad in art class right now, because as far as Giddy can tell, the squirrel drawing looks pretty darn good, maybe even great.

Jess: *awful, right?*

Giddy: *terrible*

Jess: *just feel sorry for her is all*

Giddy: *yeah*

Trinity: *look at yr boyfriend*

Giddy mentally kicks herself for looking automatically at Zach. He's working in his composition notebook, but when he sees Giddy noticing him, he grins.

Giddy turns a scowl to her phone. *That was mean and I dont even like him!*

There follows a bunch of lurid emojis from Jess and Trinity, and Giddy shoves her phone into her pocket and nods off during a PowerPoint over electron transfer. At the end of class, her teacher stops her at the door: "Are you feeling OK, Giddy?"

"Tired."

She smiles a little. "You look it."

Giddy doesn't say anything else to her. She abandons the relative quiet of chemistry for the chaos and noise of lunch.

And stops at the door leading into the cafeteria: *Do something unexpected each day.*

Jess, Trinity, and Asia sit where they always do—on the far left corner of the cafeteria close to the snack bar. It doesn't even face the rest of the cafeteria. Sitting with them, all Giddy ever sees is the matte white wall over Jess's head, latex paint over brick. She's always considered it soothing, a gift being cut off from the rest of the crowd. Only if Giddy sits there, she's not doing anything different for lunch. Of course, if she *doesn't* sit there, she'll have to explain to Jess and the others later why she didn't want to sit with them. Giddy's brain wobbles between the two choices until somebody bumps her from behind, kind of thrusting her into the cafeteria.

Giddy texts Jess: *explain later.* Then she shoves her phone into her back pocket, vowing not to look at it again until lunch is over, and scans the entire area until she targets a conspicuous pair of empty table stools. She almost missed them because they're right against the wall on the right side of the cafeteria, the side farthest away from her usual spot. Giddy winds her way between tables, stepping over backpacks, before she plops her stuff on one stool and sits on the other.

Conversation collapses. Giddy digs out her lunch amid the implosion of silence.

Then someone says: "Well, hi, I guess."

Giddy pops the lid on her Tupperware and wrinkles her nose against the odor of acrid brine. Her stomach gives a reminding lurch and Giddy takes a quick breath and lets it out slowly.

There's still that bubble of silence. Giddy can sense everyone watching, but she knows it's not really the sandwich they're looking at, it's her. Because she shouldn't be here. And somehow that knowledge provides a slight comfort.

The sandwich bends in the middle as she lifts it, and one sardine head slips out, wedged between lettuce leaves. Giddy wills her warring stomach to set down its firearms. Today's sandwich oozes less, having been subjected to a smaller quantity of condiments. Giddy takes a bite, aiming for mostly lettuce. As she does, she sees Trinity and Jess on the other side of the cafeteria stand up and stare at her as Jess furiously texts something.

Giddy's phone buzzes. She ignores it, and the bitter taste of red lettuce mixed with brine from the sardines hits her tongue. She chews with a deliberate slowness, teeth crunching leaves.

The brine with the lettuce sort of reminds her of salad dressing, salty and not *terrible*. She swallows and her stomach twists, but it seems accepting of the food. So she takes another timid bite, and this time she crunches through a little part of a sardine and mayo.

The taste is . . . unusual. It reminds her of her mother's failed Greek casserole, an internet recipe that ended soupy and gray, little black olives floating around like life preservers. Giddy might have been eight or nine. As she recalls it, nobody went back for seconds, and everyone made fun of the attempt except for her mother, who got mad and yelled that they should be happy somebody served them a homemade dinner, dammit! But later, even her mom had to admit the meal didn't compare well to its tablet-screen counterpart.

Giddy takes a third thoughtful bite and now her stomach is burning, but it hasn't rejected the food outright. By accident, her eyes lock onto the girl sitting across from her, who's staring back. Jess would make fun, because this girl's all gold, gold, gold—a little gold glitter spray on a tight dark topknot, big rectangles of battered gold earrings, gold eyeshadow, layers of gold bracelets. Giddy can hear Jess in her ear saying, *Seek attention much?*

"Why," the girl demands of Giddy, "are you here?"

Giddy shrugs. She takes another bite, burps into her hand, then keeps chewing. Almost half the sandwich is gone, and Giddy is flummoxed because her stomach is starting to burn *less*, not more, and if she finishes, she can put a check mark next to *Do something unexpected* on the list tonight.

Beside the girl is a boy, tall, skinny, hair that falls unevenly and may have been self-cut (note to self to tell Jess later), and he stares at Giddy with the same challenge in his eyes. There's a girl to Giddy's right who Giddy has just seen with a peripheral stare, yet Giddy senses the same frozen curiosity. To the immediate left of the golden Topknot Girl sits a boy who is half turned away from them, shoulders relaxed, his easy conversation uninterrupted because there is an invisible wall between groups and Giddy senses he is the line. Giddy is no interruption because she didn't take a seat *with him*, she took a seat with Topknot Girl's crew, and that's an invasion of Topknot Girl's privacy, not his.

Topknot Girl taps a long fingernail against a folded arm. The nail is pale pink but tipped with gold as if existing solely for Jess's hilarity. Then, inexplicably, Topknot grins. The broad, wide white explosion of her teeth is like a rip cord that lets something loose. The boy with the bad haircut next to her eases his shoulders in a similar release of tension, and Topknot nudges him and says: "I bet she had a fight!" There's a deliberate, plodding cadence to her words, almost like chanting. Giddy frowns. The girl says it again. "I bet she had a fight."

The boy thumps the table and snaps his fingers once. "I bet she had a fight!"

Topknot and Boy both thump the table and snap their fingers. "I bet she had a fight!" The girl next to Giddy says it with them, thumping one hand on the table before snapping, and Giddy realizes, *It's a song. They're beating to a song. I've never heard this song! Why are they doing this?* Giddy's frown of confusion grows as this goes on. "I bet she had a fight!" (*thump, finger snap*) "I bet she had a fight!" (*repeat*). It gets louder and the vibrations race from the table through her elbows and into her sandwich, whose slippery innards struggle to maintain themselves. The sardine slips, strikes the bottom of the Tupperware, and flops over, and Giddy, embarrassed, shoves as much of the rest of the sandwich into her mouth as she can without choking just so she has something to do. As she chews, she thinks, *Jess would say something cutting to make them stop!*

And then it does stop, leaving Giddy exposed in this new wash of silence. Her phone buzzes again in her back pocket and Giddy has to resist the urge to reach for it because if she gets on her phone with Jess or Trinity or Asia, then she's just sitting with the same people again, only virtually, and that's violating the list. The last gobs of sandwich slide down her throat, leaving a vaguely burning trail behind. Her stomach pitches. Giddy puts a hand to her belly and thinks, *Stay down!*

And by some miracle, the sandwich *does* stay down. Her stomach burns, but that's all it's doing. Topknot turns sideways and says to the boy: "So why'd you do it, then?"

He shrugs. "Couldn't tell you. Valentine's maybe."

"Sheryl like it?"

"She thought it was hilarious."

"Man, I told you!" They all laugh, even the girl in Giddy's side vision. Giddy makes a pretense of poking around the paper bag that held the Tupperware even though she knows more lunch isn't in there.

"I wasn't going for funny," says the boy, "but I'll take it."

Topknot shakes her head, smiling. "Dammit." She takes a bite out of her own food, a perfectly normal-looking corn dog, and Giddy feels the absence of stares, feels the wall next to Topknot extend at a right angle, closing them off from Giddy. Now it doesn't matter what they say because it isn't for her ears. She is outside of their bubble. She is a nonissue.

Giddy's anxious fingers relax as she rolls up the bag. She's not really sitting with anyone now, and Giddy guesses that's fine. She accidentally sees that Jess is texting her in all caps before she cues up an aria on her phone and hastily pops in her earbuds. It occurs to her that the low, simmering fire in her stomach is a slight improvement over the norm, and she thinks, *Maybe I need more fish in my diet?* She's about to look it up when someone leans across the table and taps her arm.

Giddy jerks her arm away and the earbuds tumble out. Topknot is standing, her bag on her back, smiling. "Bell," she says to Giddy. Then: "What are you listening to?"

Giddy silently flips the phone around so Topknot can see the screen. "*La Trav-ia-tah*. Huh." She gives Giddy a kind of *whatever floats your boat* look and walks off, and Giddy, hurriedly moving to throw her trash away, feels strangely affirmed by Topknot's acknowledgment of her existence.

As she gets up, her phone buzzes again, and Giddy automatically looks across the room to where Jess is standing next to her seat, slinging her backpack over her shoulder with one hand, the other hand holding her phone. Her expression's adamant. A rush of guilt drives Giddy's legs out the door and she heads to robotics early, ducking inside the classroom fast. Giddy plugs her phone in to charge and pulls out yesterday's design plans. Patrice and Deb are two tables away, the bot in front of them, their own plans spread out between them.

"Hey." Giddy looks over and Patrice asks: "Are you going to do anything today?" Arms folded. Stare critical but, Giddy decides, given the way she acted yesterday, perfectly fair. When Giddy shakes her head, Deb and Patrice move to a free area to collaborate over a course design that Giddy wants to point out is supposed to be independent work. Giddy adds ramps and smoke bombs to her course, smirking, imagining possibilities. How to compensate when the terrain is unreliable or hard to see? This will require a robot with flexibility. Giddy adds a stacking challenge of frozen pads of butter. Why butter? Because it starts to lose rigidity at room temperature, making the stacking challenge indirectly timed. Maybe up the ante with fire? She's still smirking over her course when she heads into the hall.

But the smirk dies when she enters world history. The class is oppressively warm again. Students fan themselves with folded papers and drink from water bottles. Giddy plops into her seat. Her teacher slaps a stack of papers on his desk with a teeth-rattling *thwack*.

"I had a poster activity in the hall where, God willing, the air-conditioning works, but then one of you thought it would be *so cute* to draw a penis around the *Lusitania*, so here we are doing classwork instead!"

The news elicits a few giggles but mostly groans. "This kind of juvenile humor is *not* funny," says the teacher, handing out laminated picture cards with the instruction: *Explain how you are emotionally impacted by what you see.* Hunter acquires extras and starts building a teetering card house. One of Giddy's photos shows the trenches. The question on the back—*How would it make you feel to be in their position?*—draws barely a breath from her assigned partner, a mouth breather named Darion who's content to draw tiny circles on his paper.

Giddy raises her hand. When the teacher ignores her, she waves it around.

"You need the bathroom pass, Ms. Barber?"

Tittering all around.

"No, I just wondered when we were going to discuss these cards out loud."

"That's what you're supposed to be doing with your partner." The teacher's eyes move right, drawn by the magnetic pull of whatever's on his computer.

But Giddy wants to discuss the cards out loud because otherwise how will anyone know she is trying? So she waves her hand around again. There is more tittering and a word of protest from Hunter. "Teacher, Giddy's trying to knock my card house down!"

"Now I want the bathroom pass," Giddy says.

In the hall, the teacher's posters are gloomy revenants over walls painted in school spirit stripes of bright gold and purple. Giddy locks eyes with front-line soldiers posing in a group, peruses a separate tableau of the dead lying barefoot, as the caption explains, stripped of their shoes. There's a terrible forced cheeriness in a couple of the photos, and of course the poster of the *Lusitania* has been taken down, leaving a gaping space between switchboard operators with helmets under their chairs and a shadowy tank squatting on a sunlit hill. Giddy still has her card in hand. *How are you emotionally impacted by what you see?*

She isn't. She puts the card into her pocket and returns to a classroom in chaos where the teacher is yelling and pointing because the cards from Hunter's house are all over the floor. Everyone's laughing except Giddy, who tiredly drapes her body over her desk and puts her head down until the bell rings.

She's one of the last out the door and of course Hunter is behind her, shooting cards over her head. "It's fifty-two pickup, Giddy!"

Then his friends repeat it. "It's fifty-two pickup!"

"Come on, Giddy, get the cards!"

"Get the cards off the floor, Giddy!"

"Come on, Giddy!"

So she dissolves into the crowd, hobbling in slow, welcome anonymity until she breaks outside and sees Jess, Trinity, and Asia. They're gathered near the wall. Trinity and Jess are on their phones, but Asia's sitting on the ground a few feet away from them, back to the wall, and there's something off about the way she's behaving. When Giddy approaches, she kind of expects at least a half smile from Asia, but all she gets is this super-wounded look.

Jess says: "What the *fuck*, Giddy?" She lowers her phone for a half second. "So you don't sit with us now?"

"Did we do something?" Trinity asks. "Because I don't remember us doing anything! Not even one text explaining."

"No! I sent one text, I just—" Giddy starts over: "Hey, remember that thing I said I was doing to feel better? The opposition therapy?"

Trinity shakes her head blankly. Jess smirks and looks back at her phone. But Asia stands up and hotly says: "No, I guess no one was really interested in *your* input, Giddy!"

"Jesus, what's your problem?" Giddy asks.

In response, Asia flips around her phone to a text chain. It's the fireplace Asia created followed by the student vomiting GIF Giddy sent yesterday in robotics.

Giddy shakes her head, stunned. "That's not—Asia, that's not for your fireplace. Jess, come on! You heard me talking about opposition therapy."

Jess smirks. "No," she says, "we must not have been listening to you."

"The thing is, I made this list and I have to do things differently for eleven days. That's why I sat somewhere new at lunch." A pause. Giddy adds, "It's nothing you all did."

For a second, nobody says anything. Trinity and Jess are still on their phones. Asia's backed up to the wall again and is ignoring Giddy outright.

"A little advance warning might have been nice," Trinity finally says.

"I kind of did warn you," Giddy says, growing increasingly aggravated. "Yesterday at lunch!"

"Well, any therapy that demands you sacrifice your friends is nuts." This from Jess. "That's not therapy, Giddy. That's a cult."

Giddy throws her hands up. "I'm not trying to sacrifice anything!"

"You didn't even answer my texts!"

That part is true. Giddy awkwardly takes out her phone and looks at the lock screen, but it's mostly just the words *WHAT THE FUCK?* scrolling in all caps over and over. "Look guys, I'm really sorry. But I need to sit away from you for a few days and I'm trying to tell you it's nothing personal."

"You know just saying something doesn't make it true." Trinity types as she talks.

"She doesn't know that," Asia says, looking over at Giddy again. "Not if she's in a *cult*."

Jess chuckles a little and looks over at Asia. Suddenly Asia's face lights up. And Giddy looks back and forth between them, wondering how she missed this before. Of course Asia sticks around despite being the one Jess and Trinity constantly criticize. Because Asia's waiting to be the girl that isn't on the bottom of the social hierarchy, which Giddy *definitely* now thinks is a thing. *And to think I thought your squirrel cartoon was cute.*

"Somebody is tongue-tied." Trinity is still typing.

"I'm a pretty forgiving person." Jess turns away from Giddy to direct her words toward Trinity and Asia. "Usually all I need in these situations is an apology."

But Giddy doesn't feel like apologizing for choosing her own seat at lunch. This seems stupid, like something grade-schoolers would do. She says: "I'm going home."

They're all three ignoring her now, and Giddy walks away, slipping her earbuds in, cranking the opera up a notch, skipping songs until she gets to one she heard this morning where the guy sounds angry, his every word a whipcrack over her ears. Giddy gets a sick satisfaction imagining him bludgeoning someone to death. She's still listening to opera when she gets to the skate park. Then she pops her earbuds out.

If you can, do something unexpected each day.

Giddy walks off the path and down a short hill to the concrete park. She sits on a bench for a minute watching some kids going back and forth on a U-shaped ramp. Occasionally, one jumps and touches the skateboard in the air, but he never gets very far off the ramp, maybe only by a few inches, and almost always he jerks his hand back up real fast like he's afraid he's made a stupid mistake.

And she thinks, *This doesn't look that hard.* Giddy walks over to the kid just getting off the ramp. He looks only a couple of years older than Tad but so much more self-assured in the way he just kicks the end of his skateboard up and grabs it without even thinking about it. He's got a helmet on and it's big-looking against his head. Giddy slows her steps because it feels weird to ask a favor of somebody who's maybe eight.

Giddy says: "Think I could borrow your board for a second?"

He looks like he never gets asked this kind of question, and for a moment Giddy thinks she's made some horrible skateboarding community faux pas. But then he drops his board to the ground and pushes it over. Giddy picks it up, head racing, because part of her didn't think he'd actually say yes.

Giddy goes up to the top of the ramp. There's not really a place to put the board while stepping on it, so she kind of just fumbles it around at the edge before sliding it back onto the flat grass next to the dipping concrete. Down below, the boy who loaned her the board is joined by a little girl about the same age as him and an older teen who might be their caretaker. There's an increasing tension on their faces as they watch Giddy get on the board, wobble, peer over the edge.

The center of the dip is a *long* way down.

The boy who loaned her the board pipes up: "Hey, maybe you shouldn't."

Giddy buckles her knees and shakes her body to nudge the board forward a little, then a little more—

For a second she is sure everything is going to go fine. The board clicks as it connects with the ramp and Giddy leans forward. But the board starts moving and Giddy has leaned over too much. She's on it for one teetering second, and then she's falling forward as the board shoots out from under her. She throws her hands up, but her knees hit first, followed by her shoulder, then she's tumbling. The side of her face strikes concrete and drags as her jacket-clad arms slow her to a stop.

Giddy rolls over onto her back at the center of the ramp.

"Did you see that?"

The skateboard kids. They've stopped everything. Giddy's the main attraction.

"Holy crap! She just wiped out."

"Look at her face!"

At that, she sits up and puts a hand to her face, then pulls it back because it *hurts.* Also there's blood. Giddy stares, mystified, at her wet hand.

Then she gets up and runs, cupping one hand in front of her face because she doesn't want to *touch* it, but she doesn't want anyone seeing it, either. And she races home to a house that's empty but not freezing, so Dougal must have adjusted the thermostat this morning. Upstairs, she gets her first good look at herself.

Her breath catches. Giddy soaks a washcloth and dabs at where the injury begins, just above her eyebrow (there's some hair missing there) to her entire right cheek, where the shape resembles the continent of Africa. Everything ends at her jawline and the side of her nose, and Giddy can tell it's going to scab over before it heals.

She's still working out the best way to deal with it when the door opens downstairs and she hears her dad come in, hears him throw his jacket on the back of the sofa instead of the rack. Giddy grabs some bandages from the medicine cabinet and goes downstairs. "I did something stupid on a skateboard ramp."

He's typing at the computer, but when he looks over his shoulder at Giddy, he flinches. He taps two keys in quick irritation and gets up, directing Giddy to the couch, where she sits patiently, closing her eyes, expecting him to maybe apply some soothing cream, since he's an orderly. But all he does is hastily slap the bandages on with some medical tape. It takes about a second and then he's back at the computer.

Giddy turns her head to test her peripheral vision, and her gaze lands on some wall shelves. They bear a couple of succulents that her mom got as presents from grateful patients at the hospital, framed baby pictures, two outdated medical journals, and, of course, her dad's copy of the novel *Ulysses*.

"They're reading that," Giddy says, pointing.

Her dad is still typing. "Huh?"

"They're reading *Ulysses* in the book club at my school. It was on a poster in the hall."

"Right," her dad says. "Best book I ever read."

Giddy's heard him say this time and time again, especially when her mom tries to declutter the den. *Ulysses* stays because it's the best book in the world. "What makes *Ulysses* so great?"

Her dad's typing slows. He stares at the screen and doesn't say anything, and Giddy thinks he's trying to remember what they were talking about. Then he pivots toward her. "Joyce is a good Irish author and *Ulysses* is his finest work."

Some time ago, an ancestry kit found Irish blood in the Barber family line and her dad has been mentioning it ever since. "What's the book about?"

"It's a retelling of the story of Odysseus set in modern-day Ireland and it has a lot to say about Irish heritage, conflict, and culture."

The book is about two inches thick, and even counterbalanced against the succulents it's making the floating shelf tilt. Giddy frowns. "If I join the book club, can I borrow it?"

"You can borrow it right now." He pivots back, eyes on the screen again. "I've been trying to get Jax to read it for months and he won't touch it."

Giddy takes the book upstairs, where she temporarily uses it to help prop up Superdoo's list. She's reading *Hamlet* on her phone when Tigs comes in. Her little sister gasps: "Giddy!"

Giddy touches her face. "It's OK, Tigs. I just scraped it."

"I wanted you to know Tad and me are both home from school now." For some reason Tigs whispers this information like it's top secret.

Giddy scrolls a little. "That's good, Tigs."

Tigs takes a step forward. She reaches up and taps the back of Giddy's phone. Once. Twice. Giddy sighs. "What?"

"Tad didn't want to go, but then he remembered it was pizza day."

"OK." Giddy's eyes return to the screen, to the part of the play where Hamlet is yelling at Ophelia in a way Giddy feels is a relationship deal-breaker. After a second or two she looks over the top of her phone.

Tigs is still standing there.

Giddy says: "Why don't you go do your homework?"

"I have three questions today. First, isn't everyone going to be mad about Halloween moving? And second, will I get two days of candy, and also shouldn't we be mad at Valentine's?"

Giddy frowns. "Halloween's not moving, and why would we be angry with a holiday?"

Tigs gapes at Giddy like she's some kind of an idiot. "Halloween *is* moving! Because Ms. Lawson says February has twenty-nine days now instead of twenty-eight and that's pushing everything, Giddy! And that's just rude of Valentine's!"

"Tigs, this is normal. It's a leap year. Nothing really changes."

"Everything's going to change! And what if the days slide off the calendar, Giddy? What if they do because they weren't ready?"

"Tigs, go do your homework!" Giddy points to the door.

Tigs deflates. "Now?"

"Yeah."

"But my questions—"

"Go ask your questions to somebody else! I'm busy."

Tigs exhales a soft breath of disappointment and looks at her feet. She backs out of the room slowly.

The second her door clicks, Giddy leaps up, locks it, and flops back onto her bed. After about an hour and a half, she sets her phone down, feeling a weird sense of disappointment at Ophelia's death. Much later, when the play ends with almost everybody dead, she closes the app and rolls her eyes, wondering that if nobody was going to win, what was the point? She puts *Ulysses* in her backpack, deciding to prioritize the history extension book, *The Guns of August.* She's reading when her mom texts her a grocery list from work. Giddy takes the book with her as she heads downstairs.

"Frozen pizzas," her dad tells her as she descends, adding items to their list. Her dad's on the phone with their mom. The front door opens, and there's just a bit of a jolt seeing her brother Jax standing in the doorframe because she almost never sees Jax anymore, wouldn't be seeing him tonight had her mother not insisted on a midweek store run. He looks distracted and weary and doesn't even cross the threshold while waiting for Giddy to grab her jacket. He frowns at her scraped-up face when they slip into the car but doesn't say anything about it. As they back out of the drive, he puts on music and Giddy pops in earbuds, *The Guns of August* open in her lap. She's still reading it when they get to the store. Giddy speeds up ahead of Jax and grabs a cart.

"What are you doing?" Jax asks. "*You're* pushing the cart?"

Giddy shrugs. She lays *The Guns of August* open on the cart as she heads to international foods.

"Where are you going?" Jax is having to trot to catch up with her. "We skipped a whole half of the store."

If you can, do something unexpected each day. "I need some things here." Actually, Giddy doesn't know *what* she needs specifically, but she's kind of excited to figure it out. She runs her finger down shelves of cans and bottles bearing names and labels she can barely identify. Her finger pauses at a bottle of borscht. She picks it up, shakes it, sniffs it, frowns. Into the cart it goes. Giddy also selects canned cucumbers in brine and a jar of gefilte fish.

"What's this stuff for?" Jax asks. "Is this a science thing?"

"No."

He picks up the gefilte fish. The white contents jiggle mysteriously. "This is for *food*?"

Giddy pushes on without answering. She grabs more sardines, and Jax, in a bigger hurry than her, veers off to grab the things her mom and dad wanted like eggs and pizza before rejoining Giddy in the meat department. "You know, one of the classes I'm taking in college is all about budgeting, and it says basically that if you buy something, you should know you're going to eat it. It's just common sense."

Giddy doesn't say anything.

"College gives you this broad perspective of the world. It opens your mind up. It really— Giddy, are those *chicken feet*?"

Into the basket they go, along with oxtails.

"Giddy, seriously, this is gross!"

"I'm cooking these."

Jax sounds exasperated. "Well, nobody's going to eat them!"

Giddy shrugs.

"Just so you know," Jax says at checkout, "*I* didn't buy the chicken feet. So if Mom gets mad later, I didn't do it."

Giddy's got *The Guns of August* open in her hands while they stand in line, and she's puzzling over why a book on World War I begins by describing what everyone wore to a funeral.

In the parking lot, Jax makes a sound of disgust as he loads the groceries. On the way home, it's too dark to read, so her mind wanders. As busy as she's been, Jax must be busier. Why else would he leave so early in the mornings and come back so late at night?

She says: "You don't have a lot of time to do the things you want, do you?"

Jax is driving. "What do you mean?"

"I mean, what time do your college classes start?"

"Seven thirty. But I like to be on campus early to study."

Giddy frowns. "But then you stay late. You're hardly ever home before midnight."

For a second, Jax says nothing. Then: "That's because I'm also in evening study groups." He hits the accelerator a little hard as they go up onto the highway, and the car lurches before settling into a new speed. "You have to work around people's schedules. You'll learn all that in a couple of years. It's not easy balancing your life around other people."

"Why not just connect with them online? You'd spend more time at home."

"Because it doesn't work like that. Geez, Giddy! Third degree much?" Jax turns on the radio and that's pretty much the end of the conversation.

Except when they go home, Mom's on the front porch looking frantic, and Giddy quickly realizes she didn't bring her phone. They don't even get out of the car before Jax lowers a window to ask what's the matter.

"Dougal! Dougal's what's the matter!" Her mother leans into the car. "Giddy, where's Dougal?"

"His room?" Giddy wasn't really listening to who was coming home since, at the time, she was lying down on her bed reading *Hamlet*. She never even heard Tad and Tigs come in.

"No, he's not in his room! He's not anywhere! And your dad didn't think to check when he came home because he was busy and—" She throws her arms up and makes a noise of such pure feral frustration, Jax says: "OK! He's probably at the park. I'll drive around—"

"You do that! Oh my God, it's nine o'clock!"

Jax pulls out of the driveway, putting the window back up. He thumps the wheel continuously with his hands, chin thrust out, eyes squinted as if peeling back the curtain of night to find his brother. Giddy finds the noise of Jax thumping so annoying, she slips her earbuds in and fills her head with a German aria.

A tenor sings, high and slow, as they reach the park, headlights making long shadows of trees. Jax circles twice, shaking his head. The tenor's words speed up and his pitch elevates as Jax guns the motor to veer off onto a street with lots of curb-parked cars and people out on lawns. Jax is emphatically gesturing as he talks, but all Giddy hears is the tenor's high-pitched, chaotic notes. When they reach a cul-de-sac, Jax parks and runs up to a door, past a couple of empty lawn chairs and beer bottles. He bangs on it, yelling. Someone answers and they both disappear inside.

In anticipation of what's to come, Giddy cranks up the aria.

Jax emerges from the house with Dougal. They yell at each other, two silhouettes against the porch light. Two of the kids Giddy recognizes from the bus stop lean in the doorway. Dougal waves to them as he follows Jax. He laughs as he climbs into the seat behind Giddy, and there's a strength to his breath, the vaping smell of fruit punch mixed with the more yeasty odor of beer. Jax spins his tires backing out of the driveway as Dougal slaps his hand against the window and waves some more.

The aria concludes. Giddy pulls her earbuds out. The car is filled with nothing but cold silence. Streetlights pool over them in rhythmic waves.

Suddenly Dougal leans over and raps Giddy on the shoulder. "What'd you do to your face?"

"Skateboard."

Dougal laughs.

Jax says: "It's not as stupid as the things you do."

"Oh yeah?"

"Mom's going to be pissed!"

Dougal says after a second: "Not at me."

"Oh, is that what you think?"

"Yeah." Dougal leans forward, grinning. "Mom's not going to be pissed at *me.*"

Jax doesn't say anything back. Giddy frowns. There's subtext she's missing. Why doesn't Jax yell some more? They both have Dougal dead to rights. But Jax is quiet. He even stops thumping his hand on the wheel. In the side mirror, Dougal looks out and twists his mouth into a hard little squiggle that's bitter and cold. He looks tired, used up.

When they get home, their mom has a warm robe tied over her scrubs and a mug of chamomile tea on the coffee table. "Where was he?" she demands of Jax.

"Just chilling in the park." Jax puts his jacket on the coatrack. Giddy gapes at her older brother as he ducks back out the door, leaving.

Her mom frowns. "Giddy, what happened to your face?"

"Skateboard."

"Dougal, go to your room *now*!" And Dougal flashes a big grin at all of them as he bounds up the stairs. Giddy's mom pulls her aside.

"Giddy, you know you're the responsible one."

Giddy does not like where this is going. She also can't help but notice Jax has already revved up his engine and is peeling out of the driveway.

"And you know our jobs make your father and I crazy busy," her mom says, "so I need you to keep better track of Dougal." She squeezes both of Giddy's shoulders and turns away.

Giddy thinks, *No.* It's a simple word, a concise declaration of independence. She's thinking it as her mother shoots her father a look that indicates they will have a private conversation about Dougal later, and she is still thinking it as she slips up to her room to read more of *The Guns of August.*

A text interrupts.

Jess: *Trinity cut her hair!*

This is followed by a grotesque GIF of a long-haired cat that's had its body shaved, leaving a puffball head. Asia sends a vomit emoji and Giddy frowns because wasn't Jess not talking to Giddy earlier? Weren't they *all* not talking to her? What do you text to someone who isn't talking to you? Giddy is trying to find a GIF of someone ripping duct tape off their mouth, but all the images are violent.

Jess: *Giddy wanna pic? Sooo bad!!*

She keeps searching. She's getting frustrated!

Jess: *she sucks so much Giddy!*

Giddy turns her phone off. She does it fast, almost without thinking, and she sets it down on her desk like it's some kind of poisoned thing.

Her eyes meet Superdoo's. He's grinning. But Giddy doesn't feel like grinning, couldn't grin if she wanted to, because it would hurt her scraped-up face! If finding a smile is the point of this, then why has doing everything different today only confused people and caused her tons of irritation?

Superdoo just keeps on grinning. Giddy scowls at him on purpose and winces when the scowl hurts her bandaged face. But she stubbornly puts a check mark next to *Do something unexpected.* Giddy angrily turns out the light.

3

When the alarm sounds at five thirty, Giddy wants to throw the clock across the room. Every time she rolled over last night, her face brushed the pillow, waking her in pain. Giddy stands at the back of the shower, cupping her hands under the cold water and slapping it onto her body along with soap. But when she rinses, she forgets, takes a tired step forward, and shrieks curse words as the cold water pours over her head and under her bandages. When she exits, she has to redo everything, but all she can find is giant square bandages and they make her look like a quilted Phantom of the Opera.

In the hall, all is quiet. Bodie hugs the wall, backing down the stairs ahead of her, tail thumping. She lets him into the backyard, and a look outside confirms all cars are gone, so Jax and her parents are already out. Giddy leans against the counter, watching the *drip, drip* inside the coffee carafe. Her stomach is oddly muted, so she eats a boiled egg with a toasted bagel and the barest minimum of cream cheese.

Her phone buzzes.

Mom: *Keep an eye on Dougal!*

Giddy looks upstairs at Dougal's closed door. Then the coffee maker beeps and Giddy pours herself a full cup. She intends to just stare at it, maybe smell it to get her blood moving.

But she takes a sip. Then another. That's when her stomach wakes up and punches her in the face. Angry, Giddy takes another sip and then another as if the mild acid of coffee might slowly eat away at the beast within. But all it does is make her stomach worse, and Giddy, further enraged, downs the rest of the cup in revenge sips that burn her mouth and tongue. As she opens the door to leave, she looks upstairs once more.

Nothing but quiet and closed doors. It's ten till six. Giddy shrugs and leaves.

She crosses a cul-de-sac, taking a path she used to bike down before discovering that going by the park was faster. The sun crests pink over two-story houses and the spiny inkblots of pine branches. An angry shout draws Giddy's eye even as she pulls the hood tight around her face.

Seven houses down the street, a teenage boy has his backpack thrown over one shoulder and he's backing down his driveway as a man, maybe his dad, yells at him from just inside the open garage door. The tension between them spills down the concrete, carried like a current to Giddy across cracked sidewalks and frosty morning grass. The boy waves off the man like he's not worth talking to and that only makes the man yell more furiously. A second later, the garage door starts to close and the boy walks alone, toward a bus stop, his back turned from Giddy. But her eyes are wide because she recognizes him.

That's Hunter. From world history. Giddy's never seen anybody except the teacher yell at him, though Hunter strikes her as somebody a lot of people probably yell at. But it weirds her out and she thinks, *That's where he lives.* It's strange to think that Hunter has a house, that Hunter lives in a neighborhood, that Hunter lives actually quite near her own home.

Giddy turns swiftly and continues walking to school. The air keeps finding ways to clutch at the scab under her bandages, and by the time she reaches school she's acutely aware of all the people who keep staring at her face as she enters art class.

Because it's Friday, everyone's kind of buzzy, talking loudly over their sculptures, making weekend plans. Alone in the midst of so much cheer, Giddy feels doubly exposed. So she throws all her focus into her work. But after two failed attempts at trying to get the ear-to-eyes-to-snout ratio to work, she sinks a fist into Bodie and watches his clay eyes dip and close together in a V.

She's rolling it out with her palms when the girl with the otter sculpture offers advice: "You know, sometimes simple is better." The tone is so earnestly helpful that Giddy stops what she's doing to make eye contact. Today the girl's added two black glass beads for the otter's eyes and they are *perfect*. In fact, everything about the otter is perfectly proportioned and ratioed.

As if embarrassed by her own competence, the girl shifts her design a few inches toward herself, and adds: "I mean, we're none of us Michelangelo." Her words come out a little jittery, and Giddy can hear Jess saying to Otter Girl: *Wow, you are committed to sympathy. Your cheeks are even blushing. Good job! No, seriously, good for you!*

Giddy rolls her eyes in a way she hopes isn't too snarky, and Otter Girl blushes further and looks down. Giddy tries to make a sculpture of Bodie again, only now his eyes are too big. She corrects it and uses a tool to make slash marks for fur. But now he looks like a reanimated corpse from a horror show.

Giddy's developed a headache and the bandages itch. Other students are turning in their projects and it occurs to Giddy that she's out of time, that the week is over, that art class is supposed to be easy, and here she is heading into the weekend failing at something simple and stupid. So when Otter Girl walks her own statue up, Giddy once again smashes what she's come to imagine as "Bizarre Bodie" and rolls her fist over and over it.

The bell rings. Students pack up. Giddy glares at the clay like it's a disobedient servant, grabs her pencil, and scrawls into the flat oval: *GIDDY'S ALL-ORIGINAL ART PROJECT—A FUNCTIONAL DINNER PLATE!* And then in smaller letters underneath: *BE IN AWE OF HER GENIUS*. Giddy peels her design up and walks it to the front table for grading. Several students look at her and she wants to tell all of them, especially the boy who fashioned the bong out of clay, to shut the fuck up. She locks eyes with her teacher long enough to make sure he witnesses her work. He frowns, looks at her design, frowns harder, and Giddy goes back to her seat thinking, *It's a plate, dammit! You wanted functional, so I at least get points for functional, right? I should get a fucking A for effort!*

Giddy throws her backpack on and hauls ass out the door.

In English, she finds herself incapable of dialing back her snark when she dashes off a response to the quick write, which asks: *What do you think Hamlet's relationship was like with his father?* So when discussion starts, no one is more surprised than Giddy when the teacher flips to her card and says: "Giddy, I really liked your answer to the quick write. Would you mind reading it out loud for us?"

As she slides the card onto Giddy's desk, Giddy feels dozens of eyes in class peeling back the layers of her ruined face. She whisper-reads: "'Hamlet probably hates his dad because his dad wants him to do too much.'"

"You know, it's funny," her teacher says, "because every other answer I received talked about how much Hamlet must have loved his father. But I actually think you may be right. Hamlet was a prince. A lot is expected of him. And now, even dead, his dad wants more?" Her teacher shrugs and sits back down. "Do you think that's fair, Giddy?"

Dozens of eyes, still watching, still peeling . . . Giddy says something her mom always tells her: "You know life's not fair."

Her teacher smiles a little. "No, I guess it's not." Then she draws another card and calls on someone else, but it takes a while for the eyes to leave her, and Giddy wants to slap the stragglers away like flies. Giddy wads her index card up, crunching it into her palm over and over, willing it into nonexistence.

In algebra II, the teacher announces they are working on their own, but he chooses a student to walk around class to help peers. As Katlyn frolics about, gleefully assisting, Giddy does her best to copy from a neighbor while the teacher urges them to locate the point of discontinuity on the graph. At the end of class, Giddy turns in her paper face down, grateful he can't see it.

But there's no such escape in chemistry, where the teacher's waiting for her. She hands Giddy her quiz at the door, right before Giddy can step inside class.

"I've graded this," the teacher tells her, "and it's as if you've forgotten basic chemical symbols."

This is the quiz Giddy turned into a joke. She says: "It'll be better in a week."

"It needs to be better *now*."

Giddy, blushing, takes her quiz and walks into the room . . .

. . . straight into the cold stares of Jess and Trinity at the back of the room. Her friends have their phones in hand, but they're looking at Giddy.

Giddy, thinking of yesterday's conversation, glares and says: "What?"

"You have something on your face," Jess says.

"A little something here," Trinity mimics, drawing a line down her cheek where Giddy's bandages are, "maybe also here?"

"Should we sign it," Jess asks, "like a cast or something?"

They both burst into giggles as Giddy shoots past them and dives into her seat. Almost immediately, Zach scoots his chair over. "Hey, happy Friday!"

Giddy scowls. "Sure."

"Your quiz," he says, "you know if it's just chemical symbols you're struggling with—"

Giddy gapes at him. "You weren't supposed to be listening to that and I can read the periodic table, thank you!"

He lowers his voice to a whisper: "I'm just saying that I could help. Maybe we could get together over the weekend. Study."

Giddy closes her eyes then slowly opens them again. "No. I'm not interested. *Thanks!*" She makes that last word so loud and definitive that Zach scoots his chair back to his table and at the back of the room, Jess and Trinity burst into peals of laughter. As the teacher lowers the lights to show them a video about English chemist Joseph Priestley, one of them, either Trinity or Jess, makes a long *smack* kissing sound that results in Giddy whipping her head around to glare at them. Because she would *never*! The very idea of kissing Zach sounds gross.

Like a sardine sandwich.

Giddy's eyes widen. The video starts playing and her hood is up so she can nod off, but now she doesn't think she *can* sleep. Because kissing Zach *is* the very opposite of something she would do, and now she can't stop staring at the back of Zach's head while the video plays, thinking, *Should I agree to study with him this weekend?*

She's still trying to decide when the bell rings. Giddy walks to lunch and plops down in her new seat, troubled thoughts circling. She takes out a Tupperware and looks up, aware of a sudden oval of silence.

Topknot Girl is no longer golden. Today she has three pink chalk stripes in her hair and it's all wrapped into a tight topknot braid. But as Giddy's staring at her, trying to figure out if it's going to be a different color every day, she realizes Topknot and her crew are all looking back at Giddy, stunned.

The skinny boy with the bad haircut breaks the silence. "What happened to your face?"

Giddy can't think of a reason to ignore him. "Skateboard ramp."

Everybody winces. Topknot Girl says: "You could not pay me to get on those things. Uh-uh. No way. Not in a thousand years." She stabs a fork into some pot roast and swirls it around on her tray, the idea pointedly dismissed. But Skinny Boy leans a little across the table, interested, and Giddy feels every muscle in her body wanting to lean back.

"I tried skateboarding," Skinny Boy says, "and I couldn't stay balanced. I never made it to a ramp. What was it—half-pipe, quarter-pipe?"

Giddy has no idea. "Steep."

Topknot Girl laughs. "Bet you learned your lesson."

"So my brother ate it on a skateboard once and almost went into oncoming traffic." This from the girl sitting to Giddy's right. "He was seven. My mom sold his skateboard at a garage sale after that."

Giddy pops open her Tupperware. The smell of gefilte fish hits her nose hard. Giddy can tell everyone at the table smells it too. She feels their eyes watching her as she lifts the sandwich, which along with the fish cake, has lettuce and tomato on it and a little bit of sour cream. Giddy bites and a taste almost like hot sauce hits the roof of her mouth. The fish cake is mushy and bits of it squeeze out from between her teeth like little tubes of toothpaste.

She looks up and just happens to see Zach leaving the lunch line with his tray of food. He sees her watching and a slow smile spreads across his face.

Giddy looks away fast. She takes four more rapid bites of her sandwich and washes the whole thing down with a juice box that does *not* pair well with the taste. Giddy puts a hand to her stomach and closes her eyes, counting very slowly.

When she opens them again, Topknot Girl says: "Are you all right?"

"Yes." This may be true, because while her stomach roils and pitches, nothing's come up again.

"I'm Ashlynn," says Topknot Girl.

"OK," says Giddy. Then she stupid-blinks. "I'm Giddy."

"That's Trey"—she points to the skinny boy—"and that's Monica"—over to the girl to Giddy's right. "When they were together, you may have heard about them—they were Treymonica. Like *harmonica*."

Monica giggles. "Only for one day and it was *not* music!"

Trey and Ashlynn laugh. Giddy's eyes pop open a little wider because—eat lunch with your ex? Why? Asia would talk about it for weeks. Jess and Trinity would explode, or maybe they would implode and collapse into a phone-shaped point of singularity. And then a smaller thought pops into her head: *Why not?*

"What were you eating?" Monica asks.

"Gefilte fish sandwich." There's a war going on in Giddy's mind, a desire for her tablemates to stop asking her questions while at the same time feeling incapable of not answering them. She thought they'd all established that she sits *near* them, not *with* them.

"Is it good?"

Giddy shakes her head. "It's just—I thought I'd try it."

Jess, in her head: *Giddy, you are proving it* is *possible to try and fail at the same time. Cute tip: if you can barely pronounce it, you don't eat it.*

But all Trey and Ashlynn and Monica do is nod, as if this statement doesn't demand the crucifixion she feels it deserves. Then Ashlynn says to Trey: "Hey, is it true you have to drop all other clubs if you want to join soccer?"

"No." Trey takes a bite of a chicken nugget. "That's a vicious rumor started by the volleyball team. You want to do soccer?"

"I don't *not* want to do it. But . . ." She twirls her fork around a little in the air and smiles impishly. "I kind of think soccer players are the new sexy and I should get in on the ground floor of that."

"You will fall on your ass," Monica says.

"I agree that you won't last," Trey tells her.

"I would look amazing in those little shorts, though," Ashlynn says, and they all kind of laugh and go back to eating.

Giddy takes the opportunity to pop her earbuds in, because usually people don't ask you any more questions when you do that. She turns on opera and the rest of lunch passes by to her quietly bobbing her head to a German version of *La donna è mobile*.

In robotics, Patrice and Deb's bot comes in second in a relay and Giddy, locked into the only corner of class that has an available outlet for phone-charging, thinks: *They came in second because they were too concerned about the robot falling apart. I would have risked it. I would have upped the torque and sacrificed stability for maneuverability.* But Giddy is just one student in a class full of kids who probably all want to be mechanical engineers just like she does. So is it really any surprise that after two days of her refusing to help, nobody asks for her input anymore?

By the time she gets to world history, Giddy slumps in her chair and stares straight ahead as the teacher talks about the exhaustion of trench warfare, about how soldiers tried their best at first but slowly tired over time. As the lights lower, Giddy watches a movie about the Battle of Verdun and thinks, *Why'd they keep trying? Why didn't they just roll over and fall asleep?*

At the back of the room, Hunter kicks a seat. The kicks travel until they reach the back of her seat. Giddy doesn't turn around. Instead she pictures every shake of her desk as if it's nothing more than stray artillery fire. She drags her heels heading out of class, and in the hall Hunter yells: "Hey, what's the matter with your face, Giddy? You hug a cat? You shouldn't hug cats, Giddy. They don't like it."

Giddy stops. The crowd she'd normally disappear into funnels into a V, bodies thrust together as if by the blades of a blender. Giddy turns around. She thinks about saying something personal like, *Saw your dad yelling at you this morning*, but she has a better idea.

"Really? My face? That's all you've got?" Hunter stands by himself, because it's Friday and his buddies never linger outside the last class of the day on a Friday. "Everybody notices my face today. That's kind of low-hanging fruit, don't you think?"

Hunter grins. "All I'm say—"

"It's not even clever. Hugging a cat? How about: 'Giddy, you mixed up acne cream with battery acid again—read a label, dumb bitch!' Or 'Aww, Giddy . . . no matter how many times you make out with a cheese grater, it's *never* taking you to prom!' Or 'I always recommend razor blades as the go-to for self-harm, but Giddy's stepped it up a notch with a blowtorch to her face BECAUSE SHE'S FUCKING NUTS!'"

She screams that last part right into his face, and Hunter lights up with so much delight that Giddy thinks his head is going to shoot right off his body. But when she turns and walks away, she hears *nothing* from him for the first time ever.

She stops at the door of the library, where the book club is meeting. She can see them through the glass doors, a bunch of students seated at a long table in the back—all girls, some she's seen around before, some she hasn't. It occurs to Giddy that she doesn't know what you're supposed to say or do at a book club. It might be like English class, in which you're expected to say just the right thing at the right time. But it's her first day. Would they look at her weird if she just sat quietly?

Giddy falters. Then she takes out her copy of *Ulysses*, holds it in front of her like a shield, and walks in.

Katlyn from algebra II sits at the head of the table. She locks eyes with Giddy as Giddy pulls up a chair. Immediately every head at the table turns, and it's like the air became solid and rushed her. Giddy senses she's the new variable in a social equation. She didn't come here to bust anything up; she just came to discuss *Ulysses*, and to make that point, Giddy deposits her dad's brick-heavy book onto the table.

Katlyn has a box of sharp pencils and a stack of note cards, and it could not be clearer who's the leader. She says: "Oh, Giddy. *You're* here."

Giddy shrugs.

Katlyn has a copy of *Ulysses*, only of course it's nicer than Giddy's and leather-bound. Giddy's eyes narrow as Katlyn stands it up on the table where everyone can see it. "So. *Ulysses*." Her eyes widen and everyone kind of grins. "What do you think?"

A girl sighs and stands up her own copy, which has rubbed-off corners and a library call number. "My English teacher says he couldn't finish this."

Someone else: "I hear it's a dare book."

"What this is," Katlyn says, a little smile on her face, "is the most influential novel of the twentieth century and I can't wait to dive in."

"I heard it's basically *The Odyssey*, so that's why I want to read it," says the girl next to Giddy. Then she looks at Giddy and Giddy catches on, that they're going in order.

Everybody waits. Giddy says: "I'm trying to do different things in my life right now."

"Right," Katlyn says, and Giddy perks up because there's a clue in her lofty voice, a tone of ominous foreboding, "because you're *depressed*."

And now Giddy knows why everyone's still looking at her. Because she was wrong: she isn't a social variable here. Variables have an unknown quality. Everyone's staring because they think they know exactly what Giddy is and Giddy can't imagine how this is happening to her or who could have told them.

Giddy says: "What?" The all-encompassing question.

"You made some kind of list," says another girl, eyes peering over glasses at Giddy, "and you're doing things to keep from being sad all the time."

Giddy's brain races backward to go over everything she's ever said to anyone ever as another girl takes out her phone, rereads a text, and says: "Yeah. You call it"—she looks at the screen again, baffled—"'the Opossum Regimen.'"

And Giddy thinks, *Jess!* Because that's the only thing that makes sense. Because Jess is all over social media. Jess, and maybe Asia and Trinity, but mostly Jess. "It's opposition therapy," Giddy mutters.

The girl holding the phone shrugs like that's basically the same thing. Meanwhile, the girl to Giddy's left says: "Well, I wanted to read *Ulysses* because it's part of the curriculum in a college credit class I want to take next year."

With that, they've moved off Giddy, but Giddy is still out there, exposed, thinking, *Jess* was *listening. But she wasn't, she wasn't really.* And Jess did this to her, put her out there on the internet, talked about her. And why wouldn't she? How is Giddy any different from Asia and her cartoon squirrels or her fancy fireplace? How is Giddy anything more than text message fodder?

And just like that, everything begins shutting down inside her again. Angry? That door closes. Embarrassed? Nope, that is too much for this. Giddy feels a terrible *nothing*, the same nothing that started Superdoo's list to begin with. She wants to feel something, but it's being held back by that same frustrating wall that keeps her from smiling.

Giddy looks at the girls flipping through their books and thinks, *I'm going to read the shit out of* Ulysses*!* So when book club ends with little more than everybody agreeing they're going to *try* to read it, Giddy already has her book open, reading as she walks, lifting her eyes to see Katlyn watching her as if Giddy only has the book open to impress *her*.

At a crosswalk Giddy waits, and some dumb jogger sees the book and gives her a ridiculous thumbs-up. But all Giddy's thinking after reading a few pages is *It's not too terrible. It's just some guys talking about stuff. This isn't a big deal.* But by the time she reaches the park, the story of *Ulysses* has shifted and now it's all about a man named Leopold and his weird life.

She ends up sitting with her back against a tree, book open, and now she understands that part of the problem with *Ulysses* is that Leopold's life is boring. Also, his wife is clearly sleeping with somebody. And maybe Leopold is too, and why are his thoughts so random? Why can't he just stay focused on one thing? Nobody thinks like this, with their brains flitting around from one unconnected thing to the next. And why is Jess such a *bitch*?

On the way home, Giddy thinks about Leopold and Superdoo and points of discontinuity on an asymptote line graph and gefilte fish, which should have had more flavor based on its horrible smell. When she goes through the door, the furnace is on, the house is toasty, and Dougal is slicing up week-old meatloaf onto a sandwich. His backpack hangs on the coatrack in the same position it was in this morning.

Giddy very quietly says: "Did you skip school?"

He gives her the same shit-eating grin Tad likes to give, so Giddy rolls her eyes and shoves past him to grab the gefilte fish jar and some saltines. She sits at the sofa eating the fish cake on crackers, thinking that it's not so bad with salt, that it's going down pretty well. Bodie puts his head in her lap and Giddy lets him lick her fingers and then the plate before depositing everything in the sink and washing up. Dougal's moved upstairs, into the cave that is his room. Giddy sets a pot of water boiling. She takes out the chicken feet and a big knife, cringing at the little curved talons poking through the plastic like the evil ends of witch fingers.

The door flings open and Tad comes in like a winter blast. He races past the kitchen and upstairs, slamming the door to his and Tigs's room. Tigs strolls inside, leaving the front door open as she sits and painstakingly removes her boots before taking off her coat. Giddy can feel every ounce of heat being sucked out the door.

Tigs ambles into the kitchen. Her eyes widen. "Giddy, what are you doing?"

"Preparing chicken feet."

"Why?" Tigs gives a little yelp and jumps as Giddy uses the knife to chop off the chicken toes, per the phone recipe's requirement. The little clawed end shoots off the kitchen island and into the living room, where Bodie knocks over the coffee table pursuing it.

"For food."

Tigs makes a big O with her mouth. A second chicken toe leaps off the cutting board before Giddy can grab it. It winds up somewhere near the base of the stairs.

"I wanted you to know that Tad did *not* want to go to school today," Tigs whispers as Giddy drops a heavy dishcloth over the toes that she cuts. "But I told him I would break all his stuff if he didn't go and then I would run to the neighbors and tell them to call Mom and Dad."

Giddy slides a few toes off the counter and into the trash.

Tigs says: "So aren't you?"

"Aren't I what?"

"Proud of me."

The knife pauses. Tigs sounds small and tragic. "Sure, Tigs."

A grin explodes on her face. "I have *four* questions. The first—"

"You mean you have one question," Giddy interrupts while chopping. "You already asked me three."

Tigs frowns. "No, I didn't!"

"You asked me what I was doing. I said I was preparing chicken feet and you asked why. You asked if I was proud of you. That's three out of four."

Tigs appears to count it up in her mind. "I have *seven* questions. The first—"

"Seven?" Giddy misses her mark and chops the chicken foot in half instead of just trimming off the claw. The amputated piece shoots off the counter and Bodie smacks his head into the stair rail catching it. "Tigs, I'm busy cooking."

"Don't you want to answer my questions?"

"I'm busy!"

"Yes," Tigs agrees somberly. "But don't you *want* to?"

Giddy stares at her. Tigs's eyes are huge. A second elapses before Giddy says: "Don't you have homework?"

Tigs rolls her eyes. "I don't want to do it *now*!"

But when Giddy points, Tigs sighs heavily and goes upstairs, and Giddy, also sighing, closes the front door, cutting off the blast of cold. Giddy mixes a marinade and watches the little chopped-up feet bob around in the boiling water like a coop massacre. Into the marinade they go and then into the oven and Giddy reads *Ulysses* as they bake. When they're done, Giddy makes herself a small plate and wrinkles up her face because while they smell good, chicken feet are the ugliest things she's ever prepared in her life.

The last thing in the world she expects when she takes a bite of the side of one is to *like* it. Giddy slurps all the meat off the bone, eyes wide, and before she knows it, she's eaten five. She made a big batch, though, definitely enough for a couple of days. She wonders if they're good cold.

Giddy puts the rest into a Tupperware in the fridge and mentally marks them for lunch the next day, maybe with some sliced cucumber. She takes *Ulysses* to her room and is still reading when her parents return, and Jax actually comes in with them for once, though she hears him go upstairs and up into his attic room after a minute of discussion downstairs. Somebody pops a pizza into the oven, because the house slowly fills with the aroma of melting cheese and pepperoni. Tad and Tigs run down. Giddy half expects to be called, but all she hears is everyone rattling around in the kitchen and arguing over the television.

After about an hour, Tigs opens Giddy's door. "Want to come over?"

She actually does. Giddy sets *Ulysses* down. The book is giving her a headache. She really doesn't understand what any of it's supposed to be about. Maybe meaninglessness? Maybe not understanding is the point or something? "Yeah, did you want me to answer your questions now?"

"I already answered them."

"You already—" Giddy frowns. "You answered your own questions?"

"I used my tablet."

"Oh." A strange pang of disappointment strikes Giddy in the chest. "Well, then what do you want to do?"

Turns out Tigs has a tiny origami book that a teacher let her have, and Giddy and Tigs spend about ten frustrating minutes trying to make bats. Tad is sitting on his bed, head inclined over a binder. He loudly announces: "I need math help!"

"I'll help you with English or history," Giddy tells him. "But I'm avoiding math right now. Why don't you ask Jax?"

Tad shrugs. He hops down. Giddy hears him beat a path up the attic stairs.

Giddy turns her bat upside down. "It's a better boat," she mumbles, and Tigs giggles, reaches out, and crushes Giddy's creation into a little tiny paper wad. Giddy rips off some more colored paper and looks up to the sound of heavy footsteps coming down from the attic.

Jax leans in her door. "Tad needs math help. Why'd he come to me?"

Giddy frowns. "So you can help him."

He looks dumbstruck. "That's your job."

Giddy's trying to remember when, if ever, anybody assigned that responsibility to her. She thinks it just sort of happened over time, probably because there's usually no one on the other side of Jax's door. "I'm busy. You do it."

"You're busy *folding paper*?"

"Bad bat!" Tigs wads up more paper and shoots it at the door, hitting Jax in the mouth.

"Yeah," Giddy says. "Super busy. Anyway, it's not hard. It's just grade-school stu—"

"Come on." Jax snaps his fingers at Tad and pivots, his little brother mutely following. The stairs creak as Jax and Tad walk into the room above, and Giddy wonders what Jax spends all his time doing that he can't spare a second for elementary math.

Her mom would say, *"College work,"* and that would be the end because as far as Mom's concerned, that's Jax's primary job.

"Bad bat!" Paper hits Giddy in the nose and Tigs squeals as Giddy retaliates. Giddy's paper hits Tigs square in the forehead and Tigs falls over backward, laughing so hard that she starts to hiccup.

All at once, this reminds Giddy of the video of her and Jax knocking over dominoes with Superdoo. A wave of exhaustion floors her and she sets her origami down. "OK, that's enough."

Tigs covers her mouth, but when another hiccup burps through her closed fingers, she explodes into laughter again.

"I said that's enough!" Giddy stands up. The paper falls out of her lap and Tigs looks up at her, surprised by the sharpness. Another muffled hiccup burps through her little covered lips.

I'm so mad! Why am I mad? "It's bedtime." Giddy kisses the top of Tigs's head.

As she leaves, Tigs says: "But what if I'm too bubbly?"

"Bubble during your sleep." Giddy closes the door. She spends an hour furiously reading *Ulysses*, but part of her can't stop thinking about how her dad managed to get through this book when he can't even resist taking out his phone during a two-hour movie. And when she turns in for the night, Superdoo, his shadow cast on the wall from the ghostly blue of her digital alarm, offers no further illumination.

4

Giddy's alarm wakes her at six thirty. She sleepily hits snooze. She's never been one to set an alarm on Saturdays. Tigs is her alarm, crawling into bed around eight to snuggle or just sitting and staring into Giddy's closed eyes until Giddy can no longer pretend and gets up to make her and Tad breakfast—sometimes breakfast for her parents, too, if they're not sleeping in from their last shift or up early for a morning shift. Dougal sometimes comes down and eats, but more often these days he's asleep or he's already gone to get a taco from the convenience store.

But Giddy's being different, so when the alarm sounds again at 6:39, she turns it off permanently. For once she doesn't flinch in the shower, and when she towels off, it occurs to her she took the time to get fully clean, that there's no soap in her hair, that the cold shower actually felt kind of *good* in a really unexpected way.

All is quiet in the Barber house as Giddy goes downstairs. Bodie lifts his sleepy head, the end of his leash in his mouth. "You have to wait for Jax to get up," Giddy tells him. She grabs a piece of bread, butters it, and sticks it in her mouth. As she closes a cabinet, a list flutters under a fridge magnet.

Her mom's handwriting. *WEEKEND: Organize pantry, take all upstairs trash out, Tigs/Tad laundry, clean rooms, brush dog.*

Giddy says: "You're shedding all over Mom's bed again, Bodie."

Bodie blinks stupidly by the front door, leash still locked hopefully between his teeth. Suddenly Giddy thinks, *Why not?* Walking Bodie in the mornings on weekends is Jax's job, but since he did Tad's math last night, the trade is only fair. Giddy would have made a face if anyone asked her if she'd like dog-walking responsibilities. She's never enjoyed being encumbered by anything that could draw her off course. Feet are made for getting you there, and the shortest distance between points A and B is a straight line.

But this morning, when the chill air hits her still-wet head and soaking bandages, she lets the hood drop because, while it doesn't feel great, exactly, it feels *awakening*. She pops the earbuds in and Bodie's tail brushes her leg in step with an aria. When they reach the park, Giddy takes off in a run down the jogging path, Bodie nipping at her heels. She slows to settle against a tree, coughing out all the cold air.

She slips numb fingers into gloves, parks it on a bench, and takes out *Ulysses*, determined to make it a third of the way through the book in advance of Tuesday. When the breeze flutters her bandages, Giddy experimentally removes them and winces as the cold slaps the still-healing wound. Giddy unhooks the leash to let Bodie wander, draws the hood back up, and reads for a while.

When Giddy comes back home and lets Bodie out into the backyard, Jax is awake and sitting at the computer. "Where the hell have you been?"

"The park." It's nice and warm in the house. Giddy takes her gloves off, hangs up her coat, and inhales the smell of last night's pizza. She's hungry. "I took Bodie out."

"I'm the one who takes Bodie out! You're the one who gets the dishes on Saturdays."

"Guess you get the dishes, then."

Jax says: "I can't do that right now. I've got work to do!"

Giddy starts up the stairs but pauses. "What kind of work?"

"College research."

"Why didn't you do that while I was out?" Giddy takes a step back down. "I was gone for an hour and a half. The dishes take thirty minutes tops."

"Whatever." He spins back around in her dad's chair and types something furiously into the computer. From where Giddy stands, it looks like he's just reading websites, but then again, what does she know about college research? Tad and Tigs's door is still closed, still quiet.

On a normal Saturday, Giddy would follow breakfast by launching into whatever chores her mom left. Instead, Giddy returns to her room. She trades out *Ulysses* for the ever-so-much-more-comprehensible *The Guns of August*, where she learns that World War I was basically driven by a handful of rich and powerful heads of countries who felt they deserved more land than they had. Never mind the countless men who'd wind up dead on the battlefield, their pants and shoes stolen. And here she just assumed wars happen because they are necessary, but no, this was all about land and getting more stuff. This knowledge makes her so angry, she wants to tear the book up. Or go back in time and commit murder. What a stupid reason to make everybody die! Just because you thought you deserved more? Giddy is wondering if any of those rich and powerful people would have still sent people out to die for land if they'd ever had to walk dogs or do dishes or take care of little brothers or sisters, when her mom yells: "Giddy!"

Giddy goes downstairs, where it smells of coffee. Jax is MIA, though the dishes appear to have been done. Her mom's fumbling in her purse for her keys. Her voice sounds foggy and disconnected. "The school keeps making mistakes. I got another text about an unexcused absence for Tigs and Tad. Now Dougal has one too. Haven't you talked to them?"

Giddy takes a breath, lets it out. "Tigs and Tad missed the bus Wednesday and stayed home all day. I don't know about Dougal." Giddy shrugs.

"What?" Her mom blinks, but she doesn't look at Giddy. She just keeps digging for her keys. "What do you mean they stayed home? What happened? Did you oversleep?" Her fingers seize the keys and she draws them out. "Why didn't you text me?"

"I didn't know about it until I got home from school."

Her mom's phone buzzes and she drags it out of a pocket. "Dammit, Giddy," she mutters, reading a text. "You can't oversleep.

You need to set two alarms. Home all day—Christ." She puts the phone away and pulls her jacket on over her scrubs. "It's a miracle those two didn't burn the place down." She pauses, a hand on the door. "My God, Giddy, *did* they destroy anything?"

"No, everything's OK."

"Dougal's a totally different—" The phone buzzes with someone's reply and her mom groans and rolls her eyes. "You're on dinner tonight."

Giddy nods.

Her mom shakes her head and goes out the door. A second later, Giddy hears tires slipping as her mom pulls quickly out of the driveway.

Giddy goes into the kitchen and unwraps ground beef. She slices onion, cracks eggs, soaks white bread in milk, and opens a package of raisins as she preps a casserole the internet says is a staple in South Africa. The kitchen air fills with warming spices as Giddy lets Bodie in from the yard and tosses a few extra raisins in his direction. When Tigs gets up, Giddy gives the leftover box of raisins to her and watches from the kitchen as Tigs runs around the room eating raisins, throwing them everywhere so they land in between sofa cushions and scatter across end tables and the computer keyboard. All the while Bodie jumps and chases after her. When Tigs comes back demanding waffles, Giddy shrugs and takes some syrup and a box of frozen waffles out of the freezer. "Here."

Tigs holds the frozen waffle box and frowns. "What's this?"

"You know what that is. It's waffles."

Tigs shakes the box. "It's not open, Giddy!"

"So open it and I'll show you how to toast a breakfast waffle."

Tigs puzzles over the edges, turning the box in her hands. She wriggles one little finger in and the box pops open. Tigs takes out a sealed bag of waffles and looks at Giddy.

"Pull hard on either side."

Tigs does. The bag expands until the glued edges part and air releases with a *pop*. Tigs holds either side of the open plastic. "Giddy, look!"

"Yeah, you can just put them in the toaster and—" Giddy stops talking as Tigs drops the open waffles on the counter, goes to the fridge, and takes out a towering stack of American cheese slices and disappears around the corner. The pantry door rattles and a soup can hits the floor with a loud bang and rolls to the back door. Tigs rushes after it and stands on tiptoe to put it back on a pantry shelf.

Giddy makes herself a cup of hot turmeric tea. A second later, Tigs reemerges, overburdened with cheese and a big box of crackers. Bodie creeps forward and sniffs the cheese, but Tigs yells: "Bodie, no!" She takes everything into the family room, where she pinches the sealed edges of the crackers like she did with the waffles and opens them with a loud pop. "Giddy, look!"

"OK." Giddy takes a sip of tea.

Tigs eats, crumbs scattering. Giddy returns the forgotten waffles to the freezer. Bodie scoots closer to Tigs to lick up cracker crumbs. Tad comes down a minute later, gets some milk from the fridge, and sits on the sofa with Tigs to watch TV. He smirks at the cheese and crackers and lifts his foot as if to tip Tigs's plate over.

Giddy slurps loudly. Tad sees her and grins. Now he wriggles his foot with swagger.

Giddy mouths *Spider-Man* over the rim of her tea.

Tad's smile vaporizes. He jerks his foot back to the floor. He sits on the sofa to drink his milk. When Tigs pokes his knee and holds out a cracker sandwich, he takes it.

Giddy finishes her tea and opens the fridge to put the waffle syrup away. Her mom's chore list flutters again as she closes the door and Giddy takes it down and reexamines it. Giddy thinks about the soup can that rolled across the floor and how Tigs automatically put it back, and Giddy has an idea.

She rips the list in half, bisecting *laundry* and *clean rooms*. Giddy thrusts one half of the list in Tad's lap and sets the other half on the coffee table in front of Tigs. "Your weekend chores."

Tad frowns as Tigs picks her section of the list up. "We don't have weekend chores."

"You do now. See? Mom's writing. And the list is torn in half so it's *fair*." Giddy folds her arms across her chest, waiting for them both to process the logic in that statement.

Tad sets his empty milk glass down and sounds out: "Or-ga-nize pantry."

Tigs shoots Giddy a dirty look. "How come I didn't get that one?"

"You can help each other as much as you like."

They exchange a bright look as Giddy goes upstairs. It's only 10:14 in the morning. Giddy flops down onto her bed, staring at the ceiling.

It occurs to her she's *never* in her room in the middle of the morning with nothing to do. There's not even her mom's scrapbook—she hasn't heard anything about it in days, so she imagines the project abandoned. She winds away the afternoon upstairs, completing an online history quiz and finishing three more chapters of *The Guns of August*. There's not a sound at all upstairs. Her dad's with Mom at the hospital. Jax's car is gone and Dougal must have gotten up early and is God knows where. Giddy's reading is only interrupted once by some heated yelling between Tigs and Tad. The origin of the argument is uncertain, and Giddy, who is determined not to investigate, only knows it's over when Tigs pokes her head through her door.

"We have a new rule about jelly," Tigs says somberly.

Part of Giddy badly wants to know more, but she just says: "OK," and looks back at her book. Tigs walks backward, placing her steps exactly as they were before, and gently closes the door. An hour later, when Giddy goes downstairs for another cup of turmeric tea, Tad and Tigs are sliding artificial sweetener packets back and forth on the coffee table as if using them in a game of air hockey. Giddy thinks for a moment and says: "You guys know to put those back in the box in the pantry, right?"

They're concentrating, but Tigs gives a mute little nod and waves at Giddy over her shoulder. Tad looks at Giddy and suddenly smirks. "Bodie wanted in the backyard, so I let him."

"OK," Giddy says.

Tad frowns. "That's your job!"

"You can let Bodie in the backyard, Tad. We can make that your job too."

The perplexing implications of this erase his frown. He thoughtfully spins a sweetener packet with his finger.

Giddy takes the tea to her room. It's supposed to be an anti-inflammatory and she guesses it might be helping, even though this morning's breakfast still burned. Actually, her stomach only seems to burn when she stops to think about it, which Giddy figures must be an improvement. She lies back on her bed, contemplating a nap. She hears Tad and Tigs burst out with laughter over something. Giddy takes Superdoo down from his perch on the desk and twists him around, playing with his articulation, positioning his arms and flying him around in little halfhearted circles. There's still no magic to him and Giddy shrugs and tosses him back where he belongs. She puts on some opera and half dozes to something called *Deh vieni, non tardar* by Mozart. A text from her mom leaving the hospital jolts her fully awake, and Giddy goes downstairs to pop the South African casserole in the oven and set the Tupperware of cooked chicken feet out on the counter.

Her dad's come home while she was upstairs, and he's now on the sofa watching television with Tigs and Tad, and Dougal is at the computer desk. Dougal's green dyslexia overlay is out across an assignment, but his eyes are on the phone in his lap. Giddy's not sure what her dad said to at least get him at the desk fake-working, but her dad has a look that speaks of such tired anger that Giddy wonders what she missed while napping. When Dougal's eyes meet Giddy's, she bares her teeth and he returns the *fuck you* look in kind.

When her mom finally comes in, looking exhausted, Dad grins: "Ooh! Looks like we both came home all 'nursed out.'"

"Well, *I* did, Scott, but you're not a nurse, you're an orderly," her mom says, kicking her Crocs off by the door.

"Right." Her dad turns down the volume on a commercial. "Let's just make that point really clear. Because it's not like we don't both work in a hospital and spend our day caring for people."

Her mom shoots him a tight smile as she hangs up her jacket. "I was just being accurate, babe."

"Accuracy's so important, so I guess I'm all 'orderly'd out' then?" Her dad clicks off the television.

Her mom rolls her eyes and comes into the kitchen, where Giddy is scrolling through a forum on South African dishes that has links to Amazon for spices. Giddy takes the casserole out and as she sets it on the table, her mom says: "Wow. Smells interesting."

"Thought you were baking a pie from the smell of things," her dad says, coming into the kitchen as Tigs and Tad scoot up on their chairs. "What is this?"

"Bobotie." Giddy cuts herself a slice, disappointed to see gray juice pooling. She scoops a dripping serving onto her plate and pops open the Tupperware of chicken feet.

Tigs says sagely: "Giddy killed a bird." Tad rears up on his knees to look at the chicken feet. Giddy can see she missed a couple of telltale claws. They look like they're climbing over one another as she stacks some into a pyramid on her plate next to the bobotie.

"Giddy," her dad says slowly, "what is this?"

"Asian chicken feet," Giddy says, sitting back. "They're super good. I don't know about the rest yet."

"Giddy, why did you buy chicken feet?" her mom asks. But Tad reaches into the Tupperware making excited *cluck, cluck* noises until his mother smacks the back of his hand. "Stop! Don't touch."

For once, Dougal approaches the table without being called. He has a shocked grin and looks at his parents as he grabs a chicken foot and takes a bite. "Oh," he says, chewing, "so good! Sooo gooood!"

"Dougal," his dad warns.

"I'm trying the casserole." Her mom serves Tigs and Tad a piece before getting some for herself. The dislikable gray pools around the edges and Tigs makes a face and pushes her plate away.

"You need to try it, Tigs," Giddy tells her. "You like raisins. There're raisins in this." Which is probably where the gray is from, now that Giddy thinks about it.

Tigs's eyes light up at the promise, and she sticks a fork in but hesitates when it comes up with ground beef. Giddy takes a bite and the flavor is . . . Well, it's not what she expected. She guesses maybe cinnamon and beef is an acquired taste, and definitely the egg needed to be cooked more.

"Giddy, this is super disgusting." This from Tad, who sits with his arms folded.

"I don't understand," her mom says. "Were they out of regular chicken?"

Dougal sticks a second fork in the bobotie and speaks through a mouth loaded with egg. "Oh, I could eat this all day!"

"You don't get to tell us what you eat all day, Dougal," her mom snaps as her dad takes a bite of bobotie and coughs a little before swallowing. "Not when you're skipping school! Tigs, Tad, I know you missed a day too."

"Giddy wouldn't take us!" Tigs complains.

"It's a *bus*, Tigs! Nobody takes you to school, you ride a bus." Her mom sighs and her shoulders sag. "I'm sorry. I'm hungry.

Giddy, this is cute, but it's Saturday night. If you didn't have the energy to cook, why didn't you pop in a pizza?"

Giddy frowns. "I had the energy. This was very difficult to make."

"It's a cultural revolution tonight at the Barber house," Dougal says. Another chicken foot pokes out of the corner of his mouth.

"Shut up, Dougal," her dad says.

"You should try the chicken feet before Dougal eats all of them," Giddy says to her mom.

"I'm not putting that in my mouth, hon. Honestly, we're not whatever or whoever eats this kind of stuff. Why . . ." She trails off, looking at Giddy. But Giddy's decided to make the best of a bad bobotie and is rubbing the chicken feet in the gray sauce, which looks terrible but it turns out it's actually the best part of the bobotie. She pops the chicken foot in her mouth and gnaws the skin and meat off. Then she stops because her mom is still looking at her. So Giddy sets the remains of the chicken foot down on her plate and looks back, waiting.

"Why didn't you just make the usual?" her mom finishes.

"Because I'm doing an experiment and I have to do things differently for a while." The time period of eleven days suddenly seems like privileged information, a duration her mother might try to shorten.

"Well, can you not do things differently when the family's involved?"

Her dad says: "Janine . . ."

"No, I'm serious! We come in very late and tired and hungry and it's Saturday—"

Giddy stands up fast, bumping the edge of her plate by accident, rattling silverware. There's a sudden quiet in the room. She picks up the bobotie and wraps it up next to the fridge. There's lots of chicken feet left in the Tupperware, but she shoves it to the back of the fridge anyway in the hopes Dougal will be too lazy to dig for it. It can be her lunch Monday. Giddy takes a frozen pizza out and lets it fall a little too loudly on the stovetop. *I'm not angry. That's not what this is. I'm not quite sure what this is.*

Behind her, her mother says: "Oh, honey, listen. It's fine. We were just thrown off."

Giddy shrugs. "OK. But the oven's still warm and the pizza should be done in eighteen minutes." Then she goes upstairs, leaving them, because the deal is that if she cooks on Saturdays, someone else cleans the dishes, and tonight she's going to hold them to it.

Giddy sits on her bed and pops a chewable antacid, not liking the way its artificial fruitiness clashes with the egg, beef, and cinnamon in her stomach. But nothing comes up, and after a minute Giddy lies back. She picks up Superdoo, thinking it would be great if she could get some spiritual guidance from him tonight through osmosis. She thinks, *Mom can be a real Jess.* It's words like *just* and *but*. *Giddy, this is cute, but* . . . or . . . *Why didn't you just* . . .

She falls asleep with Superdoo in her hands, the little edges of his fingers pressed tightly into hers.

5

Giddy wakes to find Superdoo in pieces: an arm snagged in her hair and a disembodied torso on the floor next to her bed. Also, there're little red marks in her palm where she must have gripped him tight overnight. Giddy gets down on all fours to rescue his pieces, pops him back together, and restores him to his rightful place on the corner of the desk overlooking her propped-up list.

It's 7:10. The morning sun makes jagged patterns across the textured ceiling. Giddy's mind rolls through a cycle of past Sunday assignments, the things her mom sometimes forgets to put on the fridge and thus get squeezed into this last day before the school week: *Did the leaves get raked last weekend, Giddy? We need to do it before they kill all the grass. What about the clothes all over the den—are you putting them in the laundry? Is Tad still stuffing his clothes under his bed, because their room smells! Did Bodie get his last shots?*

Can you call the vet and find out if he's due? Also, can you see if the clinic in the pet store is open today? Can you go through the mail and throw out all the junk but set the bills in a stack please, Giddy?

But she won't get these texts until later because everybody sleeps late on the weekends. Giddy's not sure why she's awake—usually Bodie wakes her by licking her face around ten in the morning or Tigs piles on top of her demanding pancakes with chocolate chip pieces and cereal marshmallows.

Giddy's stomach rumbles. She sits up, alarmed, puts a hand to her belly, feels the vibration happening again, and frowns. What did she eat last? Bobotie and chicken feet. But now her mouth waters at the thought of chocolate chip pancakes and she knows better than to try that, knows that she can't handle the sweet stuff that Tigs eats.

A few strands of her hair stick out like whiskers from Superdoo's repaired shoulder. Giddy opens her phone's calendar and, just to look at the words, types in *Reverse all your habits* followed by *If you can, do something unexpected each day.* Like what? Eat waffles? Thinking of waffles makes her think of food, which makes her think of lunch at school. And then she remembers Zach walking to his seat looking at her with that ridiculous smile.

She types *Kiss Zach* and stares at the words. The thought of his smug face leaning in toward hers turns her stomach in ways food never has, but she reasons how bad could it be, one kiss? It would be unexpected. So she scrolls through emails on her phone until she finds one from early in the year in which Zach invited her to a barbecue at his home.

Giddy copies his address to her calendar. Zach's not expecting a visit from her, but he *did* invite her over to study, so he's probably home, right? She could at least knock. But it's still early, so Giddy opens *Ulysses* and picks up at the point where Leopold Bloom decides to go into a church and kind of hates on everyone.

Reverse all your habits.

Giddy lowers the book and looks at Superdoo again. The Barbers used to go to Mass when they first moved into town, back when Giddy was only four and Tigs and Tad hadn't come along yet. Jax would scowl and kick the back of the pew with his shiny black shoes until Mom made him stop. By contrast, Dougal would be very good and quiet and squeeze Giddy's hand tight as if he were afraid of letting go. Giddy had a Sunday dress that was yellow with orange flowers, and she liked to fold the fabric to make the flowers close and rebloom. At Mass, her mom smelled of a perfume that now gathers dust at the back of her bathroom counter, and she used to rotate through a collection of pretty rhinestone clip-on earrings that Giddy played with at home. Giddy remembers there being a lot of instruction and standing and sitting and standing again. And then for some reason the family stopped going. Giddy never questioned the change.

Giddy checks the time, sees it's only 7:18, closes the book, and goes in for her cold shower, yelping only a little this time as the water splashes her upturned face. Before exiting the bathroom, she checks herself in the mirror. She slept unbandaged last night, and some of the scab has sloughed off in the shower, bisecting Africa to leave a blurry pink wave in the middle. Giddy, who lost her taste for dresses sometime around kindergarten, extracts a dark green straight-cut business dress an aunt gave her last Christmas "because every young woman needs at least one professional outfit." It's been sitting at the back of the closet, unworn. Giddy doesn't even have shoes to wear with it, but she figures sneakers will do. She goes downstairs to a house that is still so very quiet, and even the usually energetic Bodie merely lifts a head and politely thumps his tail once against a sofa pillow.

Giddy throws on her jacket, and the cold hits her bare legs hard. It's probably in the fifties, and pedaling her bike in a dress turns out to be its own challenge. The roads are nearly empty, the houses mostly dark, and the sky a low-glowing gray with a rising cloud-blocked sun. When Giddy reaches the edge of downtown, it's almost eight, and a sign at the church reads that service starts at seven thirty or eleven and Giddy, not wanting to redo everything, walks her bike back and forth before she finds a rack to chain it up. Then she quietly opens the door and steps into the church.

The warm, empty lobby smells like cinnamon. Giddy can hear a priest's loud voice coming from behind the large set of double doors leading into the pews. Giddy creeps to those doors, nervous, fingers twitching. She's coming in mid-service. Part of her thinks she should just go home.

But Giddy pulls one massive door open just a crack and to her relief, it doesn't make any noise. For a second she stands, uncertain, her back to the door, in part because she doesn't remember the room looking so big, and in part because of a change in acoustics that Giddy's rational brain knows is a fault of the vaulted ceilings. Nevertheless, the priest's voice vibrates through her soul as he points to a page in a Bible spread thick across his pulpit and reads: "'What is crooked cannot be straightened! What is lacking cannot be counted!'"

Giddy slips into an empty back pew and folds up her jacket next to her.

"'For with much wisdom comes much sorrow.'" The priest looks up and shakes his head. "'The more knowledge, the more grief.'"

Nods of heads in front of Giddy. She picks up a hymnal and flips through it, jerking a finger away from a page when the priest suddenly thumps the pulpit with his fist.

"'Laughter, I said, is madness! And what does pleasure accomplish? For the wise like the fool will not be long remembered.'"

Lots of heads bob up and down in a motion not unlike a rippling surf, and Giddy tries to track it but thinks, *If I stare at it too long, I'll be seasick.*

"And how many of us in this world of instant clicks to gratification have sensed this loss of joy in purpose? How many of us feel fragmented, disconnected, lacking?"

As if on cue, Giddy's phone buzzes in her jacket pocket. She grabs the folded jacket, but the phone slides out and clatters noisily to the floor.

"So what is the answer? What are we supposed to take from this? What is the key to becoming whole once again?"

Giddy scrunches down between the pews but can't reach her phone. Extending a foot under a pew isn't an easy thing to do in a straight-cut dress, but Giddy somehow manages it, though not without knocking her knee painfully. When she scoots the phone back into her hands and gets up, a family ahead of her has turned around—a boy, a girl, and their parents, a quartet of genetically related judgmental stares. Giddy fixes her face in what she hopes is an equally hard look until they turn back one by one, and then Giddy hastily powers her phone down. She sinks a little deeper into her seat. She wishes she had her mom's rhinestone earrings on.

"The key is what it has always been." The priest spreads his hands outward. "It is to put God in the *first* place. Then everything falls into place. First, God"—the priest holds up one finger—"then our neighbors. Then ourselves." He points to the page again and reads: "One day, we realize our root problem is we have allowed obligations to become important in themselves—"

At this, Giddy's head shoots up and she leans in, fixed and waiting.

"—whereas they are important only because they are linked to a basic obligation," the priest says, "our commitment to God, the center of all our lives."

He motions and there's the thunderous sound of everyone standing. Giddy, confused, stands as well but thinks, *You're not done! Why bring this up if you won't tell me how?* But now the priest is leading everyone in the Lord's Prayer, and though Giddy tries to mouth along with what she remembers of *We believe in God the Father Almighty, maker of Heaven and Earth*, she's still disappointed, still wondering if the priest intends to get back to what he was saying. Also, is she some kind of fraud for not feeling anything? How many recitations of holy words does it take for them to do their job?

There follows a series of priest-issued prayers with everyone repeating, *Lord, hear our prayer!* over and over, so many times that Giddy starts to scoot side to side on her feet. A flush floods her face, borne of a deep and troubling displacement from familiarity. Eventually, everyone sits and offering baskets are passed, and Giddy, who didn't bring a wallet, feels doubly bad for not remembering this part. When the priest consecrates the wafers and wine and people line up to move forward, Giddy gets up as well. It takes some families a long time to file out of the pews, so Giddy winds up in the middle of the slow-moving crowd, pressing as tightly together as when she's trying to leave the school building at the end of the day.

As she closes in on the altar, anxiety seizes her because some people are kneeling to pray after taking the wafer. Giddy doesn't remember if that's expected of everyone and what she's supposed to say if it is. Plus, everyone's going to be looking at her back as she kneels, so if she does it wrong, it's going to be really obvious. Giddy decides she's going to skip the wafer and turns to go back to her seat, but there're too many people so she keeps moving forward. She thinks about a science video she saw once of lemmings moving toward a cliff and a sudden tightness grips her chest. She looks to either side of the altar. There's an exit door on the right. Giddy edges her way to it. Before she can get a wafer shoved at her, she turns in front of the first pew and runs through the door.

It opens into a small room with table and chairs, a rack of white priest robes, a bookcase with stacks of spare offering baskets, and another door leading out the back of the room. Giddy heads for it thinking it might be an exit, but it opens before she can get to it and a priest comes out.

For a second they stand there, regarding each other. He's old, maybe in his fifties, and he has a pair of glasses on that magnify his eyes just a little, throwing them out of ratio like a reverse of the Bodie clay sculpture problem. He sounds mildly annoyed when he says: "Can I help you?"

Giddy's pretty sure she's just been caught somewhere she's not supposed to be. "I was looking for the exit."

"It's back the way you came in." The priest points. Giddy turns around and opens the door to go back out, but there are still a lot of people crowding the aisles, so she stands with the door cracked, uncertain. She doesn't want anyone to see her pass the altar without taking the wine and wafer.

"Are you a new member?"

This all very suddenly feels like the church's fault and not hers.

Giddy turns around. "You know, my mom used to say that you go to church because it's uplifting. But everything he said was about how miserable we should expect our lives to be and how we should just get used to it because there's no point doing anything. So that's all you're really telling people: not to bother doing anything."

She's expecting a rebuke. Actually, Giddy would *love* a rebuke, a chance for someone to say something sharp back to her. Then she can say something back and everything can just spiral. A good spiral sounds nice.

But the priest doesn't say anything and his expression doesn't change. So Giddy repeats: "I said, it's all about how miserable we are and how there's nothing we can do."

Another second of frustrating silence elapses. Impatience crawls up Giddy's neck when the priest finally answers. "Ecclesiastes. It is depressing, isn't it?" He indicates the table. "Have a seat."

His tone is curt and Giddy is too startled by the invitation to say no, so she takes a chair. He takes the one on the other side, facing her. It frustrates her that she can't sense what he's going to say. Giddy regards him with the kind of wariness one reserves for spam emails.

He takes a phone out of his pocket, opens an app, and starts scrolling.

Giddy says: "You're allowed to have that?"

"A phone?" The priest looks up. "Why wouldn't I have a phone?"

Giddy shrugs. "I dunno. Apps and internet and stuff—isn't there something about piety in your contract?"

"I'm Catholic," he says, "not Amish."

Giddy, suitably reproached, links her hands and fidgets with her thumbs.

The priest looks back down and continues scrolling, then suddenly belts out loud with a force that makes Giddy flinch: "'Meaningless! Meaningless,' says the Teacher. 'Utterly meaningless. Everything is meaningless. What do people gain from all their labors at which they toil under the sun?'" He scrolls down some more and reads: "'For with much wisdom comes much sorrow. The more knowledge, the more grief.'" He looks up at Giddy. "Sound about right?"

"Sounds even worse than when he said it," Giddy says.

"Ah." His eyes soften a bit. "But then later He tells us: 'Go, eat your food with gladness and drink your wine with a joyful heart for God has already approved what you do. God has given you under the Sun all your meaningless days.'" He looks up at her. "'Whatever your hand finds to do, do it with all your might.'" He clicks off his screen. "See? Even Ecclesiastes has its upbeat moments."

"But that doesn't help!" Giddy says. "Because it doesn't say *how* you're supposed to be joyful. If I knew how to be joyful, I'd have no problem." She rubs a fist against eyes that are itchy and, to her mortification, tearing up a little. "I came here looking for answers."

"So did they." The priest points to the door. "So did I. So does everybody. That pursuit is the essence of life's journey. Good words don't give good answers; they just help lead you to them." He taps the table in front of Giddy. "You are expected to do half the work here."

Giddy kind of feels like she's being asked to do *all* the work, but she looks away and shrugs. The priest gets up and goes to a shelf. "I've got some reading you might enjoy."

Giddy shakes her head. "I'm in the middle of *Ulysses*, so I don't have time to pick up the Bible."

He holds up a trifold pamphlet. "These are five-minute devotionals for teens." He frowns. "*Ulysses*? As in James Joyce?"

Giddy nods.

The priest rolls his eyes: "And you were afraid I was going to hand you a Bible." He slides the pamphlet across the table. "I wouldn't say reading it is necessary for joy. It's a tool, and tools help people look for things." He indicates the door behind Giddy. "Everyone who took part in Communion is probably either at the altar still or back in their seats, so it should be a clear path to the exit now if you want to leave."

Giddy takes the pamphlet and heads to the door.

"'The race is not to the swift or the battle to the strong.'"

Giddy looks over her shoulder. There's the wisp of a smile on the priest's face, like maybe he has the answers to joy but just feels like hoarding them. Giddy opens the door, and the aisles are clear, like he said. She lowers her head, walking back to the farthest pew to collect her jacket. The service isn't over, but she doesn't mind leaving. Giddy figures she's had more church in the last ten minutes than she's had in years.

She rides to the park, the cold slapping her face and drying her eyes. Almost nobody's there and it's frigid and lonely, the twitchy trees bare and desperate. Giddy's shoes crunch dead leaves as she sits on a bench, rubbing her legs. She takes the devotional pamphlet out of her purse. The cover's ironic, because it shows a group of beautiful, delighted teens on a blanket in a park, only their park is sunlit, lush, and green. Giddy skims the contents. It's filled with prayers and biblical platitudes like *Don't let anyone look down on you because you are young* and *Set an example for the believers through your speech, behavior, love, faith, and purity.* And then she frowns, because there's the line the priest said to her: *The race is not to the swift or the battle to the strong.* Ecclesiastes 9:11. Giddy reads it again and again, puzzling over its cipher.

She feels a surge of rage, a certainty that the pamphlet represents indoctrination and empty propaganda. But because it's religious, she doesn't feel right throwing it in the trash. Instead, she tucks the pamphlet into the empty fork of a tree and hops onto her bike.

Her new route runs through an adjacent neighborhood down a street that is not far from the house Dougal wasn't supposed to be partying at. From here, Giddy slows to read the numbers on curbs, to park her bike outside the house that has an address matching Zach's. Zach's house is yellow with a front porch with chairs. Somebody likes chickens—there's a chicken statue in the front yard, a chicken-shaped door mat, and a row of ceramic chickens inside a front window on the walk up. For some reason, it bothers her to know this much personal information about Zach. When she knocks on the door, Giddy enjoys the fervent hope that somehow Zach sent her the wrong address.

But he answers. It takes him a second to process that he's seeing Giddy. He gives her a quick up and down that reminds Giddy she's all dressed up for church.

"Can we talk outside?" she asks.

"Giddy, wow, yeah." Zach closes the door behind him. "Didn't know you still knew where I lived. What was it, um"—he scratches his head—"the barbecue maybe?"

"It was." Giddy sits in one of the porch chairs.

Zach doesn't. He crosses his arms and leans against the porch rail as if the answer to his next question isn't really that important. "So, what's going on? You look good. Green's a good color on you."

Giddy can't stop staring at Zach's pale lips. The lower one is chapped, so Giddy wonders if it's going to feel scratchy when they kiss. She wonders if she's going to taste anything and if Zach's going to try to use his tongue. This will be only the third time Giddy's ever kissed. The first time was with a cousin who kissed her on the mouth at a family gathering when they were both nine. The second was during a middle-school party at somebody's house in which Giddy kissed a boy in a closet and they both did it so fast that really only their mouths touched at the corners.

Giddy takes a breath of courage and says: "The thing I'm doing, this eleven-day-long experiment—"

"The opossum thing. You're sad, right?" Zach finally takes a seat, leaning forward, knees pointing toward Giddy. "I didn't even know you were sad. You never seem sad."

Dammit, Jess! "I'm fine! It's just an experiment. Here's the thing: Do you think . . ." She almost bails, almost says something, anything other than what she's planned, and little substitutions fire off in her brain one by one in miniature explosions that seem to take way longer than the second and a half it takes for her to say . . . "We could maybe kiss once? Nothing elaborate. I want to be clear: I don't think I'm interested in you, and I don't think this is going to go anywhere. And if I don't like it, you need to understand that it's not happening a second time, OK? Does this all sound OK with you?"

She thinks she lost him somewhere after *kiss.* Zach straightens up, looks around. "What?"

"I thought we might kiss," Giddy repeats, frowning, "as an experiment."

"Huh." He grins down at his hands. "That's, um . . . I mean, I didn't know that you—"

"I want to be clear!" Giddy puts a warning hand up. "I might not like it. And if I don't, I'm going to tell you and we're never going to do this again and I don't want to hurt your feelings."

He seems to come to his senses. He furrows his brow and nods. "Yeah, you're just being honest. I got it."

"Do you really?" Giddy asks.

"It's just"—he grins down at his hands again—"kind of amazing!"

"Zach!" Giddy says sharply, and he straightens up and looks serious.

"No, I understand," he amends. "This is just an experiment. You might not like it."

For a moment, they don't say anything. They just stare at each other, faces wary, questioning, the weight of an impending decision bearing down.

Then Giddy says: "OK." She doesn't like the front porch with the row of staring window chickens. "Can we go around to the side of the house to do this?"

"Yeah." Zach gets up and follows Giddy as she moves between his house and the neighbor's, to an anonymous brick wall right angled against a fence. Giddy's about the same height as Zach. She puts her hands on his shoulders and takes a step in. As she leans in, his face wears a look of furtive uncertainty she imagines must match hers. Giddy presses her lips to Zach's.

For a second, all she can think is that this is weirdly soft, that it doesn't seem that complicated, but it doesn't seem that interesting, either. And then Zach seems to *really* get into it, to press his mouth harder against hers, to slip his arms around her waist and run his hands up her back. When she feels his tongue against her teeth, Giddy slips her hands off his shoulders and pushes him away. "No! Not good." Giddy uses the back of her hand to wipe her mouth. "I didn't like that."

Zach looks confused, like he's drugged. "What?"

"I didn't like it." Then, to mollify: "Sorry."

Zach shakes his head. "OK. I'll change how I—" And he leans in, but Giddy puts her hands up.

"No! I said one time. That's it." Giddy walks past him. The porch seems pointless. She's headed for her bike. This experiment is over. "Look, I told you I probably wouldn't and I was right."

"Wouldn't what?"

Giddy spins around and looks at Zach with incredulity. "Wouldn't like kissing you."

"But you did," Zach says, sounding wounded and very far away, "kiss me."

"Yeah, no hard feelings," Giddy says.

Zach just stares. For a few seconds Giddy stares back, thinking maybe this is protocol, that he's going to say something, but the seconds stretch by one after the other and it becomes plain to Giddy that something has gone wrong here, but damned if she knows what it is.

Giddy sighs and gives him a little half wave. "OK. See you at school." She gets on her bike and rides off. She doesn't look behind her, because she gets the idea that the longer she stays the longer she's giving Zach a false sense of hope. But the longer she pedals, the more she starts to feel bad, because Zach's face seemed hurt and haunted. But she shouldn't feel bad, because she straight up told him what this was all about, and if he didn't listen to her, isn't it his fault?

On the way home, Giddy rides by the park, where food trucks have arrived. Her stomach rumbles and she thinks, *Really? Food truck food?* The waffle truck in particular seems to elicit the most stirrings, but Giddy's too smart to fall for a meal that would most likely result in terrible agony. So she goes home and goes straight to the refrigerator.

"Giddy!"

Giddy digs around until she locates the Tupperware of chicken feet. She pops off the lid, nibbling, and turns to her mom's voice.

Her mom and dad are in the den. Mom's got her scrubs and Crocs on, keys in her hand, on the verge of leaving for work. Her dad's got a plastic grocery bag over one arm and is still in his bathrobe. He holds one hand to keep the robe closed as he bends to collect Tad's beat-up soldiers off the floor along with handfuls of Legos and, for some reason, golf-ball-sized clumps of Bodie fur that Giddy can now see are all over the place: some on the end tables next to the couch, some on the kitchen counter and atop the island, a few hanging on to the edges of stairs. Her dad looks frazzled, hair mussed like this was a quick roll-out-of-bed sort of cleanup. When not working, her dad usually sleeps late, but he still likes to come downstairs all neat and shaven.

Upstairs, Tad and Tigs are fighting. The exact words are muffled and hard to distinguish, but the tone is one of unreconciled strife. Their door is never closed on Sundays unless they're in trouble. Giddy sniffs, but she can't smell anything bad, only the deliciously cold odor of the chicken feet, of which she has the meat and skin from one rolling around her teeth.

"Where have you been?" Her mom slips her keys into her pocket and holds up her phone. Giddy remembers her phone going off in church and that she powered it down. She'd forgotten to turn it on again.

"Yeah, where *have* you been?" Her dad pauses, stands upright. "I stepped on about five Legos coming down, and you know they're not allowed to play with their toys on the stairs. I could have killed myself and—"

"Just hold on a minute." Her mom likes to take charge of these moments, the doling out of repercussions for bad decision-making. Her father closes his mouth into a hard line with a kind of reluctant obedience she's seen in Tad before. "You just ran off this morning and didn't tell anyone."

And Giddy thinks, *Jax's car isn't in the driveway.* But that's always the case. He's never here, and there's never a good explanation except that everybody's used to it. Giddy asks: "Where's Dougal?"

Her mom throws up her hands. "Still sleeping, thankfully, because God knows where he'd be on a Sunday if he got up and saw there was no one else up. I mean, I'd understand if you were still sleeping, but to just take off? And then to ignore my texts."

Giddy takes her phone out and turns it on. There they are—the slew of last-minute Sunday chore texts. Giddy chews the meat off two more chicken feet, popping the bones into the kitchen trash one by one. If anything, the time spent cooling in the fridge only made them more outstanding. "What did Tigs and Tad do?"

Her mom looks affronted, as though Giddy interrupted her. "They were all over the place!"

"They tried to comb Bodie," her dad says, "but they left the fur everywhere, and Bodie ate some and threw it back up. Then they ran in and woke your mom." He's halfway up the stairs collecting fur.

"I said I have this." Her mom shoots a glare up the stairs. To Giddy, she says: "Why's your phone off?"

"It was going off and disturbing people—"

"And quit eating while I talk!" Her mother shoves the phone into her pocket and takes her keys out again, spinning them on her fingers. "You're just talking through a mouthful of food. It's rude."

Giddy pops the lid on the Tupperware and sheepishly pushes it far away from her on the kitchen island. She takes a seat on the stool. Her dad has come and gone from Tigs and Tad's room, but he stops on the stairs. Giddy thinks about Tad dragging his feet on the stairs on a school morning. She wonders if her dad is waiting for Mom to leave before coming down.

"So." Her mom fixes her face into her tightest *gotcha* smile and her voice bears a false loftiness when she says: "What was so important that you felt you had to leave your family on a Sunday?"

"I went to Mass," Giddy says.

Her mom's smile slips, replaced with a blank jaw drop. "You went . . . as in church?"

Giddy nods.

Her mother looks at her, momentarily speechless, and Giddy, who didn't think about what a great answer it was before she said it, notes her mother's shoulders deflate, her eyes flutter in confusion. A rush of energy flows through Giddy's body.

It feels curiously like *power*.

Giddy doesn't start eating the chicken feet again, but she does put a possessive hand atop the closed container and draws it meaningfully back toward her.

"Wow." Her mother's eyes blink again. "That's just . . . gosh." She looks up the stairs, but Giddy's dad doesn't seem to know what to add to this conversation, so he maintains a quiet stare back.

"Well, we've been meaning to go," her mom finally says. "It's just been crazy busy. How long has it been—couple of months, right, babe?"

This time, Giddy can feel all the air from her mom creeping up the stairs, prying open her dad's lips like a crowbar. "Yeah," her dad says, "it's been months at least."

"And I'm sorry I powered my phone down," Giddy says, allowing some firmness to seep into her voice, "but when it went off, it was really loud and people kept looking at me."

"It went off in church?" It's not really a question from her mom, more a horrified reinforcement of fact.

Giddy nods. She turns the Tupperware in fast circles on the table and the chicken feet leap up against the inside. She's going to eat more, but maybe she also needs to eat some of the leftover bobotie? Her stomach is really sounding off.

"So leave us a note next time and, um, glad to see you took an interest in church. That's something your father and I always believed in." Her mom's words coincide with slow side steps to the door. She opens her mouth one more time, ready, Giddy expects, to levy a final judgment. Extra chores seems likely or maybe demanding Giddy clean up the mess in the den and on the stairs, though her dad looks like he almost has it. Her eyes search helplessly around their home as if the answer might stare back at her from a heretofore forgotten corner.

But she just closes her mouth and quickly grabs her jacket. The door rattles to quiet like a sigh of relief when she leaves.

Her dad hastens down the stairs and tosses the bag of Bodie fur in the trash. Then he goes back up without saying anything. Giddy hears the shower turn on, and now she assumes all routines are back to normal. She drags out the bobotie, which doesn't reheat as well as she'd hoped or taste very good cold. She sets aside some chicken feet for school and goes up to her room. She puts one check mark next to *Reverse all your habits* and a second beside *Do something unexpected.* Eventually, Tigs and Tad settle down inside their room and Giddy hears them giggling as she reads *The Guns of August*, hears her father typing away at the computer downstairs, then gets a text saying everybody's on their own for dinner tonight and hears her dad get in his car and leave. There's the *ding* through the wall of Dougal getting the same text. Her brother responds by turning up his music.

Tigs knocks on Giddy's door and pushes it open a few inches. "I'm sorry about all the Bodie hair."

"It's OK. Bodie sheds a lot."

Tigs pushes the door the rest of the way open. "I have three questions today."

"Let's do this." Giddy sets *The Guns of August* down and twists around on her bed to face her little sister.

"The first question is: Can I keep Bodie's hair?"

"Dad already threw it away in a bag," Giddy says, confused.

"I saved some."

"Ew! No, Tigs."

Tigs sighs. "My second question is: How can I get Bodie to sit still next time in case I have to trim his bangs?"

Giddy frowns. "Bodie doesn't get bangs. His hair doesn't grow over his eyes."

"His hair gets everywhere, Giddy!"

"Yes, but when has it ever covered his eyes?"

Tigs frowns at her in a way that says she doesn't trust Giddy's answer. "*You* don't trim his bangs?"

"No, Tigs."

"You don't give him his unique style?"

"No! That's just how he—" Giddy sits up higher in bed. "Did you use Mom's hair scissors? If you did, put them back!"

Tigs's hand is still on the knob, and she's looking at the floor. "But they're dirty!"

"Clean them and put them back in her vanity." Giddy uses her lowest, sternest voice, and Tigs, nodding, shuffles off down the hall without closing Giddy's door.

Giddy picks up her book and looks at the clock. How long has it been since she's had this kind of uninterrupted time on a Sunday? As her eyes move around, trying to peel back the quiet of her room, Giddy notices her trash can, which was full of her rolled-up engineering posters yesterday.

It is now empty.

Giddy frowns and sits up straight right as Tigs ambles by her door again. Giddy calls out to her: "Did you take out my trash?"

Tigs stops in the door, thinking. "We did everything on the list except clothes."

"Including taking out the upstairs trash?"

Tigs nods vigorously.

Which means her engineering posters are in the garbage can outside. Scratch that—pickup was Friday.

"Giddy?" Tigs says. "Giddy, are you hungry?"

Giddy looks at her bare walls and tries to imagine her posters of the cheery students hard at work now crushed at the bottom of a landfill. Those posters were on her wall five days ago. They were the only thing about her room that made it very Giddy. And she rolled them up and stood them up carefully in the trash so she could retrieve them if she wanted, if she decided to. But now that decision's been taken away from her.

So she looks around at the bare-walled room, a room like a hotel's, utterly lacking in anything signifying her, and a great sense of *nothingness* rises up inside her, spreading out to expand and encompass. And at the bottom of that emptiness lies a tiny hint of terror.

"I only asked if you were hungry because *I'm* hungry," Tigs says.

"Huh?" Giddy tears her eyes off her walls. She puts fake levity into her voice when she says: "You want some grilled cheeses, then?"

Tigs claps. "Yes, please!"

And Giddy leaves her room fast to go downstairs and make Tigs and Tad hot sandwiches. And while she's in the kitchen, she thinks, *I can just get new engineering posters.* And that makes sense—they were free. Colleges probably throw stuff like that at you once you get a dorm room. Giddy tries sardines on crackers the way her dad likes and discovers they're pretty good, but also they taste best with a little chunk of sharp cheddar. Later she goes upstairs and looks at the wall again and tries again to feel bad that the posters are gone permanently. But she doesn't feel bad and she doesn't feel good. She just feels terribly *empty*. She should at least feel shocked, the way her mom was when she woke up this morning to a Giddy-less house. And speaking of that, why does she always have to be exactly where her mom expects her to be? Does her mom expect that because it's *always* been like that?

She slips into bed and reads more of *The Guns of August*, where she discovers many world leaders also expected everyone to fall in line just because they were technically in charge. She wonders why people in charge are no good at sharing power, that if they'd learned to share power, would massive wars even happen?

The thought that maybe everyone who's in charge for a long time gets like this and maybe there's nothing anybody can ever do troubles her more than Giddy ever imagined it could. It pokes at her in the way that Superdoo poked around in her pocket, and she's still thinking about it when she falls asleep, still seeing in her mind the blue glow of her alarm clock against Superdoo's face, highlighting the edges of a now-intimidating smile until it becomes villainously comical, a testimony to unchecked power and the inflexibility of authority.

6

Giddy's alarm goes off at five thirty and she slaps the top of it, rolls to a sitting position, and stares at Superdoo. Monday. Giddy sighs. Superdoo grins. She scowls as she peruses her list. *Good: Algebra II Pre-AP, Chemistry Pre-AP, Robotics. Bad: English, World History, Art.* She's supposed to flip this. But has she really? All she's really done is start to suck in algebra II and chemistry.

Reverse all your habits.

Giddy looks into Superdoo's stupid face again and tries her own big, fake grin. It feels rigid and hollow, which of course it is. And then a new thought occurs: *Fake it till you make it!* Giddy's eyes widen. Why not? If she's trying to put a genuine smile on her face, why not try a fake one today and see what happens?

Giddy heads to the shower. In the bathroom mirror, she tries the grin again, and it looks about as bad as Giddy thought it might: kind of chiseled and weak, and the angles somehow don't reach her eyes. She widens the grin and winces as a little more of scab-Africa sloughs off her face, leaving the flesh pink and new underneath. Like new beginnings?

In the shower she catches herself humming Strauss's *Arabella* and wonders if that's a positive sign, an indication that the fake smile could lead to actual cheer. When she gets out, she tries the smile again in the mirror. It's still odd-looking, but maybe that's because she hasn't practiced enough?

In her room, Giddy gets some index cards from a drawer. There's nothing she can do to prepare for success in art, but the teachers in her other classes seem to like it when students bring ideas based on the study material. So she flips through *The Guns of August* and *The Yellow Wallpaper*, writing down quotes and adding her own questions. She writes until her fingers cramp, but in the end, she has two short stacks of cards, one for English and one for world history.

Downstairs, she eats sardines on crackers for breakfast and packs a small Tupperware of chicken feet for lunch. She steps outside and pauses, looking around. Giddy tries the smile again. Wider. Wider still.

Her stomach responds by burning in agitation, and Giddy swears under her breath, pops an antacid, and puts her earbuds in.

Today's operatic melody is a French version of *Carmen*'s "Habanera." Giddy finds the mix of slow and fast tempos a challenge to walk against, one that has her alternating between slow and fast speeds on the sidewalk. When a jogger, confounded by the pattern of her pacing, speeds up to get ahead of her, Giddy flashes him what she hopes is a super-neat grin. His eyebrows knit together in worry and he looks warily over his shoulder at her as he passes.

Giddy's smile fades a touch, but maybe the problem is a lack of practice? She starts repeating a mantra of *Smile! Smile! Smile!* as she walks, trying out new grins on perfect strangers. But it's as if they can see right through her, and she barely gets more than an awkward wave back. Even worse, it feels like she's trying to seek attention, which Giddy definitely is *not* trying to do!

By the time she reaches school, she feels rebuked, her smile hanging on her like a borrowed set of clothes, ill-fitting and itchy. Giddy throws her hood up and absently reaches to scratch at her scab as she approaches the front doors. She cranks the music in her ears so high, little vibrations race down her spine. She has "Habanera" on a loop. She's not early—kids are already walking in the door ahead of her. Giddy pauses outside of art, seized by sudden anxiety.

Smile! Smile! Smile! She can do this. She can walk to her table, sit quietly, listen to opera, and just smile at people. And if they don't like it, they can look away. She doesn't even have to talk to anyone. Just read the instructions for whatever assignment the teacher has, follow it, and get an A. How bad can today's lesson really be? She nods to herself and takes a step through the door.

Giddy enters into a room in the grip of chaos.

No one's at their tables. Everyone's racing around, grabbing up bright hats and unrolling sheens of fabric. Bong Sculpture Guy is putting on blue jeweled dangle earrings while the guy next to him overturns a bucket of Mardi Gras beads onto a table so fast, they spill and bounce on the floor while a couple of other kids race to grab up the leavings. Giddy pops her earbuds out and nearly loses them when she's smacked in the face by an unrolling bolt of hot-pink chiffon. It's held by two girls arguing over whether the fabric will fray if they cut it. Giddy ducks under it and tries to get to her seat as quickly as possible, but the tables have been moved and pushed together in places, and all around her, every conceivable surface is covered with bright bags of feathers, scarves, and old hats and jackets. It's like a drag queen's wardrobe exploded.

Giddy squeezes around two tables draped in Shakespearean-style brocade dresses and finally spies the prompt on the board: *Using the items scattered about class, design a creative and functional outfit for the year 3050!*

"Excuse me!" A girl waving fabric scissors bumps into Giddy, and Giddy, flinching at the invasion of her space, jerks away and scoots back into a counter covered in yards of yellow cotton fabric and a multicolored sombrero. Giddy picks up the sombrero and puts it on her head, pulling it down in a way she hopes shields her face as effectively as her hood does, then she loops the yellow fabric desperately around her arms and hauls everything to her table, letting it spill off her. Giddy, who's never so much as lifted a sewing needle in her life, looks angrily in the direction of the teacher's desk and thinks, *This is a fucking stupid assignment!*

And sees her teacher looking back at her, a grim expression on his face. He points to her and darkly beckons, and now Giddy can see her artwork is on the table in front of him, the one that reads: *GIDDY'S ALL-ORIGINAL ART PROJECT—A FUNCTIONAL DINNER PLATE!*

Giddy approaches, squeezing between tables, and as she gets closer she can see the fire kiln has dragged out every dent and fingerprint in her plate. It's made the smaller letters *BE IN AWE OF HER GENIUS* appear jagged and crude.

When she gets to his desk, he says: "I'm not giving you a good grade for this."

"What, like a C?"

"More like an F."

Giddy's eyes widen. "But you said you'd never penalize us for being bad artists!"

"I said I wouldn't penalize you so long as you gave me your best *effort*," her teacher tells her. "Was this really your best effort—a smashed disk and a snarky comment?"

It was instead the culmination of several failed efforts to actually create something and if he could see all the squashed Bodies and the first-attempt teapot, he might realize that! *I should have stuck with the piggy bank.* "Can I redo it?" Giddy tries a smile on him, one that's not quite so wide as the one she used on the jogger this morning but not closemouthed, either, a sort of in-between pleading number.

And to her surprise, his gaze softens. He looks over her shoulder at her table. "I tell you what: you've picked some bright, bold items. Show me how they inspire you. If you do well today, I'll think about replacing the grade." And as her teacher goes back to unpacking colored tissue paper and pipe cleaners, Giddy thinks, *It worked? Oh my God, smiling worked!* Even though she didn't feel it. Even though she was just *faking* it.

It's not much, but it's enough for Giddy to feel a flicker of confidence. She goes back to her table and puzzles over her sombrero and fabric. She has no idea how to design an outfit for the future, but she unrolls the fabric across the table anyway. Then she thoughtfully turns the sombrero around in her hands.

"Know why we're doing this lesson?" Giddy looks up to see Otter Sculpture Girl has a felt jester hat and a sequined scarf. "Theater department's emptying out all their old stuff."

Giddy doesn't know what to say in response to this sudden conversation. *Smile smile smile!* She flashes Otter Girl a close-mouthed grin meant to politely dismiss and quickly turns back to her work.

But Otter Girl goes on. "Did you see we're now doing performance art every Wednesday?" She chuckles. "Sounds like something you do when you're afraid of running out of supplies."

Giddy locks eyes with Otter Girl a second time and Otter Girl seems to wait, seems to hope, for Giddy to say something back. There's a nervous cheeriness to her that confuses and irritates Giddy. Exactly when did Otter Girl imagine they'd become best friends?

Giddy doesn't say anything. She flips the sombrero upside down on the table and turns it even though it's too limp to spin like a top. After a few seconds, Otter Girl takes the hint and leaves her alone.

Giddy thinks, *What if people in the year 3050 just want to be left alone too?* Giddy grabs a stapler from a neighboring table and attaches the fabric all around the sombrero's brim so that it hangs to the floor in a cylinder. Then she staples the seam so it won't accidentally open. Giddy tries it on, wriggling until the yellow fabric falls down all around her and the sombrero locks into place atop her head.

Because it's cotton, Giddy can just barely see through. The world surrounding her is yellow, and everyone on the other side is merely shadows against the light. There's something peaceful about being secreted away like this. As long as she's disguised, it doesn't matter if she smiles. Giddy imagines doing school like this in the year 3050, the yellow fabric spilling out around her desk or billowing around her feet in the hallways. Giddy moves her hands around. She should have thought about armholes.

"You look like a tall, slender psychedelic mushroom." Otter Girl's voice.

If she were disguised, it also wouldn't matter how she sounded! Giddy tries on a lofty voice, one that might fit in well with high society. "Thanks," she says, "but this is the year 3050, and if I wanted a conversation, I wouldn't be wearing this very stylish privacy outfit."

"Oh, is that what that is?" Otter Girl sounds amused. "That's creative. But is it *functional*? Can you walk?"

Otter Girl has a point. One-half of the assignment is to make the outfit functional. As she's thinking this, someone else in the room says: "Look at the big yellow condom!"

Some kids laugh, but Giddy's embarrassed flush is thankfully hidden. *I will prove you can walk in this!* She takes a step forward, then another, bumps her hip into a table and backs up. Her elbow connects with something soft and a guy yells, "Ow! Shit!" and there's more laughter.

So maybe it needs some adjusting. Giddy mutters a *sorry* and tries to take the outfit off, but the staples catch in her hair and her blunted hands flap around like they belong to an impotent ghost. More laughter! Mercifully, somebody sees her plight and starts helping her out of it. When the outfit comes off, Giddy sees that it's her teacher.

"This is in case people in the year 3050 want privacy," Giddy tells him. "I know the functionality is lacking, but if I hemmed it and put in eyeholes and armholes—"

He laughs. Giddy's so stunned, she stops speaking. Her teacher says: "All right."

"No, I know it needs work!"

"It's actually pretty good."

Giddy gapes at him. "It is?"

"Yeah." He looks at the fabric in his arms. "It shows creativity. You're thinking of a need that some people might have. I like it!"

Giddy is even more wary. "You do?"

"This is what I was looking for! Just something to show you're putting a little bit of yourself into your art." He holds it out. "You want to work on it some more or turn it in now?"

Giddy goes back to her table empty-handed, not wanting to mess up an obviously good grade. She thinks, *Functional and creative is not the same as putting yourself into your art!* And then it hits her—she knows why she doesn't do well in this class.

Giddy doesn't *want* to put herself into her art. It's embarrassing! She *likes* that wall between her and the other students, likes them not knowing what's going on in her head. If they knew what she was thinking, they might not like it, they might start judging her, and she gets enough of that from Jess and Trinity and Asia. Her teacher once said art was "a window into the soul." But what's wrong with having blinds on a window?

She's still frowning over it when the bell rings and she heads to English. Right outside the door she stops again, because the smile worked in art class, so maybe it will work just as well here? A smile and index cards. Giddy fixes her face into what she hopes is a nice, amiable grin and ignores the subsequent itching of her scab as she takes the seat at the front of the room again. Avery comes in, sees her, but scowls back at her smile as he sourly takes a seat one row behind Giddy. He also drops his books extra hard on the desk just in case Giddy missed his irritation.

The boy and girl who sit adjacent to Giddy look at her, look back at Avery, and then exchange a smirk. Giddy can't tell if they're laughing at her or Avery or both, and this type of social uncertainty is exactly the kind of crap that would make her sombrero outfit popular!

Her smile tightens. The quick write on the board reads: *Why is the wallpaper yellow?*

Giddy takes out her index cards and flips through them. *Yellow . . . yellow . . . yellow . . .* But nothing she wrote down earlier seems to address this question. So she writes, *There is no reason. Life doesn't have to make any sense.* As she gets up to deposit her answer in the teacher's box, she thinks, *Why did I just write that life doesn't make sense?*

Her teacher underlines the word *yellow* on the board. "Why do you think the author chose this color?"

Somebody calls out: "Yellow is disgusting!"

"It's just a bad color," someone else says.

But Giddy thinks of how pretty the world looked when she was safely disguised behind the yellow fabric. She raises her hand, ready to defend the subjective attractiveness of yellow, but the teacher calls on Avery instead.

He sits up a little straighter and says: "Yellow historically is a color representing good things: sunshine, cheerfulness. Just not in this story."

"Jane *seems* cheerful," the teacher says, "so what are the signs she's not? What are the indications that, despite an outward appearance of cheerfulness, she's actually coming unraveled inside?"

The boy and girl who smirked at Giddy have their hands up, but Giddy's competitive streak surges and she suddenly thinks maybe she can win this class the way she's always winning over Katlyn in algebra II! So she waves her hand a little in the air.

The teacher points to her.

Giddy says: "Jane follows lines in the wallpaper."

"Very good." Her teacher's eyes drift away. "Anyone else have—"

"*And* she can't sleep," Giddy adds that fast. She actually knows *all* the signs in *The Yellow Wallpaper* that indicate Jane is coming unraveled. "She sees the moonlight turn into bars on her window." Giddy flips to a new index card. "And when she rides in a car, the smell of the old wallpaper follows her." She flips to another card. "She doesn't want to see a doctor because she thinks he's just like her husband, yet at the same time she says she loves her husband."

"OK. Good. But can anyone—"

"Got one more—" She flips so quickly that some of the cards slip out of her hands and spill across the table. "Wait! Just wait." She thumbs through them fast, picking them up. "Jane also sees imaginary women creeping around outside her home."

"Those are great observations, Giddy. Does anyone—"

"She's paranoid! Also . . . also, she's . . ." Giddy knows she had one more thing written down, but she can't find it. She starts arranging the cards in a quick grid on the table, searching for the one she hasn't used.

"And that is a *lot*, isn't it?" her teacher says, taking advantage of the pause to turn pointedly to the rest of the class. "Anyone else have a thought about the mental state of Jane?"

The girl next to Giddy raises her hand again.

"Yes?"

"It's like Jane doesn't know when to quit." She shoots Giddy a sideways look.

"*So* doesn't know when to quit," the boy on Giddy's other side mutters under his breath.

Giddy looks down at the cards spread out on the table. Nobody else in the room is doing this. Giddy looks up and sees the quiet faces of her classmates looking back at her, and she realizes she came on too strong. She's not winning—she's just acting weird!

Giddy slowly stacks the cards, face heated, as the teacher goes on to point to other kids. Giddy doesn't offer more input. All she did was embarrass herself. She tries to allow her silence to make her invisible, but she's still seated at the front of the room where everyone can see her. Giddy misses her old seat behind the bookcase more than she ever has in her life.

When the bell rings, she remembers *smile smile smile.* So as she gets up, she gives the boy and girl who sit near her a small, close-lipped smile—something she hopes makes her seem *normal.*

They stare mutely back before giving her a nod so ambiguous, it leaves Giddy's face burning. She probably looks pathetic! And why wouldn't she? She's currently the freak who tried to hog the floor in English class.

As she walks out of the room, head down, her teacher says, "Giddy, I thought your input today was very good," but Giddy just keeps walking. When she gets to the door outside algebra II, she doesn't feel like smiling at all. But she puts a tight grin on her face and stalks into the class anyway.

At least in here everything's quiet and normal. Nobody's ever going to put the seats into discussion formation or throw costumes around. Giddy still doesn't know how to graph an asymptote, but she's comfortable staring quietly at her unattempted practice problems when her teacher announces: "I'm assigning peer tutors for these questions. Giddy, how about having Katlyn work with you?"

Katlyn. Teaching math to Giddy.

"Giddy?" Her teacher frowns, waiting. Blood pulses at Giddy's temples. There is no circumstance under which it would ever be all right for Katlyn to teach Giddy. Giddy should be teaching Katlyn! Katlyn doesn't really know anything—she just grabs whatever formula she can find in her composition book, throws it at a problem, and prays that it works! Giddy's no mind reader, but she's certain that's how Katlyn's brain operates. Katlyn has no intuitive feel for math. Katlyn's a friggin' hack!

Her teacher frowns again. "Giddy? I said I'm pairing you with Katlyn."

Giddy shoots a glance at Katlyn, expecting her face to be lit up in victory. But Katlyn's back is stiff, as if she knows what a terrible idea this is. Giddy opens her mouth to tell her teacher, in the politest of terms, that she can do this on her own, thank you very much!

And closes it. Because the mantra *smile smile smile* is still bobbing around atop the tumultuous waves of Giddy's mind. So she curves up the corners of her mouth and whispers: "Why not?"

If her teacher detects her ire, he doesn't show it. He just goes back to assigning other tutors as Katlyn gathers up her things and pulls a chair to Giddy's desk. Katlyn's eyes remain deliberately off Giddy as she opens her composition book on one-half of the desk and sets out two brand-new name-brand pencils, lining them up until the erasers and sharpened tips are even. They are joined by three animal pencil sharpeners—a happy-looking koala, panda, and giraffe. Katlyn sets them up one by one in a neat little row above the pencils. All three are so new as not to be smudged, and Giddy can't help but close her hand around her own little pencil, which is cheap and half sharpened away because the off-brand ones don't sharpen easily, and the eraser is almost used flat. Giddy can't remember the last time she had a working handheld sharpener. Her mom buys the dollar brands and they always break the first week of school, no matter how much care Giddy gives them!

So Giddy simmers. She is coming to grips with ceding half her desktop to Katlyn when she notices the giraffe sharpener is just over the halfway mark—maybe by an inch. Giddy tries to ignore it, but she keeps looking at it sitting there, demeanor cheery over its unintentional crossing of enemy lines.

Katlyn selects the top pencil. She starts pulling Giddy's practice sheet toward her. "So if *f* of *x* equals negative *x* squared plus *ax* plus *b* over *x* squared plus *cx* plus *d*—"

Giddy stabs her pencil eraser down on the paper, stopping its migration.

Katlyn's eyes flicker up to Giddy's and she says: "I can't help you if I can't read the questions."

"I can't do the work," Giddy says, "if you take my paper."

Katlyn heaves a sigh and her eyes go back to the paper. "Where *a*, *b*, *c*, and *d* are unknown constants, which of the following is a possible graph of *y* equals *f(x)*?"

Giddy stares at the answer choices, but she has no idea. A week ago she would have known. A week ago she would have been able to complete a problem in algebra II without even checking her notes.

Katlyn circles part of the question. She says in a slow, irritated voice: "Look at negative *x* squared over *x* squared? Doesn't that tell you something?"

Giddy puts her pencil to the paper, runs its tip along the dashed lines of the graphs. Then she ever so carefully flips her pencil end upward to push the giraffe sharpener into the panda and off her side of the desk. There. She feels better.

Katlyn says: "Don't you see that this means *f(x)* is going to approach negative one in either direction?" Katlyn writes *f(x) = -1* on Giddy's paper. Then, quick as lightning, she moves the giraffe back into its original position. "Now that you know *f(x)* approaches negative one, you need to look at these graphs, because you're looking for a horizontal asymptote at *y equals negative one*."

And Giddy suddenly can't do this. It's not like she even *has* to do this. Being great at math isn't part of Superdoo's list. Being great at math is Giddy's God-given right because this is the talent she was born with! So what if she can't prove it this week? Doesn't that just mean Superdoo's list is doing its job?

"Sure," Giddy says. "Horizontal asymptote at *y* is . . . this one?" Katlyn shakes her head. "This one?" Giddy asks, moving to answer choice B. Another headshake. "This one?"

"Are you just moving from one choice to the other until I tell you which answer is right?" Katlyn asks, astonished.

"You're the peer tutor. You tell me."

"Wow." Katlyn pushes her chair back. Her mouth twists into a self-satisfied smirk. "And I used to think you were so good at math."

Giddy doesn't think. She just grabs up Katlyn's composition book and sweeps it across the table. Her practice paper soars as Katlyn's pencils and animal sharpeners fly off the desk and bounce across the carpeted floor. The bottom of the giraffe sharpener hits a chair leg and cracks open, scattering pencil shavings everywhere.

"Giddy!" Katlyn jumps out of her seat. Everyone stops what they're doing and looks. Giddy, stunned at her own behavior, drops the composition notebook. Katlyn dives for it and starts grabbing up all her things as a couple of other students reach down to help *her*—and it galls Giddy that that's where their sympathies lie!

"Barber—out in the hall!" her teacher yells, and Giddy, thankful to be anywhere but here, stomps out, hearing Katlyn whine behind her: "I didn't do anything! She just flipped out!"

In the hall, Giddy throws her back against the wall and quietly seethes. When her teacher comes out of the room after talking with Katlyn, he says to Giddy in a furious voice: "Are you OK? Because I have never seen anything like that come out of you."

Giddy rolls her eyes and shrugs.

"This is Pre-AP Algebra II," he tells her. "I don't expect to see that kind of behavior in here. Cool off before coming back in." He shakes his head at her and goes back inside. Giddy, after a moment, follows him in. Everyone's back to work, heads inclined studiously because it's like he said, it's a Pre-AP class and kids here care about their grades. Even Katlyn's bent over her practice problems, scribbling away, though her sharpeners are now piled in a haphazard heap on her desk. Giddy can feel everyone in the room deliberately ignoring her.

It's as loud as if they were screaming.

Giddy sits and stares at her practice problems. She's never done anything like this—never grabbed anybody's stuff and thrown it. Certainly she'd never do anything like that in algebra II. What's wrong with her?

When the bell finally rings, she silently slips the unworked sheet into the trash on her way out of the room. Giddy walks with her head down to chemistry, stops outside the door, takes a few settling breaths.

She walks into the room smiling. What she doesn't expect to see is Jess and Trinity smiling at her from their seats at the back of the room. Because Trinity and Jess don't smile, not really. The grins on their faces are hungry and predatory.

"Look," Jess says, "it's Giddy!"

"Wave to Giddy!" Trinity says. They both wave their hands furiously.

Giddy, unsure, smiles tightly and waves back. This makes Jess and Trinity dissolve into peals of laughter and go back to holding their phones under their table. Giddy wonders if maybe they've already heard about her meltdown in algebra II. Alarmed, Giddy eases into her seat. She hazards a tiny glance at Zach's table. Usually he looks up and waves at her or gives her a friendly smile or something.

Not today. Today he's got *his* phone under the table and he's texting something. Giddy gets the feeling that she's being pointedly ignored.

"I like balancing chemical equations," the teacher tells the class as she writes a formula on the board. "You get out of a chemical reaction exactly what you put into it—same quantities of atoms, as demonstrated by the chemical symbols, and the coefficients and the subscripts."

A soft giggle erupts from the back of the room. Giddy looks over her shoulder in time to see Trinity and Jess quickly look away from her and back down at their phones. Meanwhile, Zach has a smirk on his face and he's texting quickly. Giddy thinks, *They're texting about me! Why?*

Giddy's phone buzzes. She pops it out and looks at it.

Jess: *Stalker much?*

There's an accompanying image of some creepy guy poking his head up out of some bushes. Then Trinity texts a GIF that shows a girl licking her lips with an all-caps *I KNOW WHERE YOU LIVE!!*

Giddy thinks, *What the hell is that supposed to mean?*

The teacher goes on: "If I start out with six atoms of sulfur and four atoms of oxygen, I'm ending up with six atoms of sulfur and four atoms of oxygen even if I set them on fire or blow them up! Everything checks out. It balances perfectly. Wouldn't it be great if everything in life were that simple?"

Giddy can't stop focusing on the soft *tap, tap* of Zach's fingers as he texts under his table. To Giddy, it's as loud as firecracker blasts, so she can't understand why everyone isn't staring at Zach, asking him to stop it. She twists around in her seat again. This time Jess waves at her over the phone, that same big, bright smile on her face. Like she knows something.

"So when people go out on dates and the date doesn't work out, what do they always say?" The teacher finishes her equation, turns, and smiles. "They say, 'We just didn't have good *chemistry*.'"

Something in the text makes Zach chuckle, and Giddy sits up a little in her seat, trying to see what he's typing. And then she makes the connection, the only thing Zach could possibly be texting Jess and Trinity about.

The teacher goes on: "And I hear my friends say these things, and my reaction is to think, *Did you not measure before mixing? Did you not read the labels?*"

A smattering of laughter across the class. Zach laughs too, but it's probably not at the teacher. It's probably because Trinity just sent a GIF of a girl with red lipstick kissing a camera lens and now Giddy wants to just curl up and die!

Because Jess and Trinity must know she went to Zach's house yesterday and kissed him. They must know because Zach must have told them and *why would he do this to her?*

The teacher says: "Because if my friends had labels, maybe I could read their ingredients and understand them, right?"

Giddy gets up on her knees in her seat to try to verify that's what Zach is texting about. She barely hears the teacher say: "Fortunately, real chemistry always adds up so long as you know what you're doing. Giddy? *Giddy!*"

Giddy's head whips around. Her teacher holds out a dry-erase marker. "Come up and complete this redox reaction."

Giddy freezes, halfway out of her seat. The whole room turns to look at her, including Zach, who slips his phone into his hoodie. He wears an expression of brutal boredom as if Giddy is about to take up all of his precious texting time.

Giddy angrily grabs the marker. The equation, sprawling in languid form across the width of the board, seems simple enough, and Giddy already knows how to balance equations. So she starts off writing after the arrow $CO_2(g) + O_2H + \ldots$ and here Giddy has to look at the first part of the equation again. It's not hard. It shouldn't be hard. It's just that it's been a few weeks since she did this and she hasn't been doing any of the redox practice problems. And now she can't stop thinking about how she wore that stupid green dress to Zach's house!

"Hill system."

Giddy looks at her teacher. Then at the class. A lot of the students are smirking. "You're not following the rules established by the Hill system. It wouldn't be O_2H."

Giddy erases the *2* and makes it *OH-*. *Why did she have to kiss Zach?*

The class chuckles as a whole and her teacher shakes her head. "This isn't yielding hydroxide. Check again."

Someone makes a *smack* sound. Giddy looks over her shoulder. A couple of students sip from water bottles and smack their lips loudly. This makes Giddy think about the GIF with the girl kissing the lens and she wonders how many other kids know. Maybe the entire class knows! Did Jess just text everybody?

A few kids chuckle again and Giddy just stands there, not able to move, not able to do anything. The teacher shakes her head. "That's just rude, class! Stop trying to influence her." Then in a lower, kinder voice: "Go ahead, Giddy. You've got this."

But she doesn't have this! Because Jess and Trinity know she kissed Zach and now she looks like some kind of stalker freak. Giddy writes and erases $2O_2H$ and writes and erases *2OH + 2OH*. The students keep sipping water and smacking their lips and Giddy feels like she's missing something painfully obvious!

Her teacher starts laughing. "OK! OK! Who's going to fix this?"

And Giddy, defeated, holds out the marker as the teacher takes it and sends her to her seat. The teacher calls on Zach.

He gets up, completes the equation by reversing the chemical symbols to write $2H_2O$. He underlines it aggressively. "Good job, Zach," the teacher says. "Now, if I wanted to complicate this . . ."

As she turns to the board, Zach passes Giddy's seat and whispers, "It's *water*, Giddy. H . . . two . . . O."

And to her horror, Giddy sees he's right, *Zach's* right, and that's why everyone was drinking water and smacking their lips. Giddy's face burns as her teacher finishes another example on the board before handing back graded quizzes and some new practice problems. Over the F grade on Giddy's last quiz, her teacher has written: *Fluorine? Really, Giddy?* And next to it she's jotted down her after-school tutoring times.

When the bell rings, the words *smile smile smile* hurtle their way across her brain. So she grabs her things and smiles so fiercely, it hurts the sides of her face. Giddy breaks into a run in the hall, scooting around people to get to lunch. Trinity's and Jess's laughter follows her.

When she sits for lunch, she tosses her Tupperware onto the cafeteria table so hard, the contents jump around. Giddy notices a bubble of silence. She looks up. Trey, Monica, and Ashlynn are all quietly staring, and Giddy tenses up. Ashlynn's rocking the teal vibes today with little braided leather earrings and matching chalk stripes in her hair, and Giddy can hear Jess in her head again. *Oh, teal chalk today—wow! Pick a color for your hair, Ashlynn, and lose the earrings while you're at it; they're dragging your lobes down.* And she kind of wants to say those words out loud, just to see what Ashlynn would say if she hurt her.

"Everything good?" Trey asks.

"Everything's fine." To prove it, she grins in a way that stretches her lips tight and makes the scab on her face feel like it's about to split wide open.

They all wince. Giddy keeps the smile on her face as she pops open the Tupperware, takes a chicken foot out, and bites down on it.

"Is that tempura?" Ashlynn asks.

Giddy's mouth freezes. She lowers the food and says: "Chicken feet."

"Oh, hell no!" Ashlynn holds up her hands. "Bird feet? Come on!"

Monica looks excited. "I want to try! Oh, please let me try one."

"I have seriously never seen anybody eat chicken feet before." This from Trey, who sounds dubious.

Giddy finishes chewing the meat off one, sets the remains on her napkin. Finishes another. Starts a little pile on the napkin. Looks up.

They're all still watching. "Please let me try one!" Monica says again.

Giddy tries to read her face, to see if Monica is making fun. Jess is in her head again. *Oh, please let me try that! I've been dying to puke my guts up today, Giddy.*

Giddy slides the Tupperware over. Monica takes a bite, chews it slowly. Suddenly, her eyes pop open. "Oh my God, guys, this is better than wings!" She slaps her hand on the table. "OK, Giddy. Where do you buy them?"

"They're homemade," she quietly says.

"Did you *make* these?" Monica asks. And when Giddy nods, an uncertain look crosses Monica's face. She asks: "Was it hard?"

Ashlynn and Trey burst out laughing. Trey says: "Monica's going into law so she can make enough money to buy all her food at expensive places."

"And she's going to do this because she almost burned the school down last year," Ashlynn says.

Giddy's eyes pop open wide.

Monica slaps a hand to her face and laughs with them. "Guys . . ."

"She started an oil fire on the counter in culinary arts," Ashlynn says. "She was supposed to be making banana bread."

"And guess what she did to the fire?" Trey pops a potato chip into his mouth and grins around it. "Go ahead. Just guess."

Giddy has no idea, but she feels like maybe something terrible will happen to her if she guesses wrong so, in a panic, she just shakes her head.

"She threw water on it!" Ashlynn bursts into giggles. Giddy gapes because she thought everyone knew you don't do that to an oil fire.

Monica's shaking her head over her meal. "You guys just keep enjoying this. When I'm super wealthy and eating out anywhere, you two can be making mac 'n' cheese in a studio apartment."

"That's why we all went outside in the rain that day," Ashlynn says. "They said it was a drill, but it was really Ms. Cox dumping powder all over the counters."

"This school won't do fire drills in the rain," Trey says.

Giddy can't keep her eyes off Monica, the way she's just grinning through all this, like she's not being *destroyed* by her friends right now. Because if Jess told this about Giddy, she would want to slip under the table and die. But Monica just shrugs, eats a fry, and says: "It only damaged the upper cabinet a little. They replaced one door."

"But if you open that cabinet door, you can see black near the hinges where the paint didn't reach," Trey says. "In that sacred spot, culinary arts has its very own Monica Mark."

Monica jams her fist up in the air while eating. "Never forget my legend!"

"I want to try one." Trey holds out his hand, and Giddy, tense, hands him one. He chews, thinking. "A little spicy. Pretty good actually."

"This is why we broke up," Monica says. "You didn't cook for me."

Trey grins wide and Ashlynn draws back in her seat and crosses her arms. "Look at her! Big shot, but she needs a man to do her cooking."

Trey reaches over and grabs Monica's hand and suddenly seems to get all serious with her. "I would absolutely respect your right to do your own cooking, but at the same time I would totally do the cooking for you and yet if you wanted to share cooking responsibilities, I would be down for that, too, because, babe, that's you, and I would never try to change you. Just respect you."

For a second, they're just staring at each other, Monica looking like she's trying not to laugh. Then she says: "That work on Sheryl?"

Trey drops her hand and slaps the table, grinning. "That completely works on Sheryl! You have no idea!"

They all burst into laughter, and it's so loud that the other tables *must* be noticing. Giddy wants to jump back somehow, maybe pop her earbuds in and put up her hood. She keeps her expression neutral, thinking that this laughter is just going to go on and on around her with her being able to do nothing!

Then, as mysteriously as it started, the laughter dies away and they all go back to eating like this was some kind of nonevent.

Only, Monica slides her fries toward Giddy. As Giddy hesitantly takes a fry, Ashlynn quietly says: "Well, I draw the food line at feet."

"You always say you draw the food line at insects," Monica accuses.

"Well, now it's feet *and* insects!"

Monica and Trey snicker at that and Giddy is still braced, still waiting for some giant backlash of criticism to erupt among them. She tries to remember if she ever shared her food with Jess, Trinity, or Asia, and if she had, would they have tried it? And would they have offered her anything to eat in return? And is this *normal*?

"So why do you eat weird things?" Ashlynn asks her. "You just like weird stuff."

"No, I'm doing this thing called—" And here Giddy pauses because now she's pretty sure she's reached the part that will end in judgment and why not? Because everyone in art and English judged her and everyone in chemistry laughed at her, so why not?

They're staring, waiting. Giddy says: "I'm doing the opposite of things I would normally do for a set period of time. It's an experiment." To reinforce it, she smiles again. And she waits for them to snicker.

Instead they give slow nods of understanding. Giddy's grin falters as Trey says: "So it's a personal challenge."

"Is that why you're smiling?" Monica asks. "Because you never smile."

Giddy nods.

"OK, you need to *never* smile again if you're going to do it that way," Ashlynn says. "Like you're going to sneak up behind somebody in a dark wood and knife them."

"I can see doing opposite things to try new stuff," Monica says, "so long as you're not using it as an excuse to do terrible things. You're not being an asshole about it, right?"

Giddy shakes her head: "Oh no! I'm not—" Zach's sad words: *But you did kiss me.* And following it to rise up out of the recesses of her brain like the ghost of Hamlet's father, the internet advice: *Even though at times you may not like who you become.* "No!" Giddy says emphatically, "I would never be an asshole about it."

"So"—Monica lifts a napkin—"would you have to eat this napkin if I dared you to do it?"

They laugh and Giddy says: "No. I choose what I do." Giddy thinks about it. "I guess it's not an official rule, but I think it should be."

"Well, it is now," Trey says.

And they smile at her and suddenly Giddy feels . . . she's not sure . . . a certain tightness in her shoulders that she's never noticed before—a string that pulls the blades taut just underneath the back of her neck—she can feel it start to *loosen.* Giddy rolls her head around once as Ashlynn explains to Monica all the foods she won't eat that people like to put in salads.

But when the bell rings and Giddy walks to robotics, her shoulders draw up tight as a drum again and she can't for the life of her figure out why. So she keeps her head down, pencil working furiously on a course designed to never actually happen in real life. When she turns in her initial supply list, her teacher gives it a concerned once-over and says: "You need . . . six ounces of lighter fluid?"

"And a box of matches," Giddy says. "But stick ones, not the flimsy cardboard types you rip out of matchbooks. Those would bend too much for the robot to handle."

Her teacher frowns. "So this course you're making. I haven't seen it yet—"

"It's great." Giddy doesn't want her teacher to ask too many questions and maybe pull the plug on the design before she's finished. Just for emphasis, Giddy punctuates her statement with what she hopes is a nonchalant smile.

Her teacher goes on: "It's just that these are risky materials."

Giddy widens her smile and keeps widening it until her jaws start to ache. *Smile smile smile!*

Her teacher's lips twist. She looks *intrigued*. "That's an evil little grin you've got there, Barber. Fine." She slides the list on top of a stack on her desk. "Lighter fluid and long matches. With robots." She gives a thumbs-up. "Got it."

Giddy turns around to head back to her seat. Patrice and Deb are with their bot at a nearby table, their own design for a course in front of them. But they've been listening to everything Giddy gave the teacher and their eyes are wide with concern. Giddy shoots the same wide grin at them and Deb whispers to Patrice: "Lighter fluid? As in *fire*?"

Patrice draws a protective arm around their bot.

Giddy allows the grin to evaporate as she sits, puzzled over her teacher's reaction. She didn't expect her teacher to be *more* interested, just put off enough to allow Giddy to move forward. But then again, her teacher hasn't actually looked at Giddy's design. When she does, Giddy is confident it'll be deemed way too dangerous.

On the way to world history, the posters from last week's failed activity are still up in the hall, though somebody has drawn clown shoes on the naked feet of the dead and robbed war-front soldiers. This gives her an idea for a question, so she puts a big grin on her face and walks in, smiling at the students seated near the front row.

They don't seem to care. One or two of them look up at Giddy through bleary eyes before putting their heads back down. It's warm again in the room. Everyone looks half asleep.

So Giddy walks by the teacher, stops, raps her knuckle on his desk, and grins at him.

Instead of looking up at her, he points a single finger at the board's starter question: *How many lives must be lost for a war to be no longer justified? Share your thoughts with a neighbor.*

Giddy sighs and turns around. Hunter and his buddies are giggling over something in the back of the room. She tries not to make eye contact, but then she hears: "Hey, Giddy," and she looks up without thinking.

Hunter's smiling. He gives her this little *what's up?* chin lift, and Giddy, face red, takes her seat quickly, thinking, *My smile wasn't for you!*

"The question, if you even bothered to read it"—her teacher pushes his chair away from his computer, stands, and points to the board—"is 'How many lives must be lost for a war to be no longer justified?'" He turns to the class. "So what have we got?"

Nothing. Just the hum of the inadequate air-conditioning filtering out of a vent over the door. Giddy has an answer—and she thinks it's a good one. But when she used her cards in English, she got too into it and came off as a crazy person. So she taps them against her desk, waffling between using them or putting them away again.

The teacher throws up his hands at the room. "Really? It's a simple opinion. There is no wrong answer, guys! Come on!"

And Giddy thinks, *Fuck it! I spent thirty minutes making these!* She raises her hand and says: "What if it's a pointless question?"

Her teacher frowns and Giddy can see in his eyes he's looking for the catch or the joke. "Why do you say that?"

She pulls an index card out, sets it on top, and reads it before saying: "Because what if success alone justifies war?"

"OK..." Her teacher appears to mull it over. Then he brightens. "*OK!* Good answer. Shows critical thinking. I like it. It makes sense." He points around the room. "Anybody have a follow-up?"

In the slow silence that follows there's nothing but the thrum of the laboring air-conditioning. Giddy is quietly flipping through her cards. She sets one on top and slowly raises her hand again.

"Ms. Barber?"

"I also have a question about the red pants."

He frowns again. "Red pants?"

"Didn't you say the French army lost, like, hundreds of thousands of soldiers in this war?" When he nods, she says: "Well, some of it was because they wore red pants and everybody could see them when they fought. Everybody told them not to do it. Why were they so dumb?"

"Red pants." Her teacher sits on the edge of his desk. He looks flummoxed. "I . . . I don't—"

"Because, like, the British and the Germans and the Bulgarians—they all wore camouflage." Giddy flips through her cards to make sure, but there it is, along with page numbers from *The Guns of August* for reference. "And they told the French army—they told them, 'Hey, the warfare's different now. You're going to need to learn how to hide. And the French were like, 'Hell no! We're superpatriotic and nobody will feel like fighting if they're not looking all boss in their red pants.'" Giddy holds up her cards. "So I thought at first, maybe this is fiction, right? Maybe they didn't really do that, but I looked it up on other websites—"

"Well, that's the internet for you." Her teacher shakes his head. "You can't really trust—"

"—and I found out it was *true*!" Giddy sets the cards down and throws up her hands. "Hundreds of thousands of French soldiers died in part because the Germans could so easily see them and gun them down because of *their red pants*. How dumb do you have to be?"

There's a little bit of light laughter now. Giddy looks around her in case they're laughing at her, but everyone appears to be laughing in response to the French army's fashion stupidity, and even Hunter has shut up and he's just staring at Giddy with a bemused expression on his face.

But her teacher isn't laughing. He just looks uncertain.

Giddy thumbs through her cards rapidly, finds the one she wants, and slaps it down on her desk. "And then there's Plan XVII," and she waits for her teacher to say anything he likes about that.

Seconds elapse. Her teacher clears his throat. "Right. Plan XVII. So, what's that?"

Giddy thinks at first maybe he's kidding or the question's rhetorical. "It's Plan XVII," she finally says. And waits.

The teacher doesn't say anything. He just looks at her funny.

"You know!" she tells him. "The French army's plan going into the war." When he doesn't add anything to her words, she says: "The one where they laid out all this offensive strategy and the other countries were like, 'You're going to need a *defensive* strategy to go with this,' and the French army's like, 'No, we're all good.' But clearly they weren't, because *hundreds of thousands of them died*!"

Her teacher claps his hands together, a noise so loud that it makes several students who were sagging in their chairs sit up again. "Fine, Ms. Barber! But what about *America's* involvement? What about *our* reasons for joining in this war? What can you tell us about *that*?"

He sounds aggressive, almost resentful, and Giddy, a little confused by the rapid shift, says: "Well, Theodore Roosevelt was pretty frustrated too. It took us a long time to even commit to joining the war."

"And how many Americans lost *their* lives?" Her teacher leans forward a little.

"I don't have the exact number in front of me. . . ." Giddy starts flipping through her cards again.

"No, because you're spending time looking at websites and not reading the textbook," he says. "Because if you'd read the textbook—"

"I read the textbook," Giddy interrupts.

"I don't recall a Plan XVII being in the textbook," he tells her, "or a foray into fashion choices in France, which, honestly, sounds to me more like something you'd get from entertainment television."

"It's not in the textbook," Giddy says quietly.

"Good!" The teacher smiles. "I thought as much."

"It's in the other book you assigned on your website." Giddy takes *The Guns of August* out of her backpack. "It's the extension reading."

Her teacher stares at the book. The rest of the class stares at Giddy. The teacher doesn't say anything, but he also doesn't look like he's readying a snarky comment.

After a moment of silence, he says: "Right. Of course." He nods, but to Giddy it doesn't look like he's got anything to add. It looks like he's trying to buy time. And Giddy genuinely wants answers, genuinely wants to know why the French army didn't listen when all the other countries' advice made obvious sense, but her teacher just taps his hands on his legs, stands, and says: "You know the focus of this class is America's part in the war."

"But it's *world history*," Giddy says, "and the pants thing happened!"

Giddy doesn't realize that *the pants thing* sounds kind of funny until she hears Hunter and his friends snort and giggle. Their reaction sets something off in the teacher, because he scowls and says: "I think we're done with this topic."

"But I—"

"Know what? I give you props, Ms. Barber, for saying that 'success alone justifies war.' That's a cool quote you came up with."

"It wasn't me," Giddy says.

"You just said—"

Giddy holds up a card: "General Von Moltke said it."

Hunter and his friends explode into laughter. Her teacher's words snap out above them: "Getting back on topic! I want everyone to turn to textbook page one sixty-three. Read about America's losses and what we learned from our involvement. Write a half-page essay—" Groans. "Oh really? For only half a page? I don't know how most of you stumbled out of bed this morning."

A few kids start taking out notebook paper. Giddy flips open the textbook and starts looking over the reading, but then she sees that a few of the kids around her are just copying page 163 word for word, including Bella, who Giddy knows has a decent grade in this class! Giddy grabs her library book and walks up to the teacher's desk.

He's clicking through emails. When Giddy clears her throat, he turns a weary gaze to her and says: "You're already finished?"

She holds it up. "I want to know when we'll start discussing *The Guns of August*."

Her teacher pivots in his chair to face her. "Who says we'll ever discuss it, Ms. Barber?"

"But you assigned it!"

"As an *extension read*! You want to know more about World War I, I can't think of a finer place to start than Ms. Tuchman's Pulitzer Prize–winning work."

He sounds scornful. "Do you hate it?" Giddy flips the book around and looks at the cover. "Because I like it."

Her teacher shrugs. "Then write your essay on that." He turns back to the computer.

"But you said page one sixty-three!" Now Giddy is conscious of her voice rising. She risks a look over her shoulder, but she isn't causing a scene—really, everybody in class looks too dead to care what she says or does. At the back of the room, Hunter's folding his blank sheet of lined paper into an airplane. He lifts it up in the air, aims it as if to throw it at Giddy, and fixes her with another bright smile.

She scowls at him and goes back to her seat. The silent essay portion of class wraps up with a long, boring video, but Giddy can't nap in the dark room no matter how much she'd like to. She's quietly fuming. When the bell rings, Giddy gets up and shoves her chair into her desk so loud that her teacher whips his head around from his email, narrows his eyes, and yells: "Hey!"

But Giddy rushes out of the room, because what's he going to do, chase and tackle her in the hallway? She is shuffling behind a wall of students when someone gets up in her ear and says in a deep fake-teacher voice: "*Why don't you stay on topic, Ms. Barber?* Fucking moron!"

It's Hunter. Right there. Right behind her. Whispering in her ear. Right in her *space.*

Giddy whirls. "Call me a moron one more time—"

"I'm not calling you a moron, Red Pants!" He comes up alongside her, the sea of bodies jostling them. "I'm talking about the asshole who runs our class. He doesn't read the books he puts on his website." And then they're both out of the school and into the sunlight. Hunter vaults off in a separate direction. Giddy's steps slow.

She thinks, *Our teacher hasn't read the book?* But who does that? What teacher puts an assigned extension read on their website and doesn't read it? People aren't that dumb!

And then Giddy thinks, *The French army was that dumb.*

She sees Trinity and Jess over by the wall, texting. *Smile smile smile!* Giddy puts her grin on and considers asking them why they were behaving so weird toward her when she sees Asia come out the doors with somebody. They lean against the wall together.

And the somebody with Asia is *Zach.* She backs up to the wall facing him, and they are close, *very* close. So close that Asia has no problem sliding her hands into the front pockets of his jacket. Giddy's mouth pops open in shock. Then Asia sees her over Zach's shoulder and grins really wide. She pulls a hand out of his pocket long enough to give Giddy a little wave before drawing Zach's head down to hers and kissing him.

And Giddy backs up fast because she needs to get out of there before Jess and Trinity look up and see her. Asia looks so *happy* that Giddy saw. And Giddy thinks: *Was I supposed to be hurt by this? Is that what Asia wants?*

And for some reason, it *does* hurt. Not because of Zach. It's the intention, the thought that someone she called a friend would want to do this to her.

Smile smile smile! She does it even though her cheeks ache. Giddy pops her earbuds in, listening to *Carmen* as she takes off in a jog toward home. Someone's eating pistachio ice cream next to a food truck and her stomach rumbles, but *no*! She'd throw it up. She can't handle ice cream!

At home, Giddy drags out and dusts off an old, barely used pressure cooker and makes oxtail soup while Tad hauls an overflowing laundry basket downstairs. "Mom says I stink!" He tips the basket over and crams way too much laundry into the machine, pressing and stuffing until he has to ram his tiny body against the door to get it to close. Giddy wrinkles her nose.

"Tad, I think you do smell."

"No, I don't!"

Giddy gets up and moves closer. Then she covers her mouth because *Damn, that's ripe!* "Oh God! When's the last time you bathed?"

"Umm." Tad seems to think about it. He sniffs under his arm and his eyes pop wide. "Yuck!"

"Go bathe!" Giddy can feel the laugh coming up the back of her throat as Tad runs up the stairs, his awful odor dissipating. She opens her mouth, ready to release it. . . .

And nothing. No laugh. No smile. It's like her laugh was too tired to come out or it was overcome by gravity. *So much for fake-it-till-you-make-it.*

Giddy sinks atop the stool. Tigs bounds down the stairs: "Giddy, I have three questions."

The pressure cooker's regulator whistles. Giddy pinches tired fingers to the bridge of her nose.

"First, how much do oxen get paid for their tails?"

"Tigs, I can't—"

"Also, do they miss them? Also, do *they* grow bangs?"

She is so horrified by Giddy's answer—that oxen don't grow or change or care about anything anymore because they are dead—that she runs to her room yelling, her arms wrapped around a stuffed monkey.

7

5:40 a.m.

Giddy's set her alarm ahead ten minutes in an attempt to wake more rested, but as she rolls over, she's not sure it's worked. Her shower doesn't feel alarmingly cold today and Giddy wonders if something's wrong with the tap. But when she tries hot, that seems to work.

Back in her room, she picks up the pen and taps the list. *Do something unexpected.*

Superdoo lies on his side on the desk, looking at her, grinning. Giddy thinks, *Well, sure it's easy for you!* Fake-it-till-you-make-it day was a failure. She can't think of anything worth checking off from yesterday, and she feels no closer to genuinely smiling than she did a week ago. She looks at the part on the list where she crossed out *10* and wrote *11* because eleven is an unexpected number. She'd thought she was being clever. In reality, she was just extending a self-imposed torture by one day.

And that's when she realizes she doesn't think any of this is going to work. Giddy sits down on her bed, half dressed, and regards her propped-up list. If it were working, wouldn't there be signs of it by now? Some improvement? She's halfway through her eleven days and she can hear Jess saying, *Self-delusion is an action, so if you look at it that way, you did something. Good job!*

She closes her eyes. She didn't get good sleep. Maybe if she lies back down for a quick nap . . .

From somewhere far away Giddy hears laughter. *Her* laughter. From childhood.

Her eyes pop open. She checks her phone, but the screen is dark. Giddy pulls on the rest of her clothes and heads downstairs, frowning.

Her mom is on the sofa, feet propped up, car keys in her lap. The laughter comes from the video of Small Giddy and Jax playing with the dominoes and Superdoo. Giddy left the video on a loop and her mom is watching it on her phone.

Her mom glances over at her and gives her a small smile as Giddy comes down the last few steps and heads into the kitchen. "Hey."

"Hey." Giddy returns the smile with a degree of uncertainty. "You're still here?"

"I'm almost out the door." Her voice sounds oddly flat. "These are nice, honey. Thank you."

Giddy shrugs. She opens the brined cucumbers, winces at the smell, and pours them into a small Tupperware for lunch, packing it along with some cold oxtail soup. Giddy pours herself a small bowl and sits and sips, fingers drumming on the kitchen island, restless and eager to leave but at war with her stomach's urge to take breakfast slowly.

"Jax looks so tiny." Her mother shakes her head. "I get so worried about him. I keep thinking he's going to end up like his father."

Giddy doesn't know what her mom means because, so far as she can tell, her dad is perfectly happy. But her mom goes on: "Do you know the original plan was for both of us to become nurses? Two nurse salaries would have been nice. I already had my degree. He was going to get his. That was the plan: get married and then he'd work days and take college night classes." Her mom lets her head drop back against the couch, then turns a little to look at Giddy again. "So that first week after the honeymoon, your dad comes home from night class with books to read and homework. And he sits in this old recliner we used to own, kicks back, sets everything in his lap, and turns on the television. And he's laughing and watching late-night shows and I say: 'Can you really concentrate with the TV on?' And he grabs the remote and lowers the volume a little and says: 'No worries. I concentrate better with noise.' He opens a textbook and reads, then he watches more TV. Then he reads less, watches TV more. Turns the volume back up. By the end of the night, we're turning in and I check on the papers he had to finish and he barely did a line or two, and I think, *Maybe it's just tonight.*" She shakes her head again. "But it wasn't. He did this all week. Then the books started never making it out of the car. Then he wasn't going to all his classes. That's when I realized what I'd married."

The word *what* suspends, weighty and troubling, and Giddy's stomach starts to burn, so she digs into her purse and pops an antacid.

Meanwhile, her mom gets up, keys in one hand, phone in the other. "He was never going to get his degree. He was always going to lean on me financially. And I'd fallen for it." She chuckles as she takes her jacket off the rack by the door. "Don't get me wrong. He's a sweet man, Giddy, but that's *all* your dad is. He's not motivated like you and I are. He's definitely not someone who keeps his promises, not the important ones. And Jax is so much like him, I worry."

Giddy tosses the spoon into the sink and puts the bowl to her lips, draining the rest in an instant. Her mom says: "Giddy?"

Giddy turns. Her mom's eyes are serious. "This thing you're doing, this 'life experiment,' you called it. Whatever it is, please get it done soon." She pockets the phone as she goes out. Small Giddy's laugh dies at the closing of the door.

And Giddy thinks, *My dad is smart! He's fucking read* Ulysses*!* And as soon as her mom's car pulls out of the driveway, Giddy grabs her own jacket and earbuds and heads outside to walk to school. It rained and then froze overnight: the grass pops under her feet like glass and the hedges are sharp as razors. She cues up Handel's *Semele* and her fast feet stomp down the sidewalk in tune to a woman's angry shout-singing of an aria called "No, No, I'll Take No Less."

She texts as she walks. *Hey, Dad! Reading Ulysses. Have questions. Didn't you say this was a modern-day novel? Because so far, it's all happening in the 1900s.* Her breath puffs out in little short blasts of steam. She keeps checking her phone as she walks. No response from her dad. But that makes sense because he's probably busy on a shift. He'll text back when he sees it.

Sheets of ice coat the sidewalk and Giddy stomps on them hard, little ice veins cracking. She keeps walking. She keeps checking her phone. The minutes tick by.

Still no answer from her dad. *Do something unexpected each day.* Like what? What the hell unexpected thing can she possibly do today? She tried smiling yesterday and that wound up sucking. Her index card notes in English and world history didn't work, either.

The second the school doors open, she bolts into art class. Her teacher brightly says: "Giddy! Ready to take an exhilarating race around the art world?"

She slams her belongings on her table and collapses into her chair, head hooded, arms folded.

Her teacher stares. "Maybe just a tepid stroll, then?"

She can tell it's supposed to be funny. Giddy glares from under her hood and he says, "OK, then," and goes back to assembling his slides.

In the darkened room, they watch and evaluate work from famous artists. *In one sentence, describe your reaction—be brutally honest!* At the table next to Giddy, Otter Girl writes in languid, looping cursive, eyes trained on the screen, pausing between thoughts. Giddy dashes off her responses the second the slides change: Picasso, *a third-grader grabbed some crayons*; Degas, *ballet boredom*; Monet, *who rained on all the paint*; Dalí *taking the same stuff Picasso's on but fever-tripping.* She keeps checking her phone, but her dad still hasn't texted. When Giddy gets up to turn in her critiques, she watches her teacher read hers and sees his eyebrows rise a couple of times. He shares answers at the end of class, but none from Giddy, and when the bell rings, Giddy zips out the door and heads toward English.

On the way to class, her phone buzzes, and Giddy excitedly pulls it out of her pocket, but it's just Trinity. *Should I get this or not? Vote yes/no!* It's not even a text for her. It's a group text. Giddy's not sure she's even still friends with Trinity, thinks that maybe Trinity forgot to take her name off the group, and her fingers hover, uncertain how to respond. The item in question is a steampunk-style hooded cloak. Giddy thinks, *Yes? No? Why isn't there a* don't care *option?* As Giddy's contemplating, the phone buzzes again:

Vote yes/no now pleazzz!

Need help can't decide. 😟

Help help help? Vote now!!

There follows a ton of heart-for-eyes kitten stickers all sent as separate texts from other people and then re-sent by accident to Giddy. Disgusted, Giddy thrusts the phone into her pocket and crosses the threshold into class.

The writing prompt says: *Does Hamlet remind you of anyone you know? Discussion to follow.*

Giddy's phone buzzes again. Then it begins to loudly chime because somebody in the group text is sending a video. The entire class snickers and the teacher shoots Giddy a quick stern look.

Giddy silences her phone. The girl who compared her to Jane yesterday leans over and whispers: "You should think about just powering it down."

"Oh wow," Giddy whispers back, wide-eyed. "Powering a phone down. I never even considered it. Should I follow you for more hot tips?"

The girl's eyes narrow. "You know, you can be a real Ophelia sometimes."

"And you're Polonius *all* the time," Giddy shoots back.

"Touché," whispers the boy on Giddy's other side, and they both shoot a glare at him. He snickers and shrugs at them.

Giddy returns to her work. *No, I can't think of anybody as indecisive as—* Pauses. Flips her pencil over, erases it, and writes: *He's like my friend Trinity.* Then Giddy erases the word *friend* because she's not sure that's what Trinity is anymore. She writes: *He's like this girl I know. Like Hamlet, she keeps deciding instead of doing.* Her teacher will like that since she's already dubbed Hamlet "the Great Decider." The teacher hands out Chromebooks and Giddy makes a pretty easy ninety on a *Hamlet* quiz. There's a chance to bump the grade back up to one hundred with the open-ended extra credit question. But instead of a class discussion, the lights go down for a video. Giddy thinks she's gotten away without having to say anything until the last ten minutes of class when, while watching Benedict Cumberbatch sound off about mortality in a graveyard, her teacher makes eye contact with Giddy and beckons.

Inwardly, Giddy groans. She goes behind her teacher's desk and sits in the offered chair opposite her. The teacher says: "You didn't try the extra credit. Why not?"

Giddy shrugs.

Her teacher says: "*Hamlet* not your cup of tea?"

"I don't understand why people say this is Shakespeare's best play."

"They all don't. A lot of people despise *Hamlet*."

Then why make us read it?

Her teacher goes on: "I'm just going to ask you the extra credit question because, given everything you said yesterday, I'm curious about your response. Why do you think I wanted this class to read *Hamlet* and *The Yellow Wallpaper* at the same time?" She adds: "You should know that in my last class, nobody was able to give me an answer that I felt showed a great deal of thought."

Giddy sees the thrown gauntlet for what it is, but she's too competitive to ignore a challenge. She frowns, puzzles through it, and says: "Their families just—" And then she pauses. Why did their families come to mind? She says: "Everyone in Hamlet's family wants him, *needs* him, to do something for them." She thinks about it a little more and adds, "And his problem is, he won't. But everyone in Jane's family wants her to do nothing all the time, and her problem is she wants to do things." Giddy frowns harder. "She wants to do a lot of things. She wants to do *all kinds* of things. I guess the way they're the same is that Jane and Hamlet both go crazy from all the pressure."

Her teacher's eyebrows rise, but for a second she doesn't say anything. She just stares at Giddy.

Giddy, feeling superior, says: "I'm right, aren't I?"

"I think you might be," the teacher says. "I think that makes sense."

And Giddy feels . . . proud? Conflicted? Because now she can see a little smile at the corners of her teacher's mouth and she thinks, *I'm not the first to get this right! You just wanted me to think about it!* Giddy feels a new surge of anger, but it isn't directed at her teacher. It's kind of directed at Hamlet's and Jane's families. Suddenly she thinks she could write a whole paper on the subject! Like how everybody wants Hamlet to be something he's not and everybody wants Jane to be something *she's* not, and maybe if everybody had just shut up and minded their own business for ten minutes, Hamlet and Jane would have come through everything OK. But nobody let them do that! Why wouldn't anyone let them do that?

She checks her phone. Still nothing from her dad. She shoves it back into her pocket.

In algebra II, she's still seething, still thinking about Hamlet and Jane. The teacher gives them free seating and says they can work at their own pace, so instead of practicing graphs, Giddy tucks herself into a corner desk and reads *Ulysses* behind her math textbook, getting to a part where a guy named Stephen is getting all depressed thinking about the relationship with his dad.

Her stomach suddenly burns. Giddy gets some antacids out of her purse and texts her dad a second time in case he missed the first one: *Reading Ulysses. Isn't this supposed to be modern-day?* Her eyes flit over to Katlyn's copy, under her desk. She can see a bright bookmark in it. Giddy wants to make sure she is ahead of her before she attends book club today.

Katlyn doesn't look back at Giddy. She keeps her eyes on her work. Giddy keeps looking at her. She doesn't want to make up with Katlyn, but she also doesn't want Katlyn to be so angry with her that she kicks her out of book club. Katlyn's injured giraffe pencil sharpener sits atop her desk, Scotch tape wound around it from top to bottom like a Band-Aid. Its beady eyes judge Giddy.

When the bell rings for chemistry, Giddy drags her heels, filing in almost at the tardy bell, phone out, checking the screen. Trinity and Jess look up as she enters and start furiously texting, ridiculous smirks at the corners of their mouths. Giddy's phone buzzes. *Vote! Help me decide!* And then, from Jess, a group picture of Jess, Trinity, Asia, and *Zach* of all people, like he's part of them now! And it's weird! And it makes her uncomfortable! The quiz is on redox reactions, but it's not as simple as balancing equations and Giddy doesn't know how to use oxidation numbers. There are just too many unknowns, too many variables, and Giddy closes her composition notebook in frustration, turning in a quiz filled with guesswork because that's what you get when you don't pay attention for a week in chemistry!

Even though at times you may not like who you become.

Giddy thinks, *I've become a fucking moron!*

When the bell rings, she hurries to lunch, and Ashlynn asks: "No chicken feet today?"

"You missed out," Trey says. "They really are good." He winks at Giddy. "Giddy's going to teach us all how to make them."

Ashlynn shudders. Monica and Trey smirk and Giddy pauses, fingers on the Tupperware lid, thinking, *Is this the part where we all tear into Ashlynn?* She's been waiting for this. For days she's had difficulty determining who's at the bottom of the social scale here. She's a little afraid it might be her, so she warily says: "Yeah, total chicken foot Bake-Off at the Barber house this weekend."

Trey and Monica snicker, but so does Ashlynn. Ashlynn holds up her hand. "OK. Fine. You guys do you. I'll stick to pizza." They all resume eating.

That's it? Ashlynn doesn't even look embarrassed, *like it doesn't really matter that she doesn't like the food they like.*

"But this weekend," Ashlynn says, "I'm doing your hair."

"No," Monica says.

"Oh, come on! I know you do you, but it's so blond, girl. And it's *flat*. I could just do a little purple in it. Your hair would take color."

"Trey," Monica says, putting down her fork and wiping her mouth with a napkin, "will you please tell Ashlynn I'm not interested?"

"No," Trey says, "because you have a voice and I shouldn't try to take that from you."

Monica rolls her eyes. "Ashlynn, you should do Trey's hair."

Ashlynn lights up. "I could put some green in right"—she reaches up and drags a finger across his forehead—"through here."

"Monica," Trey says, "would you tell Ashlynn that I don't need color in my hair?"

"No, I think green would look good," Monica says.

"OK, so what are we trying today?" Trey says, changing the subject right as Giddy pops open her Tupperware.

"Oxtail soup with a side of brined cucumbers." Giddy tries the cucumbers for the first time. They're soft and vinegary but kind of sweet too. "This is like pickle relish," she tells them, letting them put a fork in for a taste.

"They should chop this up and put it on fries," Monica says.

"I've tried oxtail soup before and it is really good," Ashlynn says. Though today Trey is the squeamish one who passes on the soup, and lunch ends with Monica and Ashlynn making plans to collaborate on an English assignment, and Giddy again forgets to take her earbuds out. She lingers, checking her phone, but her dad hasn't responded. And because she hung back, she notices something she's never noticed before.

Trinity, Jess, and Asia always bolt out of the cafeteria at the bell, heads down, eyes on their phones. But it takes Ashlynn, Trey, and Monica a few minutes to leave. For one thing, Trey goes over to another table and squeezes in to sit next to a girl Giddy can only guess must be Sheryl, because they kiss each other before leaving. And Ashlynn and Monica keep stopping at other tables on the way out, leaning down to hug someone or running over when someone says hi. Ashlynn and Monica always smile back. They never ignore anybody. Giddy can't remember anyone ever trying to flag down Asia, Trinity, or Jess for a hug or a kiss.

During robotics, Giddy finishes her course design and turns it in along with a revised supply list. She watches as her teacher takes a long time looking over the design and supply list. Her teacher finally says: "I see you've swapped out lighter fluid for canned heat?" She looks at Giddy over the paper. "Too explosive?"

Giddy can't tell if she's making a joke. "Just not as efficient. You have to keep using it."

"Canned heat *is* smarter." Her teacher runs a finger down the list: "Copper sheets, marshmallow treats, butter, and"—she looks up at Giddy again—"gunpowder and smoke bombs."

"Just order a variety pack of fireworks," Giddy says.

Her teacher folds the list in half. "OK."

Giddy frowns. "OK?"

"You've submitted a very interesting, very *entertaining* course that fits the size, challenge requirements, and timing perimeters of the assignment. It's"—her teacher searches for the right word—"filled with unusual choices, Giddy, I'll give you that. But well thought out. Really well done!" Her teacher smiles.

Giddy blinks in confusion. She goes back to her seat and takes out her phone to see that Jess has texted her another picture of Zach and Asia. In this picture, they're both sitting on the ground and Asia's leaning back into Zach, who has his arms around her from behind and his chin on her shoulder, and they're both staring into the camera like some nauseating Instagram couple. Giddy thrusts the phone back into her pocket. *I should have kissed ANYONE other than Zach!*

And then Giddy's eyebrows shoot up. *I should kiss a girl.* Because why not? Maybe that would get Trinity, Asia, and Jess to stop sending stupid Zach pics.

Giddy sinks back in her seat, the genius of the idea giving way to practical application. While Giddy always knew Zach probably wanted to kiss her, she doesn't know any girls who might. She barely knows any girls who like girls. She's still mulling it over when the bell rings.

In world history, the writing prompt reads: *There is no divine plan. We choose war or peace and the results are ours to own.* But Giddy feels like she was already punished enough in this class for trying yesterday, so she stuffs a copy of the prompt into her binder and decides she'll complete it for homework. During class discussion, she folds her arms across her chest, pops her hood up, and acts like she's not half asleep.

Bella is telling the teacher: "I think the writing prompt means that we're the ones who have to own our choices. We can't just say somebody else made us do something."

"OK." The teacher points to another student. "Mr. Camacho, what do you—"

Hunter raises his hand and calls out: "I want to talk about *The Guns of August*."

Snickering all around. Giddy pulls her hood tighter around her head and shrinks down in her seat.

"We're not on that right now, Mr. Blancovich."

"But, like, I'm worried, because what if our entire school decides to wear red pants? How could we call ourselves war-ready?"

"Worry about the five assignments you still haven't turned in to me," her teacher snaps to Hunter. "We're discussing whether you can justify war by saying a country is fulfilling a divine destiny!" He turns to another student. "Mr. Portillo. Can you justify a war by saying it's divine destiny?"

Javier sleepily looks up and around. "Umm, yes?" he asks.

Their teacher rolls his eyes but asks a follow-up. "OK. Fine. Defend that."

"Defend what?"

"Defend the answer you just gave—good God, guys! At this rate, you're never going to make it through to Friday! Somebody else." He points around. Hunter raises his hand. "Somebody other than you, Mr. Blancovich."

"I want to know why Germany attacked France from all sides under the Schlieffen Plan," Hunter says.

Giddy frowns, because the Schlieffen Plan specifically *didn't* propose that Germany attack France from all sides. She whips her head around and looks at Hunter. He has a library copy of *The Guns of August* open across his desk with a page folded crudely over for a bookmark. He's grinning.

Giddy turns back around. Her teacher has the same pale expression he had on his face yesterday. "Germany did a lot of things they later regretted, Mr. Blancovich."

"Yeah, but wanting to attack from all sides under"—he checks the page again—"the Schlieffen Plan? Seems kind of ballsy."

Their teacher shrugs. "They had big ideas." He turns pointedly to the other half of the classroom. "OK, who can make an argument for war *not* being part of a divine plan? Ms. Churton!" Another student flinches, but Giddy's eyes widen and she shoots a look back at Hunter. He's beaming. He props the book up and looks over the top, but Giddy turns away before he can notice her.

"Who thinks divine plans guide wars? A show of hands." He rolls his eyes when a bunch of hands lazily go up. "Who thinks they don't?" The teacher glares around the room and finally his gaze falls on Giddy. "Really, Ms. Barber? Nothing today? Not even a hand raise?"

"I'm tired."

He makes a pout. "Oh? Too exhausted to raise your hand? Come on!"

General snickering. Giddy fumes.

When the bell rings, she bolts out. She's throwing herself into the throng of students when Hunter yells: "Giddy!"

Giddy thinks there might not be a divine plan, but Hunter's about to suffer some divine wrath. She fights against the exiting mob to get back to him. He's standing near the door to world history class. His eyes widen as Giddy bears down.

"What?" Giddy yells it into his face as Hunter takes a startled step back. "What do you want, Hunter? You want some red pants?" She keeps advancing. He keeps backing up. The edges of his mouth are turned up in shock and that only urges Giddy on. "You want to make fun of my face again? You want me to move my big fat head?" He runs out of room, backing into the wall. It feels good to yell! It feels amazing! How would it feel to throw a punch? Giddy jabs at his chest as she says: "I'm not . . . in the mood . . . for your brand of suck today!"

Hunter lifts up his arm and Giddy sees her backpack dangling. "You left your bag on your chair."

Giddy rips it away from him and pivots, throwing herself back in the crowd. She's almost outside when she happens to see the book club poster on the wall, and mutters, "Shit!" She does an about-face and runs for the library. It's ammo for Katlyn if she's late, and Giddy can just imagine her smug face.

But there's an ominous quiet at the back of the library. Someone set out cupcakes at all ten table seats, lined up on cute little paper plates with blue napkins. Only, almost every seat is empty. There's just Katlyn and a girl named Gwen who Giddy remembers Trinity talking smack about once. And there's the girl who had the old torn-up library copy of *Ulysses* last time. She introduced herself as Maddie. And now that Giddy thinks about it, she's seen Gwen and Maddie together in the hall enough times to know they're dating.

The three girls look up at Giddy from their mostly empty table. Gwen looks wryly amused, Maddie tired, and Katlyn . . .

Katlyn's fingers pluck at the edge of her own blue napkin and cupcake plate. She shoots an anxious glance at the library door. Giddy frowns and checks the time. "Am I early?"

Gwen chuckles. Katlyn's face turns an uncomfortable shade of pink. Maddie stands her book up and uses it for a lazy chin rest. Gwen says: "No, I have a feeling this is it."

Giddy sits and regards the cupcake.

"They're dark chocolate," Katlyn says helpfully. "I thought it would be cute because *Ulysses* gets kind of dark at times, and the frosting is blue like the ocean from *The Odyssey*, which *Ulysses* is supposed to parallel."

Gwen takes a bite of hers. "What's this little thing on top?"

"A boat. I made it out of marzipan." Katlyn looks around at the mostly empty table. "Not that I suppose it matters."

The cupcake is also gorgeously piped, because why wouldn't Katlyn have a professional piping kit? Giddy is still staring at it when Gwen says, "So I only made it to the second, I guess you'd call it a chapter? I made it to the introduction of Leopold Bloom."

"Ugh!" Maddie says, her chin wobbling against her book as she talks. "When that man starts thinking about eating bloody kidneys, I said, 'That's it. I'm done. I can't have this in my life right now.'"

Katlyn has her hands clasped, back straight, in a position Giddy recognizes as one she takes when facing a challenging problem in algebra II. Giddy remembers the embattled giraffe sharpener and suddenly feels a little sorry for her.

Giddy says: "I don't think the book is *that* bad."

"Seriously?" Gwen looks at Giddy over the top of her reading glasses. "What book are *you* reading?"

Giddy shows them her bookmark, two-thirds of the way in.

Gwen's eyebrows lift. "You win."

"Did you use one of those companion guides to get that far?" Maddie asks, and Giddy shakes her head.

"Maybe we're having trouble relating because the book is old." Katlyn's fingers tap the book. "I mean, we're reading something that's supposedly happening in 1904. I don't even know that much about 1904."

"How far are you in?" Gwen asks, and Katlyn holds up her copy. "I guess about a chapter and a half. Not as far as Giddy." When she says *Not as far as Giddy*, she says it fast and quiet.

Giddy asks: "When does the book change time periods?"

Gwen frowns. "I don't think it does."

"*Ulysses* takes place entirely on the day of June 16, 1904," Katlyn says. She holds up her companion guide. "It says so on the first page."

"But my dad has read the whole thing," Giddy says, "and he said it's about modern-day Ireland."

"Maybe the book changes halfway through?" Maddie is idly flipping pages, but Katlyn shakes her head.

"Look! One day in 1904. It's right here in the companion guide."

"Maybe your companion guide is wrong," Giddy says. This is starting to seriously piss her off.

"Or your dad is wrong," Katlyn says back, a little hotly. "Maybe it's not *Ulysses* that he read. Maybe he's confusing it with some other book."

Giddy's mind travels back in an instant. Her dad a year ago when he used an app to get them to a family reunion: *Joyce would have had a field day with the concept of cell phones in* Ulysses. Jax's eighteenth birthday: *So you going to pick up* Ulysses *yet? They'll probably want you to read it in college.* Griping about an administrator after attending a holiday party: *Lloyd's going on and on about how well read he is, but when I asked him what he thought of* Ulysses, *he hadn't heard of it!* But never anything about what's actually in the book. Her dad, who can walk them through every second of every James Bond movie, has never said anything to her about *Ulysses* other than it takes place in modern-day Ireland and deals with conflicts there.

Gwen says: "Giddy?" Giddy looks up. They're all staring at her. They look wary.

Giddy says to Katlyn: "Your companion guide is *wrong*."

A heartbeat of silence elapses. Then Gwen pushes her chair out. "Well, this has been a minute, but I have a thing."

"I forgot that I have something too." Maddie stands to leave with her.

It's just Giddy and Katlyn glaring at each other across the table. As Maddie and Gwen head for the door, Giddy flips her cupcake upside down and presses it until it splats all over the plate. Katlyn gasps. Giddy scowls. She grabs her stuff and runs out into the hall in time to see Maddie and Gwen give each other a quick hand squeeze and a kiss before splitting off in different directions.

Giddy says: "Gwen, can I talk to you?"

Gwen pivots and waits for Giddy to catch up. Giddy says: "You're dating Maddie."

"Yeah. So?"

"So I was wondering . . ." Giddy hadn't planned exactly what she was going to say, and now that she's here, she wonders if she should just speed through it. "You know about my list and how I'm doing the opposite of things I would normally do. I have on my list that I should kiss a girl."

Gwen makes a hard frown. Giddy can tell she's lost points, but she forges on: "I was wondering if you knew anybody."

"A girl who you can kiss?"

"Yes."

"To experiment with their feelings."

"No, not with *their* feelings." Giddy frowns. "Mine."

Gwen looks at her like she really has said the stupidest thing ever.

"I'm not looking for a relationship with anyone," Giddy says, trying to clarify.

"Yeah, I get that." Gwen looks at her for a long moment. "No," she says, "I'm afraid I don't know anybody." Gwen turns, walks a few paces, and then pivots. "Is this really how you're going to go about this? Just ask lesbian after lesbian until you find somebody?"

Giddy shrugs. "How would you do it?"

"I wouldn't," Gwen says, speaking in a tone Giddy sometimes uses when she's trying to explain something painfully simple to Tigs, "because I wouldn't want anyone to feel like they were reduced to an experiment."

Giddy doesn't have anything to say to that and Gwen doesn't seem to expect her to, because she turns around and keeps walking, leaving Giddy disappointed and, more importantly, without a solid plan. Giddy takes out her phone and texts her dad again: *Does Ulysses really take place in the modern day or does it all happen in 1904???*

Giddy stalks to the park, earbuds in, a woman screaming Mozart's *D'Oreste d'Ajace* into her head. She kicks back under a tree to read more *Ulysses*. She's not sure how long she stays like this. She only knows that Leopold's about to get into a bar fight with some guy the book calls "the citizen" when a car door slams and someone yells: "Giddy!"

Giddy has that fuzzy feeling she sometimes gets when she's been reading too long. So it takes her a second to readjust to reality as Jax stalks toward her, his car a short distance up the hill. "What are you doing in the park?" she asks him.

"What are *you* doing in the park?" He's mad, like turn-red-in-the-face mad, and Giddy gets a weird flashback to the two of them looking for Dougal that night. Jax thumps his hands aggressively over and over again against the steering wheel. "Where have you been?"

"I stayed late at school for book club." Giddy slips *Ulysses* into her backpack. Jax gapes, like her admission is equivalent to huffing paint. "Why? What's wrong?"

"Tad overloaded the washing machine and he flooded the living room."

A spasm starts at the base of Giddy's throat and her mouth pops open and her shoulders shake. It wants to be a laugh, but like the time Tad stank, it doesn't quite make it. Jax doesn't seem to notice the difference.

"It's not funny, Giddy! There's soapy water all over the place. I had to throw down towels."

"Oh, towels?" Giddy nods. Somehow she can't wrap her mind around the idea of Jax racing around the living room, fighting a tide of suds. "That's smart."

Jax throws up his hands. "No one was watching him! He and Tigs were all alone at home by themselves."

"Tad needs to learn not to do that." Giddy stands up and slings her backpack over her arm.

"No, Giddy, you need *to be home.*" Jax chops his hand into his palm three times, and this sparks something in Giddy that makes her angry again. She remembers Dougal laughing when Jax caught him where he wasn't supposed to be, and she thinks it's because Jax's face does look a little funny when he's mad, but mostly she's hung up on the words *be home.* Her feet move so fast that she reaches the car before Jax and has to wait for him to unlock it.

As she slides into the passenger seat, Giddy demands: "Where were *you*?"

"College." Jax starts the car. "And I only came home to grab dinner and run back out because I have a study group tonight, which I am now late for because I had to track you down."

"Well, I was busy!"

"Well, I was *busier*!" Jax guns the motor a little hard as he takes a turn.

"Why do I have to fix everything?" Giddy yells.

"Because when Mom and Dad aren't around, you're the adult in the house!"

"What about Dougal?"

Jax rolls his eyes. He's thumping that stupid wheel again. One thump. Two thumps.

Giddy suddenly pelts her fists against the glove box and it makes a rattling noise like something dying and flailing around in a cage. "There's no reason it always has to be me!" Giddy gives the glove box one final *thwack!* for good measure, then throws her arms across her chest and leans into the seat, seething.

For a few seconds, neither of them says anything. There's just the sound of the road. Jax has stopped thumping the wheel. He looks troubled and maybe shocked, like he never expected anything like this out of her.

He says: "Just suck it up for a couple of years and you'll be out too."

Giddy glares out the window. Jax leans on the horn when he can't get around a car. For some reason, Giddy finds herself retracing the entire conversation Leopold had that leads up to the bar argument with the citizen in *Ulysses*. She's not sure there's anything Leopold could have done to prevent it.

When they pull up the drive, Giddy unbuckles her seat belt and hops out just before Jax puts the car in park. She expects him to come running in behind her, but all he does is back his car out of the drive and take off, and Giddy thinks that is so typical of him, to just not be around when all the drama hits. She twists the key violently and kicks open the door.

The edge of the big rug in the den has been turned up and there's a lot of towels down on the floor at the entrance to the laundry room. Water has trickled out around the edge of the fireplace. Giddy thinks it's hardly the disaster Jax painted it to be. Bodie's licking jam off the lower kitchen cabinets where either Tad or Tigs must have spilled some while making sandwiches. He runs his wet pink tongue all up and down the line of it, one self-conscious brown eye trained on Giddy, waiting for rebuke. Giddy leaves him to it. The upstairs is an utter death tone of silence, meaning Dougal's not here and Tad and Tigs have retreated like mice in holes after probably being screamed at by Jax. Giddy thinks the towels by the fireplace need to go into the washing machine before the house starts to smell musty.

But she marches up the stairs instead, held by the higher calling of Superdoo and the list. So it's something of a shock to her when she flops onto her bed and rolls on her side to look at the list only to find that Superdoo isn't sitting on the edge of the desk where she left him.

Giddy leans down to check under the bed. Then she checks behind the desk and now, mildly alarmed, throws back the covers of her bed to see if she accidentally left him in the sheets.

But he's nowhere to be found. Giddy turns in a slow circle in her room, two thoughts at war. One is that she doesn't need Superdoo to complete a list. Superdoo is just an action figure and a piss-poor one at that. But the second thought, that Superdoo *is* needed, that he *is* more, drives her out into the hall.

Giddy throws open the door to Tad and Tigs's room. The room is a mess with toys and clothes everywhere, and Tad sits in a little hollow space he made on the floor by pushing everything to either side. His backpack has been emptied out next to him, presumably because Jax told him to go to his room and do his schoolwork, but Tad's school papers are just a mess of crumpled sheets and paper wads. Tad is smoothing out one crumpled paper on his knee. It has a stain on the corner that looks like jam. Giddy notices all of this, and the part of her brain that records and fixes automatically sets up a timetable of repair.

She says coldly: "Where's Tigs?"

"Bathroom." Tad keeps smoothing the paper out. It doesn't matter—the pencil he's holding has a broken tip and the eraser is chewed off, so what exactly does he think he's going to accomplish?

Then her eyes home in on the pile of toys immediately to Tad's right. She leans down and plucks Superdoo out of the mouth of a mechanized T. rex. Some of the jam that's on Tad's paper is also on Superdoo's cape and as Giddy pulls her sticky fingers away, horrified, Tad placidly explains: "I was using him for bait."

"You went into my room," Giddy says, shocked, "and you took him."

"He's mine." Tad goes back to smoothing the paper on his knee. It makes a slow *crumple, crumple*. Giddy's mind races. Superdoo's cape was never made of stellar material and Giddy can tell the jam has sunk in all the way through. She can wash it, but the stain isn't coming out. This is just another scar, the mark of a toy passed around and around until it expires.

Giddy shoves Superdoo into her pocket. Then she reaches down, grabs Tad's paper before he can make it crumple again, and throws it behind her. He yells, "Hey!" and she grabs the pencil out of his hand and throws that to the side as well. Then she crouches down so she can get as close to his face as possible without any other part of her touching this messed-up room. "You're always fucking taking my things, Tad! You and Tigs took my dollhouse when I was nine and in only five days you'd drawn all over it with crayons! You took my cars and my racetrack when I was thirteen, and when you and Tigs couldn't connect the little ends of the tracks, you stomped on them and you broke them!" Giddy doesn't even realize she's yelling until she sees how wide Tad's eyes are. He scoots back, pushing up against the bed, and all the clothes and papers and toys he has to push through just to escape Giddy knock and clatter—relics of things once shiny and new and wrapped in bright paper beside cakes or under trees. Things once tagged and gifted under the pretense of ownership but merely rented, destined to disappear without warning, a hidden clock ticking on who gets to love them next. "That's what you do! You take everything so I don't get to keep or have anything. You have systematically sucked all I love away—it just winds up in this pigsty!" She's on her hands and knees, leaning into Tad's face, as if proximity is going to make him listen. His eyes fill with tears, but like a shark smelling blood in the water, that somehow only sends Giddy into a frenzy. "You take and break all my things, Tad, so I don't get to keep anything. That's what you do. That's what you're good at!"

Tad puts his little hands up like he wants to push Giddy back from him but is afraid to. He says: "But Mom gave—"

"I don't fucking care! They were mine and I loved them and you took them and broke them, and if you cared about me, you wouldn't do that to me, Tad! You'd let me keep my things."

Giddy's voice is breaking. She grabs Superdoo out of her pocket and shakes him in Tad's face. But he's turned his head and closed his eyes in denial. "Don't you ever touch this toy again, do you hear? You got jam on him, and now I have to clean him. Don't you go into my room and don't you *touch him*!"

Tad frantically nods, eyes shut, and Giddy stands, looking him over. An icy chill breaks out on her scalp and rushes over her body, expelling through her fingers and toes, fallout, maybe, from the loss of adrenaline. Tad's knees are drawn to his chest and he's quaking and Giddy has never, ever in her life talked to Tad like that before.

The bedroom door creaks and Giddy turns. Tigs stands white-faced, wide wary eyes trained on Giddy. With exaggerated, comedic slowness she tiptoes over the messy floor to get to her bed. Then she hops up, crawls under the covers, and pulls the sheets slowly over her head until she is completely covered. As Giddy stares, Tigs draws the sheets back down to just below her mouth.

She says: "I'm pretending you're this big scary monster, Giddy."

Giddy backs out of the room, clutching Superdoo. She slowly closes the door and goes into her own room and sits on the bed. After a few seconds she puts Superdoo back in his spot on the desk, taking care to arrange him so he won't fall. He's still sticky with jam and Giddy was going to take him down the hall to clean him up in the sink, but she feels rooted, like her feet have grown into her carpet. She unzips her backpack and takes out her homework, doing a short write-up for English before moving on to the world history open-ended response question that she was supposed to turn in in class.

There is no divine plan. We choose war or peace and the results are ours to own.

Giddy can hear, just very softly through the walls, her little brother crying. *I should apologize.* But all the words she would use would undo the things she meant to say and the paradox of wanting to repair without undoing roils in her brain, a deadly rock to crash against, a soul-sucking whirlpool to try to avoid.

In the end, she tosses her world history open response in the trash and goes downstairs to eat a dinner of cold oxtail soup by herself, scooping out the fatty sections she doesn't want, flipping them so they splat to the kitchen floor. Bodie races after each, licking with gumption.

Dougal comes in while she's eating. He pauses at the door as if expecting to be yelled at because it's past seven. When Giddy splats another piece of fat to the floor, he frowns and heads up the stairs, looking at her all the way. His door closing is the jolt Giddy needs. She drinks down the rest of her meal and takes a bag of potato chips up to her bedroom, where she remains for the rest of the night.

8

Her phone buzzing on the desk wakes Giddy. She rolls over and checks the clock: 5:47. Her alarm didn't go off. She forgot to set it. Since when does she forget to set alarms? Superdoo is still on her desk, his cape sticking to the side where Tad got jam on it. Giddy remembers. Doesn't want to. Closes her eyes and drifts.

Her phone buzzes again. Giddy reaches a sleepy hand. It's her dad. She bolts upright and scoots into a cross-legged position, scrolling through text responses: *Yes, Ulysses is set in the modern day circa 1960s. You can tell by the dress and the haircuts.* Then: *Are you enjoying it?*

Giddy types fast. *I guess so. One of the girls in my book club said it was set in 1904, but I knew she was batshit. Another girl couldn't get past all the bloody organ talk that happens at the butcher shop. But that stuff is weird anyway, right?*

Giddy gets out of bed and prepares to go take her shower when the phone buzzes again.

Butcher shop?

Giddy frowns. The butcher shop is a pretty memorable scene in *Ulysses*, one that seems to start a trend of Leopold making gross comparisons between things he sees all around him and things he sees in himself. Her dad's text prickles along with the cold of her shower. When she gets back to her room, she texts: *You know! When Leopold goes to buy kidneys. It's close to the beginning of the book. Then he starts thinking about all kinds of gross stuff like bowel movements and things!* Remembering makes Giddy gag a little. It should make her dad gag too, and maybe giggle. Giddy sits on her bed and waits for his response.

Two minutes go by with nothing. Then three minutes. Giddy starts getting dressed, the phone face up on the bed, watching for the screen to light up. But she finishes getting dressed and the screen's still dark. Giddy starts to regret her last text because maybe it was too much to mention the bowel movements. Maybe her dad is spending time trying to find a funny GIF to send back.

She carries her phone out into the hall, but when she sees the door into Tigs and Tad's room, she slips the phone into her pocket and raises a hand to knock.

Then she stops. She was thinking of apologizing for how much she yelled at Tad last night, but part of her adamantly thinks, *For what?* Because Tad really was in the wrong for taking her things and he should own that.

But did she have to get in his face and yell?

Giddy's hand remains at the door, wavering.

Then a new thought occurs—why should she apologize? Her dad apologizes sometimes, but her mom *never* apologizes. Her dad likes to joke (when Mom's not listening) that it's because Giddy's mom is never wrong. And maybe Tad's forgotten the whole thing anyway. Tad's constantly forgetting stuff Giddy tells him—why would this be any different?

So Giddy lowers her fist and goes downstairs, where Dougal is eating a tin of gummy worms she knows darn good and well are Tad's. Dougal chomps on them with this big *whatcha gonna do about it?* grin that Giddy ignores as she eats a light breakfast of toasted waffles, a banana, and orange juice. Her stomach tolerates it. She grabs the bottle of borscht out of the pantry and shoves it into a bag with chips for lunch.

Still no text from her dad. A new aria loads up as she jogs past the bus stop, an icy breeze prying loose her hair from under the hood. In her ears, the woman sings with a voice of low-burning fire, notes flowing in and around themselves in looping infinity. At a red stoplight, Giddy stands and listens to the woman. And when the light turns green, she does not move.

It shakes the earth, this voice, these words, sung in a language Giddy cannot understand. The sky is navy, on the verge of gathering its energy, and around her things sluggishly stir to life and the woman's voice goes in and out of it all, poking at shadows, winking in the light of frozen puddles. It's in the grind of every garage door opening, the flicker of every porch light. It's between the rise of an early-morning jogger's step and the fall of water spinning out behind tires at the curve.

Giddy reads the song title on her phone: "Depuis le jour" from the opera *Louise*. This means nothing to her. She drops her phone into her pocket, and a bunch of grackles take off from a park tree in tandem with the song's surge. Giddy's breath catches as the singer holds a long and tremorous note that somehow lifts Giddy up with it, moving her high to a place unstoppable and untouchable.

And there it begins its descent, falling softer, fading. And now the song is gone.

Giddy yanks her earbuds out, runs off the sidewalk, and leans against a tree. She pulls her hood firmly over her head. She's *crying*. Why?

But she can't stop, so she just stands there, and it's stupid, really ridiculously stupid, to cry over a song when you don't even know the words! Giddy tries to take it apart piece by piece to figure out how it works. Was it the high notes? Was it the particular voice of the singer? Giddy doesn't have the words to describe opera. Up until now she would have just said opera is a mix of different voices and variances in melody. Up until now it hasn't been a *feeling*.

She shakes herself loose and walks in a slow, foggy state to school, phone out. She finds an English translation of "Depuis le jour" and reads words like *charming* and *delightful* and *smiling* before a horn honks at her because she's stopped at an intersection. Giddy pockets her phone and races across.

And keeps running. She goes one block. Then another, slowing her pace at lights but mostly staying in constant motion. Once or twice she slows to a walk, but only when the hammering in her heart gets really strong, and for the most part she's able to quickly catch her breath. She doesn't realize just how much she's running until she sees the school appear at the end of the block and thinks, *Already?*

And she's still thinking of the song. She gets out her phone to read more of its lyrics when an alert goes off, telling her that her name's been mentioned on one of the social media sites Jess started championing a month ago. Jess made accounts for all of them, and the email subject line matches Giddy's anonymous nickname, so she clicks the link. Giddy scrolls to a post where her name has been helpfully and automatically highlighted.

The forum title is *Giddy Barber Opposition List:*

Giddy is this girl who goes to my school. She is soooo depressed! Any normal person would take meds, but not Giddy! Giddy's doing the opposite of normal to feel better—eating gross things at lunch and sitting with weirdos instead of her friends. Would you do that—do everything opposite to feel better? Is Giddy SICK or PSYCHO? Vote NOW! There follows a series of kitten and panda emojis that have all the hallmarks of Trinity's creation. Giddy scrolls through posts, heart racing:

I vote SICK unless she jump off a cliff ha:) then PSYCHO but sick so far!

SICK!!! i should do this next week

Giddy =sick = notbesickanymore:)

I CAN'T BELIEVE ALL THE HATERS! YALL NEED T GET A LIFE AND NOT COME DOWN ON HER SO MUCH VOTE SICK SICK SICK . . .

What the fuck? A couple more posts speculate on whether Giddy's on any medication, followed by a comparison of the meds some of the posters are on, and another post that hedges their vote with *maybe psycho maybe sick dunno?*, which appears to be the post All Caps was responding to. Giddy's fingers shake.

Psycho get meds, girl!

Feel bad see doctor psycho!

Vote psycho becuz i dunno thats how I think feel better Giddy

Giddy's face flushes. She puts the phone away and looks around as if pocketing it can somehow hide the posts from everybody. Her heart is hammering. There were something like sixty posts in total, and how do any of these people even know who she is? She feels exposed, so she pulls her hood up and hurries into the building, and for some reason it's the post that said *feel better Giddy* that's getting to her the most. How dare they assume she needs their support? How dare they assume she hasn't got this? She hurries through packed halls in the direction of art, backpack swinging, dodging to get around groups. Her hood falls back as she cuts around a group of kids, and a girl Giddy has never seen before yells, "Woo, Giddy!" and tries to fist-bump her. Giddy pretends she doesn't hear. She's never been so grateful to duck inside a class in all her life.

Giddy huddles down inside her jacket. There's no starter question on the board in art or engagement activity, so she sits alone at her table. Otter Girl is closed off, playing on her phone, and Giddy feels the intense volume of the space around her, wishes she still had her yellow sombrero outfit to drape around her. Her teacher sits behind his desk, going through yesterday's art evaluations again. He looks at Giddy over the top of the paper.

Giddy fixes him with a cold stare and holds it until he breaks eye contact. Disappointingly, his face stays neutral. When everyone finally makes it in and the bell rings, the teacher calls for volunteers and gets four students to go up to the front of the room, including Otter Girl, who taps Giddy on the shoulder and whispers, "Wish me luck!"

Again Giddy thinks, *We are not friends*, and sinks down into her seat, driven by the weight of the phone in her back pocket and a growing unease as she sneaks glances at other students on their phones, wondering if they are reading about her. Her teacher instructs the students to stand one arm's length apart from each other in a line facing the room, and chuckles when he has to pause to push some paint cans back into a corner for space. Then he steps back and stares at them and the room grows silent as he waits.

After about thirty seconds the volunteers shift on their feet and one of them finally whispers: "Were we supposed to do something?"

Her teacher turns to the room. "Performance art is about using the human body as a medium for expression. If I were going to ask these volunteers to express the emotion of confusion, I'd leave them as they are and make them wait for instructions. They might shift around on their feet"—he mimics them—"they might ask me questions." He points to the one who did. "What would be another pose that demonstrates confusion that I could ask them to make?"

The next minute or so is filled with giggling as students make suggestions and the volunteers try their best to follow along. "How about a different emotion?" the teacher says, scanning the room. "How about the emotion of *rage*?" His eyes settle. "Giddy Barber."

Giddy blinks and sits up as a couple dozen heads pivot to look at her.

"Giddy, why don't you come up here and show us how you would position your classmates to demonstrate the emotion of rage."

Giddy stands. She's never been asked to do anything in front of anyone in art class before. A war wages as she makes her way to the front of the room. Part of her thinks it would be satisfying to prove it's impossible to demonstrate rage with these four volunteers. Another part thinks she should prove how pathetically *easy* it is so that her teacher sees this as a waste of time.

As Giddy reaches the front of the room, her teacher adds: "One small note: you can't tell them to speak or make facial expressions. They have to demonstrate rage to us in some other way."

There went the idea of having them run up to the teacher and scream all at once in his face. Giddy fixes her eyes on the volunteers. Otter Girl grins encouragingly, but the other three just smirk in a way that tells Giddy they don't think she can do this.

Giddy points to the closest volunteer, a boy: "Lean back," she tells him.

He frowns at her but leans back a little, back curving.

Giddy says: "Put your hands over your head."

He's still leaning this way, but now Giddy knows his center of balance is throwing him backward. He's too tough to say anything and Giddy has the satisfaction of watching his smirk vanish.

"You"—she points to Otter Girl—"stand at a right angle to him and do the same thing—lean back, arms up." Otter Girl leans until her fingers almost touch his. Giddy makes the third volunteer, another girl, go on the opposite side and lean back. Now all three have fingers touching. Giddy says: "Walk like that back three steps."

Everyone laughs to see them try to amble back toward the corner without breaking position. Giddy waits until they are just in front of the stacked paint cans before shooting a sideways glance at the teacher.

He has his arms folded and one hand to his chin, watching.

Giddy says to the last volunteer, a boy: "Now go over there and put your hands on top of all their hands."

He has to kind of squeeze between two of them to do it, and then he has to lock his fingers into three other sets of hands. Giddy says: "Press your hands down."

He starts pressing. As the three volunteers try to press back, their legs start to buckle and they do a kind of dance of balance in which they lean one way and then another for about three seconds, the class laughing.

But Giddy knows that when the students topple, they're going to fall straight into the loose-lidded paint cans and get paint all over them. They're going to be so mad, they might start yelling, might start screaming. And Giddy thinks, *Do it!* Because she can blame it on the teacher, and to her horror, Giddy realizes she kind of wants all those kids to get upset, to be hurt—even Otter Girl—who's never done a thing except try to be nice to Giddy.

Giddy opens her mouth to stop it when her teacher says: "Excellent! Volunteers, stand back upright."

There's a quick, clumsy shuffle of kids righting themselves, stumbling, coming *oh so close* to the paint—and then laughing, maybe unaware of their brush with disaster. Giddy lets out a pent-up breath. Her teacher looks at her. "So I imagine the idea was they would fall into the paint cans and then"—he makes a gesture at Giddy like he's throttling air—"rage, right?"

Giddy's breaths speed up. She's aware of every single eye in the room locked on her with laser precision.

"That's a very interesting way of demonstrating anger," her teacher says, and Giddy suddenly gets the feeling that she's Exhibit A in some kind of weird meta version of this performance. As she walks back to her seat, he's moving on, looking for someone to make the volunteers demonstrate comedy and tragedy in a single pose. Giddy sits, smoldering, in a room swiftly filling with laughter.

She gets out her phone and thumbs through more of the posts about her. She considers maybe making an anonymous post about how everyone should get a life and quit examining someone else's, but then she figures they might guess it's her posting it, so Giddy just keeps impotently scrolling through everything right up through the bell.

In English, she holds the phone under her desk. The *sick* total has grown to forty-nine, while the total for *psycho* is holding at twelve with some suggestions of how opposition therapy could be used to get out of everything from tests to relationships and Giddy thinks, *It's not about getting out of stuff!* She suddenly wants to make a post picking them all apart. She wants them to feel small and awful.

The boy next to Giddy raises his hand and says: "I think Hamlet's biggest problem is his family."

The teacher perks up, excited: "Explain!"

"I think he knows what he has to do, but he feels like he's somehow betraying his family to do it. Like his mom. I don't think Hamlet wants to hurt his mom."

Giddy posts anonymously: *Some of you guys are just lazy assholes who r looking for excuses to get out of doing hard things!*

The student's question segues into a class discussion about power struggles within families. Giddy can't imagine any meaningful input she'd have to give, so she just keeps staring at her phone under her desk and stewing.

She doesn't get a response to her post, even though she keeps checking all through algebra II, where Giddy has given up hope of ever graphing asymptotes and lately has taken to making arbitrary curved lines on graph paper just so it appears she's working. Katlyn has her copy of *Ulysses* under her desk, and from the looks of the bright blue bookmark, she's ahead of Giddy. Giddy checks her phone, but her dad still hasn't texted back about the butcher shop. There are, however, several more votes for *sick* on the forum about Giddy.

When the bell rings, Giddy heads to chemistry and lingers in the hall, dreading entry. When she finally heads through the door, she does so fast, hood up, hustling past Trinity and Jess, who call out:

"Hey, Giddy!"

"Have you checked your phone, Giddy?"

"You're trending, Giddy!"

Giddy doesn't answer them. She hurriedly takes her seat. Zach has his phone out under his table. Javier's at his table and they are both looking at Zach's screen. "I voted *psycho* obviously," Zach explains. "I mean, when she came over to my house . . . ," and he lowers his voice to whisper something that makes Javier grin and fist-bump Zach.

Horrified, Giddy flips her hood up and stares straight ahead, willing herself to be small, to be invisible, to be anywhere other than in this room. The teacher announces they can pair up for practice problems. Everyone starts milling around. Giddy waits for someone to sit next to her, but no one does. Giddy looks around the room once. *Everyone* has a partner now. Everyone except Giddy.

"You can get into teams of three if you want," the teacher says, noting Giddy's solo status. But Giddy can see everybody's settled. This is Pre-AP Chemistry. Like in algebra II, every kid in this class cares about their grades. And they aren't interested in Giddy's assistance anymore.

So Giddy fights her way through the practice problems alone. Her phone keeps sounding off. At the end of class, when the papers are collected, the teacher writes a chemical formula on the board. "This is what's known as a rapid oxidation reaction," she tells the class, "but what does that mean?"

Her phone buzzes again, and this time Giddy checks it under the table. It's Jess: *ur famous.* And she's sent another link to the forum about Giddy. Giddy looks around the room, sees a few other phones under tables. A kid Giddy doesn't even know who sits two tables over looks up from his phone and smirks at her.

Giddy shoves her phone back into her pocket, heart beating fast.

"In simple terms," her teacher says, "it means that something is about to be set off."

Another text. This one from Trinity. Another link to the post. Giddy clicks the link. Two more votes for *psycho* over *sick*.

"And when the heat is released—because we are definitely dealing with an exothermic situation—it's going to be sudden. It's going to be fierce."

Giddy shoves her phone into her pocket, but it keeps buzzing. At the back of the class, Trinity and Jess snicker loudly.

"What we have," her teacher says, "is the recipe for an explosion."

The bell rings and Giddy bolts out of her seat, rushing past Trinity and Jess before they can say anything. She runs into the cafeteria and shoves her earbuds in. Giddy is listening to "Queen of the Night" in Mozart's *The Magic Flute*. She unzips her bag and tosses her lunch onto the table.

Then she happens to glance up to see Ashlynn, Trey, and Monica quietly staring. Giddy pops one earbud out and snaps: "Do I have something awful on my face?"

Ashlynn holds up her hand. "Whoa! Whatever."

"We were just wondering if you were OK," Monica says. "Because you don't look OK."

Giddy isn't sure she cares how she looks.

Ashlynn points to Giddy's lunch. "What is it?"

They all stare at the bottle of borscht.

"What do you think it is?" Monica asks. "It's so pink."

"It's made with beets," Giddy says with a shrug, "and it's a dip, I guess?"

They each take turns scooping out the borscht with chips. "Ah!" Ashlynn says. "It's like kimchi. I hate kimchi. I don't do sour foods."

"It *is* a little sour," Trey says.

"I like it," Monica says. And when they all look at her funny, Monica slides her tater tots over to Giddy, and Giddy slides the borscht and chips over, and they both eat, happy in their trade.

"What were you listening to?" Trey asks, and Giddy pushes her phone across the table.

Ashlynn puts an earbud in. "Way too slow for me." Trey takes a listen next. Then Monica, who agrees with Trey.

Giddy gets an idea. "Hang on." She pulls up another aria, and pretty soon Ashlynn and Monica are tapping the table and grinning as Trey stupidly beatboxes to "Ma, Signor" from *The Barber of Seville.*

Giddy watches them, befuddled, the rage that had been boiling up inside slowly simmering back down again, and she thinks, *It's like they're trying to make me feel better.* Which Jess and Trinity would never do.

They stop when the song pauses for a text buzz. Giddy mumbles an apology and picks it up. Monica and Ashlynn are still clapping to Trey's beatboxing as Giddy clicks over to the forum posts and her eyes pop open a little wider. *Sick* is up to 137, *Psycho* 79, including a recent post which reads: *girl so sad so desperate think we all gonna like her now aw poor PSYCHO!* Triple vomit emojis. Giddy recognizes the username as one Jess likes to use on other forums.

Giddy scrolls, slack-jawed. There are other *psycho* vote posts, and a few have stickers that Trinity and Asia like to use. Giddy looks across the cafeteria to where Asia and Zach are sitting with

Jess. Giddy wonders what she's ever done to Jess except not sit with her. And didn't she help her with homework and with labs? It's only been a *week*!

Trey slows his beatbox and Monica quits tapping and says: "You OK, Giddy?"

"I'm fine." Giddy pops her earbuds in to emphasize the point and puts her phone on airplane mode. She cranks up *The Barber of Seville* until it rattles her eardrums. Trey and Monica and Ashlynn look at each other and finally slip into a conversation without Giddy. Giddy knows she's excluding them, but really, lunch is sometimes better this way.

She's still bobbing her head to the aria's stomping rhythm when she leaves lunch, enters the door to robotics, and stops cold.

Giant dry-erase block letters across the board read: *DESIGN WINNER, GIDDY BARBER!!* Her course diagram is on a projected screen covering half the wall. Giddy takes out her earbuds. The entire class stands and applauds.

"Congratulations, Giddy!" Her teacher steps forward to shake her hand. "I have never seen a course design so bold, so *diabolical.*" The class laughs. "I said to myself, 'What has Giddy got against robots?' and then I just knew every student here would be dying to put their bot through this challenge"—she drops her tone dramatically—"just to see if it *survives*!"

More cheers. As Giddy turns an astonished face to the class, her teacher says: "Woodshop started work on the base for the course yesterday. The science department donated copper sheets. I'm picking up the marshmallow treats, butter, the canned heat, the fireworks—what I want every one of you to do is think, *How can I protect my bot from total destruction on this course?*" As Giddy makes it to her seat, she sees Patrice and Deb are working up a kind of raincoat design for their bot and another team is adding grippers to their bot's wheels. Giddy sits mutely. For some reason, this whole day brings to mind one of the melting clock Dalí paintings they had to evaluate in art.

Patrice looks at her and says: "Well, I admit I wanted my design to win, but good job, Giddy," and Giddy thinks, *It's not supposed to be a good job! I was trying to fail at course design!*

"Do you want to help us design protection for our bot?" Deb asks. But Giddy shakes her head. She puts her earbuds in and spends the rest of class pretending to come up with further designs on paper, but all she really does is check her phone.

Sick is up to 148.

The bell rings and Giddy takes off like a rocket for world history, where Hunter has *The Guns of August* splayed open. He lifts it just long enough for her to see the title, then gives her a little grin. Giddy slips into her seat and glares at the blank board as the teacher hands out quizzes and says: "1917. Vimy Ridge." At the groans, he adds: "Oh, come on! It's multiple choice and it's all in your textbook."

A hand goes up. "Which page?"

"Use the table of contents. It's what it's there for." Hunter's hand goes up. "Mr. Blancovich?"

"I was wondering why the Russians were such big failures at trench warfare."

Giddy's eyes widen. The Russians *weren't* failures at trench warfare—quite the opposite. They invented a successful strategy against the Austrians. Hunter has a perfectly innocent look on his face. Their teacher stares at him and doesn't answer. The silence stretches, long enough for every student in the room to quiet down, to know that something's up.

Then her teacher says: "Well, the Russians had a lot of land to cross to head into battle, quite the journey to make, and especially during the cold winter, communication and organization could be troublesome."

Which has *nothing* to do with trench warfare! Giddy shoots another glance at Hunter, but while his friends have started to grin, Hunter's face remains placidly interested.

"So really a lot of struggles on all sides in the war," her teacher adds, "the Russians included." Her teacher points to the other side of the room. "Mr. Cisneros! What major battles were fought after Vimy?"

And Giddy, shocked, thinks, *He's not going to answer Hunter's question!* Giddy snorts. Then she claps her hands over her mouth as the entire class and the teacher whip their heads around to look at her. It wasn't a laugh. But it tried to be! *Did Hunter almost get me to laugh?*

"Something strike you as funny, Ms. Barber?"

No, not since I was six years old! "I—" Giddy looks around the room. "It's just you didn't answer Hunter's question."

"Oh, I didn't?" His voice edges a notch higher in a way that reminds Giddy of how Tigs's voice sounds when someone catches her in a lie. "I'm pretty sure I gave that topic all the attention it's due."

"But there's a problem with the question, because if you read *The Guns of August*—" Giddy decides it would be best to show him the page and starts digging the book out of her backpack.

Her teacher drops his textbook on the corner of his desk. It lands with a head-jolting thump. Giddy sets her backpack down and sits quickly back up. Her teacher points a finger between her and Hunter. "So, he's got you in it too. This is a little game you two have invented: quiz the teacher on *The Guns of August*." When Giddy shakes her head, he says: "No, really, it's adorable. I should put the two of you together and make you study partners."

Oh God, no!

"I would really like that," Hunter says, nodding sagely, "but I'd also enjoy more expert input from you, my esteemed teacher, on Russia's strategies during the war. Maybe I could stay after class?"

"The last thing in the world I'm doing with my Wednesday afternoon is spending more time catering to your whims, Mr. Blancovich, that deliberately draw the focus of this war onto other countries and off America's involvement!"

"It was a *world* war," Giddy mumbles, zipping up her backpack, "not just an *American* one."

Another kid raises his hand. "I agree with Giddy."

"Yeah," says a girl. "Why aren't we learning more about the rest of the world?"

"Did they ever solve that red pants thing?" another boy asks.

The teacher opens the textbook on his desk with a deliberate thud. "You want more world in your history? Turn to page one sixty-seven! All of you! I want essays on Vimy Ridge and the Battle of Arras. Fill a page and a half." Groans, but also several students are pulling out their phones, obviously intending to skip this part of the lesson. One boy Giddy doesn't even know nods in her direction and types something into his phone. From where she's sitting, she can see he's on the same social media site Giddy had opened earlier.

Giddy checks the *sick/psycho* thread. *Sick* is up to 153 votes.

The boy gives her a quick smile and a thumbs-up and turns to his textbook.

She shoves her phone back into her pocket and starts writing her essay, pen pressing down so hard that it makes tiny grooves in the paper. Her essay's good and long and contains an addendum comparing Canadian and British tactics to Russian strategies. When she turns it in, she says loudly: "There! A full page and a half on Vimy Ridge and the Battle of Arras."

The teacher blinks up from his desk at her. He looks at the clock, baffled. "There're still ten minutes left in class."

"It's long enough for you to read and grade it," Giddy says, bouncing back to her seat. She ignores Hunter's wide and shocked grin. She watches the teacher awkwardly pick up her paper and read through it. At five to the bell, Giddy is packing, ready to vault out the door. She figures Hunter will joke around with his friends for a second or two before chasing her down to say something stupid, but when she sneaks a glance back, *he's* all packed and ready to go. Their eyes lock. Giddy whips her head back around, eyes narrowing at the door and the ticking second hand of the clock above.

The bell rings. They both jump up to run.

An office aide materializes in the door, blocking them. "I'm looking for a Giddy Barber!"

Hunter and Giddy take a step back as students file out to either side of them. They look at each other for a moment before Giddy says: "I'm Giddy."

"Your parents are here." The student tosses her a pass with disinterest and walks off. Giddy frowns, slings her backpack over her shoulder, and ducks out, hustling down the hall for the central commons area.

Giddy can see her mom and dad through the glass doors of the front office. Dougal's with them. Everybody looks stressed. When she sees Giddy, her mom throws open the glass door, snaps her fingers as she walks out into the hall, and says: "Car, everyone. *Now!*"

Giddy looks to Dougal for answers, but he avoids her eyes as she falls into step with them. They get outside and into the car, her dad driving. Nobody's saying anything. Her dad maintains this laser focus on the road and her mom has her elbow up on the door, rubbing the bridge of her nose like she has a splitting migraine. Dougal stares out the window, and Giddy feels this surge of anger toward him for doing whatever it was he did that put them all in this position.

The car turns onto the road. Her mom breaks the silence. "So the school calls right at the end of my *only* work break to tell me that Dougal didn't show up for the first half of the day on Thursday and Friday of last week, and on Monday he wasn't at school at all. And today he skipped three of his classes. In fact, they had to search the school to find him. And all because he's decided not to take the bus."

"I walked," Dougal says.

"Shut up, Dougal," her dad mutters.

"But that's not the only thing," her mom says, a nervous giggle escaping her, "because why would that be the *only* thing? Today at lunch he got into a fight."

Giddy's eyes widen, and now she knows why Dougal is keeping his head turned away from her. In the reflection of the window, she can see a shiner on his right temple.

"So that's when the school calls us, not to report on him, but to say that after talking to him, they think we need to come and get him," her mom goes on, "but before we leave, they also make sure to mention that he told his math teacher to fuck off when she asked for his homework—the homework I'm sure also isn't finished!"

Giddy fixes a long, cold stare at the back of Dougal's head. She feels no sense of satisfaction in his condemnation—it's a long time coming. But she does feel irritated, because what if she'd wanted to stay after school for something today? Why did she have to leave too?

"So what do you have to say for yourself?" her mother demands.

Giddy folds her arms, glaring at Dougal, when her mother snaps: "I'm talking to *you*, Giddy!"

Giddy's head whips around. So does Dougal's. They both look at their mother, mouths popped open.

"What do you have to say, Giddy?" her mother goes on. "You've stopped taking Dougal and Tigs and Tad to the bus stop. You've stopped waiting for them to get home. You aren't checking with Dougal in the afternoons to remind him about his homework—are you even asking him if he needs your help? And what about Tad? I looked online, and his grades in math are slipping, and he says you don't help him with math anymore. Tad and Tigs are skipping baths and they are hungry in the evenings because they haven't been fed!" Her mother's voice quivers. "We can't afford your experimental cooking. You can't just buy food that only one person in the house will eat. Is it so hard for you to put a pizza in the oven or make a grilled cheese sandwich? And Tad and Tigs pack their own lunches now? When did that start?" Her mom yanks down the car's vanity mirror and locks eyes with Giddy. "Well, this all changes now. Starting tomorrow you are not only making sure everyone gets where they need to be in the morning, you are also making sure Dougal gets on that bus every single afternoon—" Her mom's eyes flash at Dougal when he starts to sputter an objection. "Don't even, Dougal! No more walking, either one of you. Got it, Giddy?"

Dougal throws his hands up and then folds his skinny arms around himself, sinking, as if he could squeeze his scrawny body into the corner of the back seat. Giddy stares at the dashboard between the seats.

Then she says: "No."

Dougal uncurls enough to look at Giddy.

A second's worth of utter silence ends with her mother saying: "Excuse me?"

"I'm not going to do any of that." A curious energy creeps through Giddy, slow and electric. "Dougal knows how to get on and off the bus. So do Tigs and Tad—Tigs is even making sure Tad gets on the bus every day. They know how to pack their own lunches. Dougal knows when he has homework—he doesn't forget and he doesn't want my help on it." Giddy shakes her head. "You don't need me to put in a pizza or make grilled cheese sandwiches, and if you don't like my food, then I'll only get enough for me and someone else can cook. I haven't been late to school *all week*."

Giddy wasn't aware this meant anything to her before now, but she discovers it does. She doesn't miss coming into art out of breath or the pitying looks the attendance clerks give her. She *likes* coming to school early, walking, being able to stay late for a club. She wasn't aware how much she liked it until someone suggested taking it away.

"You are under the impression that this is negotiable," her mom says, still looking at her in the mirror. "It isn't!"

"But I won't do these things," Giddy says. She looks at Dougal as if seeking confirmation that these very true words came from her, but he's staring at her with this mesmerized expression.

The ensuing silence is broken only by her dad's start of a slow *thump, thump* as he beats his hands against the wheel.

Her mom is just a set of mirrored eyes boring into hers; those eyes widen in a flicker of fury, or is it fear? "Wow, Giddy. Really?" her mom says, voice strangely jittery. "We'll just see about that when we get home, won't we?"

Nobody says another word. When they pull into their driveway, Jax's car is missing and it's a little too early for Tigs and Tad's bus. Everybody gets out and her mother marches up to the door and unlocks it. "Not now, Bodie." She steps around his wriggling body, and Giddy, subdued and disconnected, follows her in along with everyone else.

When the door closes, Giddy's mom whirls to face her. "You only *think* you own things, but we buy everything in this house. You really only need food, clothes, and shelter, not any of the other crap you think you own! So let's see how you feel about not doing your part when something you really love gets taken away." Her mom marches up the stairs and disappears into Giddy's bedroom, slamming the door.

Giddy imagines what her mom sees right now: Giddy's closet and dresser—filled with nothing but school clothes and the green Sunday dress. Giddy's bed—the covers a hand-me-down from her mom's college dorm days and an upgrade from the race car bed set that once belonged to Jax. Giddy's walls—bare and dotted with holes because she took down all her college posters. Giddy's desk and chair—garage sale finds. Superdoo and his list. The thought of her mother marching downstairs with Superdoo in her hands as punishment is laughable, because no mother would sense a beat-up action figure's value in the eyes of a fifteen-year-old.

For a few seconds, she hears her mother pace about. Then quiet. Then her mother comes out of Giddy's room empty-handed and stares down over the railing at Giddy as if maybe seeing something in her daughter that's put her off her game. She looks at Giddy's dad. "A little help, Scott?" Her mom inclines her head toward the room, and Giddy's dad looks shocked and ill prepared for the front lines of war. They lean, heads together, in the door of Giddy's room and Giddy and Dougal step to the base of the stairs, listening. Bodie, head bowed under the weight of the ambient tension, looks up with them.

Giddy's mom whispers: "Where is her rock collection?"

Her dad, whispering back: "Rock collection?"

Giddy remembers. Christmas. Three years ago. It came with geodes and chunks of rainbow-colored bismuth. Tigs buried the geodes somewhere in the backyard. The bismuth is somewhere at the bottom of Tad's toy box.

Her mom says: "What about her robot?"

Giddy's tenth birthday. The bot was a simple device that could only move back and forth and speak preprogrammed commands. Giddy adored it. When the batteries expired, they turned out to be too expensive to replace. Tigs dresses it up for tea sometimes.

Her dad says: "Wait—doesn't she have a telescope?"

Sold at a yard sale last year. Her mom had said, *When is the last time anybody's used this? Look at all the room it takes up in the garage! Tell you what, Giddy, you can keep the money we get for it.*

Then, as if just realizing they might be heard, her mom pulls him in and closes Giddy's door, and now there is a fevered back-and-forth whispering too muffled for Giddy to understand. She looks at Dougal, but he shrugs as if he can't make it out, either. Bodie's tail thumps in desperation between them.

The door opens and Giddy's mom and dad emerge to come down the stairs. Neither seem to want to look at her. Her mother crosses her arms, looks at the floor, and says softly but firmly: "Giddy, go to your room. Dougal, you too."

And Giddy thinks, *That's it?* Dougal gapes theatrically.

Her father yells: "Shut up, Dougal!" Dougal slaps both hands dramatically over his mouth and her dad, angrier, says: "I said, Dougal, shut up and go to your room!"

Dougal bounds up ahead of her and slams his door. Giddy follows, thinking that it almost feels like her parents are rewarding her because all she wanted out of this evening was more time in her room to finish *Ulysses* so she can have one over on Katlyn and figure out what this whole modern-day business her dad mentioned is about.

Halfway up the stairs, her dad whispers: "I thought she had more things!" and her mother shushes him. Giddy goes into her room and sits on the edge of her bed.

Downstairs there is arguing. Giddy catches limited phrases:

"I have no idea—"

"Well, you just can't allow—"

"Not acceptable! How can we just—"

"OK, let's just think it over after a meal. What's for dinner?"

Total silence. On Wednesdays, Giddy usually cooks.

The front door bursts open and Giddy hears the sounds of Tigs and Tad rushing in, home from school. Hears Tigs shout: "Peanut butter jelly and potato chip sandwiches for dinner!" Hears them giggling as they rummage through the pantry.

Giddy half expects her parents to call her back down to prepare an adult dinner, but she guesses her mother doesn't want to undo her punishment, because all Giddy hears is the clatter of pots being dragged out and the muted voices of her parents. Giddy takes out *Ulysses.* She's still reading it when her parents call: "Dougal! Giddy! Come eat something."

Giddy and Dougal open their doors at the same time. There's a moment when their eyes connect where it almost feels like they're on the same team. Giddy can't remember the last time Dougal looked at her like that. She goes down ahead of him and bypasses the kitchen island, where there's a pot of corn chowder and multiple empty soup cans in the trash. Tigs and Tad are at the island table, fingers greasy with chips and peanut butter and jam at the corners of their lips. Giddy takes her oxtail soup out of the fridge, nukes it in the microwave, and leans against the counter, eating in slow spoonfuls.

Dougal shrugs and fills a bowl of chowder. Giddy's parents eat quietly, troubled eyes connecting over their meal. Giddy polishes off the bowl of soup, supplements her dinner with sardines on crackers, cleans up her plates, and then, because no one's said she can't, goes back up to her room. She gets another ten pages into *Ulysses* when there's a quiet knock at her door.

Giddy opens it. It's Dougal.

"What are you doing?" he asks. He doesn't mean what is she doing right now. It's the quiet whisper in his voice that tells Giddy he means what is she doing in general.

Giddy closes the door without answering and goes back to her book, reading it until she's too tired to stay awake. And her brother doesn't return to ask a second time.

9

Giddy wakes to a warm house, which means someone's adjusted the thermostat. She turns off the alarm before it can sound. Superdoo grins from over the list: *Do something unexpected each day.* In the shower, she presses her forehead to the tile, the cold water coursing over her. *Do something do something do something* . . . As she towels off, she hears the soft shuffling of feet downstairs and the clinking of plates. The bitter aroma of coffee plucks at Giddy's nostrils as she gets dressed and heads downstairs.

Tigs and Tad are up and dressed appropriately, no mismatched socks or dirty clothes. They're even sitting on stools at the kitchen island with their backpacks already on, eating waffles and drinking orange juice. Dougal is with them. Another waffle pops up and he tosses it onto Tigs's plate. He pours himself a cup of coffee. Then he pours a second cup, sets it on the island, and pushes it gently in Giddy's direction. He looks at her.

Giddy looks back, confused.

Dougal takes a second plate down: "Want some waffles?"

Giddy doesn't know whether her actual brother Dougal is OK or if this diabolical replacement means her and her family harm. So she doesn't say anything. Instead, she scoots around him to grab sardines out of the fridge and goes into the pantry for crackers. She eats as she moves, packing a lunch out of gefilte fish and leftover bobotie. Then, because she's still hungry, she grabs an orange and slides it into her pocket. All the while she feels three sets of eyes on her.

Giddy zips out of the kitchen. As she opens the door to leave, Dougal says: "Have a great day, Giddy."

Giddy's hand freezes on the doorknob. She looks over her shoulder at them. Dougal waits patiently for a response while Tigs blithely tears into her waffles. But Tad sits up a little straighter and regards Giddy with a kind of quiet concern that arrests her. It occurs to Giddy she still hasn't said anything to Tad since screaming in his face the other night.

When she looks at Dougal and sees that same quiet edge, as if he's trying to pry her brain open for analysis, it infuriates her. So she marches out and slams the door without saying anything. As she walks, she scrolls through her phone. Posts she's tagged in pop up like flashes of machine-gun fire:

Voting SICK!

Going w sick not psycho

Sick is up to 179 votes, with *psycho* holding at 79, the last negative post being the one Giddy read yesterday from one of Jess's accounts. Giddy stuffs her phone back into her pocket and her hand bumps into the orange. Giddy turns it around as she walks, wondering what the hell possessed her to grab a citrus fruit when she knows what something like this can do to her stomach. But it smells good and Giddy figures there's no harm in peeling it just for the smell. As she passes the park, the food trucks are out and the mix of delicious odors make her stomach rumble pleasingly, and before she knows it she's popped an orange slice into her mouth.

It is literally the best-tasting thing she's ever eaten! Giddy motors through the rest of the orange and stares dumbly at her hands before licking her fingers and tossing the rind in a trash can. From her stomach there is nothing but the warm glow of satisfaction, no cramping, no burning. Giddy thinks, *Maybe fish oil from the sardines neutralizes acid or—*

Or maybe there's nothing wrong with her except that she doesn't eat enough.

That thought slows Giddy's feet until she stops at the park's edge, her mind tumbling with implications. Because if it's true, if the only problem is that she hasn't been eating enough, then she's been making herself sick for God knows how long. She could be eating anything: cheeseburgers, pizzas, tacos, hot buffalo wings. So why isn't she? Why would she do this to herself?

Another buzz sounds and Giddy pulls her phone out: *G. Barber is SICK!*

Up to 180 votes.

Giddy shoves the phone back and pops her earbuds in, cranking the audio up to high. She stomps to school to the sonorous rise and fall of the singer's baritone in an aria loaded with ominous foreboding.

In art, the teacher has graded her snarky art evaluations: *Giddy, you'd be surprised at how many people liken cubism to elementary school work!:) I enjoyed your comment about it "raining on the paint" with Monet. Impressionism can be described how light reflects off a surface, which results in the blurry texture you observed. A+*

And Giddy thinks, *Wait, this snark is* good? Her hands shake as she crumples up the paper. At the table next to her, Otter Girl says: "Did you get a bad grade? I didn't know he gave bad grades as long as you answered all the questions honestly."

Giddy says: "No. It's fine. I'm just—" *Sick? Psycho?* "Feeling kind of broken today."

"Did you know that even a stopped clock tells accurate time twice a day?"

What? Otter Girl is folding pieces of notebook paper into origami swans. They look a lot nicer than what she and Tigs made, but then again, why is Giddy surprised? "OK," Giddy says back to her, "I guess that's true. So what?"

Otter Girl sets a swan down. "It's something my mom likes to say. It means no matter how broken something is, there's something right going on, because if you break in every different direction, you'll *accidentally* wind up getting something right."

Giddy imagines a clock inside a three-dimensional grid with a zero point dead center and rays extending endlessly outward through all possible points. "I guess that makes sense."

Otter Girl smiles. She flicks a swan at Giddy and it hits her in the elbow and Giddy feels *lighter* somehow, maybe just a touch less angry, so she says: "Thanks."

"Don't thank me or I'm going to have to hit you with a swan again," says Otter Girl, tone suddenly serious.

"Thanks."

The second swan achieves lift and hits Giddy in the shoulder. Giddy thinks she's glad that Otter Girl isn't the unhappy mess Giddy is, because the world needs lots of Otter Girls.

When she gets to English class, her teacher is returning index card quick writes. She's written a big *Yes!* across Giddy's response of *He's like this girl I know. Like Hamlet, she keeps deciding instead of doing.*

"If we were going to study broken Shakespearian characters," says the boy next to Giddy, "it would have made more sense to read *King Lear.* What do you think?"

Giddy doesn't know what to say to that. She tucks her index card into her binder. She's still thinking of Otter Girl's clock analogy and how maybe she's right. Also, maybe things have to completely break before you can fix them.

In algebra II she's still thinking about the clock when her teacher is wearing a GET REAL, BE RATIONAL! shirt and saying: "Let's talk about points of discontinuity, places where you just can't find any information. You have to accept in life that sometimes there are impossible numbers." He writes out a series of lines and numbers. "In this rational, why can't *x* ever be five no matter what you do to it? We know *x* can't be seven because if it was—what?" A hand goes up and somebody mutters an answer.

"That's right! *Y* wouldn't exist. And *y* has to exist, right? So the point is you just have to keep looking. . . ."

Giddy thinks maybe she's not so off track after all, that maybe she just needs to keep looking. The thought settles her. She gets sleepy as the teacher talks. Then she thinks maybe it's because she's *relaxing.* The odd notion follows her down the hall into chemistry class.

Giddy steels herself and walks in. Trinity and Jess look up. But instead of hurrying past, Giddy locks eyes with them. Trinity frowns and Jess smirks and texts. Giddy takes her buzzing phone out as she sits, holds it up where she knows Jess and Trinity can see it, and powers it down. Zach looks at her and Giddy returns his stare the same way she did with Jess and Trinity—completely nonplussed. He jerks back around in his seat and falls to his work, a scowl on his face.

Giddy knows she's not supposed to be trying in chemistry, but there's something pleasing about the solo lab, one the teacher's dubbed "Franken-nail." Giddy mixes a solution of bright blue copper chloride before dropping in a pristine iron nail and taping an all-caps label of *GIDDY BARBER* to the beaker. Giddy sets it in a window, where light refracts and makes the gleaming metal appear broken but shiny and beautiful.

Giddy finishes some evaluative questions aimed at predicting what the nail will look like in twenty-four hours. She's wrapping everything up when the bell rings.

To her mild surprise, Jess and Trinity pull up alongside her in the hall. "You have so many *sick* votes right now," Jess says. "Bravo for you!"

This is Sarcastic Jess. Giddy doesn't give a damn. There's been something very freeing about this morning, something in Otter Girl's paper swan or Giddy's iron nail or the bright flavor of the orange. Truth be told, the ugliest part of Giddy's day has been the *sick* versus *psycho* crap, and that can be easily solved with a powered-down phone.

So Giddy pointedly speeds up, but they speed up too. At the cafeteria entrance, Trinity says: "Asia's going to flip out!"

"I don't know if you've noticed, but she's turned superfan for you." Jess has her phone out as they enter the cafeteria. "She gave you a *sick* vote. Did you know you're up to almost two hundred?"

"So the eleven days has to be almost over, right?" Trinity says, walking fast through the cafeteria to keep up with Giddy.

"Then you're back with us." Jess smirks. "Can't wait to see how your new peeps feel when they figure out you're not serious about them."

They've made it to the center of the cafeteria, a location Giddy believes she made famous when she puked up a sardine sandwich last week. So it seems only appropriate that she do this here. Giddy stops and turns so fast, both girls nearly bump into her. "Why on earth would I do that?"

Jess's smirk falters. Trinity stares in surprise. "Do what?" she asks Giddy.

"Sit with you for lunch." Giddy is aware her voice is elevated, aware that the noisy cafeteria has started to quiet down around their little bubble of drama. "Why would I choose to have lunch with you? All you do is gripe and spew negativity and tear everybody down. What possible reason would I have for sitting with you?" Her voice catches, and Giddy takes a moment to swallow a painful lump in her throat. Where the hell did *that* come from?

Asia's left her seat to run up beside Trinity, and because the bubble around them is quiet with curious stares, she can actually hear Asia breathlessly say: "Giddy, I voted *sick* for you!" Meanwhile, Zach is left behind at their table, half rising out of his seat, looking frustrated at Asia's adulation of Giddy.

Giddy says: "They tear you down, Asia. All the time. I know they sometimes criticize you to your face, but you should see the texts they send about you. They're never good."

A general *ooh* breaks out from the students eating and listening. Jess's mouth pops wide open, Trinity's to a lesser degree, and Asia double blinks and sputters: "No, they don't do that to *me*. I mean, we do that to *you*, but . . ." And now her own mouth is open at what she's let slip.

Giddy folds her arms. How many texts have the three of them sent about her behind her back, even before she left their table? Why did she think Jess and Trinity only ganged up against Asia? "So when I'm not around, you three gang up on me. But, Asia"—Giddy takes a step toward her—"that's what they do to you behind *your* back. And you know what? Sometimes Jess and Trinity do it to each other, too. You're all just"—Giddy looks at the three of them—"toxic. Jess, I don't think I've seen you ever say anything warm or positive. And, Trinity"—Giddy rolls her eyes—"choose something for once without asking everyone to vote on it. And, Asia"—Giddy shakes her head—"you should just sit someplace else, because as long as you're with Trinity and Jess, they're just going to keep kicking you around and stomping all over your creativity. Go with Zach to *his* table!"

Giddy points to the table full of guys where Zach used to sit. A bunch of heads turn that way. They all look back at everyone, confused and reluctant to be put on the spot.

"Oh, I don't like *Zach*!" Asia makes a face and shakes her head. Behind them at their table, Zach is still listening. His face shifts quickly from irritation at Giddy to being mortally wounded, and he slides slowly back down into his seat. "No, I just did that because—" And Asia stops, closes her mouth. "Never mind."

"Oh," Giddy says, "you just did that because you were mad at me over the GIF and the tangerine fireplace and you thought I liked him." Giddy frowns. "That is messed up, Asia!"

Asia's face lights up like she just remembered something. She whirls on Trinity. "Give me your phone!"

"No!" Trinity quickly slips her phone into her pocket.

"Give it to me!" Asia says. "I want to see if you really text about me! I want to know if you do me like you do Giddy!"

Giddy throws her hands up. "This is stupid! Has it occurred to you that you'd all be happier if you just found something nice to say about each other every once in a while?"

"Well, that's great advice coming from you, Giddy." Now Jess has folded her arms and her tone is all snark. "That's really amazingly good—"

"Oh, just shut up, kpopprincez899, bband2die4." Giddy decides letting Jess's two favorite online aliases slip is her kind of mic drop, and based on the *ooh* sound that rises up from the tables near them again, she's on the money. Giddy leaves them and walks to the far end of the cafeteria, to the table where Ashlynn, Monica, and Trey have papers spread out, and Trey is making notes on them as they eat. Giddy takes her seat.

"What . . . was . . . that?" Ashlynn asks, grinning around a slice of pizza.

"That was me ending something," Giddy says.

Trey circles a sentence on a paper. "This source is outdated." He shoves it across to Monica. "And this is what we call in journalism class an 'unsubstantiated claim,' also known as 'just your opinion.'" He makes a mark on a different paper and hands it to Ashlynn.

Monica looks frustrated. She whips out her phone and starts typing. "How can a 2008 source be outdated? It's proven science! Proven science doesn't change."

"Actually, things that are proven in science change all the time. There's new data and things get reevaluated." This knowledge bounces out of Giddy's mouth before she can think about whether to put a leash on her words. Because before the eleven days, everything she ever said at lunch to Jess or Trinity or Asia was uttered only after careful consideration. Giddy lived in the constant vain hope that appropriate forethought could avert a personal attack. But that seldom seemed to pan out, and now she wonders why she put in all that effort.

Now Ashlynn, Trey, and Monica are the ones looking at her, and Giddy freezes, waiting. And then the second passes with Monica shrugging, Ashlynn nodding as if what Giddy says makes sense, and Trey *smiling.*

"That tracks," he says, reaching for a fry, "but I also happen to know NASA updates its Mars mission objectives more frequently than every ten years." He bites into the fry and grins around it at Monica.

Monica rolls her eyes. "Who cares? Ashlynn's right. Going to Mars is a big stupid waste of money."

"And that," Trey says, tipping his soda toward Ashlynn, "is *her* unsubstantiated opinion."

"I want to see your paper!" Ashlynn reaches over to Trey. "I want to see how great your sources are."

"They are all great," Trey says, lifting the paper up for her to see, "because they are all fact-checked and current, and I left my opinion—awesome as it is—out of it."

"What if I put together a graph showing the stats on how many Americans agree with me that a Mars mission is dumb?" Ashlynn asks him.

"Then instead of one opinion, you would be interjecting a bunch of people's opinions into a paper Mr. Serrano says needs to be 'a strict analysis devoid of opinion.'"

"But I'm backing it up with a factual stat!"

Giddy resumes unpacking her lunch, but she feels lighter, almost *good*, like maybe every lunch could be a meal where she doesn't have to watch what she says so damn closely. She wonders if this is a sign that Superdoo's list is finally paying off.

Monica asks: "What's on the menu?"

"Gefilte fish with sauce from bobotie"—Giddy jiggles a bag—"and chips."

"You know, you need to bring just the bobotie and pass it around," Monica tells her, "because none of us have ever tasted it before."

"It's not great left over," Giddy tells them. "I'm just finishing it before the next store run."

Ashlynn says: "I read you can put hot sauce on gefilte fish and it works." Ashlynn looks up over Giddy's shoulder and frowns. "Hello?"

Giddy jerks her head around. It's Maddie. Gwen's girlfriend from book club. She stands over them, smirking. "I heard all that with Jess."

"OK," Giddy says, frowning.

"Just so you know, Gwen thinks this is a terrible idea," Maddie says, "but her name is Renee, and she's really sweet, so—" She places a folded piece of paper on the table in front of Giddy.

Giddy unfolds it. The name written is Renee Krueger. There's a phone number. Giddy says: "Who's this?"

"Someone willing to help you check a box on your list." She flashes Giddy a smile. "Don't fuck it up. Bye!" She leaves.

"Don't fuck what up?" Trey asks, but Giddy's staring at the paper. She doesn't know anybody named Renee Krueger. But she knows why Maddie gave her this. Her mouth goes dry and all the lightness she experienced from dumping her old friends evaporates. She gets out her phone, fingers hovering. What is she supposed to say? *Hey, I don't know you, but can I kiss you?*

Do something unexpected.

"Giddy?" Monica asks.

Giddy texts before she loses courage: *Hey. This is Giddy.* Sends. Then she shoves her phone deep into her pocket. "Sorry. What?"

"Check this out." Monica holds up her phone. "Sea urchin tacos. I had these at my uncle's anniversary party at this expensive restaurant. I didn't want to say anything, but they tasted like rotten olives." Monica frowns. "So did you have five coffees or what?"

Giddy's drumming her feet against the floor and her hands are tapping the table. She puts them in her lap. "I'm fine."

They all look at her and wait. Giddy says: "Really!" To prove the point, she pops open the bag of chips. They are a smoky barbecue flavor, something Giddy hasn't eaten since she was about ten. But they taste sweet and good and she downs the entire bag even though it makes her stomach feel slightly queasy.

She finishes her meal fast, and when the bell rings, she's on her phone, on the way to robotics, looking up *Renee Krueger* and cross-referencing it with her school. There's one profile that might be her, but there's no picture, just a couple of koala videos and some obscure British band references—Giddy would need to ask to follow her to see more and she's not about to become some creepy stalker.

She checks her phone. Nothing back from this Renee. She goes into robotics, phone still in hand—

And stops because all the tables are pushed back except three in the center, and on top of them is *her* course, under construction, sawdust under the table as shop students drill holes into copper sheets and plywood. Her course has two parts: a half-pipe on one side and a simple but steep inclined plane on the other side. The inclined plane is wide enough for a bot to travel on but lined with sharp wooden pegs. In the course's center is a circular pit about an inch deep. As Giddy watches, one of the shop students uses a pocketknife to cut the tops off smoke bombs and pour powder into the pit.

Another shop student is attaching a three-inch-deep tray to the course perimeter. A student asks: "What's that for?"

"Oh, you didn't read Giddy's design?" Somebody snickers. "It's for the canned heat. You start the canned heat at the beginning of the race, drop the cans into the tray, and because it's a copper-topped course, it slowly heats up the longer your bot's on it."

"What goes on the sharp pegs?"

Somebody points to the teacher's desk, where a grocery bag of individually wrapped marshmallow treats and boxes of unsalted butter spill over a stack of papers and a stapler. "You stack the butter on either side of the half-pipe. You stick the treats on top of the pegs."

"The pit?"

"Smoke powder."

The student's face pales. "So we can't see anything?"

"Yeah, but only if the heat reaches it and the smoke powder lights. So maybe if we ran the course really fast?"

Giddy walks around, eyeballing her design like it's a mirage. As she drops her backpack in her chair, Patrice comes up and says: "Well, the whole class thinks you *hate* us."

"I never thought anybody would actually do it," Giddy says.

One of the shop students calls out: "Are you ready to test the canned heat?"

"Yes!" Her teacher races from her desk with enthusiasm. As the shop students pop the tops and light the cans, the teacher unwraps the marshmallow treats. A soft heat radiates in Giddy's direction as she and the other students close in on the course. Her teacher sets one marshmallow treat on the copper a few inches from the tray and another closer to the center pit. Within seconds the first treat begins sweating. After a minute its square form starts to soften and sink into more of a rhombus. Sticky rivulets of sugar trickle out. When some spills into the tray, it blackens and burns and the students step back, protesting the sudden stench.

"Can we maybe add a lip around the tray so that doesn't happen again?" the teacher asks, and the shop student nods. "Looks like the treat in the center is doing OK for now." The teacher pokes the center treat critically and looks around the room. "So tomorrow's a go! I can't wait to see which activity everybody's bots choose to do first: stab the marshmallow treats atop the pegs on the ramp or stack the frozen chunks of butter on either side of the half-pipe!"

A shop student touches the copper and pulls his finger back. "This feels like it might get hot enough to start a grease fire even if nothing spills into the tray."

Their teacher nods thoughtfully. "We should perform the race outdoors just to be sure, and I'll bring that." She points to the fire extinguisher.

"My bot is going to die," a student on the other side of the course says weakly.

"What if we attach a kitchen-sized extinguisher to our bot and, I don't know, it defends itself?" his partner asks.

"This is insane," Giddy whispers.

"I'd call you a mad genius if I weren't so worried." Deb has wandered up to Giddy's other side, a soldering iron in her hands. "For the record, we're sticking with a basic raincoat over our bot to catch any drips from him carrying melting treats over his head."

"Better make sure the raincoat has a high melting point," Patrice tells her.

And Giddy thinks, *I didn't mean for any of this to happen!* And she didn't, because she's supposed to not be trying in this class until the eleven days are up. Then it's back to being on track for college and a mechanical engineering degree. Still . . .

"Forget the raincoat," Giddy tells them. "You need to worry about where your bot touches the copper. You have rubber wheels. Get a silicone baking mat. Cut it into strips. Wrap the strips around the bot's wheels."

"A silicone insulator." Deb smacks her forehead. "Why the hell don't I think of these things?" And as she and Patrice start making a list of everything they are going to need, Giddy goes to sit at the back of the room, phone in her hands, thumbing through forums (*Sick 208!*). She's also checking her texts.

Nothing yet from Renee.

After a while, Giddy gets up again to look at her course. Even the students with the most basic bots are trying to humanize them, installing decorated Ping-Pong ball eyes and making paper hats. A team two tables away has borrowed spare plywood and wood glue from the shop students. When they see Giddy watching, one gleefully exclaims: "We're making a coffin for our bot!"

The other grins. "We don't stand a chance in hell!"

And Giddy thinks, *I've made them smile!* This is what her English teacher would call irony. Giddy's grabbing her stuff as the bell rings, ready to bound out the door, when her phone buzzes.

Renee has responded: *Hey, Giddy!* A pair of smiley emojis follow. Giddy blinks at the weird cheeriness of it. Then again, Maddie said Renee was sweet.

Giddy shifts back and forth on her feet, thinking of an appropriate reply. Everyone's leaving class and the hall's going to be packed when she heads for world history. She settles on: *Maybe we could say hi after school today?* It sounds lame. Like they're in kindergarten. Giddy is in the process of regretting her words when—

How about the concession stand by the track? 3:15ish?

Giddy's fingers hover over her screen. She stands, rooted, last in the robotics room. She can end this by just not texting Renee a confirmation. But why end it? Isn't doing different things the point? She's not sure why she's so nervous. It wasn't this big a deal with Zach. But then again, she knew Zach, and Renee is some total stranger.

Before she can change her mind, she texts: *Sure!* And then regrets the exclamation point because is that too enthusiastic? But without the exclamation point, it might convey apathy, and Giddy doesn't want to be insulting to someone doing her a favor—

A text back of a smiley emoji.

Giddy pockets her phone in a rush. It's madness in the hall with students crushed together heading in different directions. Giddy is elbow to elbow in the crowd, taking baby steps along with everyone else to move forward. So she takes out her phone. *Sick* has topped out at 212 and Jess's alias of bband2die4 has posted, *How can u all pick sick not psycho? Closing comments cuz nobody shud care about this fuckd up girl!!* And that's it. The thread's grayed out with no more comments allowed. Giddy knows she should feel relieved that her brief spat of social media fame is coming to a close, but there's just this simmering need to ram her fist through something!

By the time she reaches world history, Giddy's adrenaline rush is over, leaving behind an achy, queasy calm. In just an hour she's going to be out near the bleachers at the concession stand looking for this Renee Krueger. At the front of class, the teacher reads questions from a checklist. "Which country officially quit the war in 1918?"

Giddy raises an arm halfway.

"Ms. Barber?"

"Russia."

"That's right. Russia signed for peace with Germany. And what was happening in Russia at the time that contributed to—" Her teacher blinks. "Ms. Barber, you forgot to put your hand down."

"The revolution happened."

"I would appreciate it if—" He looks down at his card. "Oh wait. That's right. There was a revolution in Russia." He slides the card to the back. "What does the eleventh hour of the eleventh day of the eleventh month—"

Giddy says: "The armistice."

Her teacher frowns. "I didn't call on you, Ms. Barber! I already know you know this stuff. Give someone else a chance and *please put your hand down after you've answered a question*!"

A few kids snicker as Giddy lowers her arm.

"OK, so what was significant about the Second Battle of the Marne?" Her teacher points to a student. "Mr. Zepeda?"

Keith has his chin on his hand and has been staring at the door. As he sleepily blinks to awareness, Giddy mutters: "It clinched victory for the Allies."

"Are you giving answers away now, Ms. Barber?" the teacher demands.

"I'm sorry," Giddy says.

From the back of the room, one of Hunter's friends snickers and says loudly: "Giddy, quit giving—"

Hunter sharply cuts him off. "Shut up."

"What?" The kid looks at Hunter, but Hunter shakes his head, indicating the student shouldn't finish whatever it was he was going to say, which Giddy knows was going to be a slam at her. She looks over her shoulder, stunned.

The teacher asks: "So what happened after the Allied victory?" A pause. "Come on, guys, I'm throwing an easy one out now!" Giddy tries to make eye contact with Hunter, but he's drawing in his textbook. One of his buddies looks at Giddy, frowns, whispers something to Hunter again.

"Leave her alone," Hunter says, still drawing.

And just like that, all his friends go back to staring into the air with disinterest. Giddy waits for some insult to materialize on Hunter's index card or on the screen of Hunter's phone, but he's just doodling, and Giddy is trying to figure out what universe she accidentally slipped into when the teacher says: "*Come on!* What happened after the Allied victory, a *hundred days* after the Allied victory, in fact?"

Giddy mutters again: "The armistice."

Her teacher throws up his hands. "I guess maybe you don't realize you're talking out loud, Ms. Barber!"

This is prime material for Hunter, but there's nothing from the back of the class, and after a second the teacher moves on to ask about the order of enemy surrender. This time Giddy manages not to say the answers under her breath.

When class lets out, she slows her steps, giving Hunter plenty of opportunity to catch up in the hall to explain himself. But all he does is walk past her. "Bye, Giddy!" And he gives her a smile and a wave like she's just some random friend of his, like she hasn't been the butt of his jokes in class all year long. Giddy gapes as he vanishes into the funnel of students. She walks out behind everyone and into a dark gray afternoon, the bulging sky on the precipice of rain. Giddy flips her hood up. Instead of walking home, she heads behind the school, out in the direction of the track and bleachers.

A sense of disconnect occurs as she heads toward the concession stand. It's mercifully silent, with only the track team exercising on the other side of the field. The stand sits lonely, door padlocked, board lowered over a window. Giddy runs her fingers through a chain-link fence. It's 3:06, so Giddy knows she's early. She sits down, back to the fence, and nervously takes out *Ulysses* and continues reading a chapter that's all told from the point of view of an attractive girl on a beach. The girl doesn't know it, but Leopold is looking at her from far away, thinking about her, longing for her.

"Hey."

Giddy looks up, confused. What the hell is Otter Girl doing out here? And then she thinks: *Who cares?* Maybe it's good that she'll have somebody to talk to while waiting for this Renee Krueger to show up.

And then she realizes she doesn't know Otter Girl's name.

Giddy slowly stands. Otter Girl drops her bag next to the chain link and smiles, shoving her hands into her pockets. Artfully torn jeans. Too tight. A black top reminiscent of the eighties, off shoulder on the side, decals from bands Giddy's never heard of. Otter Girl's striped hair is pulled back and her lips are painted pink.

And the quiet words that form in Giddy's mind are: *Oh no.*

"Hi," Otter Girl says. "So I'm Renee." She takes a couple of slow steps forward, hesitant steps, a deer at the edge of a feeder in the woods. Over their heads a crack of thunder shakes the brooding sky.

Giddy says: "Hi," even though her brain is still going *oh no oh no oh no* and then *why?* Why did it have to be Otter Girl, with her too-cute smile and her soft ways? Why couldn't it just be some stranger who Giddy didn't have to worry about upsetting?

And her brain keeps firing *oh no oh no oh no . . .*

"You're *really* surprised," Renee says.

Giddy finds her voice. "Yeah, I wasn't expecting someone I knew."

"This *is* weird," Renee agrees. But she also takes another step closer to Giddy. Now they are only a couple of feet apart.

The practical part of Giddy thinks, *Set the tone.* "I appreciate you coming out here." *Business. Be all business!* "So, you know, this is an experiment. I'm trying new things, and if I don't like it, I don't like it, and I hope"—Giddy licks her lips—"I hope that's fine." She gestures to her. "You look good, by the way. That top. It's great."

"Well, you always look good." Renee steps a little closer and looks at her for a really long moment that Giddy knows is an invitation. A fat drop of rain thuds to the earth between them, followed by another rumble from above. There're no more excuses. Giddy steps forward and leans in, carefully, gently.

Kissing Renee is soft, like with Zach, but maybe even *softer*, and it's probably because Renee's trying to be polite. But Giddy doesn't know what to call it when Renee's mouth opens against hers or how to feel about it when Renee's arms loop around her neck. And Giddy presses into the kiss hard, as she tries—really *tries*—to feel something this time. Because Otter Girl may be one of the nicest, most well-put-together people she knows. If she can't feel something with Otter Girl, then who can she possibly feel anything for? But she doesn't feel what she wants to feel and her mind won't stop screaming, *OH NO OH NO OH NO!*

Giddy abruptly stops and takes a quick step back. Mouth bruised from effort, she looks at the ground, where more fat drops of rain darken the cold earth. She wants to stare anyplace else, *be* anyplace else.

And Renee says: "That was, umm . . ." She gives a little sigh and says: "You didn't like it."

Giddy doesn't answer. A raindrop hits her head, rolls down behind her ear.

"It's OK," Renee says. But she sounds disappointed and Giddy can't say anything, can't quite bring herself to meet Otter Girl's eyes.

"Giddy, it really is OK." Now Renee sounds concerned. "I'm all right with this. We can still be art buddies!" But to Giddy, her cheeriness sounds forced. And now Giddy isn't sure she's going to be greeted by the same Otter Girl in art anymore. And why does she have to lose things just by trying? It makes her so freaking mad!

"Giddy?"

Giddy stares at a cracked and broken section of ground between the toes of her sneakers. The drops of rain stand in tight bubbles where the dry earth is too cold and dead to absorb anything.

And then she says: "At least I tried. That's more than I can say for you."

"What?" Renee says.

Giddy looks up. "Maybe the problem is you." The rain is starting to come faster, and Giddy brushes drops off her cheeks, her brain screaming, *Stop! Stop! Stop!* "Maybe you just don't know how to do this."

Renee takes a step back. "Are you serious?" She lowers her voice in a way that brings to mind someone trying to reason with a mental patient.

But Giddy's mouth is a volcano of bile, and now that it's been set off, all the bad stuff has to spew out. "Completely," Giddy says. "You suck at kissing."

Renee blinks.

"I honestly expected better," Giddy says. "Maybe if I look someplace else, put out an ad or—"

"Bitch." Renee gives Giddy an astonished look. Then she picks up her bag, throws it over her shoulder, and runs off. Giddy watches the bag bouncing against her back, keeps watching as Otter Girl gets smaller and smaller, until she's just a thumb-sized point disappearing around the school building.

Now Giddy is alone. For a few seconds she stays as she is, rooted in the moment. Then the sky cracks once more and the heavens open. Giddy puts her earbuds in and flips her hood up, running in the downpour, steps splashing as "Ebben? Ne andrò lontana" from *La Wally* sounds in her head. With every stomp, she repeats her words to Renee in her mind. Giddy knows there has to be some way Renee provoked this, some way that this isn't Giddy's fault. But her brain's exhaustive leaps of acrobatics fall flat under the repeated thwack of reason and conclusion's gavel.

She slows to a stop before a heavily trafficked street crossing, the rain drenching joggers as they race past. And her eyes lock onto the tree near the bench where she stuffed the religious pamphlet given to her by the priest a few days ago. It's soggy and swollen and if there were any words in the pamphlet that could help her right now, Giddy can't read them because the pamphlet's ruined. She made *sure* it was ruined.

The light changes and Giddy rushes across the street, the aria's crescendo blasting in her head.

By the time she makes it home, she's gulping back tears. She takes the stairs two steps at a time to get to her room. Her spiral notebook list is propped up on her bed, leaning against the side of her desk right under the corner where Superdoo greets her with his idiotic grin. Giddy grabs the spiral—

Do something unexpected each day.

—and hurls it against the wall, where it bounces and drops to the floor. Giddy picks it up, hurls it at the wall again. Another bounce. Giddy grabs it and backs up, twisting it in her hands, but just as she's about to sit on her bed, her butt bumps into something that should not be there.

Giddy yelps and stands. There's a brown paper bag on her bed. It's folded like a sack lunch. It isn't Giddy's, because she uses Tupperware.

Giddy examines the bag with caution. On one side is written: *ITS A CULTURL REVOLOTOIN AT THE BARBER HOUSE!*

There's music coming through the wall from Dougal's room. Now that she's holding the bag, she can smell fried food. Inside is a Ziploc-bagged sandwich on plain white bread, which is wet and dripping and looks like it has chicken nuggets and french fries, both probably from the school cafeteria. Giddy cracks open the Ziploc and the smell of hot sauce and ketchup hits her nose. *Aww God!* She closes the whole thing and thrusts it onto her desk, where the bag rocks back and forth, bumping into the waving hand of Superdoo. Giddy regards the bagged aberration with the horror it deserves.

Then she takes a steadying breath and takes *Ulysses* out of her backpack. She tries to resume reading, to put Otter Girl and everything out of her mind. The beach scene ends with Leopold and the beautiful girl never meeting. But then it transitions into a strange new chapter that's filled with page after page of what Giddy can only describe as incomprehensible gibberish.

What the hell? Giddy skims through the next two pages, but she can't understand anything Joyce is trying to say. It feels deliberately confusing. So she goes online and finds a scholarly article written about this peculiar section of the book. Giddy's reading it when the door opens downstairs and she hears her father drop his keys next to the computer.

Giddy puts *Ulysses* under her arm and heads downstairs. At the halfway mark, she pauses, looking at her dad as he types on the computer. Giddy takes another slow step down the stairs. Then another.

He finally swivels in his chair. His eyes meet hers and they narrow slightly.

Giddy says: "Hi."

"Hello."

"How's Mom?"

Her dad sighs. He hits a key and shuts down a web page. "She's understandably upset with you."

Giddy looks down and away, uncertain of how she's supposed to feel when she's so positive she was in the right and someone she loves is mad at her anyway. "She still at work?"

"Until one a.m."

Giddy comes the rest of the way down. She holds up *Ulysses.* "You didn't answer my last text."

He frowns. "Yeah, I did."

"Not the last one."

"Huh." Her dad seems to be thinking. He shakes his head. "Pretty sure I did, Giddy." Then he smiles a little. "You enjoying that?"

His smile, small as it is, feels like a ray of warmth in winter to Giddy. "I am, but I have a question about one of the chapters."

"Shoot!" He takes his hands off the keyboard and turns in his chair, giving Giddy his full attention. "I've been waiting to discuss this book with someone for years!"

For as long as she can remember, conversations with her dad have been held in profile. He's always had his eyes locked on something else or his hands typing away at the computer. To see him turned directly to her fills Giddy with a sense of euphoric urgency.

"So there's this scene right after Leopold goes to the beach," Giddy speaks fast, "and I couldn't understand any of it—not even one sentence."

"Can you read some of it to me?"

Giddy reads out loud: "'Universally that person's acumen is esteemed very little perceptive concerning whatsoever matters are being held as most profitably by morals with sapience endowed to be studied who is ignorant of that which the most in doctrine erudite and certainly by reason of that in them high mind's ornament deserving of veneration constantly maintain when by general consent . . .'" Giddy sits down, the book open in her lap. "It just goes on and on like that for a while."

Her dad frowns. "Uh-huh. Can I?" He takes the book from her. His eyebrows knit together as he inclines his head to the page.

Giddy adds: "I looked it up online, and apparently Joyce is using something called Latinate prose. But then he switches into some other prose and just keeps going in the order in which, I guess, prose was invented? And I'm thinking—I think he's being difficult to be funny. I think maybe he's trying to make me *smile*." And she almost does smile, only she doesn't quite, because she's not really happy and it would be just be a facsimile to underscore her point.

Her dad flips through a couple more pages. "I don't know. Joyce isn't really a funny guy."

"Sometimes he is." Giddy frowns. "This one time he spent a whole paragraph just describing how heroic this guy looked and you could just tell he was trying to be funny."

"No, you're not interpreting this right. Joyce reflects the pathos of Irish struggle. That's the essence of *Ulysses*." Another page flip. Giddy sees him mouth the word *what?* as if he doesn't recognize something on the page.

"Well, a bunch of it isn't about that. It's about religion and mortality and being Jewish."

"Joyce wasn't Jewish."

"No, the main character, Leopold, is!" Giddy gets up and walks over to him. "There's a lot of not-Irish stuff here."

"OK, but the point is Irish heritage and culture." Her dad sounds . . . mad at her now? He snaps the book shut. "And if you take your time with this, you'll see that's what's really going on." And maybe also rattled?

Giddy takes the book from him and says: "But I did. It's taken me days to get this far into *Ulysses*!"

"I think there's some stuff you're just not getting, Giddy." He turns around in his chair, hits a button on the keyboard, and the screen lights up. "I've got some work to do. This was a good talk. We should do it more."

Like when they were supposed to have dinner as a family and Mom couldn't make it and Dad blew up at Dougal. Her dad said that was a good dinner and they should do it more, even though obviously no one enjoyed it. So Giddy knows he didn't really enjoy this. Giddy puts *Ulysses* under one arm and stares at him. But his eyes are fixed on the computer and it's like she's not even there anymore!

So Giddy stomps upstairs as loud as she can, slams her door, and waits for a rebuke, some equivalent to *Shut up, Dougal!* But there's only silence. Giddy flops onto her bed with *Ulysses* in her lap. She stares at its closed spine.

And then stares more closely. Giddy holds the spine of the book up in front of her. It's a paperback, meaning there are creases in the spine to show that the book's been held open and read. But Giddy notices the creases end about halfway across the spine's width. Actually, the creases end right about where Giddy is now in the book. The rest of the spine is pristine, as if the second half of *Ulysses* has never been cracked open.

A terrible thought grows in Giddy's mind and, once begun, presses at her temples like a tumor. Giddy flips through the last pages and a couple stick together just at the very corners, a familiar manufacturing error. Giddy gently pulls at them and the corners of the pages separate with a *pop*.

Giddy stares at her dad's copy of *Ulysses* and she thinks, *He didn't read it. I'm holding a book that is being read for the first time.* And she wonders why. Did her dad start it and just not finish it? And if so, why would he lie to her? Why would it sit on their shelf while he mentions it over and over again, year after year?

It seems like such a waste of her time. She thinks about Joyce's use of Latinate prose and thinks that maybe he was also trying to waste her time. Once the idea is set, the spark of fury builds until Giddy goes to her window and unlocks it. It sticks when she tries to push it open. Giddy yells and rams her hand against it twice until it shoots open the rest of the way and a blast of cold night air hits her in the face.

Giddy flings *Ulysses* outside, where it opens midair and flops into the grass face down. And now Giddy sees her front yard isn't empty, because Hunter's standing on the sidewalk.

Hunter. Is standing there. On the sidewalk. Looking up at her window.

Giddy stares back, blank-faced. Then she closes the window as fast as she can, and because it sticks again, this takes her two curses and three hits from the palm of her hand. Giddy races downstairs, where her dad doesn't even look up from his computer as she passes, grabs her jacket, and throws it on as she runs outside.

It's stopped raining and the glow from the yellow porch light and the streetlamp wink off the still-wet grass. Hunter now has the damp copy of *Ulysses* and he's puzzling over it. Giddy yanks it out of his hands.

"You're in my yard," she says, disbelieving.

Hunter blinks at his empty hands then puts them in his pockets. "Yeah."

"You are *in my yard*!" Giddy takes a step forward and he retreats a step back. "Why are you in my yard?"

"Jess said you lived here and I needed to ask you something." He holds up a text with Giddy's address on his phone and Giddy thinks, *Dammit dammit dammit, Jess!*

"Are you stalking me?"

"No!" He takes another astonished step back and wrinkles up his face. "That's stupid. Can we talk?"

Giddy doesn't say anything. She just folds her arms and waits.

He looks down at his feet, uses the heel of one sneaker to scrape some mud off the toe of the other, and Giddy thinks that now, between her dad and James Joyce and Hunter, she has *three* men in her life wasting her time. "Wanted to ask you about the list."

For a stunned second, Giddy doesn't respond, because while she wasn't sure what Hunter was going to say, she never thought it would be about that. She shrugs. "OK. What about it?"

"I wanted to know—" He stops. He sighs. That mud just doesn't want to get completely off his sneaker. "I wanted to know if doing all these things in reverse or opposition or whatever"—he looks up at her—"does it *work*?" He hits the word *work* in a way that makes it seem like it's a heavy word, a hard word, an important word. It kind of makes it impossible to make fun of, and Giddy for a moment doesn't know exactly what this conversation is about.

Until she knows *exactly* what this conversation is about.

Giddy says. "Oh." Then: "Oh!"

Hunter looks back down at the toes of his sneakers. Giddy sees him in her mind walking down the street from his house, his dad yelling at him. She remembers the shape of his shoulders, like a clown's frown, curved and heavy.

She says: "I don't know yet."

Hunter looks like maybe this is the answer he expected, but also an answer that reinforces something terrible. He turns and heads down the sidewalk for about three houses before cutting between them, heading back in the direction of his street. Giddy watches him leave.

Then she runs upstairs and lays *Ulysses* splayed open next to Superdoo to dry. *Do something unexpected each day.* Giddy turns her attention to Dougal's bagged sandwich.

In addition to chicken nuggets and fries, it has what appears to be coleslaw, a slice of pimento loaf, peanuts, and the whole thing is drenched in hot sauce, which hits the back of her throat like lava. When she's done, she knocks on Dougal's door and leaves the wadded-up bag there for him to find. Then she lies back in bed, the hot sauce stinging her eyes, making them water.

10

Giddy's alarm sounds at five fifteen. She stares at the ceiling. Her muscles hurt and she can still taste hot sauce at the back of her throat. She rolls over and looks at Superdoo . . .

Even though at times you may not like who you become.

. . . and very slowly, very deliberately flips him off.

She groans and heads down the hall. In the shower, she frowns because the water falling down her back feels *warm.* She turns the tap off, waits for a second, then turns on the hot water, and *Oh sweet Jesus, that's boiling!* Giddy jumps out of the tub, vowing never to touch the hot water tap again in her life.

The whole house is still asleep as Giddy creeps into Tigs and Tad's room. She quietly picks through Tad's toy box, looking for the Play-Doh she knows is buried at the bottom. Giddy doesn't feel guilty for taking it, since it's supposed to help Tad with math (*Now make the shape of a number three and set it next to the four...*), but all he's ever done with it is push it into the carpet and eat it. Giddy extracts four primary-colored containers. Tad snuffles in his sleep, rolls sideways, and a broken crayon that has all its paper peeled off drops out of his hand. There's a piece of manila paper folded in half on his stomach with spaced-out letters that read *S O R R Y*.

She shuts the door softly as she leaves. She takes twenty-eight dollars from a rainy-day fund her mom keeps in the kitchen window for things like pizza delivery tips, and goes into the garage. The temperature must have plummeted overnight, because in here it feels twice as cold. Jax's bike leans against a treacherous stack of heavy furniture and boxes of stored things. Giddy wheels it out, strapping her helmet on as she goes.

Outside, the air is filled with a sharp bitterness that creeps under clothing and into skin, needles driven down into marrow, where the cold pools and settles into an unshakable pain. Giddy grits her teeth as she rides to the nearest retail store. She leaves carrying a plastic bag containing two purchases. Then she rides to the park, wheels slipping against ice, Jax's slightly oversized helmet wobbling on her head. There's a kind of excited warmth to the spicy smells from the food trucks and the mood-lifting smiles of the people exiting the lines as they eat. So Giddy lines up as well and ten minutes later she's at a bench chewing on a beef-and-green-olive empanada and washing it down with bubbly Inca Kola.

The bench is near enough to the trucks for Giddy to get some of their warmth. Couples and kids with food hustle around Giddy, merry eyes meeting, hot breaths puffing through smiles. The food wakes, warms, unites. Giddy waits to feel that same connection. She takes another bite of empanada, wanting the air to envelop her in a hug, for the ambient energy to transform her into more than just an absent piece but a critical match, a part of a whole joined with something good.

Instead, she just feels alone. Giddy licks the flavors around in her mouth, downs the last of her drink. Her stomach no longer hurts, but the begging achiness in her joints refuses eviction. Giddy throws away her trash and rides to school. The loops of the plastic bag slide back and forth on her bike handles, a troubling burden to transport and her own private albatross.

Outside of school, she reads *Ulysses*, struggling through prose she can't understand. When the doors open, she goes into art early, where the teacher has some old clay out on tables with *FREE-BUILD FRIDAY* in big letters on the board. Giddy takes out her Play-Doh and shapes it into flat, bright triangles and uses the gray clay as connecting mortar. As she works, the other students file in, including Renee.

Giddy watches Renee take her stuff down from a shelf and move to sit at a table on the other side of the classroom, far away from Giddy. Even though Giddy tries to catch her eye, Renee doesn't look at her. Two other students smile, and soon Renee is talking easily at her new table, comfortable wherever she is. After a while, Giddy stops looking in her direction, but Otter Girl's absence is like a balloon around Giddy. She expected it, but even knowing it was coming, she feels the blow of it.

She tries her best to refocus, taking some supplies out of a cubby at the back of the room and then taking out a pen and one of her purchases from the store: a blank card. Giddy writes: *I'm sorry about yesterday. I felt like shit and I took it out on you. You said you wanted to be friends. I hope someday we still can be. You're a great person and I was wrong.* She underlines *wrong* three times and stands on tiptoe to slip the card into the top of the water pitcher with the otter handle. Then she goes back to her desk and continues working with the Play-Doh and clay.

Halfway through class, Giddy takes her facsimile of a stained-glass window to her teacher and asks: "Could this take the place of my crap art?"

He looks it over. "It's nice. I'll think about replacing that grade."

"Can Play-Doh go in a kiln?" Giddy asks hopefully, but he shakes his head.

"Oh no. Play-Doh would *evaporate*. But"—he smiles at her—"this is intricate and very pretty."

Giddy shrugs. "I know it doesn't mean anything."

Her teacher looks at her for a long moment. "Sure it does."

Giddy goes back to her seat and pops her earbuds in, letting opera drown out the rest of the class. But when the bell rings and everyone's leaving, she sees Renee retrieving her otter pitcher and taking the card out, opening it, reading it. Renee closes it and slips it into her pocket. There's a twinge of a smile on her face that makes Giddy feel better, but only a little. She ducks out of the room before Renee can turn in her direction.

When Giddy gets to English, she goes directly to the back of the room to sit at her old desk. Her teacher notes the change with raised eyebrows. When Avery comes in, he stares at the open desk at the front of the room as if it's a mirage. Then he puts his bags on it. Then he walks over to Giddy.

"You're not sitting in my desk."

"No, not anymore. You can have it back."

Avery's eyebrows lift. "Is this a trick?"

"No," Giddy says. "It's your seat."

He frowns, but he takes the desk. Giddy pops her earbuds in and breezes through her final tests on *Hamlet* and *The Yellow Wallpaper.* At the end of class, the teacher announces that they're starting *A Tale of Two Cities* next week and she wants students to self-select discussion groups. Lots of hands go up—but not Giddy's—and the teacher starts writing names on the board. To Giddy's surprise, her name appears up there next to Alicia, Corbin, and *Avery*. Giddy pops the earbuds out and sits up a little higher in her seat, looking at the front of the room.

The girl who called Giddy "Ophelia" and the boy who used to sit to her right wave, and Avery, seated between them, gives Giddy a friendly mock salute. Some of the students are getting up to say hi to their groups, so Giddy gets up and goes over to them. "I'm in your discussion group Monday?"

"We asked for you," the girl says.

"Why?"

They look momentarily baffled. "Why not?" the boy says. "You've got some pretty interesting ideas."

And Giddy thinks, *I do not! I'm good at math and science. English was only an experiment!* To prove it, she goes back to her seat and slumps low. But the teacher writes the words *It was the best of times, it was the worst of times* on the board. Then she keeps writing all these contradictory statements: *it was the age of foolishness, it was the age of wisdom, it was the spring of hope, it was the winter of despair. . . .* When she asks the class how all these things could be true at the same time, Giddy waves her hand because she doesn't want anyone getting this wrong.

"Someone's confused," Giddy says, the eyes of the class on her, expectant, "because a lot's happening and their world's gotten complicated."

"So based on the first paragraph of *A Tale of Two Cities*, is the writer happy or sad?" the teacher asks her.

Giddy thinks and says: "I'm not sure they know." She doesn't try to read the teacher's face to see if her opinion is right. It's an opinion and it's hers. That makes it a thing that is real and doesn't require confirmation from anyone.

But there are slow nods from kids all around her anyway. When the bell finally rings, Giddy grabs her stuff, but Corbin and Alicia stop her long enough to exchange numbers, and Avery asks Giddy if she's ever read *David Copperfield* and then tells her she ought to. Giddy walks out the door of English class feeling different and feeling the same, feeling new but still sensing old Giddy squirming under the folds of her jacket, wriggling, shifting. . . .

Giddy has her phone out on the way to algebra II, and she's bumping into people as she walks because she's downloading *A Tale of Two Cities.* And when she gets to algebra II, the words *Do something unexpected each day* pop into her brain.

Giddy walks over to Katlyn's desk and sets her second purchase down—an owl pencil sharpener. "They were out of giraffes."

Katlyn stares at the sharpener before looking up at Giddy. "Thanks?" she says warily.

"I'm really sorry I got mad and broke your sharpener."

Katlyn picks the owl up, examines it silently.

"And if you would peer tutor me today, I would behave so much better."

Katlyn's back stiffens and Giddy thinks for a moment she overreached by suggesting this. But Katlyn gathers up her things and moves them to the side of Giddy's desk. She doesn't look thrilled about this at all, and Giddy thinks again that maybe she's making a mistake. When they are both settled, graph paper laid out, Giddy confesses: "I don't get how to graph an asymptote."

Katlyn looks at her. "Are you joking?"

Giddy shakes her head.

Katlyn sighs. "I'm going to do the first problem and you can watch." Katlyn writes on Giddy's worksheet and Giddy feels the invasion of space along with a great sense of shame. Katlyn says: "Want to try the second one?"

Giddy starts graphing. Katlyn says: "No." She taps the bottom of the grid. "It's a negative number."

Giddy mouths, *Oh*. As she corrects her line, Katlyn says: "So what's the punch line? Is it that Katlyn can't teach? Or do you have some super-awesome variant of this problem that you're going to lead the class through and everybody except for me will get it?"

Giddy puts her pencil down, confused. "There's no punch line."

"Then why are you acting like you can't do math?" Katlyn asks. "Don't even pretend this is your list, because you are always great at math. You don't even try; you're just a natural."

She sounds so bitter and it's usually true. Giddy does feel like a natural at math. But she had no idea Katlyn sensed that about her.

Giddy says: "I slacked off and now I'm behind, but I'm going to catch up." Then: "I want to keep coming to your *Ulysses* book club. I know a lot of people dropped out, but I'm still reading the book."

"Oh." Katlyn looks glum. "I have to cancel book club. I'm not allowed to do after-school stuff anymore. My grades are too low."

"Your grades are . . . *what*? Which class?"

"All of them. My rank dropped to twelve on the last report card."

Ouch! It's never occurred to Giddy to question who's behind Katlyn's push to line herself up for valedictorian in two years. "Sorry."

Katlyn shrugs like it's no big deal. She turns her eyes back to her schoolwork and Giddy stares at her, thinking that maybe she and Katlyn have more in common than she realized.

Giddy says: "I hate your stupid animal pencil sharpeners."

Katlyn blinks. "What?"

Giddy graphs the next line in silence.

Katlyn takes the owl out of her pocket. "Like the one you bought me?"

Giddy nods.

"They're super cute!"

"They super suck." Giddy finishes the graph and slides the paper over.

Katlyn points. "Your line is basically right, but you forgot to continue it at the top."

Giddy fixes it.

Katlyn says: "Do you even *have* a pencil sharpener?"

Giddy does not. She uses the clunky loud manual sharpener that's attached to the wall, the one that breaks her pencils half the time.

For a while they work in silence. When it's close to the end of class, Katlyn grabs up her stuff and says: "I might be able to do a *Ulysses* book club online."

"I'd be up for that."

"I'll let you know." And Katlyn goes back to her seat looking a little less sad than when she was talking about her grades. As Giddy leaves algebra II, she wads up the plastic bag and throws it away.

With its absence, a certain weight in her chest eases, but only a little. Things still feel off, not right. Giddy drags her feet as she heads to chemistry. She looks through the door at Jess and Trinity, who still sit at the back of the room, their stuff on the table piled high into a fortress Giddy knows well. It's a lot like Giddy's yellow sombrero outfit in art class—it makes it tougher for people to see you, but it also makes it more difficult for you to see everyone else.

Giddy tries very hard to figure out what she felt for them, way back when she first started sitting with them. Was it the way their snark kept them at a comfortable distance? Was it that she believed the Ashlynns, the Treys, the Monicas of the world couldn't really be nice but were laying some trap for her to fall into? Or was it simply that Giddy didn't think she deserved any better, that anyone who offered her more had to be, deep down, somehow less?

Giddy looks at her phone: *It was the best of times, it was the worst of times, it was the age of wisdom, it was the age of foolishness.*

She slips it into her pocket. She grits her teeth and allows her fingers to close into fists at her sides. Tighter . . . tighter still.

Then Giddy releases them and lets her hands fall flat and limp. She takes a steadying breath and boldly walks in, straight up to Jess and Trinity's table.

They don't see her. They sit hunched, C-shaped backs bent over their phones. So Giddy clears her throat and they look up, bleary eyes refocusing.

"I just want to say I'm sorry," Giddy tells them. "I quit sitting with you at lunch and I think I hurt you when I did that. I didn't mean it to be a slap in the face, but I guess you kind of saw it that way. Anyway, I wanted you to know I own that."

After a beat, Jess says: "Are you kidding?"

"She has to be *completely* kidding," Trinity says.

"Are you hoping we forgive you?" Jess barks out a harsh laugh. "Because that's just so . . . What's the word for it?" She looks at Trinity.

"Pathetic," Trinity provides.

"Sad," Jess adds. "Sad and basic."

"So basic," Trinity says.

Giddy shrugs. "I didn't expect you to do anything, actually. I just felt I owed this to you."

Jess opens her mouth to say something back, but Giddy's already turning away. As she walks to the front of the room, she hears Jess sputter something in outrage to Trinity. Giddy's chair creaks as she sits, and Zach predictably turns her direction to give her a cold sneer.

He looks utterly flummoxed when she scoots her chair over next to him. "I'm sorry I hurt you," she says in a low voice.

Zach stares, blinking. "What?"

"When I came over to your house. I ended up hurting your feelings. I wanted you to know I'm sorry."

Zach looks thoroughly off his game. His eyes flutter as he tries to piece together how to look at Giddy.

Then he looks around the room as if judging whether there are witnesses, and a slow smile spreads across his face. "Oh, I get it."

Giddy frowns. "Get what?"

"You want another shot with me. This whole Asia thing has you jealous."

Giddy tries very hard to keep a straight face. "No, I'm not interested in dating you. I just wanted to apologize."

Now he looks more confused than ever and possibly a little angry. "Then why?"

"Why what?"

"Why apologize if you're not interested in dating me?"

Giddy frowns. "Because it's the right thing to do."

"No, it isn't." Zach gives her a disgusted once-over. "You're just fucking with me!"

Giddy gapes at him. "I'm not—"

"Just fuck off." Zach turns back to his composition book, and Giddy, trembling and blinking in confusion, scoots back to her desk. She wasn't braced for this level of condemnation. Zach gets his phone out, sends a text, and several tables back, Jess and Trinity burst out in laughter.

Giddy's face grows red. She wonders if she should have phrased her words to Zach differently and if everything she has planned today is just some horrible mistake. She's nervously tapping the table when the teacher tells them to collect their beaker experiments from yesterday.

Giddy goes to the window to retrieve her nail in a beaker and flinches, because the nail, once so slick and pretty, has been distorted from its time in the blue solution. It's metamorphosed into a lumpy brown log that looks like something at the bottom of a toilet bowl. It jiggles ominously behind the tape with the name *GIDDY BARBER*.

Giddy shivers and rips the tape off. On the board it reads: *Write an analysis explaining the changes that occurred to the nail*, and Giddy, still anxious and uncertain, tries to find her old sense of calm and stability in the explanation of compounds, catalysts, and chemical reactions. Then she reads the second part of the teacher's question, which is: *Can the nail ever be restored to its original beauty?*

Giddy tries to remember everything she's learned about chemical change. It alters substances at the molecular level. So, in reality, the thing in the beaker is not a nail anymore but something new. So if there's no nail left, how can it possibly be restored? So maybe it's permanently *ruined*?

The thought yields a kind of weird panic, and when the bell rings, Giddy walks out fast, eager to put distance between herself and the ruined nail. Trinity's and Jess's snickers follow her down the hall. But when she gets to the cafeteria, a new fear haunts her and she slows down, watching her table from a distance. Ashlynn throws her hands up as she explains something to Monica, who covers her mouth and laughs while Trey smiles and shakes his head. Giddy approaches with trepidation, and in her mind she nervously recites everything she has to say.

And when she sits down next to them, she almost loses her gumption. Ashlynn's saying something about the term *pop psychology* when Giddy interrupts: "I need to tell you guys something."

It's probably the gravity in her tone that makes them immediately stop talking and stare at her. Giddy takes a breath and says: "When I first came to this table, I did it intending to go back to my old table in eleven days because this was all just an experiment to do things differently and that's what you guys were—an experiment. You're not like the people I usually hang with and I was just trying to make my lunch as different as possible."

Ashlynn's smile sinks into a wary frown and Trey and Monica look a little worried, so Giddy hastily adds: "But you ended up being the best thing about my list because you're great people! I needed you to know that I see that in you. You care about people and you . . ." Giddy tries to think of a way to put it. "You try to *give* more than you take when you have conversations. I've never had that before." Giddy has to stop and take another breath because her voice is starting to shake.

This is hard! This is the hardest thing she feels she's ever done.

Ashlynn's brow creases. She says: "So . . . you're telling us what?"

"Are you leaving our table?" Trey asks.

Giddy shakes her head. "No. I'm trying to tell you that the eleven days is up tomorrow"—she takes another breath, lets it out—"and I want to *stay*."

Giddy waits as the three of them stare quietly.

Suddenly Ashlynn laughs. "Oh my God, Giddy! Did you think we'd want you to leave?"

"Did you think we'd be offended because we were part of your experiment?" Monica shakes her head. "That's dumb! People try new things. That's just *normal*."

"We like you," Trey tells her. "None of us wants you to leave the table."

Giddy lets out a shaky breath as Ashlynn says, "Awww!" and Monica gives Giddy a sideways hug. Trey reaches across the table to quickly squeeze her hands. And the achiness that had been in Giddy's joints since this morning finally, *finally* eases in a way that makes her relieved and tired. She pulls out her food, and nothing makes her happier than for Ashlynn to switch topics and go back to an article she read in a celebrity blog. Giddy eats and listens and doesn't touch her phone or her earbuds.

For the first time in a long time, Giddy experiences *peace*. She leaves the cafeteria in no hurry, following behind them, stopping when Trey stops to wave and say a word to somebody at a different table or Ashlynn leans over to give someone a hug. She even gives her own little wave to different tables and none of the people Monica and Ashlynn and Trey say hi to seem to think that's weird. In fact, a lot of them *smile* at her. And Giddy wonders if she could have been doing this all year, stopping and saying hi to people she barely knows.

The feeling of lightness follows her down the hall to robotics, where she is promptly redirected outside by the sign on the teacher's door reminding everyone about the race. Giddy lines up outdoors alongside the school building where robots have already been collected and the shop students have turned out to help her teacher set everything up. Her copper-topped course glistens in the sun. Giddy stands next to Patrice and Deb, who took her advice and have not only wrapped silicone around the bot's rubber wheels but have turned the rest of the material into a poncho.

"To keep stuff from melting down his arm and gumming up the gears," Patrice says.

"We debated wrapping every part in silicone," Deb said. "But we didn't want him to overheat."

Giddy doesn't think anyone's really confident. One team's put googly eyes on their bot along with a sign that reads: *PLEASE GOD I JUST WANT TO LIVE!* The teacher starts up the canned heat, and the course is quickly surrounded with little heat waves. She stacks the marshmallow treats around the pit at the center, places the frozen butter chunks at the top of the half-pipe, then blows a whistle.

It's an all-boys team up first. They have a four-wheeled bot with a tall, skinny post in the middle and a spoon-lever arm. It's decorated with a purple tie and two Ping-Pong eyes with bushy brows. One of the boys makes the sign of the cross as he sets the bot down.

Everyone starts cheering, and Giddy is shoved against one end of the course as the line collapses and everyone presses in to watch. The bot, dubbed Francis, moves in hesitant jerks down the center toward the half-pipe, driven by a wide-eyed student holding a remote. Francis makes it up the half-pipe, flips a couple of butter chunks off the course before securing one on his spoon attachment, and heads to the other side of the half-pipe to deposit it.

But the butter sticks to the spoon. Teams chant: "Francis! Francis!" as his arm flips back and forth. By the time Francis dislodges it onto the target, the stack of frozen butter on the half-pipe's other side has started to melt.

"They're not moving fast enough," Deb says. "The butter's getting soft."

But the team bravely sends Francis back up for more butter, which slides easily onto the spoon, though it's half liquefied by the time Francis climbs the slope for the target, and as it oozes onto the other butter cube, some drips down the spoon arm and onto the wheels.

The class emits a low "Ewwww!" in unison. Francis slips back and forth on the way down the half-pipe. His wheels spin impotently in place for a moment. A few drops of butter spatter up to hit students standing at the course's far corner.

Next Francis scoops up a marshmallow treat, but the heat from the copper surface has rendered the treats soft and it splits in half, sending a spiderweb of goo down to the bot's base and revealing a "surprise" inside—a firecracker. Francis's spoon arm flips back and forth in a panic. The firecracker hits the center of the board and lands on copper, right next to the center pit's smoke powder.

Everyone takes an automatic step back from the course as Francis tries to reverse, but his wheels spin in place. The firecracker rolls, the wick touches copper. . . .

The firecracker explodes, lighting up the pit, smoke billowing! Francis manages to back up, but the melted treat slides down his spoon arm, knocking and dislodging an eyeball. Francis disappears inside the growing cloud of smoke.

Someone mutters: "It's like watching a war movie."

For a few seconds there's nothing but a whirring sound from inside the smoke. Then Francis emerges covered in blackening treats, wheels laboring, little bits of rubber tread sticking to the copper.

"I guess now we know the melting point of a bot's rubber wheels," Patrice says.

"To think we were going to use a plastic raincoat," Deb says.

A small fire erupts from Francis's motor as he stalls out. The teacher uses the extinguisher on him as the crowd gives a cathartic sigh.

"Well, that was kind of a bust," their teacher says, disappointed. Then she brightens. "Who's next?"

Everyone screams with a mad kind of joy and rushes the course, holding their bots up. And Giddy thinks, *I did this! I created this!* And maybe it's a little better than the nail in the blue solution. Maybe for all the ugliness that's happening, some good is coming out of this. Some kids solemnly march their bot to the course on top of the coffin they built. Giddy puts in her earbuds, Britten's *War Requiem* blasting.

By the end of class, one more bot is totaled (and an impromptu ceremony is held for it in the coffin). But Patrice and Deb's survived the course and even managed to get one marshmallow treat on a spike. The teacher announces everyone else will have a shot at the course on Monday. Giddy leaves robotics to a sea of high-fives and students chanting: "Barber Bot Barbecue! Barber Bot Barbecue!"

"You are a *legend*," Patrice tells her on the way back into the school.

"You need to get a copy of the video the teacher was making and save it for your college applications," Deb says. "It's proof of innovation!"

Which should thrill her, but Giddy's brain just goes *meh* and she wonders why. Anything that can get her into an elite engineering school should make her happy. Hasn't that been the plan ever since she got a robot for her tenth birthday? Clearly she's really good at this—she even helped Deb and Patrice save their bot!

The answer, of course, is that nothing excites her, and that's a big part of why she's doing the list, but it's *fucking day ten*! Giddy is baffled. The list obviously works because she's doing things differently, but the list is clearly *not* working because it's not making her smile any more than anything else has. And now she's going to world history, a class she's losing no matter how prepared she is, and leaving robotics, where her stupid bot-torture course is somehow *winning*?

It was the spring of hope, it was the winter of despair. . . .

A sea of girls bumps into her, giggling, turning Giddy around in place.

We were all going direct to Heaven, we were all going direct the other way. . . .

Giddy thinks, *I'm following my rules, but I'm screwing them up, too!*

When she gets into world history, she throws her books on her desk and slams her body into her chair. From under her hood, her eyes dart about in challenge. But everybody, including the teacher, is too wrapped up in their own things to notice her ire.

"Hubris." The world history teacher paces back and forth at the front of the room. "Arguably the main reason a lot of leaders thought it would be a good idea to jump into this war. Hubris and a basic lack of understanding of their fellow man."

Hunter lifts a hand. "What page of the textbook is that on?"

Their teacher rolls his eyes. "Not everything you learn in history has to come from a textbook, Mr. Blancovich!"

"I just thought it did since, you know, we're not supposed to learn stuff from *The Guns of August.*" Hunter holds up the book, shrugging, and the class breaks into giggles.

This time the punishment essay is supposed to fill *two* pages, but Giddy stares at the paper, thinking: *It wasn't hubris! It was the lack of a well-laid out plan. If everyone had planned more carefully* . . . but then she mentally shakes herself, because didn't all the countries go into World War 1 with plans they believed were well thought out? Giddy erases. Finally she writes: *You're never going to read this anyway, because this is punishment for Hunter being a dick. War is hell. But sometimes people can't help going to war. They think they've been wronged or that life's unfair. They don't realize life's unfair to everyone. And so long as they come out of it alive, they've learned something.*

It's not even close to filling two pages, so Giddy writes her name in gigantic capital letters, staggering them to fill the lower half of the page and all of the back page. She slips it on top of the stack on the teacher's desk.

He doesn't look up. He's seated, reading emails, probably counting the seconds until the bell rings so he can get all these kids out of this room. Giddy suddenly pities him, pities anyone who spends their whole day waiting for it to end just so they can start the whole miserable process over.

And she thinks, *There was no winning this class.*

Giddy reaches down and very slowly takes her snarky paper back out of the stack. She wads it up as she heads back to her desk, stopping near the door to deposit it in the trash. She looks back at Hunter, who smirks as he writes, *The Guns of August* open next to his paper. She thinks about him in her yard asking her whether the list works. And Giddy thinks, what if she had said yes? Would Hunter have his own list today?

When the bell rings, he and his friends say: "Bye, Giddy!" as they race out the door, and she leaves world history mired in a loss of identity. Because she's not winning this class, but she's also no longer the kid Hunter picks on, so what exactly is she? Outside, she dons Jax's oversized helmet and it feels weird, like she's dressed up as somebody else. She wishes she could just walk today, the way she's gotten used to. But instead, she has to ride her bike home and it's cold, the sharp chill spreading up from the handlebars through her arms and into all of her. At a stoplight, she tries to put on some opera, but she couldn't charge her phone in robotics because they were outdoors, so now it's out of juice!

When she gets home, she flings Jax's helmet into the garage. When Bodie jumps around her, she grabs him up in a big hug, the nails of his back feet clattering against the hardwood floor.

Giddy goes up to her room, grabs a pen, and starts to put a check mark on Superdoo's list. Then she counts up everything that's happened so far today.

Giddy crosses *Do something unexpected* off her list with complete satisfaction.

Then she picks Superdoo up and flies him around in the air, remembering that when Superdoo knocked over Jax's dominoes, he was being more of a villain than a hero. Giddy thinks now that was probably appropriate.

She's reading *Ulysses* when she hears the door open downstairs and her parents come in. Then the slow steps of someone moving up the stairs. Giddy freezes when her mom opens her bedroom door without knocking.

"Hello, Giddy." Her mom's face is serious. This is the first time she's seen her since the night Giddy said no to everything. Her mom steps inside and closes the door. "We need to have a talk."

At those words, Giddy reaches back for the good feeling she had at lunch when her friends told her they didn't want her to leave. She thinks about how she was wanted for a discussion group in English and how she finally made something in art class that her teacher thought was "pretty."

But all those things suddenly seem so long ago. In the seconds that it takes for Giddy's mom to sit on the edge of the bed, Giddy's walls rise, icy and as unbreachable as the yellow sombrero hat outfit.

Giddy sits, cross-legged, while her mom looks at the floor. It's like she's trying to find the best, most appropriate words.

Then she says: "I'm proud of you. You know that." And she reaches over and takes Giddy's hand.

And Giddy feels the walls begin to melt because that was the last thing she expected her mom to say!

"When I think of how much your brothers have struggled, I realize what a gift you have. You are extraordinary."

"Thank you," Giddy whispers.

Her mom's hand is warm in hers and she's enjoying how this feels when her mom lets go and adds: "I don't say it enough, but we appreciate everything you do. We're here for you. We're your family."

Giddy nods.

"That's what families do. They are there for each other."

Giddy nods harder, staring at her mom, transfixed.

"Your dad and I work hard. We're not around enough. I know that's tough." Then her mom looks at Giddy in a way that makes her feel that same tug she feels when Tigs wants her to do something. In this moment, Giddy wants nothing more than to scoot over and wrap her mom up in a big hug.

"So I'm asking you not to let me down anymore."

But instead of scooting over to her, Giddy frowns. Her mom's eyes hold hers, steady, even, and the softness is gone. Now her gaze is *hard.*

She gets up and walks around the room. "Before you got old enough, we put a lot of responsibility on Jax. But now that he's in college, we want him focused on that life. Tigs and Tad are too young to take on serious chores. And Dougal, well . . ." Her mom laughs a little. "Kids develop at different rates. Dougal's just not ready to do certain things on his own. He needs"—her mom searches for the right word—"monitoring. He needs leading. He needs his *family.*" She stops pacing and looks at Giddy. "So starting next week we'll make a fresh start. Because I know I can count on you, you will go back to the things the family needs you to do: waiting at the bus with Tad and Tigs and Dougal, taking care of the meals, making sure the lunches get packed. Only now you'll also ride the bus home with Dougal every day."

"I can't ride the bus home!" Giddy says. "I'd have to bike because I would always miss the high school bus waiting with Tigs and Tad."

Her mom lowers her voice to a patient tone. "Then you make sure Dougal gets on the bus in the afternoon and you bike *after* the bus to make sure he gets off it and comes home. This isn't difficult if you think about it."

Giddy *is* thinking about it.

"Giddy."

She looks up. Her mom looks down.

"Your experiment has run its course." And she smiles at Giddy in a soft way that tricks up the corners of her lips. It's a smile of confidence, a general expecting a soldier's capitulation. And it angers Giddy that this was how her mom imagined the conversation ending.

"No," Giddy says, voice shaking. "I can't do what you want and still make it to school on time. I'm late every day. Tad and Tigs can get on the bus without me. Dougal knows what he's doing. It's not that he isn't 'developed.'" Her words spill out faster, visions of long walks and book clubs being yanked away. "If I ride the bus home just to make sure Dougal gets on it, I'll never be able to do things after school. And I'll happily cook, but I don't see why I have to do it all the time—why can't Jax? Or why can't Dad? Or why can't *you*?" And here Giddy rips her eyes away because soldiers shouldn't speak this way to generals. "I'm not going back to the way things were before."

"It's not a matter for discussion. Your family needs you."

Which is basically what her mom said the last time, so what does she think has changed? "No," Giddy says. "I won't."

For a moment they stare into each other's eyes, locked by the taut towline of insubordination.

"So," her mom says, "you intend to turn your back on your family." The look of ease slips from her face and it's like an iceberg breaking. "Your family, who has always been there for you."

Giddy opens her mouth to say, *That's not how it is!* But then closes it because isn't that maybe *exactly* what it is? She's trying to find a better way of putting it when her mom goes on.

"This is the choice you're making?" Her mom's voice rises. "After everything your father and I do—putting food on the table and a roof over your head. This is what you do—abandon us? Abandon *me*?"

Giddy doesn't want to let anyone down, especially not the people she loves! Her hands shake in her lap. Maybe she's making a mistake. Doesn't she owe her family? They're her *family*. Giddy's brain crunches numbers and articulates compromises. *If I wake Tad and Tigs even earlier maybe I can get them to the bus stop earlier and I can leave them there a few minutes before their bus and I'll need to go back to biking no more walking but if I ride fast and go back up on the sidewalks to avoid red lights I can get to school almost on time and—*

And everything that was good about this day folds in on itself, matter squeezing, increasing density, gathering with the exponential madness of a black hole, sucking and sucking inward until everything's pulled into its center and crushed and destroyed. Because that's what a black hole does. It keeps needing and needing and taking and taking and when it can't take any more—

It reaches critical mass.

Giddy's whole body had started to tremble, but now she grows still. Her eyes, half closed, pop open. She looks at her mom and says: "No. I won't wait at the bus stop anymore. I won't ride home with Dougal. I know I have a sense of responsibility"—her mom raises a hand but then slowly drops it to her side as Giddy goes on—"but so do *they*, Mom! And if they don't, how are they supposed to develop it, if I keep doing all these things for them? I *won't* do these things." Giddy stops, chews on her lip, waits for her mom to say something back.

Her mom runs a hand across her forehead and through her hair. She walks toward Giddy's door, stops, turns, paces back the way she came in a manner that reminds Giddy of her world history teacher. It's like she's marking her territory, owning this domain.

Then she looks down at Giddy and says: "I never expected you to be a disappointment."

Words that strike Giddy. Words that sink into her like a weight and make her feel cold.

"So selfish," her mom says, edging closer. "Is that what you are, Giddy?" And then she leans down and shouts: "I need you!"

Giddy jumps atop her bed. She doesn't know what to do. In this moment she doesn't want to be here. So she grows still and locates a point on the wall where a jagged line zigzags out of a nail hole. She traces it to another line that connects and zips in another direction, then another. Giddy's eyes whip about in errant, frenetic patterns.

"I thought I had one person in this house on my side, someone who had my back!" her mom yells. "That's the part that hurts, Giddy. That someone I love would do this to me. That you wouldn't care!"

Giddy's eyes follow line after line. They go around and around the walls of the room.

"You are thoughtless and hurtful and you have made things so *hard*!" Her mom's voice breaks like she's going to cry. But she doesn't look right at Giddy. She shakes her head at the ceiling instead. It's like she doesn't wish to see, to acknowledge this section of space in the universe that Giddy takes up.

Then her mom backs out and slams the door and stomps down the stairs. Her mom says something to Giddy's dad and an argument starts, though it's mostly muted and Giddy can't make out the words. Her eyes continue to trace the mazelike designs on the wall. She doubles back and follows them again. She tries new patterns. But they are not cohesive and they don't make sense. There's something to the design, but she'd have to stare at it harder, to keep going back over and over it, to piece together what's coming out of it, to make the pattern of everything on the wall work.

Down below, the argument ends with her mom shouting something at her dad. Dishes clatter. Giddy tears her eyes away from the wall.

And shakes.

She's not sure how long she sits on her bed, trembling. But eventually she takes *Ulysses* back into her lap, reading for the comfort and the organization of words but not really absorbing anything. For minutes it's just her and Leopold Bloom and sometimes this Stephen Dedalus guy, who seems so desperately unhappy and out of place, like there's no chapter in this book in which he's really comfortable, no place in which he truly *belongs.*

So when they eventually call her down for dinner, Giddy gets up and very quietly goes downstairs and takes her seat at the table without looking at anyone for more than a second. Jax is home tonight, sitting on a stool at the kitchen island. So is Dougal. Everybody's made it. Tigs eats plain white rice with sweet and sour sauce on top because that's all she'll ever eat when Mom orders Chinese, and Jax divides a plate of noodles between himself and Tad.

Tad bounces a little rubber swirled ball in staccato beats against the table. He nudges Giddy and holds the blue-and-green ball out for her: "Planet Earth," he says.

Giddy doesn't say anything. She takes some crab Rangoon out of a bag, loads up a plate, and eats. There's nothing but the sound of chewing around the kitchen island coupled with little flashes of light from phones.

But Giddy feels the pull of eyes. She looks up from her meal enough times to notice her mom and dad sneaking glances at her. She tries not to return them. It only mildly surprises her when her mom starts talking to her.

"You know, Giddy," her mom says over her lo mein, "your dad and I have been talking about this phase you're going through, this rebellion."

Giddy takes a small container of wonton soup, opens it, and drinks tiny sips from the Styrofoam container.

"It's probably good for you." There's a kind of false cheeriness in her mom's voice. Like there's nothing serious about this. Like they're all just having a normal conversation. Like she wasn't just up in Giddy's room an hour ago, shouting in her face about how much of a disappointment Giddy is. "Kids rebel. It's a part of life."

Giddy sneaks a glance at Dougal and sees his eyes widen, sees her dad shoot him a warning look.

Her mom goes on: "But it occurred to us that maybe you aren't taking your responsibilities seriously because you haven't had a lot of exposure to the world outside of your high school. So we think you should spend tomorrow at college with Jax."

Dougal coughs out a pot sticker, catching it in his open hands as his dad glares. Dougal shoots a look in Jax's direction. Jax is eating orange chicken. He sets his fork down quickly and says: "Tomorrow is Saturday. I won't have any classes."

"But your college will be open until one," her mom says. "I already checked. So you can at least walk Giddy around, show her your classrooms. You can even introduce her to your teachers if they're there."

"I can't! I have study group Saturday morning."

Her mom lights up. "That's perfect! Scott, don't you think that's perfect?"

Around a mouthful of kung pao chicken, her dad makes a sloppy smile and gives a thumbs-up.

Her mom says: "You can introduce Giddy to your study partners, and maybe they can share stories of how difficult a transition it is between high school and college." Then her mom looks at Giddy and narrows her eyes. "Then maybe you can understand what we expect out of you now is nothing compared to what life expects out of you later."

Jax looks strangely pale. He picks up his fork again. "I don't think I can spare the time. Sorry."

Her mom hits the table with a fist, and Giddy's Rangoon jumps atop the plate. "*Make* the time, Jax! We don't ask you to do a lot because we know how college takes up your time. But this is important! You *will* take her to college tomorrow and show her around and . . ." Her mother fumbles for words. "*Explain* things."

"You are always telling us what a valuable experience you're having," her dad says.

Jax takes a bite of food, chews, stares at the table. For some reason, Dougal has this ecstatic grin on his face. Giddy doesn't care whether she visits Jax's school or not. But a vacuum of silence builds, a suction of pressure, so just to release it, she says: "OK."

Her mom's and dad's shoulders sag, the room decompressing with relief.

Giddy says: "What time do you want to do this, Jax?"

"We'll need to get up really early," Jax says. "Like maybe as early as six thirty."

"I'll be waiting downstairs." Giddy drinks the last of her soup. She eats another piece of crab Rangoon, but her stomach lurches and everything within bubbles up into a burning bile that coats the back of her throat. Dougal finishes his meal and leaves them, running upstairs. Her mom and dad move on to talk about other things while Tad and Tigs babble on about television, but Jax doesn't say anything. He just sits there, stone-faced, eating his dinner.

From time to time he shoots Giddy an intensely troubled look.

Giddy finishes her meal, goes upstairs, and immediately pops two antacids. She opens *Ulysses*, determined to bury herself in it.

That's when Dougal knocks at her door and asks if he can come in.

For a moment Giddy doesn't say anything, in part because her mom was in her room just a little while ago and that was *miserable*. But also, she can't stop seeing an earlier Dougal in her mind, a Dougal several years younger who used to ask to come into Giddy's room all the time. This was the same Dougal who wouldn't let go of Giddy's hand in church, who kept a locked grip on it as if loosening his fingers would mean that Giddy might slip away from him forever. That Dougal vanished into the ether. Giddy can't remember exactly when.

Dougal flips Giddy's desk chair around and sits backward. He taps his fingers and rests his chin on the back of the chair, grins, and says: "How'd you like your sandwich?"

Giddy's not sure what she was expecting, but it wasn't that, and the comparison of her mom's very serious words against Dougal's silly question makes her almost smile with relief. *Almost*. "That was inspired. The whole fried chicken nuggets with the buffalo sauce—it's not a bad pairing."

"But the coleslaw and the peanuts?" Dougal says.

Giddy considers it. "Texture. Crunch. Kind of nice. Hot, though."

Dougal smirks. "I'm going to make you more sandwiches."

"You do that!"

"Good! I will."

"Good!"

Dougal thumps the back of the chair once. He says: "I told Tad to lay off you. That whole bathroom clog thing. I told him it wasn't funny anymore. I'm pretty sure I'm the reason he stopped."

Giddy is pretty sure the Spider-Man comforter is the reason he stopped, but if Dougal needs this win, why not? "OK."

"What Mom said in the car to you, that wasn't right. Just so you know. I know what I do is my fault."

Giddy doesn't want to talk about her mom right now. She looks down at the covers on her bed. She says: "So why do you do it?"

Dougal shrugs. Then he says: "The stuff they put on my forms at school—all that stuff about staying organized, checking my binder, taking my assignments in chunks, using colored overlays—that kind of worked a lot of the time, but I've stopped doing it."

Giddy frowns. "Why would you stop doing something that works?"

"There's this teacher, Ms. Pearlson. She assists in the class for the kids who fall behind," Dougal says. "When she leans over to talk to me, her voice gets all *sweet. Oh, Dougal, honey, how are we doing here? Did you skip this one? Let's cover half the problem with our hand and now let's look at the second half* together." His voice gets squeakier and squeakier until it's almost a bird chirp when he finishes his sentence. "She talks to me like I'm four years old and everyone in the class hears her and they listen to it."

Giddy's heard this voice before, but she's never really thought about it. She says: "Well, are the other kids making fun of you, because she should say something to them if they are."

Dougal throws up his hands. "They are *listening*, Giddy! The whole room can be talking, but when she leans over to point something out on my paper, it's total *silence*. And I have to sit there while she baby talks to me and they just listen and enjoy it and I know what everyone is thinking. So they don't have to make fun, Giddy. They're doing it in their minds."

Giddy's first inclination is to say how crazy that sounds, but when she thinks about it, is it that crazy?

"It doesn't help that you're perfect," Dougal adds hotly.

Giddy's eyes pop.

Dougal goes on: "Your grades are good. You get everything done. Giddy never fails at anything!"

And Giddy can see her mom standing where Dougal's sitting. *I never expected you to be a disappointment.* Giddy shakes the image out of her head. "So the answer's what? Flip off a teacher and wind up in detention?"

Dougal puts his chin back on the chair and looks serious. "At least it gives them something to talk about other than how stupid I am."

"Dyslexia isn't stupid."

Dougal shrugs again. "Anyway, I'm fine with seeing Tad and Tigs off to school, so don't worry about them." He looks at her book. "Have fun reading *Ulysses*."

Dougal stands and Giddy suddenly doesn't want him to leave. She hasn't had a conversation with her brother that didn't end in yelling in God knows when. So she sputters out: "I'll have fun getting up early on a Saturday to go to college with Jax."

Dougal pauses. He looks . . . Giddy's not sure . . . worried? "Yeah," he says. "That'll be interesting." And he doesn't explain what he means as he leaves and closes her door. Giddy sets her alarm and goes back to reading about Leopold and his exploits. She's beginning to think Katlyn was right: this whole book wraps up in one day. That's weird considering how thick the book is. She closes her eyes for a second. . . .

11

• • • and opens them to the six a.m. alarm, which feels absolutely inhumane on a weekend. She shuts her eyes briefly in obstinance, slaps around her clock for the button, and winds up striking Superdoo. The action figure slams to the wall and slides behind her desk.

"Shit!" Giddy rolls out of bed, silences the alarm, and crouches to retrieve Superdoo. He has split into his respective parts—both legs are off at the hip and one arm is off at the elbow. Giddy gathers up his pieces and quickly snaps them together before setting him back on the edge of the desk.

She tiredly showers before heading downstairs. The coffee is just starting to drip when Jax very softly closes his door and rushes downstairs, jacket already on, keys in his hands. He sees Giddy and stops. His shoulders slump and he continues down to sit across from her at the kitchen island, where he stares glumly at the carafe.

It's only 6:14! Giddy says: "Were you about to leave without me?"

"No." Jax watches the coffee. *Drip. Drip.*

About ten minutes later they are fed and Jax is muttering under his breath as he clears ice off the windshield. It's especially frosty this morning, and Jax's car doesn't have good heat, so Giddy puts her arms inside her jacket.

As they pull onto the highway, Giddy expects Jax to start griping about how Mom's making him do this, but he's just *quiet*. He's not even thumping the wheel. There's nothing but the hum of the car on the road.

Giddy says: "So what are we going to look at?"

"The campus and stuff."

"What kind of stuff? Classes?"

"What do you want me to say?" Jax snaps. "I'm going to show you around campus."

"OK!" Giddy rolls her eyes. She pops in her earbuds for the rest of the trip, almost nodding off to a soothing aria.

They reach campus right as the sun's coming up, and Giddy views the immaculate landscaping and evenly spaced brown buildings through a curious eye. Giddy's been to a college campus before—she went to an old university on a field trip. This place is a new community college built all at once, so the buildings look the same. There's a quiet ease to the students wearing their backpacks and sitting on benches with their breakfasts in their laps. Giddy imagines Jax navigating the landscaped courtyards instead of the crowded halls of their hectic high school and experiences a stab of envy.

"Here we are," Jax says flatly. He gets his college ID out and drops the lanyard around his neck. Giddy follows him down the sidewalk, her hands shoved in her jacket pockets. When they get to a big open area, Jax gestures around: "This is the commons. Kind of where we eat lunch sometimes." He points to the cafeteria. "Or in there."

Giddy is shivering and she expects they're going to go into a building soon, but Jax just walks her a little farther outside. "That's the engineering building, where I guess you'd take classes if you went here. Across the way over there is the business school, where I go."

"Can we go inside?" Giddy's rocking back and forth on the balls of her feet. "I'm freezing."

Jax doesn't say anything for a second. He's watching kids walk up and down the sidewalks. Then: "No, there's no point. None of my professors are going to be in today."

"Where's your study group meeting?"

"That got canceled."

"Seriously?" Giddy gapes at him. "Then why'd we get up early?"

"They canceled this morning."

"Then why did we leave—"

"You ask a ridiculous amount of questions." Jax walks ahead of her again. "Anyway, the library is that direction and that's basically the tour."

"I want more coffee," Giddy says, looking at the cafeteria. "Let's go inside and get something warm to drink. Come on!"

"I'm budgeting my money."

"I'll pay for it!" Then Giddy frowns. "Do you not want to go inside anywhere?"

Jax doesn't say anything. He looks down at his ID, mutters a curse.

Giddy says: "Jax?"

"My ID card won't unlock the cafeteria door," Jax says, "or any of the other doors."

Giddy just stares. But Jax isn't looking back at her. He says sharply: "I'll explain in the car," and walks ahead of her.

Giddy follows him, flummoxed. When they're in the car and the motor's started, Jax says: "You see, technically I'm not a student this semester."

Giddy keeps staring. She finally says: "You have an ID."

"That's from last semester." Jax thumps his hands on the wheels. He pivots in his seat. "Giddy, have you heard of biofuels?"

Giddy doesn't say anything for a few seconds. Her mind is stuck on the words *technically I'm not a student.* "You mean like ethanol?" she says.

"Yeah, but from stuff other than corn, like soybeans." Jax speaks faster. "So a friend of mine has a cousin with a startup here in the city and it's biodiesel. I'm already on board. I'm in charge of sales." He seems to think about it for a moment. "Well, I'm one of three people in charge of sales. His cousin has two brothers who are also going to sell this fuel. When it's ready."

"It's not ready?" *Technically I'm not a student technically I'm not a student technically* . . . "You're in business school so you can learn how to be a part of things like this."

"That's where we met. Business school. Giddy, imagine never having to fuel up at the gas station again!"

"But it's biofuel," Giddy says slowly, "so you still have to fill up somewhere."

"Yeah, but since it's going to be *exclusive* to our company, we'll need our own fill-up places and there won't be the big lines you see at gas stations. We already have drawings of how it's going to look." He taps something open on his phone.

"You have drawings." Giddy shakes her head. "But there's a business, right? So you have more than just ideas and drawings. You have investors and a building where you meet somewhere and—"

"We're getting investors now." He opens a website. It has a logo and there's a bio with Jax's photo.

"How many investors do you have?"

"We're working on that! Jeez, Giddy! It is literally always the third degree with you." He shakes his head. "You should be thrilled because this is huge for me."

Giddy doesn't say anything, not because she doesn't have something to say—she has *plenty* to say—the delay is figuring out what to say first. But what spills out in a loud and shocked voice is: "Dougal knows. How the hell does *Dougal* know?"

"He found our website," Jax says. "We used to have this banner that said, *How can four college dropouts change the future?*" He sighs. "We took that banner down."

"But Mom and Dad are paying for college for you," Giddy says. "Right?"

"Most of the money's still in my account," Jax says. "I just used a little to help get us set up."

And by *us* he means a company that has no building, no investors, and no actual developed product. Giddy opens her mouth to say more when Jax says: "Please don't tell Mom and Dad. I'm going to tell them. Really! And I'm not lying—I haven't touched most of the money they set aside for business school."

"But stuff like this is why you go to business school!" Giddy says. "To figure out how to do things like this without losing money!"

"I hate classes, Giddy. They're not for me."

And Giddy thinks about what her mom said about her dad, about how he sat in front of the television instead of studying and that's why he's an orderly and not a nurse like her. And what Jax is asking is for her to keep a big secret and Giddy feels like she doesn't need this right now. "Take me home," she says.

"Not until you promise not to tell Mom and Dad!"

"Are you going to hold me hostage in this car?" Giddy snaps at him.

At those words, he backs out of the parking space. For a long while Giddy is silent as her brother drives. But then Jax starts his *thump, thump* on the wheel and the noise is like a little hammer knocking thoughts around in Giddy's brain.

She says: "So last Saturday when you got mad at me because I walked Bodie and you had to clean dishes instead of studying—"

"I *was* studying, Giddy!" Jax says. "Studying successful businesses, reading about them, getting ideas."

"And instead of taking classes or attending study groups, you're never at home because . . . ?" Giddy holds up her hands in an exaggerated *why?*

"Know what, Giddy?" His hands hit the wheel *thump, thump, thump-thump!* "You've got it all figured out. Why ask me?"

At that, Giddy bundles up inside her jacket and thrusts her earbuds in. Only now instead of dozing, her mind roils the entire way home. Their parents' car is gone as they pull into the driveway. Inside, Giddy rushes upstairs, tosses her jacket to the floor, and slams the door to her room. On the desk corner, Superdoo topples, falls to the floor, and this time all his arms and legs come off, so Giddy has to get down on her hands and knees to gather him up. She's shoving the pieces into her front pockets when she hears her mom and dad come in and yell, "Kids, get down here!"

It's probably the smell of doughnuts that gets Dougal to open his door and go downstairs ahead of her. Tigs gets up too, barreling past Dougal and Giddy to grab the first French twist out of the box. Dougal looks at Jax and gives Giddy this meaningful eyebrow raise, but Giddy doesn't respond.

"Did you enjoy college today, Giddy?" Her mom smiles as she takes milk out of the fridge. "You see anything cool?"

"Did you maybe stop at the engineering building?" This from her dad as he unpacks napkins. "Jax, you showed Giddy the engineering building, right?"

"Sure." Jax gets a doughnut, turns it in his hands, sits in the office chair, and looks at Giddy with so much doubt and apprehension on his face that Giddy doesn't know what to say or do. She knows what she *wants* to do. She wants to scream her head off.

"Did they have orange doughnuts?" Dougal pipes up. He digs through the bag. "I love the orange doughnuts." He looks at Giddy for a long, meaningful moment, eyes bright and questioning.

Giddy doesn't reach for any doughnuts. Once, in chemistry, she plugged a test tube so hard, the rubber stopper wouldn't come out. That's how her throat feels. Like there's a rubber stopper blocking everything.

Tigs reaches for the second French twist and her dad picks up her hand and lightly pulls it away. "Uh, uh, missy! That's your brother's. You better call him down before his twist gets cold."

Tigs grabs a frosted doughnut and shoves it into her mouth. She tries to call out: "Tad, come get doughnuts!" but it mostly emerges as a garbled spittle of chocolate icing.

"Ew, Tigs!" Her mom grabs a napkin and tosses it to Tigs, who takes it, stares at it, and makes an attempt to clean around her mouth while still eating. Her mom wipes her hands on a towel and grins at Giddy, but it isn't warm. It's a cold grin that says she has Giddy exactly where she wants her to be, trying to keep her head up in the sea of Jax's *responsibility*. "So, did you meet Jax's study group?"

Giddy shoots a quick look over at Jax. He seems quietly angry, like this is Giddy's fault, as if Giddy is the one who made him quit college, finance a dumb startup, and lie to his parents. Giddy queues up everything she can say: *Jax's study group couldn't meet us because they were too busy doing college without Jax* or *Remember that discussion about responsibility and me being a disappointment? Well, Jax has some fascinating insight into a nonexistent biofuel company. . . .*

But she doesn't say anything, can't say anything, and she doesn't know why. So to buy time, she selects a maple-frosted doughnut out of the box because there was a time when maple doughnuts were Giddy's favorite, when she'd rush to grab them before anyone else. But now doughnuts burn Giddy's stomach, so she hasn't partaken of a Saturday morning doughnut run in what seems like ages. Not that anyone's ever said anything. Not that anyone's ever even noticed.

Jax jumps in and says: "Study group canceled. Somebody's sick. We'll try again next Saturday."

"Aw." Her mom looks profoundly disappointed. She reaches over and grabs a cherry-filled doughnut. "Then I guess you'll take Giddy to meet them *next* Saturday."

Jax's mouth pops open. "Mom, I can't just keep dropping everything to take Giddy along!"

"It's one thing, Jax," her mom says, licking cherry filling off her fingers. "*One thing* I'm asking you to do. Don't make a big deal about it."

And Giddy has a flashback to about a year and a half ago. Giddy's mom is saying, *I need you to start taking on more of the cooking in the evenings so that Jax has time to get his grades up— Oh, come on, Giddy! Don't look at me like that. It's just one thing!* And on another day: *Do you think maybe you could do this one thing for me: Start sorting the mail on a schedule, maybe every Tuesday and Friday, so it doesn't keep piling up on the counter?* And then: *Bodie needs regular washing and brushing and flea treatments, and Jax is kind of busy these days, so I'm going to need you to do this one thing for me on the weekends. . . .*

Because it's never one thing. It's one thing *after* one thing. And my God, is the tide turning? Is Jax back to being the one who has to do all the *one things* because now Giddy's become unmanageable? She looks at Dougal, but he's sitting near the box of doughnuts, quietly grinning at all of them. Tigs finishes her chocolate doughnut and reaches, again, for the French twist.

Dougal slides the box farther into the center of the kitchen island counter. "Quit stealing stuff, Tigs!"

Tigs groans in frustration. Their mom rolls her eyes. "Tad!" she shouts. "Come get your twist before your sister eats it!"

Jax says: "Mom, I can't really afford the time to chauffeur *Giddy*!" And he says her name like she's so toxic, so unbearably difficult. It makes Giddy gape because it's as if he's forgotten how easily she could get him into trouble!

Giddy takes an angry bite of maple doughnut. The sweetness of it burns.

"Yeah, Mom," Dougal says. Tigs has climbed onto a stool in an attempt to reach the doughnuts and is giggling as Dougal slowly drags the box back and forth out of her reach. "Jax is super busy." He looks over at Giddy. "Isn't he?"

Dougal is waiting for Giddy to drop the hammer. And Giddy wants to, badly! But part of her just can't. She tries to tell herself that it's not because her mom is mad at her and she doesn't need Jax to be mad at her too. Instead, she thinks she's going to hold this over Jax to get things the same way Dougal does. That doesn't make her a bad person, right?

The doughnut hits her stomach like a torpedo. Giddy puts a hand to her belly. She wants to vomit.

"Dougal," her mom says. "Quit teasing Tigs! The box is empty anyway."

"No, there's the twist left." Dougal swipes the box viciously to the side, and Tigs lunges across the island, still giggling. Dougal yells at the stairs: "Tad, come get your twist before *I* eat it!"

"Tad, will you eat your damn doughnut!" Her dad stops thumbing through the mail. He frowns at Tigs. "Is your brother in the bathroom?"

Tigs shrugs. She plops back down in her seat and starts licking her fingers.

Her mom shoots a stern look at Giddy and snaps: "Where's Tad?"

Giddy throws her hands up. "I've been out with Jax!"

"Dougal, where's—"

"Christ!" Dougal rolls his eyes, wipes his hands on his jeans, and bounds upstairs. He opens and closes a couple of doors and comes down, frowning. "Tigs, when did you see Tad last?"

"Oh my God! He's not playing with Bodie? It's freezing outside!" Her mom rolls her eyes and opens the door to the backyard. Bodie bounds in. Her mom pokes her head out, ducks back in, closes the door. She says to Giddy's dad, "Scott?"

Years later, Giddy will remember that it wasn't the volume of her mother's voice at that moment that made them all stop eating and turn to look at her. It was the tone. Her dad tosses the napkin onto the table and opens a downstairs closet door, rifling through the jackets, Giddy guesses, because Tad used to hide there when he was smaller. Then her dad goes and opens the door into the garage.

Tigs, popping her fingers out of her mouth, suddenly says: "Oh, Giddy! Your toys!"

They all look at Tigs. She claps her hands over her mouth and parts her fingers to whisper: "It was supposed to be a surprise."

"Janine!" Giddy's dad shouts from the garage. They all run through the door, into the garage, where the cold hits Giddy with the thrust of a sledgehammer. When Giddy was in here the day before, all the boxes were stacked to the ceiling. Only now a bunch of them have toppled and there're toys and old school papers, things Giddy hasn't seen in years, spilled all across the garage floor. Two old stuffed chairs that were close to the ceiling yesterday have fallen into a collapsed pile of cardboard.

Her dad shoves the two chairs aside and there's Tad.

"No no no." Her dad kneels, blocking Giddy's view. Their mom stares for a dumb second before grabbing her phone. "Kids! Blankets! Now!"

They all rush back inside.

Their mom barks out orders: "Dougal, grab the comforter off my bed! Giddy, take the couch afghan and get the rest out of the closet. Jax, grab all the towels from the bathrooms!" And then she's back on the phone as they all split off in different directions. Giddy loads her arms down and runs into the garage, Jax behind her with towels. Their mom whispers low, urgent words to a 911 operator.

"Move!" Dougal shouts, and bumps into Tigs, knocking her back on her rear as he drags a heavy comforter through the garage to her dad. Tigs blinks at Dougal and then tries to pile in under the comforter with their dad, but he and Dougal shout at her at the same time and Jax swoops in to scoop Tigs up, to lean against the wall and hold her tightly to him. Jax is mute and still and so utterly helpless in his shock while Dougal practically vibrates, bouncing back and forth on his feet near the garage door, his urgent soul begging for something more to do. As their dad bundles himself and Tad up, he has this stricken look that he wears when he comes home from a bad night at the hospital. *I swear, Janine, just when you think you get used to all the sadness, there's another gut punch. . . .*

Giddy takes a slow step forward. She walks around her dad and Tad to where a box has ripped in half, scattering toys all across the garage floor, toys Giddy didn't even know were in the garage. There's the broken bismuth from her old rock collection. Over here are the little toy cars she used to treasure along with some bent sections of racetrack. There are worn children's books and a broken game console. And finally an old robot—*the* robot—the one Giddy adored when she was ten. The one that was a present for her, not a hand-me-down. The one that made her first decide she wanted to become an engineer.

She taps it with the toe of her sneaker, rolling it over. It's dead, the little screen cracked and black, its arms coated in green and red from when Tigs went through her tempera paint phase. Giddy believed, really believed, that all this stuff was still buried in Tigs and Tad's room. Her mom must have boxed it up during the last summer cleaning. So Tad lost things too. But he knew what had happened and where they were and how to get them. And now here they are, everywhere, the spoils of war, the men without shoes on the battlefield, fragments of Giddy's past life, scattered, lost, heretofore unreachable.

When the paramedics arrive, everybody presses back against the sides of the garage as they unwrap Tad. Tigs has wriggled out of Jax's arms, and now she comes over to Giddy and whispers: "Is Tad going to be all right?"

"Yeah, he's just knocked out because it's cold and he needs to get warmed up," Giddy tells her.

"OK." But it's not, so Giddy reaches down and picks Tigs up. Tigs's arms tighten hard and fast around Giddy's neck. Then Tigs mumbles: "It was going to be a 'surprise sorry.'"

Giddy pats Tigs's back, rocks her, stares at the paramedics as they take Tad out of the garage.

"Tad has a card for you," Tigs says. "He made it himself."

Now Giddy's following everyone out the door and into the front yard, where Tad's being loaded into an ambulance. And Giddy's remembering a folded manila paper lying on top of Tad as he slept, remembers a crayon rolling out of his sleeping hand.

Giddy's mom gets into the ambulance and says something to their dad before the doors close. Their dad grabs his keys and heads for the car. Giddy follows, still carrying Tigs.

Tigs mumbles, her little lips pressed against Giddy's neck. "He said he was going to get you your toys back."

Giddy stops. Everyone else is getting into the car ahead of her. Giddy's just standing there in the yard, holding Tigs. Jax slides into the passenger seat. Dougal climbs into the back, opens the door, and leans out, shouting: "Giddy, get in!"

Giddy flinches and moves. She straps Tigs into the seat between her and Dougal. They follow the ambulance and everyone slips into this very terrible quiet.

The ambulance turns on its sirens to get them through a red light. The traffic is heavier than Giddy thinks it ought to be for a

Saturday and it feels like they are moving too slowly. She counts the breaks in the concrete sidewalk outside, the way she counted when she was measuring the blocks on her first walk to school. One . . . two . . . three . . .

Dougal reaches across Tigs, takes Giddy's hand, and squeezes it. She looks over at him and there are no words between them.

Their car lurches forward as they pull out of a traffic gridlock and follow the ambulance down the shoulder of the highway. Giddy looks out the window again and thinks, *Cold is good when you're injured because it slows everything in your body down*, though she doesn't know if that's true or not. Then: *They wouldn't put him in an ambulance and take him to the hospital if they didn't think they could help him*, but Giddy doesn't know if that's true, either. She's counting the lengths of concrete barriers on the side of the highway now. She's up to thirty-six.

It feels like it takes a year to get to the hospital and another three months to park. By now Tad and her mom have already gone in. Giddy and her family get out and run through the doors into the waiting room outside emergency. And just as they come in, Giddy's mom comes out through the door from the ER. She has this horrified look on her face. She puts her hand over her mouth and runs to their dad, who takes her in his arms.

In that moment, Giddy's world careens like a planet thrown off its axis.

But then her mom lifts her head and says: "Tad's core temperature is back up, but he's still not conscious, so they're doing a brain image."

"OK," her dad says.

"They want to know how long he was in the garage." Her mom looks at them all with great urgency.

Giddy shakes Tigs's arm. "When did Tad say he was going in there to get my toys?"

Tigs blinks at her.

Giddy says: "You're not in trouble. When?"

Tigs shrugs.

Giddy snaps: "Tigs, *when*?"

"I don't know, it's a surprise, sorry!" Tigs yells out, jumping a little on her toes.

Dougal looks at Giddy: "Wait. Why was he going after your toys?"

And now everyone looks at Giddy. Dougal, Jax, Tigs, Mom, and Dad . . . they're all just staring at her. And Giddy thinks, *This can't be my fault. What did I say? Something like . . .*

"You take all my things. I don't get to keep anything. You take all that I love away."

But how could Tad think she meant it?

"Giddy?" Her mom's voice breaks as she says Giddy's name. Now Giddy can feel the stares of *everyone* in the emergency room. All the families are looking. And Dougal's right. It's most cruel when everyone's just quietly listening.

It's not my fault I didn't do it it's not my fault!

"Giddy?" Her dad reaches out, puts a hand on her shoulder. Giddy flinches and looks at the floor.

Stop looking stop looking stop looking . . .

Tigs tugs at her leg and now Giddy can't look down. She tries looking up, but . . .

"Giddy?" Her brother Jax. She tries to look someplace else, to find a spot over their shoulders.

But there's nothing and there's nowhere left for her.

So Giddy looks at her dad and says: "You've never read *Ulysses*."

He blinks, taken aback. They all kind of stare at her, confused, and her dad says: "What?"

"You've never read that book." As soon as Giddy begins, the words spill forth and she no longer has any control over them. "You don't know anything that happened in it and the last pages are stuck together. It's never been read. You've been lying for years, telling everyone you've read it. But you didn't. You're just a liar."

"Giddy!" It's a sharp rebuke from her dad but also a startled one, and her mom opens her mouth like she's going to say something, and Giddy tells her: "Jax dropped out of college. He's spending your money on a startup business that doesn't even have a real product. He's been pretending to go to class all this time." She looks at Dougal. "Dougal knows and he didn't say anything."

Jax was already ghost white on the whole ride over, but now he just stares at her and swallows hard. Dougal's face wrenches up and his fingers work at his sides, opening, closing, eyes pleading, *Giddy, what are you doing?*

"Dougal's not using any of his accommodations at school," Giddy says, looking him in the eye. "He's trying to fail because he hates being different."

Dougal's eyes widen. But there's more. There's so much more! Giddy knows her words have become real things that have weight and mass. And these have only been the small words, the ones on top. But now that they've crawled out, been wrested free, seen the light, broken loose with all the haste of a sliced-open artery, there's nothing to hold back the big ones anymore. So before Dougal can open his mouth to say anything, Giddy whirls on her mom.

"And you don't love Dad!" she says, her voice breaking.

"No. *No!*" her mom says. "No, that is *not* true!"

"Yes, it is!" Giddy yells this part, because now it hurts. It's nothing but pain coming up and out of her. "You're embarrassed by him because he wouldn't finish college! You *told* me! You said *what I married*!" It's out. It's expelled. And now it's everywhere. Giddy feels pain everywhere she can think to feel. "And you make me start things you don't finish! You'll never make that virtual scrapbook. Remember when you wanted to learn sign language and you made me look up all those courses? Remember when you were going to start painting and you had me go buy all those supplies? But you never do it because you're busy! That's all you're ever going to do—work and wish you did fun things!"

And she looks down because Tigs is pulling on her sweater and crying, big fat tears dripping out of her eyes, Tigs who never does anything wrong, who is nothing but sweet, and Giddy says: "Why weren't you watching him? Tad is *your brother.* You share a room. Where were you?"

Tigs gulps in air. "Giddy?"

"If you'd been with him, this never would have happened." It's those last words that slither up and ooze out like slime the way they oozed out of her mom. *I never expected you to be a disappointment.* Giddy sees Tigs take the words in, process them, watches her eyes grow big and change with knowledge.

Giddy sees a nail in a blue beaker solution, brown and scabby, jiggling and monstrous, the marked label: *GIDDY BARBER.*

And she laughs.

It's a big laugh, harsh and horrible. It hurts to the core. Giddy levels a shaking finger at them all and says: "I know I'm a disappointment, but guess what? So are you! It's a Barber family trait!"

And she laughs again. And again. She can't stop laughing. They're all just looking at her. Tad's the one in the hospital, but they're all looking at *her.* And her laughs are coming so fast that Giddy starts hiccupping between them.

"You are all"—she laughs—"such *fucking disappointments*!"

She can't be part of it anymore. Giddy turns around and runs. She bolts straight out the sliding glass doors of the emergency room and outside into the cold air. She runs through the parking lot. She can hear her family shouting after her and the stumble of feet as someone gives chase. But Giddy doesn't stop. She just keeps running, moving faster than she ever has, scooting around car after car. She runs until she's out of parking lot. Now there's just a stretch of trees, an easement with a highway in the distance.

So Giddy runs for that and just keeps going.

And the priest is in her head, warning her, *The race is not to the swift or the battle to the strong*, but Giddy doesn't think she can stop being fast, though she definitely isn't strong. When she reaches the highway, there's a lull in traffic and she races across. She runs into another neighborhood, up and down streets she doesn't know, running until she isn't sure where she is or what she intends to accomplish.

Only when she is out of breath does she slow down to think about it. She walks, head down, arms limp. When the neighborhood meets another major road, Giddy sees a city bus at a stop and gets on.

She watches the fenced houses go by, forehead pressed to glass, thinking about the day Jax picked up Dougal and *he* did nothing but look out the window as if imagining himself someplace else. Giddy changes buses at another stop and rides to her neighborhood.

She disembarks and walks. Giddy sticks her hands into her front pockets to put in earbuds but realizes her phone is in the jacket she flung to the floor of her room. She doesn't even have her house keys. Instead, Superdoo's pieces poke her and she remembers shoving his broken parts into her jeans this morning. She thrusts her fingers in after him, forcing him down all the way to the bottom of her pocket.

Giddy walks around her neighborhood, down one street and then another, until her aching feet slow to a stop and she stands there like a questionable point on a map. She closes her eyes and thinks, *YOU ARE HERE*. Then opens them.

And sees Hunter's house.

A surge of energy shoots through her. She runs up to it and beats on the door over and over with both fists. After a few seconds it opens, and Hunter stands there, looking stunned. He had a scowl on his face like maybe he was going to tell whoever was knocking so hard to fuck off. But now he just looks confused.

"Giddy?" He steps out, closes the door behind him, looks behind her and around. "What's going on?"

Since she doesn't need to knock anymore, Giddy's fingers close into fists at her sides. She squeezes them tighter and tighter until the vibrations racing up her arms cause her whole body to shake.

Hunter asks: "Are you OK?"

Giddy shakes her head, dislodging tears she didn't know existed. She doesn't say anything. She just keeps shaking her head.

He puts a hand on the door. "Want to come in?" And when Giddy doesn't answer, he adds: "My dad has a beer fridge in the garage. I could raise the door. You could grab one if—"

"I do not want to go in the garage!" The scream bursts out of Giddy and so do more tears.

Hunter says: "OK! OK! What do you want? What can I do?"

"I want to go to the park," Giddy says between sobs. "Will you go to the park with me?"

"OK."

And as they walk to the park, Giddy is crying, crying more than she thinks she's ever cried in her life. Hunter doesn't say anything, doesn't try to stop it. He just walks next to her with a kind of scared expression on his face like this has never happened to him before, like he doesn't know what to do.

When they reach the park, Giddy stops and sits on the grass under a tree at the far edge. The food trucks are also out, but she doesn't want to go to them, either. Giddy hates that she enjoyed food truck food, hates that she ever took pleasure in anything. Hunter sits down next to her and Giddy just shakes and cries and shakes some more and cries some more.

Then she thinks, *I should call and check on Tad!* She forgets she doesn't have her phone. She shoves her hands into her pockets and—ouch!—there's nothing there again but Superdoo's pieces.

So Giddy takes Superdoo out—poor, old, much-abused Superdoo. She turns the pieces around in her hands and says: "My little brother is in the hospital because he went into our garage and stuff fell on him. It was cold. We don't know how long he was there. I don't know if he's going to be OK." Superdoo's cape is all twisty around his head. She straightens it out, turns his head around, sees his big plastic smile. "He was in the garage because he wanted to give me back some old toys. I'd yelled at him. I told him he took everything I loved. So he was in there trying to give me back something." Giddy pops Superdoo's legs back on. She tries to put his arm back together, but the pin has fallen out and the joints will no longer connect at the elbow. "I'm supposed to watch him. I'm the only one they ever ask to watch him. They never ask Jax or Dougal. It's always me. I stopped because I didn't want to do it anymore. I'm supposed to watch Dougal too, and he's only a year younger than me. I'm supposed to keep him out of trouble. But I quit because I didn't want to do that, either." Superdoo's other arm is broken at the shoulder. Giddy can't reattach that one either because the actual plastic is snapped. "My mom treats me like I'm the maid. I'm even supposed to organize fun stuff for her, and I spend time doing it and then she never does any of it anyway. And my dad's been lying to me. And my mom hates my dad. And my older brother was lying to both of them because he was supposed to be at college but he dropped out and he's spending his college fund on some stupid business that doesn't really exist. And I'm not sure what to do with all this information!" Giddy gives up on the arms. She needs replacement parts and hobby shop glue. And even if she gets those things, she's not sure Superdoo will look the same ever again. She says: "And I really hate that I wasn't watching my brother. And I hate that my stupid list made me a bad person. I hate myself so much!"

In the distance, skateboarders perform stunts on the half-pipe and people line up for the Peruvian food truck and another truck that's selling ice cream and waffles. Giddy considers flinging Superdoo's pieces as far as she can throw them. But all she does is tuck them one by one back into her pocket.

She looks at Hunter because she's honestly surprised he's still there. But he's looking off into the distance at the food trucks, staring into space the way somebody does when they are processing something very difficult. He shakes his head. He says in this kind of shocked and angry voice: "Wow."

Giddy blinks, keeps looking at him. But Hunter's still processing, still thinking. She can see his eyes moving back and forth, mulling it over, piecing it all together.

Then he says: "Giddy, that's terrible." He shakes his head. "No, I mean that's seriously fucked! That's *a lot*! It's fucked-up, Giddy."

Giddy nods because it *is* fucked-up. She looks down at her hands. She feels . . . How does she feel? Empty? Worn out? Like everything's spilled all over the place.

"No wonder you're sad."

Giddy looks at Hunter, but he's saying these words with a frown on his face like they're only just now making sense to him.

"Giddy, *no wonder you're sad*! Think about it. That's some seriously messed-up shit!"

Giddy nods again.

"I'm sorry," Hunter says. "Jesus Christ, Giddy, I'm so sorry!"

Giddy looks back at him. He looks a little bit like the way she imagines she must look—worn out, dumped on, expended and depleted. And when things are that empty, what do you fill them up with?

Giddy keeps staring at him. He frowns and says: "What?"

And then she does something that she never saw coming.

She scoots over and puts her head on his shoulder. When he doesn't do anything, she lifts her head up and looks at him. She doesn't know how to give an invitation that isn't planned out at least a day in advance with all the pros and cons weighed. But when he doesn't move away, she lifts her head and presses her mouth as gently to his as she can.

And for a second he's too stunned to do anything. And then a second later he's *kissing her back.*

There's part of Giddy that just wants to stay in this place, in this section of universe where she finds herself right now. Because while it's not good yet, Giddy feels it approaching good, like good is available and ready for when Giddy's ready, whenever that might be. And isn't that maybe what it's all about? Isn't it possible that the reach is just as important as the grasp?

Giddy very slowly stops kissing him and stands up. Hunter's looking up at her, baffled, and Giddy says: "I need to go back to the hospital."

"I'll go with you!" Hunter starts to get up, but Giddy shakes her head, backing away.

"No. I've got this." And she turns and runs. Giddy runs to the nearest bus stop and waits, hands thumping against her legs. When the bus arrives, she takes it all the way to the medical district.

And her thoughts are a jumble of radiating matter as she looks out the window. They are particles flying in different directions and some of them are quite terrible. Giddy thinks of the worst that might be waiting for her, and once that thought is targeted, it's the *only* thought.

When the bus reaches the stop, Giddy runs down the block and across the highway. She winds through the same parking lot she ran through before. She nearly bumps into the glass before the sliding emergency doors can finish opening.

Her family is no longer in the emergency waiting room. Giddy runs up to the desk and says: "I need to see my brother Tad Barber!"

The woman behind the desk is on the phone. She holds up one finger and eyes Giddy sternly. "Wait."

But Giddy's done waiting. Giddy beats her fist on the desk and shouts: "I need to know the room number for Tad Barber!"

"You need to keep your voice down!" The woman goes back to talking on the phone, and Giddy, frustrated, sees the button on the woman's side of the desk that opens the ER doors, leans over, and pushes it.

"Wait!" the woman screams after her. Giddy runs to the slow-opening doors and squeezes through. She runs down the hall, because how hard could it be to find Tad? "Tad?" Giddy yells. A woman in scrubs carrying a clipboard sees her, says something, and puts her hands out like she's going to stop Giddy.

Giddy breaks out into a run, shoving past her, hitting the woman with the edge of her shoulder so hard, it knocks her aside. "Tad!" Giddy rounds a corner, keeps running. Now there are voices behind her. Giddy's shouting: "Tad! Tad! *Tad!*" More voices. Somebody puts a hand on Giddy from behind. She shoves them off her. But it's a security guard, and he grabs her arm. Giddy struggles, kicking, screaming. "Tad! *Tad!*" The guard is trying to talk to her, but Giddy won't have any of it. She keeps fighting him even as he pulls her arms behind her and starts pushing her down. Giddy flails and kicks, rubbery sneakers squeaking against the slick floor. "Tad!"

"Get off her!" Her mom's voice. "Oh my God, *no*! That's my daughter! I've got this! Please!" The grip loosens. Giddy is sitting on the floor when her mom drops down and throws her arms around her. "Oh, honey, Tad's going to be *fine*! He woke up. He talked to us. All the imaging's good. They're just keeping him overnight to be sure. Shh . . ." She rocks her. Giddy trembles. Her mom holds her.

"Shh!" Her mom rocks her. "Shh! Shh! OK. OK, Giddy."

Giddy doesn't say anything. They stay like that on the floor for a little while. Then they get up. The security guard has stepped back and there's a couple of people in scrubs near him, watching her, and the tense quiet fills the air with a sense of unreality. Giddy's arms and legs wobble. They hurt. They feel like they're going to fall right off.

Her mom walks her in to see Tad.

Giddy's little brother is in a hospital bed. The room is dim, lit by the sun through closed curtains. Tad is sleeping, but there's enough light for Giddy to see that his lips aren't blue anymore and except for a bruise on his temple, he looks perfectly normal. Someone put a gift shop teddy bear in his arms. Giddy puts a hand on the rail, watches his chest heaving in and out.

Dougal's in the room in a chair next to the window. He gives Giddy a little wave and a half smile. Giddy's mom is holding her hand. She squeezes it and kisses Giddy, tugs on her. "Come on."

Her mom takes her to another waiting area down at the end of the hall. It's nicer than the ER one, with soft couches and vending machines. Her dad's there, sitting, on his phone, one arm around Tigs. Jax is coming back from one of the vending machines, a coffee in his hands. He puts the coffee down on a table when he sees Giddy, and her dad sits bolt upright and Tigs's eyes get wide. And here in the brighter light of the waiting area, she can see that they all look terrible, including her mom. They have gray under their eyes. They are pale and exhausted and Giddy senses she may have missed some fight between them all.

Giddy looks into Tigs's wide eyes and the words *If you'd been with him, this never would have happened* rise up to shame her.

And then Tigs runs over to Giddy and throws her arms around her legs, and her dad and Jax come over and put their arms around Giddy. And Giddy has never felt so surrounded in all her life.

But she pushes back against them, not violently, but just enough to wriggle her way down to Tigs, to look in her face and tell her: "You didn't do this, Tigs. This wasn't your fault. I was being mean."

"I know," Tigs says, eyes huge and wise. "Dad told me." Her young voice speaks with uncomplicated conviction. Relief washes over Giddy and she is suddenly tired, more tired than she can ever recall being. She doesn't resist when her mom pulls her over to a quiet sofa and they sit together. Her mom doesn't let go of Giddy's hand and Giddy tiredly regards the connection with great wariness. She senses there are words to be said, but Giddy has no breath for them.

So she leans a heavy head against her mom's shoulder.

And Giddy sleeps for a long time.

She wakes to a crick in her neck. When she looks around, she sees the arrangement of the waiting room has shifted, with new seats taken and others vacated, with toddler toys strewn about over old magazines and scuffed tables, snack wrappers from vending machines and lipstick smudges on cooling coffee cups. And all these strangers look lost in their own struggles, have tired eyes that pass over Giddy. Giddy rubs the back of her neck and sits up.

And notices her mom is still holding her hand. She looks at Giddy. Her mom's eyes are owllike, circled from not closing. Giddy pries her fingers loose and withdraws her hand to her lap, making a pretense of stretching, but really all she's doing is scooting away from her mother, putting an inch or two between them. Giddy folds her hands together in her lap in the same way storm shutters lock down windows.

Her mom stiffens. For a second or two they stay as they are, saying nothing.

Then Giddy's mom says: "I'm the disappointment, Giddy. Not you. And I'm the one who's selfish."

Giddy knows this to be true, but knowing it doesn't make Giddy feel any better. To the contrary, it makes her angry. But she sits, tense, locked down, wanting to be anywhere except here listening to this confession.

"This was never your responsibility," her mom says. "I put it all on you. I put *everything* on you. I didn't leave any room for you at all. I'm so sorry."

Giddy doesn't care. She sits stone-faced, waiting.

"What I said about your dad," her mom says, "was a thing that never should have been said. And just so you know, I do *love* your dad. And he loves me even though I can be very awful."

Giddy can tell her mom is forcing these difficult words out, can feel them crack and break under the weight of their own rigidity.

"Can you forgive me?" Her mom's voice shakes. Little vibrations tremble through the fabric of the sofa, invading Giddy's space.

Giddy doesn't answer her mother, doesn't tell her that she'll forgive her. But she also doesn't say that she *won't*. As far as Giddy's concerned, that's a good enough answer. They sit like that for a few seconds, Giddy's thoughts racing around as fast as her body in the hospital parking lot.

Finally, Giddy says: "I don't want to become a mechanical engineer."

Her mom looks like that's the last thing in the world she expected Giddy to say. She blinks, surprised. "Oh?"

"When I was ten, you and Dad gave me a robot for Christmas," Giddy says. "Every time I got it to do something new, you and Dad would fall over yourselves saying how great I was. You called me your 'little engineer.'"

Her mom doesn't say anything to this. She waits, tense, listening.

"That was the only time I remember you paying more attention to me than you did to Jax," Giddy says. "And I think I just figured this was me—I was an engineer. Finally I'd found something I was good at." Giddy shrugs. "Engineers are good at math and science, so I became good at math and science. But I'm starting to become good at other things too."

Her mom reaches up to try to brush a strand of hair out of Giddy's face. "Baby, you can be good at anything you want to be—"

And is forced to lower her hand when Giddy reaches up and slaps it away. Her mom draws back and Giddy feels the gulf between them expand with tectonic power.

"But I don't know what I want!" Giddy says, looking at her hands in her lap. "I don't smile, like, *ever*. Nothing makes me laugh." She looks up at her mom. "Why?"

"OK." Her mom's eyebrows are locked together and she looks around the room, seeking, as if she knows she needs to say something brilliant right now. Giddy knows she's never told her mom how she feels and maybe she's expecting something that her mom isn't capable of ever giving.

Then suddenly, her mom says: "Do you know why you are named Giddy?"

Giddy frowns. "You just said you liked how it sounded."

Her mom shakes her head. "That's not true. When I became pregnant with you, something bad happened. I woke up one day late in my pregnancy and I wasn't happy about anything. I thought it would pass, but it didn't, so, at your dad's urging, I saw a therapist. But nothing changed. It got so bad, I would shut down for days and your dad would take care of Jax and run the house."

Giddy's eyes widen because she can't imagine her dad running anything, can't imagine him taking the reins of the family even for a minute. Giddy says: "What did you end up doing?"

"Nothing," her mom says. "It ended naturally the day I had you. You were born and I heard you cry. And I just started laughing. And it was over. It felt so good. Because while I was like that, it felt like I wasn't really living, like everything was grayed out and just bad. So when it was over, how could I not name you after happiness?"

Giddy's heart starts racing because she thinks she knows this feeling. She thinks about all the times she's lain in bed with Superdoo staring at her like it was natural to be smiling all the time, natural to be happy, and says: "Why have you never told me this?"

"I don't like to think about it." Her mom's voice changes with those words. She says them in a way that is final, and Giddy can tell she doesn't want to talk about it. Instead, she pulls Giddy into a hug that Giddy doesn't fight, even though she's not interested in hugging.

She says into her mom's neck: "I'm still not taking Tigs and Tad to school and I'm not monitoring Dougal ever again."

Her mom laughs. "I know."

And when her mom finally lets her go, Giddy gets up and walks around the room, stretching her legs, her brain wrapped in a surreal fog. When she comes back, her mom is leaning into the corner of the sofa, eyes closed. She's making little snorting noises and Giddy imagines her mom napping like this on an overnight shift, wonders if her mom spends most of her sleeping time on hospital couches.

Giddy's dad is tucked into the corner of a sofa on the other side of the room. He has his phone plugged into the wall. Giddy's eyebrows lift to see that Tigs has somehow acquired her tablet. It's also plugged in and she's watching Disney videos.

Her dad sees her. "Jax went out and brought us some stuff from the house." He reaches into a bag on the floor and retrieves Giddy's phone, earbuds, and charger, handing them to her. Then he reaches in again and this time retrieves his copy of *Ulysses.*

He holds it out to Giddy. She takes it, but she isn't sure what to do with *Ulysses* anymore. This is a book that mattered when she thought her dad had read it. Now it's just any old book. Her dad says: "My senior year in high school, I had an English teacher who said this was a life-changing book. So I bought it and I started reading it. I don't know how far I got in—not far, probably. Anyway, I think maybe I found it confusing?" Her dad frowns a little, scoots back into the corner of the sofa, turning a little so he can face Giddy fully. His eyes look pleading. "I *was* going to finish it, I swear I was! But I watched the 1967 movie first. And then, I swear to God, I was going to finish this book! And I know this next part sounds a little nuts but . . ." Her dad shrugs, rolls his eyes. "I honestly thought I *had* finished it. Like I remember picking it up again and again and flipping through it. I think I even read the end because I remember there's some stuff with Molly that gets interesting." He shakes his head. "I just really remembered reading it. And I remember my teacher said that it was all about Ireland and Joyce was influenced by Irish conflicts and maybe I just believed *I'd* come up with that." He shakes his head again. His shoulders sag under the weight of truth. "Maybe I just really wanted to believe I'd read *Ulysses*."

And Giddy thinks, *That's no excuse for lying!* For a second, she wants to find another window to throw *Ulysses* out of. And then it occurs to her that maybe her dad means it—that he really thought he'd read it. So he was lying, but he wasn't lying to Giddy. He was lying to himself.

Her dad stares off in some indeterminate direction. He looks confused and sad like something important has been taken from him. Giddy is pretty sure she knows shame when she sees it. A war wages within her, wanting to stay angry and wanting to hug him at the same time.

Instead, she says: "There's a movie?"

"Yeah, I'll show you." Giddy sits next to him as her dad gets out his laptop and finds a copy of the movie streaming. He puts his arm around Giddy and they watch the beginning of the movie, which is in black and white and all the haircuts and suits are like her dad said, from the 1960s.

It's not bad, but Giddy thinks she likes the book better, and she falls asleep again sometime while the character of Stephen Dedalus is trying to teach a kid a lesson at school.

When she wakes, it's dark out. Her dad's also asleep, the computer open in his lap, the screen dark. Tigs has crawled up to fall asleep against Giddy, and they are all lined up on the sofa like a row of knocked-over dominoes. Giddy's legs hurt, so she extracts herself, dragging Tigs's little form over so she has their dad to sleep on, and Tigs, dead to the world, doesn't wake. Giddy walks to the window, notices for the first time that the waiting room is much bigger than it appeared, that it goes around the corner. Sitting on a sofa at the far end of the adjacent hall are Jax and Giddy's mom. They are awake and talking. Giddy hears Jax say the word *biofuel*, notices that he's very animated and excited, moving his hands around a lot while her mother is rubbing her fingers against her temple as if everything Jax is saying is giving her a headache. As Giddy watches, her mother interrupts, puts a hand on Jax's knee, and says something very softly to him. Whatever it is, it seems to deflate him, and his expression sours as he sags back into his seat.

Giddy leaves them to it. She goes back into Tad's room, where Tad is sleeping and Dougal is in a chair playing a game on his phone. He looks up at Giddy.

Giddy says: "How is he?"

"He was up a while ago. You missed him eating dinner."

It suddenly feels unconscionable to Giddy that she should have missed that! Dougal sees the stricken look on her face and he comes over and puts his arms around her. "Hey! He's good. He'll be out tomorrow."

Giddy thinks it's time to fess up. She pushes her brother back, looks into his face, and says firmly: "It's my fault. Tad went into the garage to get me toys because I accused him of taking all my things."

"What?" Dougal blinks. Then he laughs. "He's so dumb!"

Giddy stares at him, confused.

He adds, "No, seriously. I'm going to hold this over his head for the rest of his life."

Giddy can't believe Dougal is ready to dismiss her confession with just that simple statement. She pulls away from him. "But it's my fault!"

Dougal looks at her like she's lost her mind. "Giddy, it's nobody's fault." He grins. "We're all disappointments, remember? We're all human."

But Giddy can't dismiss this so easily. She's heard from her mom and her dad, but now it's her turn to apologize. She needs this! She needs absolution!

She says: "Well, I'm sorry I told Mom about what you said about school."

Dougal laughs even harder. "So I'm stupid too," he says. "So what? Want to be stupid?" He holds out his hands expansively. "We can all be stupid together, the stupid bunch of Barbers!"

"But none of this is funny!"

"But it kind of is, isn't it?" Her brother sits back down in the chair and takes his phone out again. "I mean, *isn't it*?"

Giddy looks down at her brother, confounded, because she's not getting the joke that he's getting. He suddenly stands up again. "The cafeteria hasn't closed yet. I'll make a coffee run. Maybe get us some burritos. You look hungry." He pats Giddy on the shoulder and goes past her, leaving her there in the room, and Giddy, not wanting to wake up Tad, not feeling like she has any *right* to disturb him as he sleeps, quickly backs out of the room and softly closes the door.

In the waiting room, her mom's scooting Tigs over to sit next to her dad. He wakes and gives her mom a groggy kiss. Her mom smiles a little but frowns at the darkened computer in his lap. He taps a key to restart *Ulysses.* Her mom draws up her knees and curls up against him, wraps her arms around Tigs in her lap. She begins to watch.

Giddy goes to sit down, and her dad scoots over to let her sit on his other side. Jax walks back from a vending machine and stands behind the sofa, watching it with them, crunching his way through a bag of chips. When her mom asks their dad a question, Giddy jumps in to explain the scene, comparing it to a longer chapter in the book. She's not sure if her mom gets it or not. Her mom just quietly nods to everything Giddy tells her as Tigs stretches out to sleep across their laps.

And when Dougal shows up with coffee and food, they all wind up watching *Ulysses* right through to the end. Giddy's mom declares the movie outdated and sexist, while her dad counters that Joyce's views on women were actually ahead of his time. Jax doesn't say anything, and Giddy thinks he was just confused by the movie. Dougal quietly tells Giddy that if she really wants to see a good film, she should watch the third Transformers movie.

Then her mom leans back against her dad and takes her phone out and that's it—everybody's on their devices. Even Tigs wakes and reaches a sleepy hand for her tablet. Giddy decides to leave them and read, sinking into a chair on the other side of the waiting room. She skips to the end of *Ulysses* to read the scene her dad mentioned. It winds up being a similar version to what happens in the movie, and it all takes place in the head of Leopold's wife,

Molly, as she reflects on her lovers and why she chose her husband. Giddy closes the book, confused, because, this is it? This is how it ends? It's just a list of everything Molly wants—all her hopes and her desires and all the things that made her happy back then and might make her happy right now. Molly's just there and she's just so sad. And what's the point of that? That she's *human*?

Katlyn, at book club. *Right. Because you're* depressed.

Jess: *There's a lot of that going around, so you're not special.*

Her hands start to shake, so she tightens her grip on the closed book to slow them down and shoots a nervous look around the waiting room to see if anyone notices, but they're all focused on themselves. *If you can't spot the crazy person in the waiting area, maybe, just maybe, it's you.*

The eleven days are up. The data is in. Her fucked-up family is the problem. It's not her. And if she's still a little sad right now, she can just will it away, right?

Barbers solve their own problems.

Because if the eleven days didn't fix this, then what does that prove? That she's broken? That she's going to end up like Jess or her mom?

Her own words at lunch rise up to haunt her. *Things that are proven in science change all the time. There's new data and things get reevaluated.*

A light goes off in her head, one that makes her sit up sharply in her seat. Maybe all this needs is another round of reevaluation. Maybe the whole eleven days didn't solve anything, but it did expose things that need to be dealt with. And isn't getting on a skateboard ramp when you don't know what you're doing and falling on your face kind of a sign something's up? Also, making yourself eat a sardine sandwich atrocity when you know your stomach wants to hurl? Aren't these things kind of a version of self-harm?

That thought *terrifies* Giddy!

Her breath catches in her throat. She digs out her phone, and her fingers keep shaking as she types *call therapists* in her calendar for Monday. Then she shoves the phone into her back pocket and crosses her arms before she can delete the entry. She thinks, *What this requires is a second experiment with an outside point of view to minimize bias and error.* Therapy could work or it could fail, but that doesn't matter because every good scientist knows you experiment again and again for precision and accuracy. Every failed experiment gives you something to learn from. Every failed experiment gets you closer to the truth.

Satisfied, she gets up and slips *Ulysses* back into her dad's bag. Then she goes to check on Tad again. It's late, almost one in the morning, and Giddy thinks she might take the chair Dougal vacated and fall asleep in it. But she winds up standing over Tad and staring at him for what seems like ages. Giddy digs Superdoo's pieces out of her pocket, unties a ribbon from around the neck of the teddy bear Tad was snuggling with, and uses it to tie up Superdoo into one piece. He looks a little bit like C-3PO in the trash in Star Wars with his limbs all strapped against him, but at least he holds together. Giddy tucks him in under Tad's arm.

And Tad lets out this long, loud, smelly fart in his sleep. Giddy gags and steps back. Tad squirms, face screwing up in obvious disgust. But he doesn't wake. His expression just relaxes into one of utter contentment. Meanwhile, Giddy is covering her mouth and nose, opening the door behind her and fanning her hand through the air, thinking, *Damn you, Tad!*

And then she laughs.

It just slips out of her, like it was always there. And it's not a horrible laugh. It's a good laugh. It feels so good, she does it again. Then she covers her mouth as if laughs are precious things she can't let slip away.

When she lowers her hand again, she is smiling from ear to ear.

Then she sits down in the chair, tucks a hospital pillow under her neck, closes her eyes, tries to get more sleep, and . . .

12

Acknowledgments

I would like to thank my agent, Jim McCarthy, for his tireless efforts at finding a home for this book and for believing in me and my writing so strongly. Many, many, *many* thanks to senior editor Ashley Hearn for loving this book as much as I do and working so ardently to make sure the finished product was as polished as possible. Thanks as well to copy editor Kaitlin Severini and editorial assistant Zoie Konneker for their very detailed work on this book, and to designer Lily Steele for an amazing cover.

Interns Keara Watkins and Mya Bailey—you both singled out this book from huge piles of reads! I'm honored that you thought so highly of it. Also thank you to Terry and Michelle and the entire marketing team at Peachtree, especially Sara and Elyse in publicity.

Thank you, Deborah, Gene, and Mike, for reading my works over the years and providing wonderful feedback. You made me a better writer. Much thanks and love to my husband, Shawn, for brainstorming and reading, for your brutal honesty in critiquing, and for holding my hand as I agonized over every project.

And finally, thanks to all the Giddys I've taught over the years, who have way too much to bear and are on that precipice. Hold on a little longer. Help might be just an experiment away.

About the Author

Dina Havranek hails from Houston, Texas, where she teaches science to the excellent students at Timberwood Middle School. A former TV news reporter and local actress, she loves being onstage and has been a speaker at the DFW Writers Conference, where she is a regular attendee. She lives with her husband, her daughter, an out-of-control Lego collection, and a pair of extremely ungrateful cats.